Something Followed Us Home

Something Followed us Home

Tales of Latiné Horror

EDITED BY

Cynthia Pelayo

PRIMERO
SUEÑO PRESS

ATRIA

New York Amsterdam/Antwerp London
Toronto Sydney/Melbourne New Delhi

PRIMERO SUEÑO PRESS
ATRIA
An Imprint of Simon & Schuster, LLC
1230 Avenue of the Americas
New York, NY 10020

"Ángel de la guarda" previously published in Argentina in *In Fraganti-Cuentos 2* (Mondadori, 2007), edited by Diego Grillo Trubba. Published in agreement with Schavelzon Graham Literary Agency.

"The World from Above and the World from Down Below" previously published in Spain in *Las Voladoras* as "El mundo de arriba, el mundo de abajo" (Páginas de Espuma, 2020). Translation rights arranged by Agencia Literaria CBQ.

"Pomelo" previously appeared in *Kweli Journal* (November 2021). Published in agreement with Creative Artists Agency.

The authorized representative in the EEA is Simon & Schuster Nederland B.V., Herculesplein 96, 3584 AA Utrecht, Netherlands. info@simonandschuster.nl

This Primero Sueño Press / Atria Paperback edition September 2026

PRIMERO SUEÑO PRESS / ATRIA PAPERBACK and colophon are registered trademarks of Simon & Schuster, LLC

Interior design by Esther Paradelo

Manufactured in the United States of America

1 3 5 7 9 10 8 6 4 2

The Library of Congress Cataloging-in-Publication Data has been applied for.

ISBN 978-1-6680-9194-4 (pbk)
ISBN 978-1-6680-9195-1 (ebook)

Contents

Foreword

Brenda Lozano
Translated by *Heather Cleary*

The stories contained in *Something Followed Us Home* remind me of a conversation I had recently about the differences there might be among ghosts, depending on where they appear. What differentiates a ghost in Latin America from one in the United States, or another that appears in Europe? Given all the vague and imprecise terms that attempt to group the countless spaces that make up a continent or a country, what distinguishes a ghost on one side of a border from the other, or on one side of the ocean from the other? Reading the myriad of voices in this book, you might come up with several interesting answers, as well as a few more questions. Could it be that Latin American ghosts are connected to histories of colonialism, to state and narco violence, to dictatorships and various other forms of repression, to femicide? Could it be that telling any story connected to any part of Latin America—even in English—is intrinsically linked to the political history of Spanish, as if rooted in the language? I like to think that languages have their ghosts, too. In the alphabet shared by Spanish and English, the behavior of the letter *H* is revealing. In Spanish, the letter is silent, silent like a ghost among the sounded letters around it, a visual apparition like a stealthy black cat, like a presence that appears when a photograph is developed, a written but inaudible existence, a ghost letter, a mysterious and ever-mute *H* that in English is pronounced forcefully, vigorously, like when a ghost shrieks into the frame in a Hollywood movie.

In the United States, ghosts are not necessarily connected to political history. There, they might be more closely linked to personal, individual histories. Let's say, for example, that a ghost appears in an old house. Let's say the family who had previously lived in that house lost a seven-year-old child under tragic circumstances, and we see this child as a ghost in the story of that home's new residents, who are in the process of renovations. Let's say we see how the child appears, how the ghost bursts into the present because it wants the living to know something, to see something. In the Anglo-Saxon tradition, ghosts appear in the tense space between the rational and the paranormal. In Latin America, which is predominantly Catholic, faith entails a suspension of logic by which miracles and demons are made possible. Moreover, in Latin America, the appearance of a ghost is connected to class struggle, oppressed cultures, Indigenous communities, and, therefore, to rituals and sometimes mysticism. And just as happens with borders, which blur each time they are crossed, ghosts from either side might find similar reasons for returning to the world of the living: a shared class struggle, for example. Both ghosts bear a message—in Spanish or in English—but those messages have different origins.

In Europe, ghosts are connected to family lineages and the thirst for revenge, as was the case with the ghost of Hamlet's father, the O.G., the Ghost of Ghosts. A brief digression on this great ghost: in his brilliant *Specters of Marx*, Jacques Derrida recounts how Marx and Engels, writing history's first manifesto in 1848—the eternally beautiful and still potent *Communist Manifesto*, at Le Cygne in Brussels—decided to call their work *Specters*. The title was not a casual decision or a youthful whim. Let's remember the first line, with which they ignited the nineteenth century: "A specter is haunting Europe—the specter of communism." The specter here is political, and threatening. Its apparition is imminent, just as the beginning of *Hamlet* announces. I find it fascinating that the creation of such a powerful political ideology, with so many diverse interpretations—including many misinterpretations and many fortunate starting points, from the constitution of entire countries to discussions among young people even today—began with a figure from fiction, with a ghost in Shakespeare's play. This brings me to something else that is extraordinary about this Ghost of Ghosts, and about the power of fiction more broadly: every masterpiece becomes a ghost that appears time and again in many later works. And the stories we tell, like the ones in this book, are also haunted houses in which the ghosts of other stories appear.

Despite the differences among ghosts depending on the site of their appearance—in Japan, for example, they wear white kimonos, have long black hair, and float around tormenting the living—all ghosts have a few things in common, no matter where they're from. Ghosts are the past barging in on the present, often with a message. But why, then, is the appearance of a ghost so terrifying? What frightens us so much about the past asserting itself? Perhaps because the message never comes on its own, in the abstract: there needs to be a messenger; therefore, ghosts are necessary. We are shocked by their form, on one hand, and on the hand terrified, because we can't control when they appear. They come to us when they please, which is to say, when we least expect it—that is, until we cross the threshold of fear and summon the courage to say their name three times.

Horror is related to what we do not know but believe we do. Cue Freud's hologram. What was familiar ceases to be familiar, and terror takes over. For centuries, monsters were thought to exist in places that remained unexplored, unconquered; just as monsters occupied the oceans many years ago, aliens now hover above the Earth. We have a need to give these beings shape, materiality, and the forms we assign them are often terrifying. In any case, both monsters and ghosts appear before us without our active participation, and both are the material manifestations of essential concepts: space and time. Monsters are to space what ghosts are to time.

The past materializes in the present in the form of a ghost, whose message we struggle to hear because terror stops up our ears. This is why fear plays such an important role: we cannot listen to the ghost, we don't want to, but the ghost won't rest until it delivers its message. A message of revenge, of resolution, of finally finding closure, of farewell, of terrible family tidings, of a hidden truth that failed to come to light in time, of a posthumous call for justice. And what is it about these stories of murmurs and ghosts that draws us in, tugs at us, captivates us? In lieu of an answer, we have this extraordinary book, which invites us to disappear into that question time and again.

Blue Flowers

Agustina Bazterrica
Translated by *Sarah Moses*

"I make fans like small wings,
dragging my feet along the dry earth."
—Nicolás Nucciarone, "El Propósito"

"There are ghosts in the shed," says my sister, placing her hand on the wood of the closed door. She looks at me with eyes that always seem to be smiling, but her voice is serious. I notice her clenched mouth tremble slightly. "No," I say, "there are no ghosts, ghosts don't exist." She moves her hand, and though it seems like she's whispering, she yells: *But I saw them*. She points to the pile of two boxes she climbed to reach the dirty window. The morning sun shines on her, setting her hair aflame, as though it were made of something brilliant, almost unreal. It's the color of the golden nuggets we find on the riverbank when we gather blue lilies. "All you saw were shadows, and shadows aren't ghosts," I tell her, even though I know that's not true. My sister bites her lower lip with her tiny teeth whenever she doesn't believe me.

We see Mother go into the milking yard, and my sister runs off through the dry grass. She raises her arms like a bird in flight. Her dress has blue flowers on it and fades as she gets farther away. She likes to pet the cows while Mother milks them. I stop to look at my reflection in the stagnant rainwater we store in metal drums. I don't like my eyes because they're too big for my face, and my black hair is the color of a crow's dirty feathers. That's why I keep it neat and tie it back. I brush it in the water's reflection because one day, all the mirrors in the house broke, and Father had to remove them. My sister liked to look at herself in those mirrors, but I never did. In one of Brother's books, I'd read that the image in a mirror can kill you, that it's not really you, but someone else, and you have to be afraid of that person, as they just want to take your place.

I look at my reflection in the stagnant water that lifts in small waves in the summer breeze. On my face, I think I see a smile that isn't mine, that's not really a smile, and only looks like one because my lips are spread wide and my teeth show. But it's something else. The mouth in the reflection is trying to say something, but I don't want to look, or know, so I touch the water and erase my image.

I hear Brother's axe chopping wood. The sound hurts, as though the axe could wound me. With every strike, my body trembles.

It's time for me to do my chores so Mother doesn't get mad. Before I leave, I touch the silver lock on the shed's door. Father locked it one day. Only he has the key. Sometimes I climb onto the pile of boxes to reach the dirty window and look inside. There's a staircase with a broken railing, old furniture, things we don't use anymore stored in two big trunks, a lot of dust, and the shattered mirrors. Sometimes I think I see shadows like the ones my sister saw. Sometimes, if I keep very still and quiet, I think I see the other girl in the broken mirrors, the one who lives in them. My other self.

I run off to collect the eggs, clean the chicken coop, count the hens, and check to make sure they're okay, because one disappeared this year, and we found another with a broken neck. I have to do the laundry and help Mother knead the dough. We keep the dirty laundry in baskets in each room, but I don't like to go into the house. I like it better outside. It's cold in the house, even in the summer. The cold hurts like tiny, freezing teeth piercing my skin, biting me again and again. Even with all the lights on, the gloom absorbs the brightness. And there are the voices. In the dark.

I go to Mother and Father's room. They left two sets of sheets in the laundry basket. The sun's rays don't penetrate the windows; it's like they disappear on entering the house. I quickly grab the sheets and though the room is empty, I hear someone say my name. I don't want to look around and I run to Brother's room. His laundry basket is full. Always full. Brother hates me. He dirties more clothes than he should. I sit down on the bed, a little frustrated, because I don't understand Brother's disdain. The cold hurts my hands. Someone or something is breathing in the shadows. I think it might be Brother, watching me in silence, but I hear the axe, the unmistakable sound of him chopping wood, the rage he unleashes with every blow. I shut my eyes tightly and run off with the basket full of clothes.

I never go into my sister's room because it's Mother who washes her dress. My sister is obsessed with the dress, the one with blue flowers on it, and she never wants to take it off. Mother must have made a few dresses with the same fabric, because when they tried to get my sister to change it, she ran away, and they spent two days looking for her. They found her asleep in the shed, in one of the old trunks. The trunk was locked on the outside. My sister didn't say anything to Father, but afterward, she told me that I'd whispered she should hide in there to teach Mother a lesson. No matter how hard I try, I can't remember saying anything to her.

Mother calls me to knead the dough, and I pull on an apron over my dress. I like to touch the dough because when I move my hands I don't feel the cold as much. Mother doesn't look at me, she barely speaks to me. It's better that way. I focus on the dough so I don't look at the shadow behind her. The shadow isn't new, it's been with Mother for a while, causing her to stoop beneath its weight. The shadow is black, but it's a black I've never seen before. It's a black that's blacker than the black of the black stones by the river, blacker than the black sky in the dead of night, blacker than the black circle in Father's eyes. Father also has a shadow that follows him, but since he spends most of the day working the land, I only see it at night, and not always. Sometimes I think Father's shadow is now a part of him.

My sister is still too little to knead dough. I remember when Mother brought her home in her arms. I was just a girl and I'd never seen anyone so fragile and beautiful. I touched my sister, and she grasped my finger with her tiny baby hand. Now she's sitting on one of the stools and her small face comes up to the edge of the table. I dust a little flour on her nose, and she laughs with her eyes, but her mouth is closed. Mother doesn't look at us, and I see the shadow place its fingers on her shoulder—stretching out, growing long, until they cover her chest like the legs of a deformed spider. Mother stops kneading the dough for a second and dabs at her eyes with the edge of her white apron. I think she's crying, but I can't be sure.

While Mother puts the bread into the clay oven, I go down to the river with my sister to gather water for the laundry. Brother is still chopping wood, and when we walk by, he places the axe off to the side. He looks at me silently, his eyes hard, filled with green stones like the ones covered in moss in the woods. We nod hello, but he ignores us, as always.

I put effort into doing the laundry. My sister goes to look for flowers. I watch her from a distance while I try to get the sweat stains out of Brother's shirts. Her image blurs among the trees.

I stand up and shout her name, but she gives me a perplexed, unfocused look and disappears into the woods. I run after her, look for her, call her, but all I hear is the water in the river flowing furiously. She'll be back, like always. I keep scrubbing and the sun warms my freezing body. I throw myself into the work so I'll be tired at night, so I'll give in to exhaustion, so that when my body touches the sheets, my eyes will close and they won't see what lives in the dark.

Night has fallen and I search for something to do indoors, to keep myself busy, but everything's clean, all the chores are done. Everyone is asleep, and though I don't want to, I go to my room.

I close my eyes and pull the sheets over me so I won't be cold. I'm tired, but I can't fall asleep because tiny, sharp teeth are gnawing at me, freezing my skin. The sheets are strangely heavy, as though someone were sitting on them, and I try to move them, but I can't. My body won't respond. All I can do is open my eyes and blink. I'm a prisoner in my immobile body. I feel the weight of the sheets shift onto my chest. It's hard to breathe. I close my eyes, try to move a finger, a leg, but my body won't react. I don't want to open my eyes because something is touching my face. The touch is not soft, it's like ice burning my skin. I try to scream, but I can't. I hear Brother's axe. He can't possibly be chopping wood this late. My body trembles with every blow, though I'm unable to move. I can't stop the tears that fall from my eyes and wet my cheeks, my neck. Something whispers in my left ear. It's not a human sound, but it says my name. I open my eyes, and now I can move. I scream, light the oil lamp, throw the sheets onto the floor, feeling disgusted and desperate. I sense the axe striking harder, faster. I jump out of bed and flee my room, leave the house, run through the dry grass. I run without stopping until at last I turn around. From a distance, I see the darkened house, no shadows, no axe. I fall asleep on the ground.

I wake with the morning dew. The day has dawned cloudy. I clean myself with water from the metal drums, shake the dirt and dry grass from my hair, and try to neaten it. When I look at my image, I see bags under my eyes. It's hard to open them, so I rub them, yawn. I don't want to remember what happened last night. I think I imagined it, that it was a hallucination, that I'm exhausted. But my body knows it was real.

I go back to the house, walk quickly to my room, take off my dirt-stained nightgown, and put on a clean dress and apron. I wait for my sister at the door to the shed, wanting to say hello before I get started on my chores, but she's not there. I don't see the wheelbarrow at the entrance to the house either. Mother and Father use it to go into town. Yesterday I saw Mother with a small bouquet of blue flowers, but when she saw me, she hid it in the pocket of her apron. I look at my reflection in the stagnant water and there's no expression on my face. I slap the water with my left hand and my image vanishes.

I hear footsteps, and it's Brother coming with the axe. He walks slowly, staring at me, not blinking. The stones in his eyes are cold. He says nothing, raises the axe, and breaks the lock with one blow. I open my eyes and mouth, but no sound comes out, my only thought is that Father will be angry. Brother grabs my arm forcefully and shoves me into the shed. I want to hit him with my free arm, but he shakes me and throws me onto the dirty floor. I get up quickly because I'm angry, because I don't want to talk to Brother on the floor. Before I can yell at him, before I can ask why he hates me so much, he points to the broken staircase and says, "Today's the anniversary." I don't know what he's talking about. Brother gets mad and kicks one of the trunks where we store the things we don't use. The lid opens with the impact, and I see my sister's dress, the one with the blue flowers on it. I go over to the trunk, kneel down, and very carefully touch the dress. It's starched and someone has folded it delicately. The flowers shine like tiny shooting stars. That's when I remember everything.

I'm struck by a pain that feels like my chest is splitting open, like it's being slit in half. The pain is so intense that I lie down on the dirty floor and curl up in a fetal position to hold back my screams. In my mind, I see my sister in the dress with the blue flowers. I hear Brother's axe outside, but the blows don't affect me. I see myself calling to my sister from the top of the staircase with the loose railing that Father never fixed. But I'm not myself, I'm the girl who lives in the mirrors. Like me, her eyes are too big and her hair is black. But hers is shiny, and she doesn't tie it back. My sister climbs the stairs, and the other girl pushes her. She watches my sister fall until she hears her neck snap. Brother's axe stops. The other girl smiles constantly, it's an inner smile no one can see. She smiles even when she sees Brother run in screaming, and she says it was an accident, that their sister slipped; she smiles even when she hugs Mother, who's crying; she smiles even when she comforts Father, who's screaming with rage and blaming himself for not fixing the railing; she smiles even when she cleans up the shards of the mirrors someone broke on the night of my sister's death. She smiles even when they cover the small coffin with earth, even when she sees the people dressed in black leave. Then she stands over the grave, spreads her lips wide, and truly smiles. She smiles showing her teeth, while she drags her feet and draws small wings on the damp earth. She moves as though she were dancing, but no one sees her.

I lie still on the dirty floor. I want to disappear, but I get up. I look at Brother, neaten my hair, and hold back my tears as I shake off my dress and apron. I gaze into the broken mirrors but see nothing. I close the lid on the trunk and leave the shed without saying a word. I walk to the river. I feel Brother's steps behind me. He's the one who gives me stones to slip into my apron pockets. They're heavy. I want to look Brother in the eye, but I don't because he already knows, because he's always seen the other girl inside me. I step into the river. The current is strong. I'm cold, but this cold is different because it doesn't hurt. Before I sink down, I see my sister on the shore. She looks at me with those eyes of hers that seem to smile. The sun isn't out, but her hair is shining. The blue flowers on her dress get bigger until they disappear. Then only water surrounds me.

The Hand That Feeds

Isabel Cañas

This one begins as most stories from my great-grandmother do: with a mother in a kitchen and food on the stove.

But this one also starts with someone shrieking. With a hand pointing an accusing finger.

"Madre de Dios, what is that *thing*?"

That pitch pierces the delicate flesh of the wolf pup's ears. It shatters the aromas of human home: comino, bubbling caldo, woodsmoke.

The boy tightens his arms around the pup protectively, even as his mother towers over them, her stance aggressive, her wooden spoon an outstretched weapon.

"But, Mamá, she's hungry."

"Get it out of my kitchen!"

Hands seize the pup and toss her into the refuse behind the house, into the dry cold of the night. Doors slam. The sound shudders through her bones.

That is the last the pup will ever see of the boy who dried her rain-soaked fur and moth-delicate ears, who brought her scraps from his pack's table. If she had lips, they would tremble, her eyes welling with a weakling's grief. But she is fangs and paws and patchy, half-grown gray fur and a snout still speckled with rice that the boy gave her.

That snout smells that the refuse around her has gifts to give.

The boy's pack is too poor to throw out food, but she catches the scent of bone on the air. A hint of spirit once living. She hauls herself to all fours, ribs aching from where she struck hard-packed earth, and pads in the direction of the smell.

She paws ash aside and finds her quarry: bones. Ribs, to be precise, and from a pig, if the lingering tendrils of scent are to be believed.

Behind her: a flare of light. She shies away, but not quickly enough.

"¡Vete!"

A rock hits her shoulder. The breath cracks out of her as she stumbles sideways.

She snatches the pig rib between her teeth, turns tail, and flees.

The pup digs a shallow den under the mesquite grove—out of sight of the house, but close enough to still taste the woodsmoke and the warmth of pack gathering. Her belly aches, its emptiness barely sated by a handful of rice. Her heart's ache twists deeper.

She turns the rib between her paws with practiced care: thrice to the left, finishing with it pointed toward the east, where the moon rises and drenches the chaparral in sweet silver.

"You never listen to me."

She looks up, and she is no longer surrounded by mesquite. Instead, she stands before the dying embers of la Huesera's fire.

La Huesera: creator of monsters, mother of bones.

The pup hangs her head and dips her tail between her legs.

"I made you stronger than this, Lobita." But la Huesera also made her alone. Packless beneath cold stars. "You know what men say of wolves: they will bite the hand that feeds them. You cannot trust someone who gives nothing himself."

Lobita paws at her face. Itchiness grows up her snout, as if she were going to sneeze; then her claw catches skin, and she yanks.

Sinew snaps and disconnects from muscle. Gristle stretches and slowly rips. A warm dribble of blood, as always, runs over her teeth as she pulls her skin away.

It collapses before her, a soft pelt in hands that are bare and declawed and red in ember light. She runs her tongue over teeth. They are slick with copper after the kill, but flat. Smooth. Speech-ready.

"But I don't want to be that strong," she murmurs. Her throat catches, dry as tumbleweed, old bones splintering in the desert. "I don't want to be alone."

La Huesera leans forward. Her braids are swinging steel ropes. Her skin smells of sun and age, but her eyes crackle with an ageless fire that would bite even the Devil's heels with heat. The monsters of the world are her pups; her love for them is both harsh and, with a cruel, swift twist of the wind, achingly tender. She tucks a lock of black hair behind Lobita's ear.

"You are never alone if you can call for me." La Huesera braces a palm on one knee and plucks the pig's rib between time-gnarled fingers. "What will I make with you?" she coos, admiring its curve.

Bitter wind stings Lobita's bare skin. Make, make, make. A creator obsessed with creation, but not with caring for them. Not as Lobita aches to be cared for.

For that, she will need a pack. No matter what la Huesera says.

The sun rises and sets over the desert a hundred times, a thousand times more. Cattle low. Coyotes scuttle through the night. Lobita becomes la Loba, and la Loba hungers as prey becomes scarce and frost nips the northern slopes of the hills. But more than an empty belly drives her toward the scents of kept animals—goats, sheep, cattle—and guard dogs.

Jubilant music eggs her on for miles; soon, it is joined by the smells of sweat and the thrum of rhythmic feet.

There is a party on this ranchito.

She once stole a dress for a time like this and hid it deep in the chaparral. Now she carries it in her jaw, fabric draped ever-so-gently over fangs. Once within sight of jumping firelight and dancing, she sheds her skin and replaces it with silk as red as heart meat.

The throngs of humans are so thick that she thinks no one will notice a strange woman enter—black hair pouring down her back, her feet bare and red from the cold.

She was wrong. One notices.

She could never claim that he is the same boy who loved her when they were pups, but he smells enough the same: kitchen, caldo, café. He smells like he has a home. But he does not smell like woman—and that might mean he has a home to share.

He takes her by the hand, dark eyes alight as the bonfire, glinting with a yearning that could be akin to greed. She feels its echo in her breast. She is greedy for touch, for someone to *see* her.

You know what men say of wolves: they will bite the hand that feeds them.

La Huesera's words strike a warning note in her bones, a shudder so soft and nameless she nearly misses it.

It is easy to brush away.

"Do you dance?" the man asks. What he means: Will she step into his arms? Will she follow him into his world?

"I can learn," she says.

And she tries. Oh, she tries. She tries harder than any woman human-born: she braids her hair tight; she forces herself to become accustomed to the weight of skirts to her ankles; she teaches clumsy fingers to grind maíz and café for her new husband.

Their house is a worker's jacal on the broad sweep of a rich man's rancho: it is all bright, airy patio with tipichil floors on the outside and dark rooms within. She sits on the patio in the pale sun and smells the wind. She remains in the outdoor kitchen long after meals, when the wood settles into slumbering embers, and does not think about the back room.

Her wedding night was calloused palms on bare skin, the rake of teeth over throats and shoulders. But when that hunger was sated, she had another: she itched for her wolfskin. Her breath felt thin without it. And so, flush with love and the hubris of having won man and home, she drew her skin from where she had slipped it beneath the bed. Her husband, propped on elbows between sheets, frowned; then, as she slipped into the change, he leaped to his feet.

She had stared down the barrel of many a gun.

But never that close.

She tore herself bare again, human flesh slick and dripping with the blood of the change and sour with panicked sweat.

The back room is slim, dark, and shallow, barely more than a cupboard.

That is where her husband strode when he seized her wolfskin from the floor, still naked, gun over his forearm. He knelt before a simple wooden chest, wrenched it open, and thrust the wolfskin inside.

Later, la Loba learned that a chicken-footed witch had sold it to him in Tampico. It was spelled so that it would only open with his hand.

He never locked it.

He never had to.

• • •

When winter closes its jaws over the land, la Loba knows she should retreat inside, but she longs for the caress of its cold fangs. She slips out of bed. Leaves her boots at the door.

"I am grateful," she tells her reflection in the moonlit creek. But the woman's face is strange to her—she doesn't recognize the pinched skin at the corners of mouth and eyes. The reflection shifts, as if it is frowning, as if it means to ask: *Do you not lack fangs?* So la Loba adds: "I finally have a home. A pack."

When she returns to the jacal, she is reunited with her husband's palms. They leave bruises.

Spring. Her husband drives the cattle to San Antonio. A cold bed suits her. She sleeps easy. She never tosses, never turns, and never, ever thinks about that back room. Nor about her skin thirsting in the dark.

At night, she drowses in the cold bed, listening to the skin claw at the inside of the chest. She imagines gouge marks. She dreams of the give of the wood beneath claw, the splay of her toes against an immovable surface. She hears the crack of splinters.

She wakes in the back room, on her knees, splinters beneath shredded nails. She rests her cheek against the chest and feels the crack of salt drying on her cheeks.

A heartbeat thuds inside the chest.

Her own breast is silent.

White sun fills her head with buzzing. The women of the ranchito notice la Loba's bones growing prominent.

Lovesick, they cluck knowingly over merienda. They ply her with sweet breads and promise that her husband will return soon and fill her belly with a baby.

La Loba promptly vomits behind the kitchen.

She tries a machete. She tries a butcher knife. She tries stones. The floor before the back room is spotted with dried blood.

She paces. Each step hitches, hobbled by the ever-desperate need for another two legs. Her breath pulls ragged. Her brow burns with fever.

With her tail between her legs, she stumbles to the kitchen refuse. A bone—a pig's rib. *How fitting*, she thinks as she collapses before the small table. She turns the bone thrice to the left, and when it points east, the jacal around her ripples, but it does not disappear. There is no sign of la Huesera's fire.

"*No.*" It's a dry, broken bark, too exhausted for tears, too parched for anger.

She turns the bone again. Again. *Again.*

"I raised you stronger than this."

La Loba whirls, gasping, eyes wide. She sees nothing unusual about the kitchen . . . but it is la Huesera's voice that snaps in the embers of the dying fire.

"I'm dying," la Loba croaks. "Help me."

"Help you, chamaca?" La Huesera's voice is drier than the kindling. "You, sinvergüenza, who took my loving advice and tossed it to the wind? I told you this would happen, and yet here you are. Why shouldn't I sit back, wait until you waste away, and then make something useful out of your bones?"

"You," la Loba says, and it is so dry, a dry rasp that it is barely speech, "are my mother." Her breath barely keeps the blackness from the corners of her vision now. "I can call for you still. So I am not alone."

Warmth ripples off the fire. A murmur; perhaps it is a harrumph, perhaps it is even affectionate.

"Tell me what happened."

La Loba does.

La Huesera considers these pieces: the gun, the spelled chest, the machetes and stones and blood on the floor.

"Well," she says at last. "It sounds like only his hand can open the chest."

The kitchen fire is low when la Loba's husband returns at last. Boot heels on the patio, a click of spurs. The long creak of the door opening.

The dusk has long since melted into velvet black. The vaqueros returned triumphant to the ranchito after their long drive north. The husband's smell sweeps into the jacal's central room: sweat, leather, horse, aguardiente. Roasted red peppers and the burnt spots on tortillas and marinated puerco. La Loba did not join the other wives preparing the meal to welcome the vaqueros home.

She waited here.

She masks her scent in the cross breeze of the open kitchen. She masks her silhouette in shadow. Darkness has been a ghost haunting her footsteps, hand in hand with hunger and thirst; now she draws it over her shoulders like a cloak and creeps forward.

Her clawless hand curls around the handle of a knife. She runs tongue over teeth: they are flat and slick, but not for long.

A wolf like her doesn't bite the hand that feeds. She was always too famished for tenderness. So starved that she kissed the offering palm, wrapped though it was in thorns.

Weak, la Huesera would say, and perhaps she would be right. Even la Loba is not so sure.

But she is sure of this: even without wolfskin, her leap will be a silent thing. Even without her good nose, she knows where fragrant blood runs hot and close beneath the skin.

This time, when she limps to the back room, her breath pulls jagged with anticipation. Instead of a machete, or a stone, or a knife, her fingers curl around her husband's wrist.

She kneels before the spelled chest. Gently—tenderly, even—she places his palm against the latch and splays his fingers wide, not caring how the severed wrist weeps sluggish blood on her skirt.

A long moment passes. Thundering heartbeat. The drip of blood on the floor.

Then the latch clicks.

La Huesera hums to herself as she tallies her latest offering. The dry bones of a man's hand click against one another in her palm. She pokes them with the tip of her carving knife, squinting in the red light of embers.

"Monstrous in life, monstrous in death," she murmurs. "What shall I make out of you? A key to the underworld? Dice carved with faces that foretell death? Or perhaps a simple pipe?"

She cackles. She speaks to no one. There are bones and woman and knifeshine, and a long, distant echo of wolfsong on the wind.

Her First Cruise Ship

Ann Dávila Cardinal

Ileana smoothed her clothes for the hundredth time that morning. She didn't know why she was so nervous; it was a simple retail job for fuck's sake, but there was something about the day's impending tourist invasion that upped the tension in the normally tranquil atmosphere of the small store. To calm herself, she kept busy arranging and rearranging the hand-painted coconut shell jewelry in the rectangle of glass cases that was the main counter.

It was her third day working at Artisanal Puerto Rico, and she had begun it feeling confident. The summer job in Old San Juan was a placeholder, after all, until she figured out what to do next: graduate school, travel, work for her father's soul-sucking investment firm. Actually, that last one absolutely wasn't on the menu, not even on the table; she just pretended it was to keep her tyrannical father off her back.

"You okay, mija?"

Ileana jumped a bit. She hadn't realized her manager, Carmen, was standing next to her. "Oh! Yeah, sure."

Carmen smiled warmly and patted the younger woman's arm. "The first cruise ship is always nerve-racking, but pretty soon it becomes pan comido."

Ileana tilted her head. "Eaten bread? Eww."

Carmen laughed. It was a light, bell-like sound that had a calming effect. "It's like 'piece of cake.' 'Easy.'"

"Still gross. I keep picturing gummed bread mush in an old person's toothless mouth or something."

Carmen chuckled. "You'll get it, amor."

Ileana smiled back, though she couldn't help but wonder if there wasn't some judgment tucked under Carmen's kindness. Like "Check out the gringa dissing our Spanish" kind of thing. But Ileana knew that was just her insecurity talking. Everyone was so patient with her sluggish attempts at her father's language. Truth was, she understood way more than she spoke, but it was the regional idioms that always tripped her up. That's why she decided to get a job in the city while she was on the island. Otherwise, it would be too easy to settle in with her bilingual cousins and jabber away in English (though, truth was, she felt like an outsider even with them). It was embarrassing to be Puerto Rican and not speak Spanish fluently. She planned to remedy that this summer.

The coqui song sounded—the recording of the beloved tree frog's voice was how they knew a customer, or customers, had come in—and Ileana looked up to see the handsome face of David, who worked next door at the cosmetics store. He had this wavy chestnut hair that moved when he talked, and when he smiled, it went all the way to his eyes. She was a sucker for boys who smiled with their eyes.

"Buenos días, señorita," he said in his oddly unidentifiable accented Spanish.

She flushed a bit, and it embarrassed her. "Good morning, David." Those dark eyes brushed her up and down with their thick black lashes, and she felt heat rise again behind her face. But Carmen had warned her off him on her first day. "*They hire particular people because they're so seductive, mija,*" she had said, and it was true. Yesterday had been quiet and Ileana had watched through the store's large front window as the handsome guy worked his charm on the tourists who walked up and down the street, flirting with men and women alike, gently leading them inside the store and into his floral-scented web of two-hundred-dollar hand creams. There was something . . . vampiric about all the pretty people who worked in that store. So, she would settle for a little flirting and admiring David from afar. Besides, a venereal disease was not the souvenir she needed from this summer.

"David!"

Ileana looked toward the door, and Vanessa, a leggy girl with silky mahogany hair, was leaning in. They locked eyes, and the woman gave her an equally seductive smile.

Maybe they *were* vampires.

He answered, but didn't take his eyes off Ileana. "What? Can't you see I'm busy?"

"The ship's already docked. Get your ass back in here."

David sighed, then picked up Ileana's hand and pressed his soft lips to her knuckles as he stared into her eyes. He smelled spicy and warm, like summer cinnamon.

After she watched him saunter out the door and out of sight, she reached for the bottle of rainforest-scented sanitizer on the counter and applied it liberally to her hands. No judgment, but who knew where those lips of his had been?

"Ileana, do you want to watch them come into the city, since it's your first time?" Carmen now stood by the store's open doorway. Misty air-conditioned air escaped around the woman like horror movie fog, tumbling out the door and over the blue cobblestone street.

The assistant manager, Sol, yelled from the other end of the counter, near the books, "Ooh! The virgin gonna get her cruise cherry popped!"

Ileana rolled her eyes at them as the other staff hooted and hollered like a bawdy Greek chorus. She didn't mind, though. Sol ribbed her, but they were kind and patient during Ileana's training and made her feel at home despite her not being island-born. Damn, her own father couldn't even do that.

She waved her hand dismissively at their continued cackling and turned back to Carmen. "I'd like that."

She stepped out from behind the glass cases and followed her manager out onto the street and down to the corner of Calle Fortaleza. The city was quiet and almost cool in the midmorning calm, but soon the sun would blaze down, heating up the cobblestone until it felt as if you were walking through the fires of hell. Hence, the incredibly wasteful open doors releasing their seductive chill to lure unsuspecting passersby. But Ileana had chosen this store to apply to when every piece she picked up had *Made in Puerto Rico* stamped on the bottom. It only carried work from Puerto Rican artisans, none of the mass-produced plastic crap that was peddled in so many souvenir stores throughout the city. She was proud of that. Besides, it helped her justify to her father that she had taken a retail job for fourteen dollars an hour after he "spent a hundred grand on an art history degree." God, she hated that she could so easily conjure his judgmental voice in her head. But the fact that he didn't get it? It only made this work more appealing to her.

When they got to the corner, they looked down the hill and toward the docks, and Ileana gasped at the sight of the twelve-story, gleaming, white-and-blue behemoth that had appeared at the base of the city. The many decks were stacked like layers of an overly elaborate cake, and figures flooded the two gangways, like the red ants she stumbled on when she was five and visiting her abuela's house in Bayamón. They had covered her lower legs, their bites spreading like fire as she screamed and ran to the house.

"Beautiful, huh?" Carmen asked, pulling her back into the moment.

Not the word Ileana would have chosen. "I mean, I guess so."

"Well, the money they spend sure is beautiful. I'm going back inside; you can stay for a bit if you like. But come back before they reach Fortaleza, okay?"

"I will, thanks." Ileana watched her boss walk away, then took a deep breath of morning air. The smell of the city was clear and new at this hour, with only a slight hint of spilled alcohol and urine from the previous evening's partyers. But it smelled like life with a capital *L*, not the curated scent of her father's gated community that she returned to each night.

As she waited for the disembarking to begin, she gazed off into the San Juan Bay behind the ship, its water a deep azure and the sky a ridiculous bright blue, and she understood why people flocked here. So much natural beauty and history in one small city. Directly across the street from where she stood was the historic Tapia theater building with its colonnades and, supposedly, two ghosts. Directly behind her? She could see the tops of the old-style black cast-iron lampposts of Plaza Colón, while she caught the buttery scent of Mallorca sweet rolls and dark, rich coffee brewing.

When she looked back toward the docks, the passengers had been cleared and began to funnel down the planks and spread onto the docks like sand in a just-turned hourglass. These tourists were the main reason her father questioned her choice of summer jobs. "*They're like locusts, Ileana, hungry and totally out for themselves. I offer you a corner office in the cultural and economic center of the island, and you choose that?*" When he made statements like that, she would look into his calculating brown eyes and wonder how they could be related. What she'd wanted to say in response but didn't—in truth the man frightened her a bit—was that she'd always choose being down here with the people over up there in his company's glass tower.

The passengers crossed the highway near the piers and then surged up Calle Paseo de Colón. It was odd, Ileana thought. They really did look like a swarm of insects, almost moving as one. She shuddered, despite the warmth of the sun, but it wasn't until the first few passed the post office that she began to notice something was wrong.

There was a man at the front, around her father's age, overweight in the way so many American men of his generation were—the large, round belly leading in front like a basketball hidden beneath his striped, button-down shirt. His face was red and his nose enlarged, and Ileana could picture him in a recliner, yelling at a football game on the television, beer in hand. A typical American tourist, but . . . he kept stumbling. Not like he was drunk, but more as if he were falling forward, *up* the hill. A taxi swerved to avoid him as he stepped into the street without looking, and he didn't even seem to notice the cacophony when the driver leaned on his horn. As he rounded the curved street and passed the Starbucks, he lifted his head, and his eyes caught Ileana's. Locked onto hers. They were red-rimmed and huge, almost . . . hungry. Then a smile snaked across his lips, his mouth opened into a round, black void, and he let out a guttural moan that echoed against the sixteenth-century buildings on either side. Not long after, the other passengers behind him seemed to notice her, too . . . and they all picked up speed.

"Jesus Christ!" Ileana screamed, then took off up Fortaleza and back toward the store. Her heart threatened to beat its way out of her chest. She risked a look back over her shoulder as she tore across La Tanca. An absolute herd of passengers spilled up the street behind her like a spreading bloodstain, their clothes a riot of tropical colors, arms waving in a macabre form of semaphore, the rising scent of decay announcing their arrival. The chorus of moans grew louder and louder as more of them turned the corner and onto Fortaleza. As they marched, some broke off and stumbled into open doorways of shops and bars along the way. Others headed straight for her, limbs jerking them forward.

Terror wrapped itself around Ileana's chest like a tourniquet, her sneakered feet pounding the sidewalk beneath her in retreat. She literally threw herself through the doors of the store. All the employees looked up as she stood, breathing heavy, eyes wild.

"Are you okay, honey?" Sol asked as they rubbed their hands up and down Ileana's arms as if she were cold.

Ileana struggled to get words out of her mouth as panic tightened around her throat. "No!" She pushed their hands away. Couldn't they hear the moans? "Sol! We have to close the doors! There's something . . . wrong with the people on that boat!"

They coughed out a bitter laugh. "You're telling me, girl?" Then they sighed and looked at the other staff members, clapping their hands. "Places, bitches! It's showtime!"

Ileana stood, sputtering. "What the fuck?" How could they be so nonchalant? The moans were getting louder, closer, and she felt like screaming. She grabbed Carmen as she walked by, the keys on the spiral stretchy around her upper arm stabbing Ileana's palms. "Carmen! Listen to me! We have to lock the doors! Put bookcases in front of the windows, anything to keep them out! Those *things* aren't human!" Tears filled her eyes, but Ileana ignored them. She didn't have time to cry; monsters were loose in the city!

"Sure they're human! Or were . . . Besides, either way"—Carmen patted her on the cheek—"you'll be fine." She stepped away toward her usual position near the door, pausing to whisper back, "But whatever you do, don't piss them off." The last word was still hanging in the air as the first cruise passenger shambled through the front door, the tree frog song mockingly innocent beneath the man's strangled groans.

Ileana jumped over the counter and ducked behind the glass case, bashing her knee against the top in the process. She dropped low to the floor, ignoring the pain in her leg, breathing heavy.

But she still felt vulnerable. She needed to see what was happening. She shimmied forward, grabbed the counter's edge with her fingers, and inched up, peeking over the glass top.

The red-faced man dragged his legs forward, flanked by two women, one painfully thin, her bright orange resort-wear garish against her brown wrinkly tan. The other one, closest to Ileana, was plump and squeezed into a tight-knit dress, her face pale with two pink splotches painted on either cheek. Ileana stared, fear paralyzing her limbs, as the plump woman turned and looked straight at her, though only her eyes were above the counter. Ileana couldn't move other than to tremble.

The cruise woman leaned over the counter, bending at the waist like a doughy Barbie doll, and her thick-lipped, over-Botoxed mouth fell open as if the hinges on her jaw suddenly gave way. A creaking sound emerged, then Ileana could discern words among her moans . . .

"C-c-c . . . cruis-uh disssss . . . count."

The last *t* was percussive, like an arrow hitting its mark, and she slammed her pale, bloodless hand on the glass counter.

Ileana jolted and jumped to her feet, stepping just out of reach. The woman's fingers, plumping around her gaudy rings like rising bread dough, clasped a bright green piece of paper with a drawing of a cruise ship and *20% discount* written on the corners as if it were currency. The woman just stood there, fetid, ragged breath steaming up the counter. She smelled like rotting meat and . . . sunblock.

Ileana knew this creature was waiting for something, but her desire to run was overwhelming. There were more of them in the store now, the aisles bustling with shambling figures. Maybe she could make it to the door, she estimated, but then she looked out the front window. Among the moving mass of passengers stalked a man in a bright Hawaiian shirt, awkwardly juggling a bunch of

Polo Ralph Lauren shopping bags and waving what looked like a dismembered human arm, torn flesh waving at its end like the casing on a just-bit sausage. Was that . . . *his* arm? Or someone else's?

Ileana put her hands on either side of her head and tightened them, as if she could squeeze it all away. *This is a nightmare; it has to be!* The voice in her head was more confident than she was. But she used the analytical mind, the only good thing she inherited from her father, assessed her situation, and determined—absurd as it was—that the only choice was to go along with this.

Ileana swallowed through her tightened throat and took one step forward. "Y-y-es, we accept those vouchers." Her voice croaked, not unlike her customer's.

The woman's round face lit up in a weird, lopsided smile, and she began to point, seemingly at random, to things in the case, indicating individual pieces of jewelry with a simian grunt.

Moving as if underwater, Ileana grabbed each item, scanned them, and shoved them into a store-branded shopping bag while the woman muttered words among the noises, "daughter-in-law," "niece," and "dog sitter."

When the bag was full, Ileana said in a small, choked voice, "That will be three hundred and twenty-six dollars with your discount."

The woman smiled—it was actually more of a grimace—and Ileana realized her teeth were broken off and covered with muck. She dug through her filthy straw purse, pulled out a Coach wallet, extracted a credit card, and held it out.

Ileana took it, wishing she didn't have to touch it. Couldn't the woman just use the tap function? Well, Ileana certainly wasn't going to suggest it: the sooner the woman left, the better. Ileana ran the card through before handing it back. "Th-thank you for shopping at Artisan Puerto R-rico . . ." Her voice went up at the end, as if she were asking a question.

The woman grunted and shambled out and onto the crowded street.

As soon as she left, Ileana took a deep, shaky breath, her eyes filling with relief. Although it didn't last long.

A young, blonde woman in a sheer pink cover-up over a bikini appeared in front of her and slammed a hand-carved wooden Don Quixote sculpture onto the counter. Ileana jumped at the sound, wondering if it had cracked the glass. That's when she noticed that the long metal sword the Cervantes character held was impaled through the woman's hand. Dumbfounded, Ileana could only stare as the woman awkwardly shook the statue, trying to fling it free, but all it did was tear a larger hole in the center of her palm. Shaking herself out of her stupor, Ileana reached out and held the base of the sculpture down on the counter as the cruise passenger ripped her hand free with a wet, popping sound.

"Ra . . . raaaa . . . puh . . ." The newly freed woman struggled to get sounds out, the muscles around her mouth seemingly not working.

Through her terror, Ileana struggled to discern meaning, while the woman's cloying scent of tuberose fought with her base note of rotting flesh. "I'm sorry?" She asked it gently, afraid to anger the woman.

"Rah . . . puh . . ." the woman said again, frustration twisting her face into a caricature of a Karen-can-I-speak-to-your-manager expression.

What is she trying to say, damn it? Sweat broke out on Ileana's forehead as she felt the woman's anger growing. *Shit! Shit! Shit!* She glanced around, desperately wanting to buy time and figure out what she wanted, when her eyes fell on the roll of palm tree wrapping paper. "Wrapped? You want it wrapped?"

"Yuh," the blonde woman muttered, nodding.

Ileana let out a long breath. "Of course! I'll do that right away."

It was unsurprisingly hard to wrap neatly when your hands are shaking, but after a few missteps with the tape dispenser, Ileana finally finished, tucked the package into some bubble wrap, and into a shopping bag with the store logo embossed on it. She placed it in front of the customer. "That'll be one hundred and seventy-eight forty with your discount."

The woman fumbled with her tiny purse, struggling with the zipper. When she finally zipped it open, it tore away a length of skin across her index finger, the flesh pale and jellyfish-like in the store's unrelentingly bright lights. No blood rose to the surface, Ileana noticed, which was both a relief and terribly disturbing. Then the woman pulled out an Amex Black card and, fumbling, tried over and over to get the machine to read it, with only its angry beep in response. The woman grunted, then held the card out for Ileana, the strip of skin hanging off the card's shiny surface.

Ileana hesitated, her throat tightening and vomit pushing against her gullet. She swallowed hard and took the card, attempting to avoid touching the woman without looking like she was attempting to avoid touching her. When she turned around toward the machine, she tried to discreetly shake the gelatinous skin off the card. It took a few tries, and she gagged a bit as it thwapped wetly onto the pile of paper bags behind the register. She ran the card through, tore the receipt off unevenly, and handed both back.

"Thank you for shopping at Artisan Puerto Rico. Please . . . come again." She forced a smile that was also probably more of a grimace, and the woman stumbled away, flipping the shopping bag over her peeling arm. Her Gucci flip-flops were twisted, their bottoms flailing back and forth, the toe posts straining to hold on.

Ileana looked around and saw Carmen patiently holding a

man's bag while he tried to pop his dislocated arm back into its socket. Sol was calmly ringing up a thousand-dollar order for a white-haired, thin elderly woman who howled continuously through her toothless mouth, holding her loose linen skirt on with one hand and slapping the counter impatiently with the other.

"I'm in hell. For real," Ileana said to nobody as another moaning customer stepped up smelling like coconut and . . . hamster cage.

This went on for what seemed like days but was only a few hours—a blur of transactions with what the day before she would have considered monsters. However, none of her coworkers seemed the least disturbed. About halfway through her shift, there was a loud commotion outside. Ileana had no customers in that moment, so she ran to the front of the store and peered out the large window to see what was going on.

A group of cruise passengers mobbed the cosmetics store next door, their manner agitated. They shifted as one out into the middle of the cobblestone street, and Ileana could see they were carrying something on their shoulders. It was then she heard David's voice, shrieking, "Okay! I'll throw in the eye cream . . . for an extra sixty dollars!" But the words devolved into a piercing scream as the mob yanked and pulled back and forth on his limbs. The group closest to the store tugged hardest, until his left leg ripped free, blood splattering across the window right in front of Ileana's face. She screamed and jumped back. Silence fell over the store behind her, and she slapped her hand over her mouth. *Shit!* Ever so slowly, she turned around to find every eye staring at her, staff and cruise passenger alike.

She paused, the urgency of the immediate threat overpowering the image of David being torn apart. Ileana took her hand away from her mouth and forced a nervous giggle, though it came out a bit strangled and panicked. She waved at them flightily. "Sorry! Uh, I just saw that the"—spinning around, the nearby display of ceramic tiles caught her eye, and she pointed at them—"that the decorative tiles are on sale!"

A pause.

I'm dead, she thought.

Then, everyone in the nearest group of customers lurched toward her, and she choked back a shriek of terror, until she realized they were descending on the trivets as if they were starving and the tiles were the last steak at the buffet. There was a struggle, before one woman took her wooden souvenir machete with inlaid mosaic glass and shoved its dull tip into a man's stomach, over and over. Afterward, she grabbed the hibiscus flower tile from the victim's hands and stepped away, slipping on his intestines that were now spilling out onto the floor.

Holy. Shit.

The adrenaline was roaring through Ileana's body, but she forced herself to stay still. After a few minutes, and ever so slowly, she extricated herself, stepping back as the cruise passengers growled at each other, occasionally holding up a hard-won square of ceramic and moaning in triumph. When she felt her back hit the counter, her shoulders slumped with relief and tears sprang to her eyes.

"Nice save, chica," Carmen whispered from behind the register.

Ileana wanted to whip around and scream at Carmen, demand to know what the fuck was going on, but she was beyond bone-tired. Not to mention she had no desire to draw any further attention to herself while this ship was in port. Instead, she just nodded, then straightened her skirt and made her way back around the counter. The image of David's body being pulled apart seemed to be permanently tattooed inside her eyelids, and she could still hear the echo of his dying screams. But she shored her shoulders and kept going. What else could she do? To go home she'd have to pass through so many streets of those . . . things. *You worked at the mall on black Friday, you can certainly handle this*, but even as she said this to herself, she knew how ridiculous it was. No one was tearing someone else limb from limb over a discount on a flat-screen TV. At least, not during her shift.

Eventually, the last of the cruise passengers took their bags of purchases and stumbled out onto the sidewalk, blinking in the bright afternoon sun as they slowly made their way back down the hill to the docks.

Ileana's knees gave out, and she slunk down in the corner behind the register next to the cleaning supplies. She stared off blankly, her heart gradually slowing from a gallop to a trot.

Carmen yelled across the store, "Nice job, everyone! That was the only boat coming in today."

Ileana could hear choruses of "Thank God" in Spanish and exhausted laughter.

Deep breath in, and out . . .

"You okay, mija?"

Ileana jumped at the face that peered over the counter. But it was just the manager.

She opened and closed her mouth like a guppy, trying to moisten her dried-out tongue. She wasn't sure, but she thought she might have a spray of blood or intestinal fluid on her face from the tile fiasco. "I think I'm okay?"

"Good!"

Sol's grinning face appeared next to Carmen's. "Girl handled her first cruise ship like a champ! Let's hear it for the new girl!" they yelled out, and the other staff whistled and shouted their own words of support.

Sol held their hand out to Ileana. "Honey, hand me the

Windex, if you please." They turned to Carmen with a roll of their eyes. "The fuckers got blood on the front window again."

Still dazed, Ileana handed them the bright blue cleaner and a roll of paper towels, and they were gone.

The front window . . .

That's when Ileana remembered the handsome face contorted, his usually smiling eyes huge and full of abject terror. "D-David! They . . . they tore him . . ." But she couldn't finish; her thoughts were awash in his blood.

Carmen leaned her back on the counter, folding her arms across her ample chest. "Yes, that was sad. He didn't deserve that. But it doesn't happen all that often, and only at that store. The staff get greedy and try to take advantage of the cruise passengers." She glanced down at Ileana. "Sweetie, that was one of the reasons I told you to stay away from him. There's a revolving door of pretty salespeople, and every few months, one of them gets it." She patted Ileana's hand. "So, it's better not to get attached to any of them."

This was just not making any sense. "You mean to tell me you've never *lost* anyone here? In this store?"

Carmen waved her fingers in dismissal. "No! Of course not!"

Ileana let out a long breath. At least that was some relief . . .

"Well, unless you count Armando."

She was afraid to ask. "Armando?"

"Oh, I should never have hired him. Bit of a player type from Bayamón, ¿tú sabes? Tried to get some extra money out of a skeletal Texas woman with big breast implants."

Ileana swallowed. "What happened to him?"

Carmen's eyes looked far away as she remembered. "The woman kind of . . . ripped his tongue out. Then the mob finished him off."

"Ripped his tongue?" Ileana's stomach was somersaulting.

"Yeah, it was a shame." Carmen shuddered. Then she stood up straight, shook it off, and grabbed a mop and bucket. She yelled back into the store, "Good work, everyone! This afternoon should be nice and quiet—we earned it."

They all applauded having survived, and Ileana stood up and gaped at them. "That's it? That's all you have to say?" She gestured wildly to the open front door where a street sweeper vehicle scrubbed up the pieces of flesh and blood that used to be handsome-but-sleazy David. "Someone was murdered! Right in front of us!"

No one responded. They looked somewhat chastened but resigned. Like they were hardened soldiers who had long ago made their peace with the horrors of combat.

Finally, Carmen leaned the mop against the counter, walked up, and took Ileana's arm. "Amor, every job has its risks, ¿verdad?"

Ileana cackled maniacally. "Yeah, papercuts! Tweaked back muscle, maybe! Not getting torn apart by your customers!"

"Everyone freaks out the first time. It's a shock, but you get . . . well, not used to it, more like . . . tolerant of it." Carmen's voice took on a Miss Frizzle level of calm patience.

"But the police, the government, I don't know, the CDC? They all know about this?" Ileana looked over at Carmen, hoping for clarity. Or at least a clue.

"On the mainland? They don't give a shit what happens down here, but locally, of course they know. But we need the tourist dollars. It's a huge part of our economy in this city. Besides, if the cruise passengers get what they want, they leave. But not before dropping hundreds of millions of dollars a year in our coffers."

Ileana snorted. "Yeah, zombie dollars!"

Carmen shrugged. "Live, undead, doesn't matter. Their money is still green."

"But at what cost?" Ileana hated that this was starting to

make sense to her. "That money won't do David any good! Or Armando!"

"Ah, but it was their greed that got them killed." Carmen looked at Ileana, who was about to respond, when she continued, "Honey, my cousin Ines worked her ass off all forty-two years of her life. She cleaned houses of the rich in Finca Elena in Guaynabo—"

Ileana flinched: her father lived in that very community.

"Last July she developed a terrible cough, though she never smoked a day in her life. Then, a few months later, she drops dead. Doctors said emphysema from the cleaning chemicals. There's always a risk, particularly for those of us in the working class who don't have many options."

Ileana felt that one like a blow. She had a choice to work a cushy job with her father, something that her co-workers didn't have. She choked back a sob.

Carmen seemed to notice the tears in Ileana's eyes. "Honey, it's okay if you don't want to stay. None of us would blame you. Hell, if I had a choice, I doubt I would." She touched the younger woman's face with her palm, the way Ileana's mother used to when she was little. "I hope you choose to stay, but you have to do what's best for you. Just let me know what you decide, okay?" She patted her cheek, smiled, and was off to mop up the remains of the man's guts by the ceramics section.

Ileana stood there for a long while and pictured working for her father as he barked orders at her and criticized her "inappropriate office attire." Imagined weathering gossip in the office kitchen about nepotism and hearing her credentials (not unjustly) questioned. Then she tuned back into the store, the strums of the cuatro guitar and heartbeat of the conga drum reaching her from the speakers on the ceiling, accompanied by the familiar and comforting music of Puerto Rican Spanish all around her.

As she stood there in thought, a family came in. Normal tourists, all smiles and enthusiasm. The young boy loved the sound of the coqui frog and began to jump back and forth in front of the sensor, setting off a continuous string of *co-kee*, until his father gently ushered him in with a chuckle.

Sol walked back in through the front door, shuffling fistfuls of bloody paper towels behind their back as they passed the family. When they reached Ileana, they put the Windex on the counter and smiled big at her. "You did great, hermana."

"Thanks," she said as she returned the cleaner to its rightful place on the shelf. It was then she noticed the piece of skin hanging off the bags. She *tsk*ed a bit, then flicked it off and into the wastebasket. "Let me know if you have any questions," she called to the family with a cheery voice.

The mother smiled at her. "We will. You have so many beautiful things here."

"Thank you! They're all handmade by Puerto Rican artisans." When she turned around, Ileana saw Carmen watching her with a smile. The manager gave her a nod, and Ileana nodded back. Then she got to work cleaning handprints off the glass cases.

When she next looked up, she saw Vanessa, the leggy salesperson who had worked with David, out on the sidewalk, talking to every tourist or local who walked by about their skin, her full lips smiling their glamorous smile as if nothing had changed.

As Ileana worked to make the glass shine, she realized that nothing, in fact, had changed. Nope. It was just another day in the colony.

My Boyfriend

Gerardo Sámano Córdova

I'm aware my boyfriend is possessed. He was possessed long before we met. Kind of why I think he was determined to date me. He's hot (midnight-fantasies-can't-sleep hot), that demon glow—*Oof*—the violent sharpness of his bones, a hairiness close to fur, his beastly ravenousness, et cetera. Would he be as hot unpossessed? No. (Still turn-your-head handsome.) He's also nice, the non-demon part, like cinnamon roll nice—gooey, sweet, and a great comfort in the mornings: he remembers what I say better than I do, has framed three of my drawings and taken one to his office (to look at, I presume, as some sort of talisman). Sometimes he stares at me so happy I exist, like I'm a veritable godsend. I squirm. I'm no godsend. I took him possessed, and he took me milquetoast (I wouldn't even say ugly, ugly has panache).

My boyfriend doesn't slaughter people. He doesn't lure them to evil either (cheating or stealing or murdering or whatever). He condemns some to hell, but we all do that, "Go to hell!" to someone who cuts you off in traffic, that type of thing, except when he does it and his voice changes pitch, I imagine he actually damns them, their souls irreparably doomed. The best demonic he does is fuck like it's a competition and the prize is paradise. At least, he used to. He's lost his moxy. My boyfriend seems content in routine: work, come home, prepare a healthy snack, and watch cooking competition shows in shorts and socks.

• • •

The curandera took one look at my boyfriend and "Yup," she said. "Possessed." This was a few months ago, two years into our relationship. He was tired of waking up in the night speaking in several pitches of unintelligible grotesquerie, of the persistent neck soreness from gyrating 360 degrees, of the projectile spewing of blood from every orifice (nasty business, lots of mopping, sheets like Kleenex until we decided we didn't mind keeping them bloodstained). Mainly, he said, he wanted me to have him and only him. No demon, no more. My Felipe wants me all to himself, how cute. But I don't mind the demon—two boyfriends for the price of one.

The curandera lit her candles, spoke her incantations, did the herb-shaking cleanse and the egg cleanse (yolk came out like tar). "Very dark demon," she announced.

My boyfriend paled, and I hid the pride I felt.

If I was dating a demon (semi-dating? Dating by proxy?), it better be the darkest, foulest.

My grandma used to say, "Isidro, listen, better alone than badly accompanied." She was right (she should be; her husband died twenty years before she did, and she was never livelier), but when you're me—a guy who's been alone for a while, early forties, and an uncannily pretty man offers to buy you a drink at the bar you swore you wouldn't go to anymore because you come out more depressed than when you go in, but you still go because, what the hey, what else are you doing on a Friday night—you say yes to the drink, and you say yes to going back to his apartment, and when in the middle of heavy making-out, naked and groping each other's asses, thighs, cocks, as if grabbing were breathing and your flesh oxygen, his body spasms and it looks like eels are crawling beneath his skin and his voice lowers to a cavern-like book and says who knows what in a primeval-sounding language and his eyes darken like black marbles and you're sure that this is it, this is the moment you die, and the only thing that comes to your mind is that you forgot your laundry in the dryer . . . you give in; you relinquish your life and hope the demon does a better job of it than you.

We can't have dinner parties. Though my boyfriend's demonic demonstrations happen after midnight, he doesn't want to risk alarming our friends. His friends. My friend is singular and she moved three hours away to Querétaro: husband, two boys, SUV, house in a gated complex—the middle-class dream. She used to be fun. The first of us to get a tattoo, the one to score coke, the one who slept over on Sundays to avoid the weekstart gloomies. Now she gets bored and calls me to announce her husband is cheating (he's not), and when doubly bored, she calls to confess she's the one who's cheating (she hasn't, but it's only a matter of opportunity until she does).

When I tell Felipe's friends I'm a political cartoonist and their eyes go wide and they say something clichéd but genuine like "That's so cool," I answer with "It pays the bills." Is it so hard to say, "Yes, super-duper cool" and puff like a puffer fish? My therapist argues I don't believe what I do is "super-duper cool" and that's why I can't puff about it. He may be right. Then again, he nods off half my sessions and snaps back as if he were a staunch listener. I should change therapists, but the idea of starting anew, erasing all the hours invested in this guy (even if he remembers only a portion of my inanities), exhausts me.

My boyfriend works at a bank, financial something or other. I joke that's why he's possessed. Banker: demon, the analogy checks. He hates the joke. He's not high up enough in the organization to warrant evil taking residence in him . . . His position doesn't even have the power to ruin people's lives. I work in cafés around la Nápoles—sometimes I walk up to Escandón, or take the metrobus down to Coyoacán. People sneak glances, curious to know if it's them I'm sketching. They're seldom right, but their stares are thrilling. I like to imagine their mouthwatering jealousy at learning I am in a relationship with a demon.

Sometimes after a demonic demonstration, after we've mopped up the blood, put the sheets into the wash, and replaced them with a stained but dry set, my boyfriend weeps and I hold him. His shivering is deep, a jackhammering in his marrow. I encase him the best I can, like I'm Tupperware, like I won't let him spill.

My boyfriend goes to once-a-week sessions with the curandera. Her place is enchanting. An old casona in Coyoacán with a courtyard brimming with potted plants, bougainvilleas prowling up the walls. I accompany him to all appointments, reading in the courtyard while he gets cleansed.

He doesn't get cleansed. The demon, as the curandera warned from the get-go, is too powerful. Still, the curandera holds hope. Felipe holds hope. I hold hope Felipe will learn to enjoy his demon, let it loose once in a while without regret.

Today, I read a lovely novel about divorce. I'd forgotten the pleasure of a good book, and his sessions have become my special reading time. Alone in the curandera's courtyard, it's as if I don't need anything else but my book and my heartbeat. It's as if I once knew how to be by myself . . . some ancient mastery (pre-forties, when lonesomeness is still a choice and not a condition). The afternoon sun warms the terra-cotta floors, the plants sway, a soundtrack of birds, this cushioned Acapulco chair swaddling me like a womb.

Today, Felipe comes out sprightlier than ever.

"The demon weakens!" the curandera announces. I adore the rattle of her piling necklaces and bracelets, her one missing tooth, the way her salt-and-pepper hair poofs wild. I believe everything she says. "The demon loses its hold!"

I could've told them that. The demon has been losing its vim for a while.

I wait for Felipe naked. Our one-bedroom apartment consists of the one bedroom, one bathroom, and an open space made up of living room with TV, kitchen, and dining table. I stretch on the living room sofa. La maja desnuda right when he comes in. I don't know if this is sexy . . . at least it's a clear message. Wind from the open door rushes against my naked skin, groping, as if it too wants to partake in the sexiness. He watches me with the same strained effort he looks at art, a puzzle to solve. I bend over, ass up. I'm not art. I'm not a puzzle. I'm not a formal exercise hiding a sociopolitical message. I just want to get fucked.

"Nice," he says, sets his briefcase down (This is it! About to get rammed!), slides his apron on, and begins emptying the dishwasher. "Did you eat today?" He opens the pantry. I'm watching all this unfold from under my spread legs. "We have jicamas, I could prepare them with honey-lime dressing."

"Demon, demon," I call in my boyfriend's ear while he sleeps. "Demon, demon." (I don't know its name.) The demon doesn't answer.

• • •

My friend who lives in Querétaro tells me on the phone that I'm not the center of the universe. She's on the treadmill, winded. "People have things going on, you know. If I don't call, it doesn't mean I've stopped loving you."

"I know. It feels personal sometimes though."

She huffs, puffs. "It is, sometimes."

"How can I tell when it's personal?"

"You can't. Unless you ask. But do you really want to be asking people why they don't want to talk to you at any given time? That, right there, is reason enough to cut you off."

"Yeah . . . that'd be annoying. By the way, Felipe is possessed."

"You wish."

"I'm serious."

"Since when?"

"I met him possessed."

"And you're only telling me now?"

"He doesn't want anyone to know. I was being a good boyfriend."

"Why are you not being a good boyfriend now?"

"The demon seems to have fallen out of love . . . lust . . . I don't think demons do love."

"So no sex, huh?"

"No, nothing. Just blah. It hates me."

"See . . . this is what you do, Isi. Everything is your fault, no? Well, no. Maybe the demon has problems in hell. Maybe it's not doing its job correctly. Maybe it'll get fired. Maybe the demon is sick. Why do you think everyone must hate you? You're not that hateable. Geez."

"I guess not."

"The demon must be starving. Don't demons need sacrifices to stay alive?"

"We do the sacrifices, of course! A chicken every new moon. When the night is darkest."

"Lovely."

"It is actually a charming ritual. Candles, chants, we dance naked, drink chicken's blood, lather in it."

"Ew. You do it, too? How does it taste?"

"Warm."

The time we didn't do a sacrifice (out of curiosity, testing what would happen), my boyfriend seethed, shrieked, smashed half the apartment, clawed his skin. I watched: at first huddled in a corner, then I got in his way. I wanted to see if he would smash me like the dining chair, our blender, and all our plates. I offered myself. Break me, too. His black marble eyes scanned me. He grunted and flung me out of the way. I flew, not because he used that much force, but because I needed to know what it felt to be hurt by him, if he could ruin my enchantment. He couldn't.

The next day he felt so bad among the debris, he called in sick and cried while I tended to his torn skin. My enchantment relies on his duality: the terrifying excitement of his wildness giving way to softness, the way he embraces me, ear to my chest, my heartbeat a salve lulling him to sleep.

We brunch with Felipe's friends on a sunny patio in la Roma. People wear sunglasses, fashionable jeans, lean back like there's nothing better to life than this Saturday, this patio in Mexico City. His friends, a couple who brew beer in their backyard, hug me like I'm an old friend. There's an exquisiteness to my boyfriend when he's having fun: louder, more rotund—smacking down his enfrijoladas, nothing tastier, the slurping of his coffee, the delight as he nibbles on his concha, a contagious savoring. I wonder what part of passion is demon. The hunger is demon, the savoring Felipe. He holds my hand. His friends coo "Adorable," and I soak up their jealousy. It might be genuine warmth. Whatever the case, my palms sweat. They know Felipe. They don't know the demon. The demon is all mine to love.

Next morning, we're in bed. Even if we're not cinematographed in sweeping light and the ambient noises are uncurated (I could do without the motorcycle roaring past), this is the kind of scene I believed only happened in movies: our whispers intimate, our pauses romantic, his breath a stinky delicacy, his eyes so gorgeously dark I want to lick them.

"Isi, who do you love, me or the demon?"

I love both. I don't think I can love one without the other, like an ice cream swirl—you can't lick only one flavor. You must enjoy both.

"You," I say.

"How can you tell?" he says, and I part my mouth so I can taste his words. "You don't know me without the demon. I don't know myself. What if I'm boring? I'm probably boring. Would you stay with me?" (Maybe? Probably not. I don't know.) "I catch myself watching TV for hours and my demon screams *Stop it*, but I don't mind. Work is the same I've done for years, but why would I quit? Another job would be the same. I have one set of skills. I can picture my life in five, ten years so clearly, same everything, with you but demonless. Is that bad? Sounds predictable, but doesn't feel so bad."

"I think we should stop going to the curandera. She's killing the demon."

"Isn't that the idea?"

"It was. But what if you're not supposed to be without the demon?"

I find Felipe in his eyes: streaks of a lighter, brownish hue. Brilliant only because of the darkness that surrounds them.

My boyfriend agrees to pause his sessions, but a month later, his demon remains weak. Weaker. Its night spewings have become mere trickles, his neck barely turns past his shoulders, his black onyx eyes have lost their glint of damnation. Felipe wanes, too. Mopes. We order out more often, decline brunches. He watches reality TV without his usual zest: doesn't tear up at a wannabe singer's performance or shout at the foibles of hot people dating. We certainly don't fuck. The curandera really did her job, five stars, and now we need to reverse it.

Felipe suggests we skip the month's chicken sacrifice, poke the demon, anger it. I'm on board. We hide our valuables and the furniture we can fit into the bathroom—can't afford a half-destroyed apartment. Past midnight, the demon awakens. It thrashes, growls, and I'm hopeful. He picks up a chair (cheap and expendable) and hurls it. We want the demon to remember the thrill of smashing. The chair breaks, but it doesn't smash proper. The demon thrashes a bit more, growls out some grotesqueries, more like an obligation than true relish, and folds on the floor. It speaks its tongue, but its voice, though adequately grave, doesn't shake the foundations of our building.

It speaks and speaks, its black onyx eyes annoyed, like how am I so ignorant to not understand it. I suggest miming. Charades. The demon holds an imaginary knife and mimics plunging it into my stomach. I ask if it wants to kill me. The demon flaps its arms like a chicken. "You want a chicken?"

The demon wags its finger. No more chickens. It points out the window, at the empty street, at the city. A man hurries on the street, a late-night jogger. The demon points at him.

"You want him? I can't catch him."

It points at different spots where people would be if it weren't so late. It wants us to sacrifice someone . . . not a chicken . . . human.

I suggest we sacrifice Felipe's boss. Not his immediate boss—she's a delightfully foulmouthed divorcée—but his boss's boss, the bank director. The times Felipe has met the man, he's been exceptionally friendly . . . "*Can't we pick someone nasty, mean, rude?*" But I say we Chucho el Roto this business, class consciousness and whatnot. Maybe we'll lead a revolution, although we'd have to get caught, wouldn't we, to claim our role as rebels, and I don't plan to get caught.

Prison wouldn't suit me, or Felipe. May suit the demon.

I suggest the easiest way to sacrifice the bank director is for Felipe to seduce him and lure him to one of the sex hotels around the city. I'll be there and together we'll sacrifice him.

"He's straight, though."

"So? You're possessed, use your demonic wiles."

Felipe practices summoning his demonic wiles in the bathroom mirror. I stand by his side. "Open yourself up," I coach. Less a summoning than a "letting the demon work its magic."

Felipe is timid. He's spent his whole possession worrying that if he lets the demon play too long, too heartily, it'll fully take over. I assure him I won't let that happen. I love the Felipe-demon swirl, not one without the other. I have no clue how I can prevent the demon conquering, though I imagine calling Felipe's name, *Felipe, Felipe. Come back to me. I love you.* Love is infallible. Is it?

"You can do it!" I say.

Felipe smiles at his own smile in the mirror, a self-seduction. He wavers. Felipe holds on to the bathroom sink, breathes. He and the demon are tired. "Do this for your very existence!" I cheer.

Felipe straightens, licks his lips. The mirror responds with a come-hither grin. A wink. More lip-licking. It's all very porny. I'm getting hard. Felipe's skin radiates pheromoned heat; his eyes glow like only this moment matters; his muscles contract. Felipe makes out with himself in the mirror. I remind him I'm there. We have sex. Like Sodom-and-Gomorrah sex, like curse-an-entire-people sex, like break-the-bathroom-sink sex. We'll have to call a plumber. Later. Tonight we sex like damnation.

I go to the Cineteca by myself. I used to do this all the time pre-Felipe. The artsier the film, the better. I fancied myself above the junky delights of commercial cinema and companionship. The film is Indian and tender and, by the end of it, I want to cry but am unable. The cinema empties except for a woman and me. The credits keep rolling with bare-bones piano music, each note stark like a pinch in the soul. I envy this woman . . . crying alone, using Kleenex after Kleenex, like I would've done without Felipe. I miss this lonesomeness, so intimate, so unshareable . . . but it's only nostalgia, this luxurious pining for oneself.

Felipe is exhausted, bags under his eyes, cracked lips, his skin, once vibrant in sensuous oils, now ashen and saggy. He's one unkind word away from crashing. All his energy is being sucked by the demon and stored for demonic seduction. I let him rest. Stroke his head on my lap. We have a mission, the three of us.

• • •

My boyfriend texts: he and the bank director are in room 203. We chose the hotel with most neon along the viaducto. There's commotion at reception, three people shouting at each other; someone has been caught cheating. I slip by easily unnoticed and take it as a sign our plan is blessed . . . or whatever the equivalent of *blessed* is when dealing with demonic sacrifice.

Damned? Doesn't sound right.

As per plan, Felipe has jammed the door open, a piece of cardboard on the lock. Basic schemes often work best. The bank director and Felipe make out naked on the bed. I wonder if I should be jealous instead of turned on. Whatever. I relish my horniness.

I hide in the bathroom. From my backpack, I take a roll of plastic covering, a butcher knife, zip ties, and a pack of tea candles. I jump up and down, like boxers do. "I can do this," I tell the three different mirrors. My jumping evolves into a psyching-myself-up interpretive dance. I'm lithe for once, my movements graceful, my face beautiful. I'm powerful. I can do this. Fuck yeah.

The room is pistachio green (carpet, wallpaper) with a pink armchair, pink cushions, and pink tassels on the pistachio brocade curtains, so wonderfully garish they should be charging triple. My boyfriend and his boss's boss writhe and moan interlocked in each other. We should've come up with a signal . . . I don't know what to shout: *I'm here? Hello? Excuse me?*

"Hands up."

They don't seem to hear me.

"Hands up."

I unearth the power I just discovered dancing in the bathroom.

"Hands up!"

They unwrap from each other. The bank director's mouth shines red from all the making out. He looks at Felipe for guidance. Am I part of this sexy adventure?

"Hold him," I tell Felipe.

Felipe is befuddled. One second ago he was kneading this man's flesh, and now . . . right! He straddles the man and pins him down. The man complains: "What is this?" . . . "Get off" . . . et cetera. I ask Felipe to flip him over; I need to zip-tie his hands. Very difficult with a squirming man. He kicks. Throws punches. Breaks my nose. I stumble. I'm so into this plan, the pain barely registers even though the blood flows torrential. At the sight of my beaten face, Felipe's demon surfaces—eyes turn onyx black, he growls. The bank director yelps. Felipe, now demonic, flips the man over, easy like a flapjack. I zip-tie his hands together. Feet. Gag him with duct tape. I cover a patch of floor with plastic, light tea candles in an oval as wide as the space allows. Felipe, demon strong, carries and lays the man at the center.

"How do we do this?" Felipe asks. "Is there a chant?"

I pinch my nose to quench the blood, and my voice comes out muppet-like. "I think we just kill him."

"But what if we kill him and didn't follow the recipe and it doesn't work?"

"What recipe? Is there a recipe?"

The demon jabbers in its language.

"What does that mean?" I ask Felipe.

"How should I know?"

The demon growls, stabs the air. I imagine it wants us to get on with it. I hand Felipe the knife. The bank director squirms. His shouts come out as muffled squeaks. Before I gagged him, he pleaded, "I have a wife, kids. I'll give you money, how much? I never do this type of thing . . ." as if I were some vengeful angel or crusading psych-prude.

"What if it gets stronger?" Felipe asks. "With a human sacrifice, it might just take over me."

"I told you I won't let that happen. Trust me." I wave the knife. "Take it."

My boyfriend grabs it. "How do I do it?"

"Stab the heart, I guess."

"Here?" Felipe points the knife's blade at the bank director's sternum.

"More to the left . . . his left. Down a little bit. You'll have to be strong, Felipe. One potent blow, yes?"

Felipe straddles the man and raises the knife with both hands. He's a vision naked and knife-wielding. The man squirms, squeaks, drips in sweat. He cries, thrashes. Snot and tears fly.

He pees himself.

"Oh no." Felipe drops the knife, climbs onto the bed, covers his face with one of the pink cushions.

Sacrificing a human really is a harrowing endeavor. The fluids, the shaking, the sobbing, the breaking down. "Yikes."

Felipe's eyes turn onyx black, the demon roars, and I figure he'll jump down, all fours, and finish the job, take over us fiddling chickens. But it is Felipe who wins over the demon and retreats farther into the bed.

"You do it," Felipe says and chucks the knife to me.

"Did the demon say that?"

"The demon doesn't mind who kills him, as long as we kill him in its honor."

"Are you sure?" I ask. "We don't even understand it. What if I kill this guy and the demon dies anyway?"

"Isi, I'm sure."

I grab the knife, slash one of the man's thighs, quick, to see if I can actually bring myself to hurt him.

I can.

He bleeds.

I touch his blood to know it's real, warm and thick and awesomely crimson, to know that I'm not in some sort of delirium, that I'm actually about to murder someone. A necessary sacrifice, I tell myself. I can do this. I'm ready. I'm pumped!

I lift the knife. The bank director's whimpers cease, like he's resigned, like he knows this is what I must do, like he's offering himself to our demon, to the flourishing of our relationship, Felipe, the demon, and me.

I thrust. Felipe tackles me. The knife skitters.

Have I killed the bank director? Nope. He's still alive in a puddle of blood, piss, and sweat.

I could grab the knife. Finish the job. But Felipe sits on the floor naked and his skinny legs are long and hairy and he doesn't cry. He looks at me, like Felipe, like Felipe unpossessed. He's cute, undevastating but adorable, and his eyes are his, kind and light and boring, and I realize he truly doesn't want me to kill the man. He may have never wanted to; he only wanted to hold on to me.

"Do you hate me?" he asks.

I scooch over and hold him. This will be the last time I kiss his head and smell him—his shampoo, his scalp's delightful sebum—the last time I get to boop his moles, pull at the hairs on his back, relish the raspiness of his five-o' clock shadow.

A year later, I see Felipe at brunch on a patio in Coyoacán, far from his usual haunts. He's with another man, cute in all the ordinary ways, like Felipe, my ex-boyfriend. I'm with a book. Relieved to be near a plant, semi-camouflaged. For a bit, I considered moving to Querétaro, buying a little house close to my friend, but Mexico City's pull is too strong.

After Felipe left the hotel, I slashed the man's other thigh, for symmetry and to make sure he remembered not to rat us out. Of course he agreed to keep his mouth shut. He was lucky to be alive. He had seen the demon, felt it, hell, he'd been seduced by it. He would take this night to his grave if it meant the demon never came back to visit him. Plus I told him I had video of his tryst (I didn't).

A waiter serves Felipe enfrijoladas. A concha sits on a side plate, Felipe will save it for the end, to dunk in his last coffee. I imagined Felipe would've quit his job. Maybe he has and moved on to another bank, but maybe he hasn't and he got promoted, employing the one relic of power the demon left him. I ask for the check. I can slip out and avoid a scene: *Oh my god, hi!*

. . . Hi, oh my god! . . . How have you been? . . . Let me introduce you to bla bla bla and whatnot.

I'm signing the check when Felipe lifts my book, inspects the back cover.

"Good?" he asks.

"Excellent."

"I was going to ask you to join us but you've finished eating."

"Were you really?"

"No." He winks.

I don't understand this wink. I try to catch a hint of demon. A wild hope. There's none.

"You know," he says, "how people say they would kill for someone but no one actually means it? You meant it. You would've killed for me."

"For you and the demon."

"Right. Nevertheless, I will keep thinking it was all for me."

"Even if you're wrong?"

"Even if I'm wrong."

"Okay."

He returns to his boyfriend. The guy is probably asking about me. Felipe says . . . What does he say? An ex-boyfriend . . . ugh, too banal. A former lover . . . a bit better.

He says: *A demon I dallied with.* And the boyfriend says: *So you dally with demons* (trying to be sexy). And Felipe answers, *Not anymore.*

I walk out. I drank too much coffee. I'm jittery and my nose itches, but the sun is high and the plaza pleasant and there's a lonely bench under a tree where I sit and finish my book.

The Immaculate Rebirth of Nicki Duran

Zoraida Córdova

There was this one time in the ninth grade when my friends and I cut school for no reason in particular, other than we were restless and young and wanted a place to be ourselves. It was the dead of winter, and my family had just bought a new house in Queens Village, New York. There was no heat. The walls prepped for renovation. We tested our strength by punching manicured fists through brittle sheetrock and moldy wallpaper in search of a black hole and doorway to anywhere else, as if there existed a place for lost girls, savage girls, fucked-up and quiet and troubled and loud and unruly and unfixable girls. When we tired ourselves out, we gathered under our North Face jackets, passing around a slender bottle of vodka, a joint, and a book of fairy tales I'd checked out from the Jamaica Public Library.

"The real stories," I'd said, not yet understanding every story is older than it thinks. "Not the glittery bullshit cartoon ones."

And so, my friends let me read to them about unhappy endings. Princesses raped in their sleep, butchered limbs, cannibal witches, hungry wolves, mermaids turned to foam over basic boys.

"What the *fuck*," Leticia said, then passed the cheap Bud she'd stolen from her brother. "That's crazy."

"I think I prefer the Disney ones," Chrissy said before she threw up purple vodka slushie and pizza chunks.

A few months later, she found out she was pregnant, and her parents pulled her out of school. Sent her back to Guyana without so much as a goodbye call or letter. That was before we had complete access to everyone. Before slender cell phones and unread notifications and DMs from classmates you were never friends with desperately trying to hook a line into fast-fading memories.

On the morning I woke up three months pregnant with no memory of what, or who, might be the cause of my predicament, I found myself thinking of that cold, cold day over two decades ago when, for a little while, the scariest thing about the world was reading a book of fairy tales.

The intake nurse at my doctor's office looks more and more haggard every time she reenters the examination room. When I arrived at the clinic, there was a line out the door, but it was flu season, so I didn't think much of it. Everything after I woke up and felt the . . . the . . . I can't say it, let alone think it.

Everything after the *baby bump* was a blur.

I'd just seen nurse Kayla a few weeks ago for my pap smear and checkup, and I was decidedly not pregnant. She runs through a list of questions she must ask, dabbing her forehead with the back of her hand every few minutes. Stuff like what brings you here today? And when did you first start to notice your symptoms? When was your last menstrual cycle? Family medical history? Sexual history? And you're sure, you're absolutely sure you were not pregnant before today?

"It's not something I would forget," I say, and even as I say it, I know that isn't always true.

There are stories—fairy tales and nightmares alike—of slumbering girls, chosen girls, unlucky girls who find themselves in compromised positions. But this isn't some immaculate conception shit, and I am not in a rom-com where a doctor inseminates the wrong patient.

The nurse untucks a necklace from beneath her scrubs. I can't see the detail, but I know it's a saint or a Virgin Mary. I have a similar one at home. Nurse Kayla rubs the gold pendant over and over, her brown eyes affixed to the bump beneath my clasped hands. I didn't realize I was holding my own belly until her penetrating stare makes me self-conscious, and I want to ask her if she is staring so long because she knows what I'm growing inside, and maybe that is why her face is so full of pity and fear and awe.

She snaps out of it. Stretches a smile that cracks her chewed-up lower lip. A ruby drop hangs there before she laps it up, and hands me a cup to pee in. After, I wait. The room smells sterile. I try not to move even as something inside me stirs. I imagine it like a tadpole swimming in a pond. A fly trapped in the bulbous lamp fixture on my ceiling. A fat worm working its way through loamy soil.

When the doctor comes in to confirm that I am, in fact, pregnant, I don't believe her.

"That's not possible," I say, and then I say it again. "There's no way."

Dr. Zaynab shifts in her seat, her mouth open; pink tongue stuck prodding against the inside of her lower lip. I'm unsure if her pause stretches like taffy or if I'm imagining it, until she finally says, "The test is ninety-nine percent accurate." Her even tone edges on confrontational, brow furrowed at my challenge. "You're not on birth control."

"I'm not dating. Or sexually active." A desperate laugh bubbles from my chest. "Unless you count my toy drawer."

She doesn't laugh with me.

Chrissy once said her cousin got pregnant from jerking off

her boyfriend in a hot tub. Claimed another girl got pregnant from cleaning herself with the same T-shirt her guy had used to wipe semen from her back. Another girl, whose parents had refused to sign the permission slip to watch a sex-ed video, believed babies were made from tongue kissing. When you're young and stupid and know shit about the world, you find answers in gossip. What is gossip but communal warnings? And what is a fairy tale if not a warning in a tulle dress?

I'm not naive anymore, but even I find myself grasping for those innocent explanations, because believing the alternative is not an option. "Give me the test again."

"Ms. Duran, can you think of any incident when you might have—"

"When I what?" I lean forward, defensive. "Might have forgotten protection and wound up *pregnant*?"

"It's very rare but has been known to happen. Teen girls giving birth after not having realized they hadn't been menstruating."

"I had a bloody period two weeks ago."

She shakes her head, but repeats my hormone levels at me and adds, once again, "It's very rare but has been known to happen. Though"—she rubs a trembling hand down her face, as if she can reset her worry into medical indifference—"less and less common these days."

I don't understand what she means by that, so I sidestep it. "I'm thirty-nine. I've done a pretty good job avoiding getting knocked up this whole time. So what is it? A tumor? Immaculate conception? Did I get raped by a ghost? Fucking aliens? What the fuck?"

When I was twenty, I went camping with a guy I was obsessed with. I hated camping, but I lusted after him in the way someone does before their frontal lobe matures. I wanted him to think I was cool and sexy. I let him fuck me in a tent, a canoe, a hammock. I let him do everything to me except consider that I might produce a bowel movement, so I plugged myself up with Imodium. After I got back home, my guts had to be flushed out at the hospital. For a moment, I consider if this was a repeat of that, but now I'm grasping.

The doctor shifts in her seat before asking, "Is there a possibility that you were passed out?"

"No," I say, pressing my palm over my racing heart. "I don't think so. How can I tell if I'm missing time?"

"We'd need more tests."

"For now. Please." I swallow but my mouth is dry. "Please."

"Walk me through your routine," Dr. Zaynab instructs, cold and distant, even for a doctor who's grown tired of the world. "Anything that sticks out as unusual."

My thoughts skitter, recalling everything I did yesterday, the day before, a week ago, two weeks, a month. I'd been laid off after NovAmerica Airlines went belly up six months ago. My most frequented places were the movie theater, the gym, and the library—all within spitting distance of my apartment. I'd been on three dates, none of which had resulted in kisses, and only one in conciliatory sex because it was Christmas, and I always get maudlin on Christmas, missing every life I never got to live. Then there was Vinny, the last pilot I'd fucked before the layoffs. But I misremember the last time I saw him and there was no such thing as a delayed pregnancy.

Hadn't I read a news report of a man who'd intentionally impregnated one thousand women after one-night stands? There were other stories: dark fairy tales. Warnings. Breaking news after dinner—ugly little pills that put women to sleep. Fists. Weapons. Monsters who only found power when their prey was unconscious. Was it so different than that version of *Sleeping Beauty* where the prince rapes her in her sleep?

We conclude I'm not missing time.

I really am pregnant. Or at least, something is growing inside me. My whole body is numb. I can't stay in this bright room for much longer without wanting to scream.

"So what am I?" I ask. "A medical marvel?"

Dr. Zaynab wheezes a brittle laugh. I thought she was distant and cold, but I see the truth in her eyes, the tight furrow of her brow and flat line of her lips. She's scared. Of me? Of what's inside me? Of how it got there? Slowly, she starts, "One instance might make a marvel, but you're not the first patient today to come in with this condition."

I'm unsure I heard her right. I reach for my phone, but forget I'm still in a hospital gown and I'd only grabbed my keys and tiny purse on the way out. "How many?"

"Six," she says. We repeat the word at each other.

Six?

Six.

Six. How can six people wake up suddenly three months pregnant?

"You're my number seven, but the news reports keep increasing."

"Increasing? W-what's the total?"

"Three hundred," says the doctor.

I remember the line of anxious patients spilling out the clinic doors and around the block.

"And counting."

Ten hours later, I'd been poked and prodded just about everywhere. Drained of blood. Slathered with cold jelly for a sonogram that showed absolutely nothing. Do you know what it's like to have a black hole inside you? Not in some teen-goth-angst poetry way, I mean the complete absence of light and life that confirmed the *thing* inside me was real.

There was no sound. I've only ever seen the imaging done on TV and in movies. Most of my friends were women who'd chosen careers or themselves over motherhood. I wasn't always there for Leti after she found her suburban prince, and Chrissy had long become a fairy-tale warning, and the reason I was scared of sex until I was twenty. Yeah, some of my cousins had kids, but we weren't close enough that I was there at doctor's checkups and birthing classes. I didn't know what to expect when someone tried to see through you, into you, and found nothing.

On the way home, I clutch tight to my souvenirs—a bill for four grand that the insurance won't cover, a strawberry lollipop, and a picture of the negative space in my womb. It reminds me of trying to make photocopies that one summer I worked at my college's English department.

When I walk inside my apartment, I shrug off my puffer coat. Kick my sodden snow boots into the corner. I check every window to make sure they're locked. I shove all my clothes aside in the closet and knock all over the walls. Perhaps I have always been searching for a way out, a way to another land, but this time, I'm looking for how a monster might have come in. Every time I knock, I wait a beat. My heart shrivels with every second I anticipate someone, something, might answer back. Only after I've made sure I'm secure do I take my clothes off and hop into the shower.

It takes six pumps of soap before I feel like the sonogram jelly isn't on me. I cup my hands around the swell of my belly. I can feel something inside me. I wonder if that is what it feels like to be an astronaut floating in the dead of space. I wonder if that is why this is happening to me, because for so long, my life had felt like a big empty, like I was adrift in a great big nothing. Nihil. Nihilnaut.

After, I microwave some dinner, then put on my comfort pajamas and curl into bed. The best part of living alone is that I don't have to explain to anyone that I'm going to sleep at five p.m. after eating pizza rolls. I turn on the news just to have pundits in the background while I deep dive my situation.

They say upward of 1,634 women have reported waking up twelve weeks pregnant. In other countries, the World Health Organization has dispatched teams to handle the crisis. In the United States, health gurus are going viral with mushroom tonics; churches are setting up tents to shelter and guide these "Immaculate Ones" from dreaded government testing and, heaven forbid, abortions.

There'd be no point. The abortions aren't working, according to my doctor. A woman who underwent an immediate procedure claimed they dilated her uterus, that they inserted the vacuum and scooped her out, but there was nothing there. And yet, all her tests signaled she was still pregnant. A Rorschach blot swimming in her uterus.

I leave my phone face down on my nightstand next to my glass of water. I stay curled up in the fetal position, legs tangled in fresh sheets as my phone buzzes off the ledge. My upstairs neighbor is pacing in a circle, and I can't even summon enough energy to hate her heavy tread as usual. The school across the street lets out early. Helicopters fly too low, and the soliloquy of New York City traffic mutates into a raucous scream of confusion.

I rest my hands on my bump, trace the knot of my belly button like it's the thing that holds all of me together.

"What are you?" I whisper to it.

And I feel a tug, as if it wants to answer back.

• • •

Over the course of four weeks, 756,332 Immaculate Ones are reported, at least the ones who come forward. That's what they call us. Immaculate Ones, coined by the friggin' pope. I hate it.

My mom, who'd used my meager wedding and baby fund to buy herself a retirement condo in the ass-end of Florida, calls me crying. She only knows how to cry in Spanish, and I put her on speakerphone and let her get it out. Twenty minutes later, she's still talking about "el milagrito" and I can't help but think that turning a miracle into a diminutive transforms it into a scream. Part of it, at least. Milagrito. Mila. Grito. Milagrito. *Little miracle.* But I only focus on the end of the word, separate in meaning. Grito. *A scream.*

Did a part of me scream? Cry out into the universe for a baby? I want to say no. I'm not one of those women who chose a career over a husband and kids. I just like being alone too much. But now I'm not alone. I have my miracle. My little scream.

I name the black void inside me Mila. I jokingly say I don't have to have a gender reveal party because I already know I will give birth to an abyss. That sets my mother crying for another twenty minutes in which I am reminded that I am a terrible child, and she came all this way from Ecuador to suffer at the hands of her cold, distant daughter.

"I'm sorry," I tell her because I don't know what else to say. I don't know how to talk to her. I don't know how to unscramble the conspiracy theories that have rotted her brain out of empathy. I know I still love her, even when I sometimes don't like her, and I think that is why I never wanted to have a child. I couldn't stand it if I disappointed someone I loved.

Now there is this inexplicable thing inside me, and I want to hate it. I want to be repulsed by it. I want to be afraid, like the women in the news, like Heather Bishop, who went to work only to go to the roof of the building and jump, or like the cruise full of Immaculate Ones who chartered a yacht, sailed to international waters, and dove into the Atlantic with weights tied to their ankles.

But I don't.

When Leticia visits me, she brings enough Chinese food that they send six sets of forks and chopsticks. At first, she hesitates to hug me, like she might catch it.

"You were like that when Chrissy got preggo, too."

"This shit is *viral*, Nicki. I read they're rounding up the Immaculate Ones to study."

"Hence why I haven't left my apartment in three months." I feel my back crack when I sit down, but in a good way. Everything about me feels swollen and sore. I'm in my body, but it isn't quite mine anymore.

"What do you do with your garbage? Your mail?"

I shrug. "My super has a crush on me, so he does it."

"Better be careful. Sometimes men will propose to pregnant women."

"*What* men?" I shout, laughing so hard the pigeons on my fire escape take flight. "Shut up. Thank you, I needed a laugh."

But Leti isn't smiling. She's staring at my comically spherical stomach. When we were in school, we used to put basketballs under our skirts and look in the mirror to see what being knocked up would look like. Now pregnancy is as alien to me as it was back then. Only difference is I thought growing up meant having answers.

Leti and I shovel noodles and rice into our faces and watch music videos on YouTube.

"You're scary, you know that?" She sets her carton of food down and fishes a blunt from a designer cigarette case.

"How?" I rub my belly.

"Because you're acting so normal. You don't even know how this happened to you. No one does."

"What should I do?" I snatch the blunt from her coffin-shaped nails and watch her pretty face twist in disgust when I light it. Take a puff. "Kill myself? Shoot up a hospital like that 'Gods Warriors' group who think I'm carrying the devil's spawn inside me? And also don't know where to find an apostrophe."

I try to hand her the blunt back, but Leti holds her hand up. "Keep it." Plucks another, one that won't have my saliva on it. She lights up. "Oh, I brought you some stuff."

She points to one of the many bags she toted into my apartment. A pink onesie sleeve sticks out from between the zippers.

"It's just a few things I held on to from when the kids were born."

I wonder what a black hole will look like dressed up in tulle dresses and bows. There's a swirl inside me, and I think Mila is pleased. Sometimes I wonder if she can see through my eyes, or if she can read my thoughts. I've gone on a deep dive into pregnancy forums online, and the whole experience feels textbook. Discomfort. Hot flashes. Swelling. Appetite. Mood swings.

I've eaten my entire carton of lo mein, and reach for seconds when Leti chuckles. "Damn, girl."

"Don't shame me. I'm eating for two."

"You look great, actually. That's what's so freaky about all this. Not to mention how insanely normal you're acting. Did you hear that there's an eighty-five-year-old pregnant *nun* in Germany? And an eleven-year—"

"We have a group chat," I tell her. We, in fact, do not have a group chat.

"Are you serious?"

"No, but I've been invited to a few support groups."

"Why won't you go?"

I don't know how to explain to her that I don't need to be around a bunch of strangers just because we're experiencing the same weird science. What are we going to share? The fear of our alien bodies? The fear of what will happen when we all crack open or hatch or burst or splinter open in less than three months? I don't need support. I need food and rent money and maybe a hug.

"Because I can deal with it the same way I've dealt with everything. I'll figure it out."

Leti sighs, tips her head back, grinning the way she does when she's outer-space-high. "Yeah, we always do, don't we?"

But because Leti was Leti, she couldn't let it go. Before she left and drove back to Hampton Bays, she handed me a piece of paper with an address.

"You know I don't believe in that bruja stuff," I said, but she wouldn't take no for an answer. Left me there with bags of secondhand baby clothes and take-out, which won't last long.

I've never been this hungry before. I toss Leti's scrap paper into the trash, then hunch over my laptop to search the message boards. I'm in the middle of typing *What is a normal appetite* but get a text from a pilot I used to hook up with.

Vin is all like: *U up?*

I grimace at his spelling, then grin. I know a booty call when I see one. I text him a mirror selfie. Leti was right. I am glowing. My hair longer, darker than ever. My tan skin flushed. My belly tight and round and hanging out of my favorite crop top and fuzzy pajama shorts. It is ridiculous, but I want to see his reaction.

I go: *Immaculate #7*.

I don't really know my number, but I go by the number I was in the doctor's office that day.

Vin shoots back: *Nice.*

Then: *Hot.*

Finally: *Can I see u?*

I say: *Don't come empty-handed.*

An hour later, I'm freshly showered and letting him into my apartment. I had a third lock chain installed. It won't change anything, but it's nice knowing I really need to want company or a delivery to undo all the locks.

"Welcome aboard, Captain Cordero," I say, saluting him.

Vin's got a tipsy smirk and is still in uniform. He sets his hat on my head, and I inhale his sweet sweat and ambergris and woodfire smoke. He parks his anemic overnight bag by the pile of shoes and comes in, holding up an offering of greasy take-out and fast food. I press a kiss on his cheek and lead him into the small living room.

The reason I've always liked Vincent Cordero is because he likes being alone just as much as I do, but he only comes up for air to eat, fuck, and fly. All of which his job affords him, sometimes all at once.

"Fuck. It's real," he says, undoing his tie, his top buttons.

I kneel at the coffee table and begin to lay out our smorgasbord. "Why do I feel like I ordered a stripper?"

"Who says you didn't?" He shrugs off his jacket, his belt, his trousers. Each move makes me forget about the food, despite the hunger that hooks deep into my belly when Vin settles me on the couch and buries his face between my thighs.

On one of the message boards I'd read in the middle of the night, there was a thread of the new kink going around. People who got off on Immaculate Ones. Different than ordinary pregnant people. The more I read, the more I understood it was something about being inside a woman while they were creating the unknown. One fucker said he thought of it as an alien turducken.

I don't want to be someone's perverse kink, but I haven't been with anyone but myself in months and every part of me is touch starved. Something hot twists right at the core of my body, and all I can do is want him. Vin digs into the tender flesh of my hips and devours me, filling me with his fingers first. I feel pried open like an oyster, my pink meat exposed.

Vin thrusts his penis inside me and groans, "God, what are you?"

He's asking me, but he's *not* asking me. His eyes are shut, his brow furrowed like he's playing that game—you know that game, the one where you're blindfolded and stick your hand into a bowl of cold noodles and have to guess. He sticks his tongue out, panting, as if he's trying to guess at how deep he needs to go to feel for himself. I am a pregnant sex doll contorted and smashed into the cushions. He sticks a thumb in my mouth and I bite down on it hard, harder. He reels the hand back and grabs my chin, slips his other hand down to grip his root as he comes, screaming and rubbing the slippery mess of him back onto himself.

"God, what—"

His voice cuts off. Vanishes like someone who has dropped off a cliff, leaving behind a puff of dust and the whistle of air filling the empty in their wake.

Pleasure spreads through me, and I have to hold on to the cushions so I don't shudder onto the floor. For the first time in days, maybe months, maybe forever, I feel full. Panting, I reach between my thighs. Sore and wet. I blink slowly.

"Vin?"

The rumble of my neighbor walking around with brick sandals (probably) makes the ceiling creak. My living room is empty.

"Vinny?" It's worth a shot because he doesn't like being reminded of being a kid.

I am alone, and I wonder if I have lost time again. If I was drugged and left behind. If I passed out from the way he held me, even though I wasn't ready to use my safe word and I never have with him.

"Vincent," I try again, though I know he isn't here.

And he didn't leave. His suitcase is still by my door. His shoes and tie. Everything he was wearing when he vanished went with him. I rub my stomach. Clench against a sharp cramp. My little scream is stretching. Growing.

Full.

When my heart stops racing, I clean myself up and curl into bed. In the morning, I decide to visit Leti's bruja.

Botanica Santana is a quick train ride to the Lower East Side. The city feels dead, worse than COVID. Back then people were hacking their brains out without covering their mouths. Now it's masks all over the place, even men. Cops cluster in corners, more than I've ever seen before. A few of them nod along at a middle-aged man preaching about the end of times, while a warring nut-job spews unintelligible dreck. The only word that is clear when I walk by is "Whore. *Whore. WHORE!*"

I hurry inside the botanica and the bell jingles hard. It's crowded with people buying candles, sage, palo santo, and agua de florida. A couple of teen girls load up on bath bombs that promise money and protection and baby-soft skin. The only employee, whom I assume is Santana, gestures to denote she'll be right with me.

I linger, waiting for the other customers to clear out. I busy myself picking out pretty crystals based on my favorite color. The owner returns from the back with a spray bottle to water the dozens and dozens of plants covering every surface.

She spritzes in my general direction. "Immaculada?"

I nod. I hand her the paper Leti gave me. In Spanish, I say, "She didn't tell me what you do exactly."

"I let you see." Santana taps her forehead and then her abdomen. She's in her late fifties with brown skin and frizzy curls shot through with silver. She wears a button-down and jeans and a dozen slender necklaces. Saints and goddesses I have no name for. Crystal beads polished and cut to glitter in any light.

The bruja points to a back room. I hesitate, holding my belly at the sides. I feel so heavy I might sink right through the floor. What can this woman do that scientists and pseudoscientists haven't already tried? But I think I ate a man last night, or my black hole did, so what do I have to lose?

The back room is a lush greenhouse. There are rows of flowers and glossy plants. A tiny mouse scurries behind bags of dirt. Butterflies flit from bud to bud, lapping up nectar. It reminds me of Vin last night, and a dull ache spreads from within.

"Back here." Santana waves at the end of the flower rows. There's a long chair, like from a dentist's office or spa. The only choice is to sit or leave, so I sit. She places sticky tabs on my chest, wrists, and belly. I can't help but feel that one of the conspiracies was right—aliens are harvesting us for parts. Using us as incubators. Now I've walked right in.

"What's that for?" I manage to ask.

"To read your hearts," Santana clarifies, bustling all over. Boiling water, brewing a smelly tea.

I drink it. Not that bad. Kind of like drinking the gunky water in a forgotten flower vase. I wonder if Mila even has a heart that can be measured. There is not a sonogram or NASA-designed machine that has been able to peer into the Immaculate bellies. I kind of want Mila to have a heart, but don't want to say it out loud in case this is another bust.

I know the tea hits when my tongue swells and I lose control of my arms first. Before I can try to stand, I hear the chaotic rhythm of my heartbeat. It is everywhere. My throat, under my nails, the tip of my blackheads, and that one stubborn pimple. And right behind it, like one of those little bear cubs trying to catch up to its momma bear, is a second pulse. Mila's heartbeat. She's there. My little black hole. My little miracle. My perpetual scream.

When Santana the bruja said this—this ritual—would help me see, I don't know that I believed her. I do now.

A baby's cry rings through a rainforest maze. My damp curls cling to my temples and neck. My heartbeat is distant in my ears as if I'm underwater. There are four paths, two ahead and two behind. The sky is gray. And for the first time in months, I am not pregnant.

"Mila?" I place a hand on my stomach, flat but soft. Is it weird that I miss her? I know I said I was a loner, but I miss her.

Drawn to the cry, I pick a direction. The ground crunches under my boots. I've had nightmares where I look down and I'm dressed in the same clothes as when I was in high school, and there they are—my Payless knockoff Timbs trampling mulch.

There's a baby in a basinet made of knotted roots. For a moment, I close my eyes. *God, what are you?* What is she? What is the thing tucked beneath that soft forget-me-not blue blankie?

When I was born, my grandmother came into the hospital to inspect my hands. To make sure that I was fair like my father, instead of like my mother. I wish my uncle had never told me that, because it's the first thing I think of when I let myself look at Mila for the first time.

Leti's kids are each a carbon copy of her, and it seems I have done the same. She is me. Ten fingers and ten toes. I hold her in my arms. She makes those sweet baby noises, and I tell her, "I thought you were going to have tentacles or a hunchback."

I don't know why I'm crying. I didn't even want or ask for this child, this changeling wearing my baby face.

I take a deep breath, and she is gone. The rainforest becomes an airport. It's like looking at the world through foggy glass. I squint at the little girl disembarking from a plane.

It's Mila. She's around ten. She wears the same clothes I did when I came to this country. It's the same plane, too. The same bell-bottom pants and clogs with white socks embroidered with little yellow flowers. She holds someone's hand—a shadow. The shadow leads her onto the tarmac and away from me.

"Stop!" I run after them and it's like running through a cloud. I keep my eye trained on the shadow, swallowing the light around it.

I manage to grab Mila's wrist and yank her to me. We stumble and fall backward. I wish clouds were solid, big memory foam pillows taking on whimsical shapes. Instead we go through them until we hit something firm. Beneath us is a pile of black North Face jackets. I get up first, then help Mila.

We're in my old house post-renovation. In the mirror, I'm younger. Seventeen, maybe.

So is Mila.

When she opens the liquor cabinet, I realize she doesn't just take after me. She is *exactly* like me. She knows where Mom's husband keeps his nice alcohol, and she pours us two large glasses.

"I can't believe you thought I was an alien." She looks skyward and hands me a drink.

"Not me. The conspiracy bros. But, God, what are you? For real, real."

"I'm yours, the way Athena was Zeus's. Would you want me then? Would you be less afraid?"

"I'm not afraid. I've been absurdly calm about this."

"I ate your fuck buddy."

I frown. "Vin was simple."

"People are anything but simple."

I blink and Mila is older now. About the age I was when I thought my life was going to be something, anything more than it is, but somewhere along the line, I ran myself into a black hole. Every day is a different version from the one that came before. There is a man without a face grazing my thigh as I serve his drink. There is a pilot who thinks that just because I fuck Vin, I'll fuck him, too. I became a stewardess because I thought I'd be on a route to France or the Caribbean. When I got onto my first flight, the KLM stewardesses were tall and beautiful and smiling, and it might be stupid to base a life choice on a childish assumption, but it got me up into the air and away from everything permanent, even if my route ended up being LaGuardia to Rochester three times a day. I live my life on the go, rootless, because my mother ran away from her past and I am filled with a black hole and I will birth a black hole that consumes everything. I am another story; another warning of a girl who didn't make perfect choices, who was always unsatisfied, who never wanted to settle down.

"It's always the end of the world with you," Mila says. "But I like when you read to me."

She holds my hand. Lines feather at her—my—face. I have the sinking sensation of moving through time. I am five. Cool Pacific water washes over my feet. I scream. The area around me is covered in dead, washed-up jellyfish. The sun is so bright, I can only see flashes of color against the bleached sky. Salt and sand abrase my milk teeth.

"Can you feel it?" my little scream asks.

I can. We can feel the other Immaculate Ones getting ready to give birth to their miracles.

"I want to go home," I say, but I know I want to do more than that. I want to cut a hole in the womb of the universe and crawl back inside, where I am star stuff, an extension of the creature I carried inside me. An exit. After all these years, I found my way out.

"Then let's go." Mila picks me up and I curl into her side, watching the world from over her shoulder as we walk into the waves, weightless, embraced by the ocean at last.

Guardian Angel

Mariana Enriquez
Translated by *Megan McDowell*

The two of them were killing her.

Marisa lay awake all night, waiting to hear them. Once they thought Mom was asleep, Inés opened her bedroom door and let him in. But Mom slept even less than Marisa, because she could not rest: her lungs were full of fluid, her heart was heavy, her one leg deformed by swelling, the amputated one still very present with its phantom pain. Obese, Mom sat in bed and listened to them fuck all night long, even though they tried to keep the noise down. Each morning, when Marisa brought her breakfast in bed and saw her crying, she knew that her mother had heard it all, every moan and every grunt, the running on tiptoe, the stifled laughter. And that she said nothing because she was too horrified and sick and disgusted. Maybe she also knew, as Marisa did, that it wasn't their fault.

It was that devil on the ceiling, thought Marisa. It had first sprung from a stain on the plaster. Dad was always fixing cracks in the ceiling, climbing a ladder to cover them with mortar. One of the repairs was right above Marisa's bed, and she had seen its transformation clearly: first it looked like a bird with outstretched wings, but then it shape-shifted until the wings turned into horns and the little feet joined together to make a nose, and the body formed the devil's face. That had been some time ago. The more the stain looked like the devil, the fatter her mother grew. To the point that she had to have the bed to herself: Dad couldn't sleep with her anymore, because she took up the whole mattress. Besides, he bothered her. He moved into the junk room next door to Inés. And when the stain grew horns, Dad started going to Inés's room every night.

But they're not evil, Marisa told herself. She prayed beneath the sheets, because the devil was staring down at her from the plaster. My sister isn't evil; my father isn't evil. It's the devil.

She started to lock her door in case Dad got the idea to visit her as well. She knew that if he touched her, he would pass the devil into her. By now she could tell when Dad wasn't Dad. His eyes turned doll-like, as though made of plastic, and his stiff eyelids closed with a *click* when he turned his head. Even his eyelashes looked fake. She didn't talk to him when he had the doll inside him. But she would hug and kiss him when he was normal, to see if all her love could drive the devil away. She didn't dare try that with Inés, because she was too belligerent. Every weekend, she'd rinse her hair with Coca-Cola and take the 45 bus downtown. The neighbors said she stayed there all night, picking up guys. Those were commands from the devil, Marisa was sure, and she started to pray at her sister's bed, kneeling. But Inés made fun of her, shouted *goody-two-shoes*, and snorted cocaine off the nightstand.

One night, a hammering sound started in Mom's room. Always three blows, and they rang out when Dad went into Inés's bedroom. "I don't know why the neighbors would hang pictures so late," Mom complained, but she didn't insist, because it was only three blows, after all. Marisa wanted to check it out, but when she politely asked the neighbor, he assured her that everyone in his house was asleep at that hour. Marisa believed him, but she said nothing. Oh, if only she knew how to help them, but all she could do was pray to God. And her mom had gotten worse since the hammering started. Her phantom leg hurt more than ever. There were several nights when they had to call an ambulance because her heart was failing. When she was hospitalized and out of the house, the hammering stopped. It didn't come back once she died in the hospital, after the hammering had gone on for two weeks.

Marisa knew Mom was dead before anyone else. Dad was in the Capital, working at the hardware store; money was so tight he couldn't even take time off to care for his wife. Inés was minding the kiosk where Mom used to work before she was confined to her bed. Marisa had gone home to get clean clothes for Mom, and as she was packing the bag, she heard a noise in the living room. First it was just a flapping of wings, but then there came a whisper and then a thundering sound that made her cover her ears and scream. She was so terrified that she ran out of the bedroom. And in the living room she saw hundreds of sparrows, a brown-and-black cloud of birds crashing into windowpanes and walls and the TV, squawking, and some fell dead onto the sofa. The winged devil, the devil that had once been a bird.

Marisa went down on her knees and folded her hands, *Our father who art in heaven,* and suddenly, as if they'd never been there, the sparrows disappeared. They didn't fly away—it was the dead of winter, and no windows were open. They disappeared as though they had never existed. *But I'm not crazy, not at all,* Marisa thought, and, trembling, she checked under the chairs and on the shelves until she found a single dead sparrow—proof—which she hid in her nightstand drawer. Then she unpacked the bag: Mom wouldn't be needing it now.

Dad tried to soothe her, but he couldn't. He said things like "Mommy isn't suffering anymore," but Marisa didn't listen. She scratched his doll-like face, then lunged at Inés. "You witch, you witch, you killed her, the two of you killed her." Dad gave her a pill and sent her to bed. When she woke up, Inés was gone. Dad promised everything would be different now. He also announced that they would be moving to the Capital to start a new life. Too many memories in this house, he said through his tears. Marisa was delighted, and she kissed his cheek, his neck. The doll had left him: he was Dad as he'd been before, like when she was little and he came to pick her up at school or made chocolate milk for her friends. Sweet, lovely Daddy.

The worst part was dismantling Mom's room: the stench of medicine and urine, the mattress sunken from the weight of her enormous body, the orthopedic leg she never got to use. The neighbors helped them move: everyone in the neighborhood loved them and no one wanted to see them go, especially Don Kiselevsky, the Polish man who had rented the kiosk to her mother. "She was such a good woman, it's such a shame," he said. He was helping move the wardrobe out of the sickroom. On the wall behind the wardrobe, Marisa saw it. The outline of a fat woman drawn in charcoal, a nail driven in where the heart would be. Marisa opened her mouth and screamed. Don Kiselevsky went to get her father, saying, "What's wrong, what's wrong? The poor girl is in bad shape. It seems she can't get over what happened to her mother." Marisa pointed to the wall, but Don Kiselevsky couldn't understand, he didn't see anything there. Dad pulled Marisa's hands away from her face because she was scratching herself, digging her nails into her cheeks. But it wasn't Dad anymore: he had the doll's plastic eyes. "There, look, they killed her," Marisa screamed, and Dad's rigid eyelids opened and closed and told her, *Honey, that's a stain from dampness, there's nothing there, nothing there*, but it wasn't Dad.

• • •

The new place was in Saavedra, far away from Lomas de Zamora. Marisa liked it anyway. It had two floors, and although it was at the end of a corridor, the sun shone into the backyard and the upstairs bedrooms. But above all, she liked it because there were no devils on the ceilings or silhouettes drawn on the walls. Besides, Inés wasn't going to live with them. Maybe Inés had taken the doll with her, or maybe all that had been left behind in the old house. Dad seemed to have gone back to normal. Marisa kept a close eye on him. She went to pick him up every day at work, and he introduced her to his coworkers, proud because Marisa had declared a law major. When she got A's in her first two classes, Dad took her out to eat at a very expensive restaurant in Barrio Norte. Every night, Marisa prayed to God and thanked him, though sometimes she also got angry: Why did Mom have to suffer like that? Why had the devil chosen her to punish them? Maybe it was a test. She bought a rosary and decided she would never take it from around her neck, in case the birds came back.

But the birds never did. It was Inés who came back. Dad let Marisa know ahead of time, over dinner. He told her that they needed to rebuild their family. That Inés had suffered a lot, too, but she was rebellious, and Marisa had to try to understand her. That Inés had finally gotten a job and was also in school, but she wasn't making enough to pay rent, and he wasn't about to leave a daughter of his in the street. That the two of them had to forgive and love each other, because they were sisters, and it's what Mom would have wanted. Marisa spent the whole night vomiting and praying. But the next day, when her sister arrived with her suitcases, Marisa received her with a hug. Maybe Dad was right. He hadn't had the doll's eyes when he'd talked to her.

Sure, there were fights during the first weeks. But they were mostly because Inés wanted to listen to Metallica, while Marisa preferred Ricky Martin. Dad laughed and said he would buy another stereo—*Let there be peace, girls.* Three days later, Dad picked Marisa up at school and told her he had a surprise for her. In the back seat there was a cardboard box and, inside, the promised stereo. But the surprise lay elsewhere: Dad had doll's eyes. Marisa held herself back. She couldn't cry or lash out; she couldn't let them realize she knew. She had to act her part. There was a reason the devil didn't seek her out. She was pure. She had never had a boyfriend. No one had touched her. She needed to save her family, though she had been unable to save her mother. She owed it to her, poor thing, who'd died with a nail in her heart.

Inés moved into their father's room because, she said, she heard noises when she was in hers. Marisa heard them, too. Running steps on the stairs, and again, the hammering. Then there were Dad's groans in the night, *Kiddo, you're divine*, and then Inés, *Daddy, eat it up, eat my pussy just like that.* Even when Marisa covered her ears, she still heard them. She could hear the smacking of their kisses and their tongues, and she heard Dad a little while later, his low voice begging Inés, *Suck it for me, sweetie, suck it.* What could she do? Guide them, perhaps, through suggestion. Over breakfast, for example.

"Dad, do you hear the noises Inés talks about?"

"Yes, who knows what they are; there are a lot of apartments here. You know how people are . . ."

"But do you hear the footsteps on the stairs?"

"Oh, I thought that was Rocky. Poor dog, he discovered the steps, and he plays at night."

It wasn't Rocky. Even Inés knew that. Her sister no longer had the devil in her all the time. Marisa could tell. Dad passed the doll to her when she went into his room. During the day, she was normal.

"Mari, let's go ask the owner what's up."

The two of them went. Dad tried to make light of it, but he was clearly a little uncomfortable. *I'm going to help you, Daddy dear*, Marisa thought.

They asked the landlord, who lived in the apartment across from them, if anyone had died in the house. He told them that no one had, at least since he had bought it. Marisa was reassured until, a week later, their food started to rot. Even the food in the freezer. They couldn't cook. They had to buy ready-made food at the grocery store and eat it fast because it would start to stink on the plate. Dad insisted it was that shitty refrigerator, but without conviction, timidly, just to say something. When he didn't have the doll in his eyes, he seemed frightened. Marisa convinced him to pray. "Come on, Daddy, let's pray. Strange things happen sometimes, and we can also pray for Mom." The three of them knelt down in the bedroom with Marisa's rosary every night. But the noises continued. And sometimes, even after praying, Dad got back into Inés's bed.

Help them, help them. In the morning, Dad looked at Marisa with his real eyes, which seemed to plead with her. She had seen him crying in a corner of the living room, saying in a low voice, "My God, what is happening to us?" To help them, Marisa took a bus downtown. She was looking for the address of an angelology center. A brochure she had found stuck to a wall on campus claimed they could help you cast out demons, find your Guardian Angel, end corruption, and find the Divine Light. Marisa signed up without a second thought when she saw the place: silent, filled with white candles and with peace. She also signed up Inés, though without telling her. She would tell her later, if the course worked.

In the first class, the teacher said that every person was a being of light, and that everyone was capable of expelling darkness. Marisa took notes. It was possible to help those who moved in darkness, whether from corruption or a curse, because the devil lurked everywhere, but he was not invisible. She heard some wonderful stories of people who had suffered so, so much, and were now free through the grace of God. But it was essential to invoke and find the angel. We all have one who accompanies us in silence, but we can learn to speak to them. The teacher said that he could even see a few there today, floating above the students' shoulders. Marisa asked if he saw hers. Not yet, the teacher said, but with a few instructions that he would give her, she could meet her angel soon. She also asked him how a person reached the light. The teacher personally handed her a small book—just folded photocopies, really, but it contained the method of Purification. "With faith and the Angel's help, it always works," and he squeezed her shoulder with real affection. Marisa went home with her book and her instructions pressed to her chest; she didn't dare read them on the bus.

She ran up the stairs and started to read sitting on her bed. There were so many angels to contact! She hadn't expected that. Michael, Gabriel, Raphael, Uriel, Chamuel, Jofiel, Zadkiel. She had to choose one. But first she took note of the purification rite. She copied it in full into her notebook so she would remember it, the way she did with readings at the university. That way she memorized them better. She was struck by the words at the end of the instructions for the rite: "Sometimes it is frightening." She was very afraid. But she had to help them, help them.

Before going to sleep, she invoked Zadkiel.

"May the evil spirit be definitively annihilated
and may love reign among us
as Your love for us is manifested fully and inexhaustibly
Amen."

• • •

She found him in the morning at the foot of her bed. He didn't look like what she'd expected. No mantle or wings or youth. He looked to be around forty years old, with black, gelled hair, a dark blue suit, and a white shirt.

"Zadkiel?" Marisa said, and she tumbled from her bed to the floor. There, kneeling, she prayed.

"But my dear, I've been waiting *years* for your call. Stand up, please. Or sit on the bed, it doesn't matter."

"Zadkiel?"

"No, he's busy. I'm Nicholas."

" 'May your love . . .' "

"Thanks, hon, but there's *no need* for all that ceremony."

The angel gave a snort. He had green eyes and a broad forehead. He looked around while he waited for Marisa to stop crying and sit down on the bed.

"Oh, Lucifer, Star of Morning, you are *obsessed* with this neighborhood, aren't you? You're so obvious! It's clear that your sin was pride. 'There is a border region where the city and the desert come together in a combative embrace, like two giants engaged in a singular battle. Saavedra is the name that cartographers assign to this mysterious region, perhaps to avoid its true name, which must not be uttered.' The geography has changed a little, to be sure. Not that you care, I know."

Marisa was staring at him, entranced and terrified.

"Sorry for the tangent, my dear. But who thinks it's a good idea to live in Saavedra, just tell me that. Anyway, let's get *to work*. How old are you?"

"Twenty-one."

"Whole life ahead of you. Good. Lucifer Morningstar has been cruel with your family, right?"

"We need your help, beloved Zadkiel . . ."

"Nicholas. Of course you need it, and *I have no choice*."

The angel stood. He was very tall and thin. He did not radiate light.

"It's going to be *hard*, Marisa. Very hard. Unfortunately, you've gotten caught in the middle of a battle between angels and demons who are fighting for the soul . . . Well, *to work*. I am Nicholas, the Purifier. You and I must work together until the end. Take heed: your father and your sister, with their lust, have been filling the city with incubi and succubi. For a *long time*. They don't even know they're doing it. I am going to guide you, every step of the way."

Marisa was sobbing with fear and gratitude. She cried so much that soon she heard knocking at her door. "Marisa, are you okay? What's wrong, honey?" Dad asked.

Marisa looked at the angel, who shrugged.

"He can come in," Nicholas said. "He can't see me. I'm *your* guardian angel. Invisible to other people."

Marisa opened the door, and, trembling, she saw the angel was telling the truth. There he still was, sitting on her bed; her father sat down beside him and didn't notice his presence at all.

"What's wrong, honey?"

He had the doll's eyes. Marisa looked at the angel, who nodded.

"Daddy, we need to pray."

"Marisa, that's enough. Enough!" He stood up angrily, his eyelids rigid. Marisa trailed after him. "Leave me alone, I'm going to the bathroom." But still, Marisa followed him. When she went in, she saw the true doll reflected in the mirror, the one she had previously seen only in her father's face. It was smiling. "There he is! It's the devil," she screamed. Dad, furious, punched the mirror and it broke. Then Inés came in, half-naked. Marisa began to scream and call Nicholas's name. Dad started talking about psychologists and sedatives. Inés murmured, "Crazy-ass bitch," and left.

The angel floated over Marisa, who was screaming as she lay on the bathroom floor.

"To bed," he said, and for the first time his voice sounded powerful. It filled the world, shook the mirror shards on the floor, and made Rocky start to howl as he went up and down the stairs. "To bed. Tomorrow is another day."

The angel Nicholas told her that he would make sure neither of them would resist. At midnight, he brought Dad and Inés to the room they shared. He seemed to have taken away their will. With a single gesture he had them get on their knees and pray, and they did. Then he sent Marisa to have a talk with the landlord. "We must not be interrupted," he explained. She tried out an excuse: "My family and I started attending a religious center, and we're going to say some prayers."

"Twelve hours," Nicholas said, "until the final Purification." He instructed her to close all the doors and windows and to turn on all the taps in the house: they would need a lot of water. "Flowing, flowing," he said. And they would need to pray. The three of them holding hands, naked in the bedroom, the mattresses on the floor. Marisa could feel the force, and she saw Nicholas's feet hanging at the level of her eyes. Now he gave off a black light, a shadow that outlined his body like the charcoal silhouette that had killed Mom. Nicholas himself had lit candles in all the upstairs rooms and on the ground floor. He spoke, but Marisa didn't understand him, except when he gave her curt orders. *Psalms*, he would command. And Marisa and her sister and her father prayed, with the Bible open.

All the wicked of the earth you discard like dross;
therefore I love your statutes.
My flesh trembles in fear of you;
I stand in awe of your laws.
I have done what is righteous and just

"Justice for Mom—be gone, Satan," Marisa screamed. She cried when she saw her father was excited, even though every time he tried to approach Inés he received a kick from the angel, who was floating in the air, wrapped in black light. Dad's face, the doll's face, started to get deformed from the blows, but the angel kept going: *My dear, this is not real, when it's over, you will have your family back, as before, as it should be.*

They prayed, holding hands, until the angel stopped them and enfolded Dad and Inés in his arms again: he was so strong; he could lift them both at once. They were as though dead, so lax that excrement and urine dripped from between their legs, and soon the whole hallway reeked, in spite of the candles and aromatic herbs.

"I'm going to hold him on his feet," the angel said.

And Marisa knew she had to be brave.

Inés merely looked on, though she didn't seem to see.

Marisa went to the kitchen and came back with a knife, the first one she found, a small knife with a wooden handle and serrated blade. She looked at the angel, who had closed his eyes. And she stabbed the knife into the doll's face. Once, twice.

It will come out through the chest, the angel said, though his lips did not move.

"Daddy, I'm sorry," Marisa said. She used the knife to draw a circle in the flaccid skin of his chest.

And now the neck, the angel commanded, and he dropped Dad. Marisa received the jet of blood on her face and slipped in the blood that covered the floor. She felt the hot liquid drench her groin, and with it she felt an unfamiliar shiver. *This is what Inés feels*, she thought, *when Dad is the doll.*

Again in the face, to get the doll out. *Those stiff eyelids*, she thought, and she yanked them off. Dad's mouth was open. Was he screaming? She could only hear the angel, who was now beside Inés, holding her up. Her sister seemed to be awake. It didn't matter. The angel dropped her. Inés fell into the blood and rolled around in it. She was laughing.

Lucifer in the face, the angel said. *Do it!* And Marisa knelt and bit the doll to tear it out once and for all, once and for all. Again, she felt a hot wetness between her legs. *It's blood, it's blood*, she thought, and she spat out flesh, cheek, lips. She turned around, teeth clenched, and she saw the doll in Inés's face. Inés was smearing the blood over her breasts, so dirty, so impure, whore, Mother-murderer, whore.

Then the angel opened his eyes, and his shadow outline bellowed. Intruders, Marisa knew. How had they gotten the door open?

"Be gone! This is not real!" the angel cried. When the intruders tried to stop Marisa, the angel intervened. With a swipe of his hand, he sent them flying across the room, over and over. Marisa still had the knife raised high.

"I am the Purifier!" the angel screamed. "This cannot be stopped!"

But Marisa felt her knees go slack. She tried to stave off the intruders who wanted to bind her hands behind her back; she struggled to lunge and bury the knife in Inés's face, which was the face of the doll. It was in her sister, but it was also everywhere, and it was screaming something impossible to understand, something that made the black light around the angel disappear, the angel who was no longer floating, whose feet now touched the floor, whose head was down, and who was saying, *Stupid, weakling*, but without any rage, now resigned. Marisa looked at the intruders and said, “The devil was in Dad. Mommy, Mommy, now Daddy will be good again.”

The intruders pushed her toward the front door. She screamed the angel’s name, but there was no reply. The last thing she saw, before a blanket was wrapped around her and she was blinded by the midday sun, was the blood-spattered ceiling, and the doll’s laughing eyes in the eyes of her sister.

The Return of La Muelona

Carolina Flórez-Cerchiaro

Santa Elenita del Mar was a town that could only exist in the shadow of the land's own curse. If you closed your eyes and breathed in deeply, you could almost taste the rot that seeped from the soil—the blood of the land, spilled by the hands of those who had worked it for centuries. The smell of ripe bananas wafted through the streets, cloying, too sweet, like a graveyard of fruit left to spoil underneath the scorching Caribbean sun.

The flies, black and buzzing, thickened the air in the clouds, sticking to everything—your skin, your food, the walls. They clung to you no matter where you ran—hovering, relentless, like hunger given wings.

It was as if the town crawled, something twisting just beneath its skin. As if Santa Elenita was alive with decay.

I had lived here my entire life. All of us had. The ghost of the Spanish conquerors still lingered in the cracked facades of the town's old houses, framed by cobbled streets, their red-tiled roofs and crumbling stucco walls weighed down by centuries' worth of history—a history of bloodshed, exploitation, and secrets that were never meant to be unearthed.

And yet, that history began to resurface the moment Isabel arrived.

I had heard her name whispered among the women since I was a child. They called her La Muelona, but not with affection. No, Isabel was a creature most people feared. They said she was a bruja. A fortune-teller. A gitana. A corrupter of hearts.

She claimed to see beyond the veil, between the living and the withered buried beneath our feet. To communicate with the spirits that lingered in the remnants of our town. But those who sought her counsel quickly learned that her gifts were more than mere fortune-telling.

She knew things. Dangerous things. Things she shouldn't know.

Some said she could cure sicknesses that the doctors couldn't, that her bebedizos and potions were more than remedies—they were magic. But others, like Mamá and Abuela, whispered darker things, always with warning: that she was a harbinger of curses who bound the souls of the dead to her will. They said she took blood from the living, offering power in exchange for sacrifice.

"She's brought nothing but ruin to this town. She's sacrificing babies. Drinking people's blood like it's rum." Mamá's voice was low but sharp with conviction.

I stared at her, unsure if I was more disturbed by the rumors or by how much she seemed to believe them.

I told myself they couldn't be true. But that didn't last long.

As I got older, I began to wonder about Isabel. There were rumors that she had once been the wife of one of the plantation owners. A woman shut away behind four walls while the banana crops fattened under the blazing sky. But when her youth faded, his gaze wandered. And greed, more than love, set the course for what came next.

The land was already flourishing, heavy with fruit. But he wanted more, more yield, more gold, more proof that he could wring even the earth dry. So he turned to old whispers. A priestess told him the land could give twice as much, but only if fed something in return.

He gave it Isabel.

He thought her worth ended with her beauty. But the land remembered differently as soon as it consumed her.

He led her into the fields at dusk, kissed her cheek, and slit her throat with the same blade he used to reap. Buried her underneath the oldest tree, where the roots coiled like veins. Isabel's blood seeped into the soil like an awakening, as had the blood of the many workers before her who had broken their backs under the sun, who had died feeding this place with their sweat and lives.

The earth drank her in and recognized itself in the woman. And with her, it finally found its voice, vengeful, full of decay and memory. Through her, it could rise, not only show the town what had been done to it, but to make them feel it in their bones.

But the ground doesn't keep secrets. And nothing stays buried forever.

Days later, Isabel returned. Not as a ghost. In the flesh. Quiet. Changed.

She didn't speak of what had been done. But the land did.

And it spoke in her voice.

The day I first met her, I was seventeen years old.

The sun was already high in the sky, its heat pressing down on everything, smothering the town in an unrelenting grip. It had been a sleepless night, my mind wrestling with the realization that I couldn't stay in Santa Elenita. Not anymore. It was the weight of tradition, of the life I was expected to lead. As the daughter of the mayor, I had to marry a plantation owner, the son of Señor Andrews, give my body to him, like every other dutiful wife, and bear children I didn't know if I wanted.

The women of Santa Elenita knew their place: wives, mothers, daughters. We were born to serve, to labor, to give birth. And when we gave birth, it was often to children who would one day serve the land, the plantations. Without question, without protest.

But I dreamed of something else—of freedom, yes, but not just that. I dreamed of never again being dragged between rows of sugarcane, of the bruises left by rough hands and rougher laughter. I dreamed of never again smelling rum on someone else's breath, of never again tasting blood in my mouth because I'd bitten down too hard just to stay quiet.

I fantasized of tearing down the skin that had been passed from man to man, a transaction sealed in handshake and cigars.

There had never been a moment of choice, only expectation. A knowing look. A nod. A locked door.

I was a body promised before I knew how to say no. A debt paid in silence.

And though I never spoke of it—not to Mamá, not to Abuela—something inside me changed. It didn't break. It opened. In our family, the women stitched their anger into quiet things: a hem, a prayer, a sealed mouth. I'd been taught silence was safer than teeth. But the urge to bite back rooted itself in me, bleak and stubborn, even as I was already steps closer to the altar, toward a wedding day that felt less like a vow and more like a burial.

The land must have felt it.

And so did she, as if the same thread had been tied to us both, one knotted by fate, the other by choice.

Isabel's house sat on the edge of town, near the dense jungle where the flies seemed to come from, hidden among vines and trees, far from the eyes of the men who owned the land. The air there always smelled different—a mixture of herbs, blood, and something rotting deep within the earth. I had heard stories of people disappearing into that jungle and never returning. All stories starting and ending with her: La Muelona. Alas, if I disappeared, if I could vanish, wouldn't that be a form of escape, too? Wasn't that what I wanted?

I should have known better than to get involved.

La Muelona's house was a withering structure, leaning as if it were about to collapse under its own weight, with darkened windows that seemed to stare back at you, even if no one was inside.

I hesitated, considered my options, but I had none.

I knocked on the door. It opened immediately—no creaks, no hinges, no stalling—revealing Isabel inside.

She was standing at the doorway, her black eyes glinting with something ancient and cold. Her skin was pale—too pale—and her curly brown hair hung around her face. Isabel was tall, almost unnaturally so. She didn't smile, but she didn't need to. I could feel the pull, like a hook in my chest, urging me to step inside.

"You're here." Her voice soft but sharp. "Come in." As if my arrival was never a question, only a matter of time.

I obeyed, my heart pounding in my chest as I took a step forward.

Her house was coated with murk that seemed to writhe when you weren't looking. Inside, the air was no better than outside. But there was something else, far worse. It was the smell, the stink of a thing older than decaying wood and mold. There were glass jars, dozens of them, filled with stuff I couldn't name.

Though it was the flying bugs that unsettled me the most. The flies were here, too. They crawled atop the jars, across the table, and along the walls—swarming in thick clouds, so dense it almost looked like the room was moving.

"I . . ." I didn't know what to say. I didn't even know what exactly I came here looking for. How could I ask for freedom when my body had never truly been mine? When men's hands still lived in my skin like something spoiling, like something buried that wouldn't stay dead? Suddenly, I felt a stirring inside me—old, sharp, waiting. "I—I want to know my future," I said, my voice hollow as I spoke.

Isabel's lips curled into a smile. "You already know your future," she said. "You know what it holds. You're the mayor's daughter. You'll marry the son of Mr. Andrews and birth light-eyed kids. In exchange, your father will continue to hold power, prestige, even though everyone knows who has the real power."

Them. The banana plantation owners. The settlers. The invaders of our land. The snatchers of resources, of names, of bodies.

"But you want to change that, don't you?" Isabel's voice snapped me out of my own thoughts.

I didn't know how to answer. Yes, I did. But I didn't know what she was offering—or what it would cost. I only knew I didn't want to live like my mother, like my friend Clara. I didn't want to continue to be traded like fruit. Touched like land someone thought they owned. Smiling while something inside me spoiled.

"What you seek isn't simple," she said sternly. "It comes with a price. Everything does. The land demands it."

Isabel's eyes locked onto mine, and for a moment, I felt as though she was seeing straight into me—beyond my skin, beyond my soul, into the deepest parts of me I hadn't dared look at.

And maybe she was. Because, according to the stories, Isabel knew what it meant to be offered up. She was once the wife of a powerful man, then nothing, then something worse, hidden under the soil.

I felt my heart skip. If there was a price, I didn't have money to offer. I was unwed, had no man to provide for me other than Papá, and he'd certainly give me no penny to spend on brujería, not even if I begged. But maybe it wasn't coin that she wanted. Maybe it was something else.

I swallowed, each breath scraped down like ash. Still, I dared to ask. "What price? How much?"

"Blood," she answered. "Always blood."

I frowned. "I don't understand. What do you mean?"

"Blood is the currency of power," Isabel replied, her voice as smooth as honey. "It's what Santa Elenita has been built upon. The land demands it. The land takes it. And it will give in return."

I felt the sting of her words, even if I didn't fully understand them. I'd heard whispers of blood magic, of curses passed down without asking, but I never imagined it could be true.

"What do you want?" I asked, my voice trembling.

Isabel didn't respond right away. Instead, she stepped closer, her eyes never leaving mine. Then, almost in a whisper, she said, "You don't have to give it now, if you don't want. But someday, it will come for you. The land, the blood—it will all come for you. Your blood. For the future."

Blood. Perhaps just a few drops. Papá had already sold me—no ceremony, no vows. Just quiet agreements behind closed doors. He let men touch me, use me. Promised me to men with hands like rope and voices like mud.

And still, he expected me to stand at the altar and smile.

I was desperate. But it wasn't only desperation. What they did to me hadn't faded—it festered, a slow hunger crawling through my skin.

Maybe that's why Isabel hadn't looked away when I came through the door, because she saw the scorch of rebellion smoldering within me, a wild flame unraveling the silence and the bones that held it.

So, I held out my hand to her. "Do it," I said. "Take it."

Isabel turned away, gathering herbs and powders from her shelves. The room was prickled with the scent of crushed leaves, earthy and pungent. She stood in front of her wooden table as her hands and fingers—long and graceful—moved swiftly, each motion deliberate as she kept adding to a stone mortar.

"These will do it." Her voice low, almost soothing, though there was a quiet intensity masked in her words. She leaned over the mortar, her breath steady, and added drops of liquid—a gooey, amber oil, and a touch of something that shimmered faintly, almost silver in the candlelight.

My stomach growled, sickened by the scent invading my nostrils.

"This will help you." Isabel carried a small vial with the inky brew in it. "Drink up."

I reached for the vial and emptied it in one gulp. The dense liquid felt like drinking rust, metal. My stomach complained, and bile quickly pooled in my throat, but I swallowed it all down.

"Good," Isabel said, grabbing my arm.

The sting of her blade sliced through my skin. The blood welled up, hot and sticky, as she caught it in a vial.

I had offered it freely, but now that it was leaving me, I wasn't so sure. Still, I let her take it. I had nothing else to give. Not my name. Not my body. Those had already been claimed. This—this was the only part of me that still felt mine.

The room shifted. Not suddenly but subtly, like the walls had inched closer. I swayed where I stood, the edges of everything blurring. The smell of iron and herbs clung to the inside of my throat.

Isabel's eyes never left me. Her gaze was steady yet piercing, as if she understood the weight I bore, the pain, the fury, the refusal to be broken, as if she'd seen it coming long before I even knew it myself.

"You will see," she whispered.

I didn't know then what would happen next, but I woke up in my bed hours later, my skin throbbing where Isabel had cut me. The heat inside my bedroom was nothing compared to the fire that now lived inside me.

The memories of what I'd done came first, overwhelming, suffocating. Then came a vision.

The land. The plantations stretched endlessly across the horizon, an ocean of green and yellow. Beneath the surface, the dirt was cracked and dry, veins of corruption pulsing through it, stained red. The workers, men and women, drifted through the fields like hollowed shells, unaware of their own lifelessness.

Their eyes were dull, bodies bent and ragged, broken by the endless weight of their labor. They were ghosts, their lives stolen by the land that owned them.

And in the center stood Isabel. Silent. Still. Her eyes found mine like she'd been waiting.

The stories had always said her husband gave her to the land because his greed hungered for more—more profit, more power. He listened to the whispers and offered her up to feed that insatiable thirst.

I used to think the tales about her husband and what he did to her were superstition, a story meant to scare us.

But now I could feel it—what the stories had left out: her marrow-deep ache.

She remained. The land held her. She became its roots and its poison. Its fruit and its craving. She was the land that kept growing. And the curse that would soon make it bleed.

Not as a punishment, but as a witness. As memory. As reckoning.

She wasn't a monster. She was what was left behind when a woman refuses to disappear.

I woke with a sharp tightness in my chest—something inside me changed, felt wrong. The sheets stuck damp against my skin. Then came the sound. A tremble in the walls. A thin, jittering whine.

I held still, heartbeat racing, eyes straining against the gloom. Wings flicked throughout the room like razors in the heat.

The stink followed, sweet and sour, heavy as syrup. It settled in my throat. I swallowed it down.

Had I brought this on? Was this what the blood had called?

The sound rose, sharpened.

As if something had awakened.

As if it had heard me.

And somewhere below the floors—or deep inside me—something began to pulse in return.

The following days were more unbearable than usual. The town had fallen silent, eerily quiet. There was no sound of children playing in the dirt, no gossiping women by the markets or after la Misa de media mañana, no laughter in the streets. It was as though the very life of Santa Elenita had drained away, leaving only an emptiness, a hushed silence filled by the incessant buzzing of the flies.

It was worse by the banana plantations. The workers, the ones who would toil in the fields every day under the burning sun, had vanished without a trace. The plantation owners, once eager to increase their profits, now moved erratically through the streets. The train went around with empty wagons. The very crops that fueled the town's economy were left to wither on the vine, their fruit turning black and diseased.

I walked through the abandoned plantations in the sweltering heat, the oppressive silence making every step feel like a betrayal. It was in that stillness that I saw them. The swarm—restless, their buzzing like a chorus of death. They blanketed the sun-bloated bananas, their skins split and oozing, the flesh inside gone gray and weeping. The things crawling over them weren't just feeding—they were blooming.

It was then that I understood what Isabel had meant. The land was angry. It was not just the crops or the workers. It was the very ground under our feet that was reaching out. Isabel was the land that remembered, and the curse it sent to make us pay.

That truth weighed on me as I made my way back to Isabel's house. I had no destination, no purpose beyond fleeing the stillness that hung over the town like a shroud.

She was standing in the clearing near the jungle, waiting for me. Her eyes glittered in the moonlight, and the black-winged things hovered around her, like sentinels guarding a secret. Her face was as calm as always, but I knew, deep down, something terrible was happening.

"You saw it, didn't you?" she asked, her voice cold. "The truth woven into the earth."

The air grew heavy around us. The ever-present humidity made it hard to fill my lungs.

"The land always takes back what was stolen," Isabel said, her voice barely more than a whisper. "Invaders came with soft words and sharpened steel. Planted hunger. Harvested bodies. Turned daughters into dowries and sons into shadows."

Something in the trees seemed to stir.

"They thought the earth would forget. That blood would sink and stay. But it rose. Always."

"What is happening, Isabel?" I finally asked, my voice trembling. "What is all this?"

"The flies," she whispered. "They are a sign, a symptom of what has been festering here for generations. The land is sick, poisoned by greed, by lives ground into the soil, forgotten. And now it's come to collect."

"Collect what?" I asked, though the answer already twisted in my gut.

"What was never laid to rest," she said. "The debt of comfort built on suffering. The cost of looking away."

I was struck by the intensity of her words, by the certainty in her eyes. She didn't just speak of the land—she spoke *like* it. Slow and low, something ancient in her breath. Like the earth itself had borrowed her mouth to speak its wrath.

Physically, she looked changed, too. Not sick, exactly. But weathered, worn through, like someone who had survived a fire only to smolder from within.

"You brought me here for this," I said, my voice shaking. A spear of pure terror rooted me to the ground. "To . . . witness this? To . . . become part of it?"

She stepped closer. "You already are," she said softly. "The land knows who's been broken. Who's been used and discarded. It remembers."

I flinched, every nerve screaming to turn away. Her words scraped against the truth I carried like a bruise.

The fields. Papá's deal. The men. Their hands. My silence. And in the center of it, the shame I could never name.

I wanted to deny it. Wanted to run. But something in me had already cracked opened.

Maybe that's why I had come.

Her voice dropped to a low murmur, almost drowned by the humming around us, but I heard her still. "I will help you," she offered. "But you have a choice to make. You can let the land seize you, drag you down like all the others, blood spilled and drained, lose yourself in its depth. Or you can rise, become part of it, lead it."

"Lead it?" I whispered, my throat raw.

She nodded once. "You already belong to it. The land *heard* what you couldn't say. All you have to do is accept it."

I opened my mouth to speak, but no sound came.

A rush of cold surged through me, sharp as glass. Like fingers threading through my marrow, searching for the part of me I'd tried to forget.

Isabel closed the space between us without a sound. Her presence pressed in, vast and quiet and unbearable.

Suddenly, the thought struck: becoming like her—ancient, unknowable—should've filled me with terror. And maybe it did. But there was something else, too. An ache. A pull.

Was this what freedom felt like? Not the kind I had once imagined, all open skies and running. A freedom that didn't mean forgetting but becoming the thing they feared.

The world changed when I stepped outside, the night growing still and watchful around me.

I left Isabel's house, and as I moved through the streets, my steps mindless, I felt the weight of her power forcing me onward. People didn't notice me, didn't look at me with the same curiosity they once had. I was no longer the mayor's daughter. I was different now, and I could feel their fear from a distance. They didn't know what I had become, but they sensed the gloom lurking within me.

It didn't take long for me to stumble upon Papá at the town square. The midday sun burning above us against a canvas of clear skies. As if today was another regular day. But this was far from regular.

"What happened?" I asked, my voice quiet but certain. "Everything seems . . . out of place."

My father's face, once carved from stone, cracked with disbelief—no anger, no hate, just cold, empty fear.

"Something is wrong," he muttered, trying to shove the thought away like a bad smell.

His eyes darted past me, toward the dusky jungle swallowing the road out of town—the place where freedom waited, just out of reach.

I saw through him. Saw him for the coward that he was.

I wasn't his. Not anymore.

A wildfire roared within my ribs, born from every scar he pretended not to see.

I hated him with a fierceness that felt holy.

And now, I was something else entirely: dangerous, unyielding, alive.

"The land, it's come to take everything back," I said, my words slightly dissonant, almost like they'd slipped from somewhere beyond me. "All this will be gone."

The hum swelled, low at first, then denser, thicker, those black wings vibrating through the air like a warning. Not loud. Just steady. Certain.

Papá recoiled slightly, but it was enough. I caught the flicker in his eyes, the far-off stare, like he was watching something ancient unearth itself, something he'd long pretended to forget.

And within me, I felt a pressure. Power. Something waiting. Isabel's presence.

"*Let them see. Let them feel it.*"

It wasn't a whisper. It moved through me like smoke—slow, clinging, impossible to hold or escape. I tried to resist, to keep myself separate from her. From it. But hadn't I, for once, made a choice of my own?

Still, the more I pulled away, the louder it became. A call I couldn't quiet. A tug I no longer knew how to refuse.

I turned to my father, voice steadier than I felt.

"Tell the people to leave. The land will take them all, one by one, until it's satisfied. Until it gets what it's owed."

Days had passed, and a lingering haze curled around me like a living fog. Murmurs rippled through the people of Santa Elenita, their eyes wide with unease, but no one dared to move. They were trapped in a silent fear.

I left them behind, drawn to the edge of town, the clearing near Isabel's house. Dusk folded into darkness, swallowing the last light. Near the jungle, Isabel stood motionless; her eyes caught the fading glow, cold and unreadable.

"You feel it now, don't you?" she asked, her voice calm but full of something deeper and harsher than the wind that blew through the trees. "The hunger. The power."

I couldn't find the words. They caught like stones in my throat, heavy and cold. A bitter taste lingered on my tongue. Deep down, I knew Isabel spoke the truth.

"You've chosen," Isabel repeated, a smile playing at the corner of her lips. "Now it is time to fulfill your purpose."

I nodded slowly, the finality of it sinking into me.

Isabel raised her hand, and as she did, I felt a shift once again. It was as if the land itself were moving with us, responding to our call. The chill deepened, shapes flickering unnaturally around us, and then in the distance, I saw them.

The workers. Their families. The natives. Centuries-old victims, players in the war for the land.

They were emerging from the grasp of the jungle, their bodies stiff, their eyes empty. They were dead, but they moved like they were alive, their limbs jerking awkwardly, their faces contorted in agony.

"They have risen," Isabel whispered. "The land has claimed them."

The dead were coming, slipping from the earth's cracks, their hollow eyes burning with a hunger that would not be sated, drawn to drag down those who dared hide their sins below the graves of the forgotten.

"They will follow us," Isabel said, her voice rising with the growing sound of the flies. "You will lead them, just as I have led them here."

The dead began to move, slowly at first, but then gaining pace—an unstoppable tide swarming through the town, heading straight for the heart of Santa Elenita, where the rich men lived, where the plantation owners sat in their mansions, their wealth built on the backs of those they had enslaved.

The time for the reckoning had come.

Santa Elenita shifted uneasily as the dead advanced. Blinds fluttered, doors creaked, small signs of growing dread. The throng's noise deepened as pale faces appeared at windows, watching the procession snake through the streets.

I watched from the edge of town as the dead shuffled through the winding lanes, their features twisted with fury and despair. It was as if the history of Santa Elenita had risen from the ashes of its own sins.

Now, Isabel whispered within me. *Now is the time.*

I stepped forward, my footsteps sure and steady. The flies trailed after me, crawling through the heat, a smear of motion that never broke apart. Their sick hum pressed into my ears, like something gnawing at the edges of thought. I could still hear the distant cries of the townspeople, faint, scattered, just barely rising over the whisper of wings. Some had seen what was coming and tried to flee. But there was nowhere left to run. The land was done waiting.

I raised my arms. The dead stopped. One by one, the ruined bodies turned toward me, heads tilting, eyes vacant yet knowing.

Waiting.

And I gave them what they wanted.

They poured ahead of us—twitching wings forming a veil that dimmed the light—slowly at first, but then with increasing speed, their bodies jerking forward in a wave of relentless hunger.

The town continued its screams, but there was no escaping what had been set in motion.

I lifted my hands, and something moved through me, vast and old and final.

The dead moved faster now, their footsteps dragging but purposeful. They reached the first house, Señor Andrews's estate.

At the gates, they didn't pause. Blighted hands pulled, twisted, tore. Wood splintered like bone, and the iron gave way.

Then came the infestation: flies spilling through the shattered windows, slipping through doors, burrowing into walls. They filled the house with a sound that wasn't quite buzzing, more like a low, endless shriek.

The estate writhed, alive with fury. Nothing inside was spared.

The air turned dense and rancid, pressing in from all sides as the dead advanced, drawn not only by rage but by memory.

I moved closer, my steps light, the ground no longer resisting my presence.

The front door burst open before I could even reach it.

Inside, Señor Andrews stood, trembling, his face bleached with terror. Behind him, his wife and sons huddled, their eyes wide with disbelief. They had heard the screams, had felt the ground tremble, but they believed their wealth, their power, would shield them.

They were wrong.

"What is this?" he barked in his mediocre Spanish. "What do you want from us?"

I stepped in. The room tightened around me, every silhouette seeming to lean closer. Isabel's power surged through me, her voice curling through my thoughts.

Make them feel it, she said. *Make them remember.*

I opened my mouth, but it wasn't my voice that spoke, it was hers. Cool and precise. A blade wrapped in silk.

"Do you remember the blood that was spilled on this land, Señor Andrews? The lives broken to build your empire? The hands that bled for your harvests? The lives spent beneath your feet, festering while you dined above them?"

He sneered, but I saw it, a hint of fear in his eyes.

"I don't know what you're talking about," he blurted. "I haven't done anything. You're just . . . just mad. I can't believe your father wanted my son to marry a madwoman like you." He spat the words, and then he froze as I reached out to him. My hand closed around his wrist, cold and steady as stone.

"Mad?" I echoed, Isabel's venom coating every syllable. "You call this land yours, but it was never yours to take. You made it a grave."

He yanked his arm, but I didn't release him. Instead, I grinned—a slow, splitting smile that stretched too wide, pulling at the corners of my mouth like something unhinged. My cheeks ached, but I didn't stop.

A cry tore from his throat, a raw, ragged thing, as the dead surged inside. They pulled him from his family; limbs wrapped around him like roots reclaiming stolen ground. The hunger had found him.

His wife screamed, his sons clutched at her skirts. But none of them moved to help. They were part of it, too.

And then, quiet. Just a breath. Just the sound of tearing. And nothing left but what the land remembered.

But even as the dead sank back into the soil, I stayed still.

Not haunted. Not possessed.

Changed.

What Isabel began didn't end with her. It lodged in me, not as a guest, but as the rage carved into generations.

People would tell the story of Santa Elenita, long after the town was no longer part of a map.

How Santa Elenita was never the same. What had once been a thriving community had become a hollow shell, its streets empty, its buildings crumbling into dust. The flies wouldn't leave. They'd hover like ghosts, a constant reminder of what had transpired.

Some would even say the dead still walk the town's streets at night, that they are led by a woman with eyes as bleak as eternal dusk. Others would say that La Muelona still lurks around Santa Elenita's ruins, hidden in the shadows, waiting for the next souls to claim.

But the truth was darker.

The girl who once longed for freedom was crushed into dust, fed to the roots, swallowed by silence like all others.

Vengeance floods my heart and soul.

I am La Muelona now.

I smile wide, and then I feast.

Pomelo

Xochitl Gonzalez

Once there was a man with an insatiable thirst. He had pockets filled with coins that he clutched in his extremely tight fist. With his fist and the weight of his coins, he wielded great power in the city on the wide river where he lived. With his other hand he controlled the comings and goings of the large house where he dwelled on the outskirts of town. The man held many secrets, therefore he was prone to suspicion of others and built his large house out of glass in the shape of a horseshoe so that from nearly any vantage point he could see two things: what everyone else was doing and his beloved grapefruit tree, which sat in the center of the courtyard. The tree had been born of a cutting taken from the grapefruit tree at his father's home, whose tree had been born from a cutting of his father's tree before that. And so on and so forth, going back to the time when this place belonged to a different country, and even, perhaps, to when it belonged to no country whatsoever. The tree was the centerpiece of the courtyard, taller than most grapefruit trees, towering over the orange trees and lemon trees that surrounded it. Only the ahuehuete tree eclipsed it in size, but that majestic tree did not bear fruit, and that was what the man valued. The grapefruits of his tree were one of the few things that could quench his thirst.

Every detail of the man's personal needs and homelife was tended to by his wife and the household servants, with one exception. Each morning, upon rising, he would walk through the glass doors of his bedroom, cross the courtyard, and pluck a grapefruit from his tree before tearing into its pale-yellow flesh. The only time he unclenched his fists.

Most mornings he clawed off the rind and bit into the taut, thin flesh with his near-perfect teeth, the skin casually discarded for someone else to dispose of. Some days though, he delivered it to the kitchen, silently setting it in front of his wife, who always took her coffee at the small table there. She would rise, dutifully, and juice it. Alma, the cook, would have done this, of course, but the man enjoyed his juice more when he knew his wife had wrung out the flesh with her own hands. He couldn't, he lamented, see her from the dining room table, where he sat and read his paper. The kitchen one of the few blind spots in the home. But he could picture her. Her delicate hands working the fruit, arm muscles contracting as she twisted the pulp around the ceramic juicer, attempting to extract every last drop. Straining the seeds with great care. For him. He could smell her before she entered the room, the grapefruit's dirty, sharp scent wafting in like the sweat of a beautiful woman. He took great pleasure in the sight of her on these mornings as she walked through the rounded doorway into the sunlit room. The glass full nearly to the brim, balanced on a small saucer to prevent any spills.

"Your juice, my love," she would say, smiling demurely as she set the glass down in front of him.

He would take it up with a grin, flashing the near-perfect teeth whose whiteness was set off by his just-tanned-enough face, before examining the juice admiringly and taking his first long, slow sip. His throat, his heart, his soul, dry like smoking brush about to spark flames. The juice dousing it all; a cleansing. Then he would release a sigh of satisfaction he otherwise reserved for the bedroom.

"How was it, my love?"

"My tree gives the most delicious juice," he would always say, gazing only at the glass, as if to purposefully look past Marlen and her efforts. From the corner of his eye, he could see her trying to recover herself, pick up the tiny bit of hurt feeling that dripped onto the floor, no saucer there to catch it.

"What does your day look like today?" she would ask as she leaned over him to brush crumbs from the table. This was when he would usually look into her eyes.

"Ah, Marlen, very busy. Very busy. I won't be home until very late."

Just as she would cast her gaze down, sad because they both knew what he really meant, he would laugh and grab her ass, take her into his broad arms, and pull her slim frame onto his lap, sending a smile to her face. And it would all be erased. For a moment.

From the kitchen they could hear her singing, their daughter Pilar. Her voice clear as a bell. Marlen jumped up—fearful to be caught being so intimate with her husband.

"Apá!" Pilar called as she bound into the room, trailed by Alma carrying a pot of fresh coffee for the man.

Pilar ran and kissed her father's cheek. She was, he thought, a very beautiful girl: round, amber eyes, noble nose, a mouth that turned up naturally in its corners. Every good thing inherited from her mother, with the fortunate exception of Marlen's melancholy disposition. It dragged on his wife like tiny weights on a fishing net. She had not been like that in the beginning. Certainly not on the night that they first met; both guests at a dinner party thrown by a mutual family friend. She had sat across from him at the long, narrow table, and he remembered how bright her eyes looked, the light of the tall tapered candles reflecting off them. How her long waves of brown hair cascaded against her bare shoulders, the color of a rich crème. How she would throw her head back when she laughed, which she'd seemed to do often that night and throughout their brief courtship. How he'd leaned into her and began to whisper slightly ribald jokes to see if she could handle it—but also to glimpse the perfect pink flick of her tongue when she giggled. How it had tantalized him that night. Now the sadness hovered around her like a cloud that chilled his bones unnecessarily. But Pilar? Pure light. Beautiful and bright with a jovial personality that reminded him of his own youngest sister, long dead, and for whom she was named. It was this tie that lived in his mind, between his small Pilar and his favorite sibling, that elevated his daughter and allowed him to see past the fact that she was not a son.

"Apá," she said, jumping onto his lap, "Alma said there was juice today."

"Yes," the man replied.

"I came for a sip."

"Just a sip, mija," he said.

The juice glass so big in her seven-year-old hands. With the reverence of a devout disciple, she purses her lips, taking just a few drops before throwing her head back and dramatically smacking her lips.

"Ahhhhh!" Pilar exclaimed. "There is no grapefruit tree like ours, Apá."

"I think that's true, mija," he said, "except, maybe Welo's, because his tree is the father of my tree."

"I can't wait to grow up and have my own grapefruit tree so I can have juice every morning!"

Marlen shifted her weight and looked out into the courtyard while the man chuckled lightheartedly and tugged at his daughter's impeccable braid. Her hair, sable-colored and thick, the one trait of his she carried.

"Pilar, only sons can take cuttings from the grapefruit tree, you know that. Besides," he said, hugging her close to him, "you're the youngest girl. You're going to stay here and take care of Apá and Mamá."

A look of upset crossed Pilar's face.

"I'm the oldest!" she cried out.

"Mija," said Alma as she cleared the man's breakfast plate, "you are the only. Which makes you oldest *and* youngest."

"Pilar!" her mother exclaimed, more tightness in her voice than she'd intended. "Go get dressed; we need to go soon. Alma! My husband needs more toast."

Alone, the man noticed his wife had pulled her cloak of sadness tighter to her, attempting to bind the wound he knew had just reopened. The one they both knew had never truly healed.

She leaned closer to him, taking the napkin from his lap, refolding it into smoothness.

"You're going out?" he asked.

"I need a bit of money, my love," Marlen stated demurely.

"For what?" he'd replied, taking his eyes back to his paper. "What could you need that this house doesn't already have?"

This was (and Marlen would concede if asked) generally true. Fresh vegetables, the best cuts of meat, newly caught fish, the freshest of bread, wines, tequilas, and whiskeys were constantly delivered to the glass house. Everything the man might ever want or crave. If she had to accompany him to a business function or a gala, he almost always picked out a gown for her and had it delivered to the house. He loved her hair a shade more auburn than its natural brown, so a colorist came bimonthly to keep it just so. Her lingerie, her perfume. All of it chosen by him. Everything that Marlen or Pilar could possibly need or want. At least according to the man.

"Pilar's communion is coming up; I have to take her to the city for a dress."

The man gladly paid for Pilar's Catholic school, because it

was the very best and was filled with the daughters of other important men whose gardens held trees sprouted from the cuttings of their ancestors. But he shunned religion. Feared its hellfire and brimstone. Disdained its disdain for his larger thirsts. His wife knew this.

"All the families from her school will be there," she added flatly, pressing her lissome body into him.

The man scoffed, irritated that she knew this was the button to push. He shoved himself away from the table—away from her—and begrudgingly took his billfold from his pocket, thumbing out money onto the table before he got up and walked away.

During the days, the man looked down upon the city from his perch of power. Money delighted him, but paled against the thrill of money earned, which gave him influence over another. For this reason, his interests mainly lay in the acquiring and leasing of land and, of course, the lending of capital. Through the glass of his office, the people wandering the streets were far away and invisible to him, but he knew that scores upon scores of them were in his debt. People anxious to run into him unexpectedly, people lamenting favors needing repayment. This gave him a feeling of calm satisfaction, while also presenting him with a sense of unease on this particular day. Below him was a world of chaos. Of indifference and desperation. Most days, he found a comfort in the pit of his stomach knowing that his wife, his daughter, his household, were safely ensconced from this. But today, they were out there, somewhere, down below. Shopping.

He prided himself in anticipating their every need, in knowing the intricacies of his household and in that knowledge enabling him to keep his family apart from the chaos of the city. This was an urge provoked less by fear of their harm than by his desire to preserve their contamination. To know that his home—his jewel box and the contents within—was truly not a part of this filthy world. That no matter what depths of debasement he might traverse in the course of his days doing business or his nights seeking to quench his other, more carnal thirsts, when he was home, this was a space that was pure.

His lapse in memory around this communion frustrated him, not only because it took his wife and daughter out of the home, but because it exposed for him his blind spot. He had blocked the communion out of his mind because he liked to block the church from his mind. He abhorred the performative piousness of the faith and the cottage industries of superstition and sorcery that had cropped up around it. How many indulgences and blessings had he paid for while Marlen was trying to conceive another child? For forgiveness of his perceived sins, for prayers to heal her suddenly barren womb. How many ofrendas had he made the gardeners dismantle that she and Alma erected in little corners of the house and garden? As though he wouldn't notice or would approve.

Marlen was a faithful woman; he had known this when he met her, when they married in a ceremony filled with smoke and wafers and wine—he himself had come from a faithful family—but the desperation with which she clung to God being able to give her another child repulsed him. When he came home early one day and found her under the grapefruit tree with the old woman, the stranger in his home, rolling an egg around her . . . an egg! As though that would be the thing that, after doctor upon doctor and specialist upon specialist had investigated his wife inside and out, would help her get pregnant? Well, it was all so ridiculous, he had to put his foot down. He threw the old woman out onto the street and smacked Marlen so hard she fell, but he needed to make it clear. Enough was enough. This nonsense was over.

There was a knock on the door to his office, and Victor, his most trusted employee, the one to whom he gave all his work that required discretion, entered.

"Sir . . . Gloria came by today, wanting to see you."

The man sighed with heaviness, looked at the clock. Poured himself a drink.

"I sent her money," he said, aggravated.

"It wasn't for money, sir," Victor offered. "The girl was with her."

The man threw back the scotch and set the glass down.

"She only left after I swore I'd bring you to see them. Soon," Victor added.

"Fine." The man gazed back out the window, down to the street. So many people in his debt. "I'll go tonight."

It was well known among the well-heeled women of the city that Calle Princesa had the finest clothing stores—all the latest fashions imported from Europe, the most trendsetting designers from New York. But Marlen didn't direct their driver to Calle Princesa, but rather to a no-name mom-and-pop store that sold children's special occasion wear in a working-class part of town, on Calle Siete, down from the unnamed alley that Marlen had heard whispered was a red-light district. She wouldn't know. She rarely was out of the house at night, except for the occasional social outing with her husband. Certainly never to this part of town. Indeed, Marlen could not help but notice Pilar's exhilaration as she looked out onto the frenetic streets just past the car windows. To school and back. The poor girl's world so very small.

The car pulled up to the shabby boutique, and Pilar bounded out as soon as the driver opened the door.

"Alma," Marlen called out to the older woman as she hoisted

her plump frame from the front seat. "Remember, dotted swiss, maybe a lace. Tasteful. Something my husband will like." Marlen peeled off four bills from the stack the man had given her, keeping one for herself. "Afterward," she now whispered, "take her for a treat or to a toy store or something. I'll be back here in an hour."

"Of course, Doña Marlen."

And the two women stood, pretending to small talk and window-shop until her husband's driver pulled away.

Marlen stole away down the alley, gazing up and down at the house numbers and the piece of paper that Alma had written the woman's address down upon. In her nervousness she tripped on an uneven piece of cobblestone and fell into a puddle, dirtying her dress, the anxiety of which made her start to perspire. She could feel the moisture gather at her temples, beads of sweat streaking her foundation, the frizzing of the roots of her smoothed-out hair. The walk from the car to the woman's house was not long, but when she arrived, she was disheveled. Nervous.

"Doña Viviana?" Marlen asked, though no doubt existed that the ancient woman across the threshold was anyone but. Her brown skin wrinkled and spotted with age, her thinning white hair, pulled into a bun, showed her scalp. But her eyes, pale and gray, were still clear, and as the old woman took her in, the gaze was so penetrating, so piercing, Marlen felt tears come to her eyes.

She led Marlen to a small table in her dimly lit kitchen, thick with the scents of cooking and incense, fetched her a glass of water, and, only once Marlen had calmed herself, did the woman begin to speak.

"So," Doña Viviana said, "what is the problem with your daughter?"

Marlen startled at the woman's sorcery, causing Viviana to laugh.

"Please," she said, "I'm a bruja, not a mystic. I'm also very, very old. Your kind of panic can only be induced by a daughter."

Somehow knowing her pain was so visible twisted the knife in Marlen just a bit more.

"My daughter," Marlen said, "is perfect. She is light and song and laughter and curiosity. The problem is . . . there was supposed to be a house full of children. Sons. More daughters. So that someone, by choice or chance, would stay home with my husband and me. But . . . my body failed me and, because of this failure, my girl, with her enormous spirit, will be confined to this minuscule world."

There was a moment of silence. Marlen could feel Doña Viviana looking on her as the wheels of her mind churned. She cast her own eyes down in shame.

"I've seen every priest and curandera in every city and town along this river," Marlen continued. "Except for you. Can you help me?"

"And why should I help you? You insult me to my face by telling me I'm your last resort—"

Marlen had feared this might come up. That Doña Viviana would take her act of desperation as a slight when it was anything but. All the women in the area knew that her witchcraft was the most powerful. All the women knew how estranged lovers had been reunited after her interventions, how sick relatives had been brought back from the brink of death, how families on the cusp of fiscal ruin would suddenly find themselves flush after a visit to Viviana. Marlen, like all the other women in their city by the river, knew this. And she, like everyone else, knew these miracles came with a dark side. That the lovers would reunite after one had been struck dumb or blind and needed care. That the relative on the brink would come back to full physical health, but with the mind of a vegetable. That the family, suddenly flush with cash, would only find themselves so after compensation from a fatal accident would reverse their fortunes. The desired outcomes, yes. But always with an edge of darkness to it. The edge that Marlen had wanted to avoid, until her torment eclipsed her fears.

"Doña Viviana," she now said with contrition, "it wasn't a slight. Not at all. It's just that only now did I realize that I would give anything to give my Pilar freedom in this world."

"And how do you want to do that?"

"By having another child."

Doña Viviana looked at her and laughed. "And what about this child? You won't care about them being free?"

Marlen felt punched in the gut. She had never thought about it that way. She had been so fixated on this as her solution, on castigating her body for betraying her in providing it, she had failed to see the flaw at the root of this plan. She now suddenly felt trapped.

"Don't worry, mija," Doña Viviana cooed softly as she placed her gnarled hand over Marlen's smooth one. "I have a way to help."

Later that night, the man's car dropped him by a children's clothing store, unable to make its way down the narrow alley illuminated by the red lights of the district. He walked quickly, wishing to be done with this errand. He glanced up at the numbers on the doorways and, in his distraction, nearly tripped over a loose cobblestone, his whole foot falling into a murky puddle, further souring his mood. At the doorway, Gloria greeted him, all smiles, draping herself on him. Brushing her dimpled brown cheek against his graying five-o'clock shadow. Raking her fingertips through his thick, black hair. And his annoyance and frustration with her and the situation were overtaken by his insatiable thirst. She led him into the bedroom.

Afterward, while he was lying there, resting his eyes, he heard Gloria walk out of the room and emerge a few minutes later, the weight of her sinking the edge of the bed. Even with his eyes closed, he knew she had the girl with him. He refused to open them, to play this game.

Why? For her to point out the almond-shaped eyes they shared? The similarity in their wide grins (which he never showed when the girl was before him). For Gloria to ask, sadder and sadder each time, the dimple transformed to a sad pockmark on her face, why the girl couldn't be claimed as his own. To have a chance at the life his Pilar had. To be the one to stay and care for him as he aged. In these moments, the man felt pity for her. She really didn't see the difference. He could tell. The difference between a woman like Marlen—who despite all her flaws had such polished beauty and an established family and a world-class education—and poor Gloria, who he knew through little fault of her own had been born the fatherless daughter of some kind of charlatan witch and mainly worked private dance clubs for cash like the one where he met her. No, he would keep his eyes shut until she understood his intention.

When he made his way to leave, into the hallway of the apartment thick with the scent of cooking and incense and his recent sex, Gloria's mother stood there, waiting for him, the dimly lit kitchen transforming her to silhouette.

"In the end," she called out to him, "you die alone."

Outside, a strange fog had descended upon the river valley, quickly thickening, so much so that were it not for the glow of the lights in the glass house, the man's driver would not have been able to find their way home. And with the fog also descended upon the city a peculiar sadness. Young women cried over memories they had not yet lived, young men wept for lost lovers whom they hadn't yet met. And the elders? The elders of the city were stricken with a sense of regret for choices not made, for roads not traveled, opportunities not pursued so severe, they were left noxious in the wake of their regret. In the glass house Alma wept in the kitchen as she prepared breakfast. Marlen's tears fell into the juicer as she wrenched the grapefruit for her husband. Pilar suddenly could only remember the words to the most melancholy songs and found herself unable to stop singing them. And the man? In the morning, when the man stumbled his way through the courtyard in the fog to pluck his grapefruit, his body was overtaken with a physical pain. The recollection of every hurt he had ever inflicted upon others flashed before him. By the time he made his way into the kitchen and handed the grapefruit to Marlen, his body was shaking with sobs.

After three days of this, a storm descended on the river valley, cutting through the fog. There was a loud crack of thunder, and it seemed, almost immediately, that the sky opened up. It came down in sheets, bouncing off the normally hard, dry earth. The sound woke Pilar up in the night, and she watched the rain filling up the courtyard with fascination. She had never seen anything to rival it. Each drop seemed heavier than water, larger than she'd known a raindrop could be, each falling perfectly straight down from heaven. Over the sound of the rain, she did not hear the door to her parents' room slide open. So focused on the raindrops themselves, attempting to locate one and track its descent to the ground, she did not notice her mother crossing into the courtyard. Not until she lost count and looked past the drops to the grapefruit tree.

Her mother wore her long white nightgown, the one Pilar

thought made her look like an angel. A thin, voluminous cotton confection, now stuck to her thin body, soaked wet from the rain. Her auburn hair hung down; limp, wet ringlets plastered to her shoulders. The sight of her filled Pilar with a strange anxiety. The little girl slid open her own glass door and called out to her mother, but the downpour drowned her voice. Pilar wanted to go to her, but her feet were stones. She could only watch as her mother lay down at the foot of the tree and melted away in the rain.

In the morning, the sun was bright and shining again. The storm had washed away the fog and with it the grip of sadness the fog had brought. The man found himself humming when he woke up, not even minding that his wife had left the door to the courtyard open. Today, he did not want juice. Today he wanted to sink his strong teeth into the thick rind, hear the ripping sound as he tore it away from fruit. To feel the bright burst of citrus as he punctured its thin, papery walls and felt the meat of the juice sac with his tongue.

With great care, he chose the grapefruit that seemed the most ripe, the most robust, the most comely and plucked it down ceremoniously. For a moment, he felt the weight, particularly heavy, in his large hands. Luscious with juice, he thought as he gazed down upon it. He took the fruit into his open mouth, biting down and releasing a howl so raw, the entire staff came running into the courtyard to see about this injured beast. There, the man stood, mouth bloodied, hovering over the abandoned grapefruit and the scattered remnants of his perfect, beautifully white cracked teeth on the ground.

The tree never stopped bearing fruit, but the man never touched it again.

• • •

After the fog, when everyone's melancholy had lifted, Pilar had found herself only able to remember the sad songs. After her mother washed away in the rain, nothing left behind—not even the threads of the white nightgown—she found herself, in fact, unable to make sounds unless she sang them. Try as she might to tell her father what she had witnessed of her mother's demise, words were unable to come out of her mouth. For her father's part, when his wife did not rush to comfort him after the grapefruit stole his teeth, he knew something was wrong, but absent her being ill—and she was nowhere to be found—he could imagine no other cause for her disappearance but infidelity. He raged. Gardeners and housekeepers were dispatched in informal search parties around the city. He had Victor interrogate every man who worked for him—at the offices, in the back alleys, at the house—and finding no one who could possibly be his wife's lover, he concluded it must be Victor and had his other men pummel him before throwing him out into the street.

With her mother melted away from her and the house turned upside down by her father's antics, Pilar found herself increasingly frustrated. They had to dig up the tree! Her mother had melted into the tree and the only possible way to find her was to look beneath it. Unable to make the words come from her mouth and unaware of any songs that precisely suited the situation, Pilar decided to write down exactly what she had seen, explaining how the only way to save her mother was to destroy the tree, whose grapefruits were clearly no longer any good. She wrote down what she saw and ran to her father at his breakfast table with urgency, but he simply tore her note to pieces, renouncing whatever sorcery had possessed his daughter to make up such stories in the first place. He was less generous when, days later, he found her on her hands and knees, school uniform filthy with earth, knee-deep in a hole she had dug at the foot of his grapefruit tree. She shrieked and cried as he yanked her by a frayed braid, pulling her away from the hole where she knew her mother was. He beat her until her nose bled and her arms were reddened with welts where his hands had been. Later, when Alma cleaned her face of dirt and tearstains, Pilar sang herself to sleep.

Vuelvo a ti, madrecita
A llorar en tus brazos
Y a curar si es posible
Mi alma ya echa pedazos

II.

Over the following years, as Pilar evolved from girl to teenager, her mother's worst fears for her daughter appeared to manifest. The man, whose anger grew in conjunction with his daughter's beauty, was at first certain his wife, once settled in her new life with this other man, would return and take his Pilar away. Then, as that possibility diminished, his daughter began to appear less as a girl and more as a woman. He grew increasingly certain that, if given the chance, a young man would steal her away.

First, he stopped excursions to her friends' houses. Then, as the months went by and she remained unable to do anything but sing—and the saddest of songs, at that—he decided there was no point in sending her to school, instead employing a private tutor to try to coach Pilar's speech back and, at the very least, keep her well-read. Indeed, the only time that the girl left the house was for choir practice with the school—that she at least could be able to use this gift for God, the sisters had pleaded with the man. Truthfully, they felt sorry for her, and he felt their pity and resented that it implied he was not enough. The guilt (their terrible, judging gazes) proved too much, and he relented. And so, three times a week his driver took Pilar to choir practice and, other than that, for many years, she did not leave the glass house.

The tree never bore an edible fruit again, and now, in the mornings, he did not cross the courtyard to get to breakfast, but went through the house instead. Grapefruits now came regularly with the delivery of mangos and pears and pomegranates and, as Pilar grew, she would, as her mother once did, make her father's juice as she sang melancholy songs. His waist thickened, his hair thinned, and his teeth were replaced with an equally perfect pair, but he was self-conscious where once he was confident. His thirst, unquenchable without the fruit from his grapefruit tree, had led him to seek satisfaction in darker corners of his city, causing him to spend more and more time away from home. Alma and the tutor were his daughter's sole companions. This may have been for the best, as no vice could fill him as the fruits of his grapefruit tree once did. His frustration grew, his anger at the very sight of the tree vexed him in a way that made him cross with everyone who came into his path. And it was in this mood that Alma entered the dining room one morning to say that two of the Sisters from the school were there to see him.

"Uninvited?" he asked as he cut into his breakfast, his juice glass there, untouched.

"They said it was urgent. They wanted to catch you before you left for work."

He nodded reluctantly and motioned for Alma to take his plate away. A few moments later, two nuns from the school his daughter didn't even really attend anymore were before him. He vaguely remembered them from when his wife disappeared. The tall one he remembered as Sister Beatrice. She was larger than him and broad, but had a face that could have been pretty had she chosen another occupation. The other, Sister Dorcas, was small with a face that looked like an armadillo.

"Señor," Sister Dorcas said, "we're so sorry to bother you unannounced."

"We tried to make an appointment at your office," Sister Beatrice said, looking down on him. "But no one has returned our calls."

He vaguely remembered now ignoring their messages, assuming they were calling to ask for more donations to this thing or that. His heart, and ego, had been shattered by Marlen's disappearance, but one thing that had gone with it—largely—was the presence of the church. Minus Pilar's singing in the choir, he was now free to mainly ignore its existence.

"Apologies, Hermanas," he said now, "but what could be so urgent?"

"Well, it's come to our attention that Pilar's fifteenth birthday is approaching," Sister Beatrice began.

"And?" the man asked.

"And," Sister Dorcas picked up, "there've been no plans begun with the church for her quinceañera. And we are running out of time."

The man let out a sigh of recognition. He did not want to have this quinceañera at all. Not the church ceremony, not the party. But just as the Sisters recognized his daughter's impending milestone, he knew so too would the wives of his colleagues—all of whom paid far too much attention to his daughters' welfare than he felt was appropriate. He hated being the subject of gossip and knew ignoring the birthday would be fodder for it among the families of his social class, who had only just ceased whispering behind his back about Marlen.

"We understand that normally this would be something her mother would—"

"I can handle this just fine!" he said defensively. In the river of canards that flowed through this town, the nuns, he found, were always the source. He decided to use this opportunity for an out. "I just . . . I thought perhaps I should spare the girl. What friends does she have to invite? She's been a mute for seven years for God's sake!"

"Señor!" Sister Dorcas chastised.

"Pilar is no mute!" Beatrice exclaimed with near-personal injury. "She has the voice of an angel—"

"If you like sad songs," the man interjected.

"She sings the songs of God at church—"

"Same thing, no?" he said, chuckling at his own joke. The Sisters were not amused.

"Despite her difficulties," Sister Dorcas said firmly, "your daughter is quite popular with the other students in the choir. I'm sure you'd have no shortage of guests. Unless . . . well, unless finances are the issue?" And with this, her beady black eyes darted around the dining room of the glass house to the courtyard behind the man, to the custom ceilings, to the artwork.

"Fine," the man said, resigned. "We will have a quince."

"Wonderful!" Sister Beatrice said with a broad smile. "And since we're here, we might as well get the deposit for the ceremony."

For six months, Pilar got a taste of what she could not wait to fully savor: a life! Preparations for her quinceañera insisted that she be out of the house. To select invitations, to choose flowers, to go shopping for her gown, for Alma's gown (which she convinced her father to buy), to practice for the religious ceremony, to practice her waltzing, and, naturally, to practice the songs she would sing: at the ceremony, and again at the reception. And, of course, the best part, to practice her entrance and dance with her quinceañera court: the fourteen friends and relations who would be her damas y chambelanes on the special day of her fifteenth birthday.

Oh, they were miserable dancers, all of them. Chela couldn't step without stomping on Rodrigo's toes. José needed to be led. Carmen had no sense of rhythm at all. Rather than be upset, Pilar was delighted, because her ragtag crew meant more time out of the house. More time required to practice—because with all these friends and family and associates at the house watching, she knew her father needed it all—them all, her—to be perfect. And getting to perfection also meant more time with Dagoberto. Dagoberto, whose tenor was the perfect complement to her soprano in the chorus the girls Catholic school and boys Catholic school had formed together. Dagoberto, who had shoved his tongue down her throat (to her delight) in the moments between when practice ended early and Apá's driver showed up to retrieve her. Dagoberto, who would be going to a music program in New York that summer, to which she sent an audition recording and was accepted and knew she would never be able to attend.

Also, even when at the house, things were different in these months. Afternoon after afternoon, Pilar would gaze out of the wall of glass, down the sloped hill the edifice sat atop of, onto the long and winding drive that led to the thoroughfare below. Normally, minus her father's car and the occasional delivery, days could go by without any movement on this road. Lately, however, on any given day there were minor traffic jams. The hustle and the bustle of the party planner's visits. (A foppish man Pilar selected from the bunch she was presented with largely because she was amused by how he got under her father's skin; his mere arrival signaling to her father that more money was about to be spent.) The florists made several visits, and of course the caterer. Then as the day itself drew closer, the house was a hive of activity—the band, the people bringing the lights, the tables and chairs, the gardeners to trim back the lush greens of the courtyard. Pilar could not sleep. Not with anxiety (if anything, she was excited for her moment in the spotlight), but awake with the buzz of life. Of receiving the attention of so many people. Of eavesdropping on all the workers talking about their lives or their bosses or her father as they did their part to put this party together. Of the . . . joy.

When the party was over—after she had danced with her father and Dagoberto and the rest of her court under the twinkle of fairy lights, after she had sung "Madre Abandonada" and everyone had a slice from the grand tiered cake, and after the band had ended their second encore and her father was sleepy from too much tequila with his cousins and colleagues—Pilar stayed up. First milling in the courtyard as dirty plates were put onto racks, soiled linens were dropped into laundry bags, tables folded back and thrown onto trucks. All that had just been magic, in what felt like moments, was disassembled before her eyes.

From the wall of glass, she watched in the darkness as the taillights of all the cars and trucks made their way down the long drive and turned, this way and that, onto the main road, getting smaller and smaller. And, for the first time really, Pilar understood that down the empty driveway there were lives being lived in houses far shabbier than her father's glass castle, working jobs far harder than her father probably ever had to work, but that these people had far better lives. For the first time in her short existence, she felt in herself a sense of longing to be a part of that.

It was nearly three in the morning and the last of the trucks was long gone when Pilar returned to the courtyard. All was still and, save a forgotten champagne flute stained with lipstick, it was as if the whole thing had never happened. Beneath the grapefruit tree was the depression of the hole she had dug all those years before, hoping to find where her mother had gone. It fit her body perfectly now, and with everyone else in the house asleep, she sat in it. She often felt her mother was here and now, desperate to talk to her, to ask her why she felt so lonely, how she could have a life of her own, that she found herself—stripped of traditional speech—humming. Humming a tune to a song she had never heard before. One that came from her sorrow, she felt. Still in her party gown, lying on the ground, she was about to lull herself to sleep when she heard someone else humming along with her. In harmony with her voice.

She sat erect, but did not stop humming. She quietly sang a phrase of an old church song and, from above, heard the melody repeated back to her. She hummed a new tune, a sad one she'd heard on the radio, and, from above, heard it reflected back to her. Frantically, she began looking for the source of the sound, humming and singing as softly as possible to not wake her father or anyone else in the house. She inspected the grounds near the tree, searching for a drunk guest who might have found sleep wherever the night took them, but found none. She began to look up to the boughs. The hum was coming from there. The life. She climbed up into the tree in a way she hadn't since she was a girl, since before her mother slipped, like water, through her grasp. And there, as she hummed and sang, she realized the sound was coming from the fruit. Not just the fruits, but one grapefruit in particular. She was able to spot it because it vibrated when the humming came not only from it, but from her.

She plucked it from the tree.

The next morning, knowing her father would be hungover from the party, she woke early. She took the fruit into the kitchen, made coffee for Alma, and waited until the woman, now stooped with age, shuffled into the kitchen. When she did, Pilar laid the grapefruit on the counter and began to sing "Itotiani" to the citrus.

"Mija, that isn't a sad song," Alma noted.

Pilar shrugged. *It depends, I think*, she wrote on a piece of paper.

Pilar sang to the grapefruit, and Alma watched, astonished, as the flesh of the rind slowly rippled beneath the surface, undulating in time with the music. Alma let out a shriek, but Pilar put her finger to the old woman's lips and moved into the chorus of the song as she leaned in closer to the pomelo.

"*Uiuiuiui Uiuiuiu*," Pilar sang softly, cooing to the fruit.

"*Uiuiuiui Uiuiuiu*," the fruit replied.

Alma grabbed Pilar's wrist, stunned for a moment into silence as Pilar and the grapefruit harmonized with each other.

"Pilar!" she whispered. "What is it?"

Pilar again shrugged. *I think we need to peel it and see*, she wrote.

"No!" Alma exclaimed. "What if we hurt it?"

But the grapefruit, sitting now on the counter, began to roll itself toward Pilar, and both women took it as a sign.

The fruit was large in Pilar's delicate hands. It vibrated in anticipation as she, as gently as possible, dug the edge of her thumbnail into the smooth, yellow skin, cracking the oil sacks and sending the sharp fragrance into the air. When she could feel the thick albedo firmly under her nail, she quickly inserted her thumb between the pulp and the rind, and the fruit moaned softly.

Alma let out a cry and crossed herself, but Pilar shot her a look and went back to her midwifing. She ran her thumb now in a strong motion away from her, and as she tore the rind from the flesh of the fruit, the pomelo cried out in a true yawp of pain. Pilar moved quickly, no need to drag it out, ribbons of yellow rind dropping to the brown tile floor. The fruit now cried continuously;

Alma had to look away from the pained thing, but Pilar continued with her work, undistracted, until the fruit was naked but for its thick white albedo. Its crying ceased, but it shuddered as Pilar went on with the delicate task of peeling back the layers of fibers, cleaning away the last of the fruit's encasement, until both she and Alma could clearly see what they had each come to suspect. That inside was no fruit at all. In her hands, curled up in the pinkish-veined sac of a grapefruit, was a man.

Pilar looked at Alma, bewildered at what to do next.

"Well, finish it!" Alma said. "You have to let him out!"

Tears welled in Pilar's round amber eyes. She was afraid to hurt him.

"Pilar," Alma said softly, "all birth hurts."

Pilar nodded, lifted the fruit to her mouth, and punctured the wall of the sac with her teeth.

The juice—the most flavorful, delicious grapefruit juice she had ever tasted—came dribbling down her chin, soaking the front of her dress. But what didn't spill, Pilar drank up, sucking the papery thin sac dry until it was nothing more than a translucent blanket covering the man's naked body. Pilar set him down on the counter and peeled the blanket away. The women stood in awed silence, which quickly turned to anxious worry for now, after all that commotion, he did not move at all.

"I killed him," Pilar whispered, shocked at the sound of her own voice aloud. A voice neither woman had heard in over seven years.

"Mija!" Alma said, wide-eyed in the presence of so many miracles, unsure which to focus on first. She looked at the small man as his light brown body covered with tiny bits of grapefruit pulp shivered slightly in the cool of the morning. His tiny chest moved up and down gently with breath. She would celebrate the return of Pilar's voice later. "Mija, he just needs a little help."

Alma cradled the curled-up man in the palms of her hands and carried him over to the sink, where she washed him clean with warm water, just as she had done with Pilar fifteen years before. She took her pinky and cleaned out the man's mouth, noting it full already with teeth, and cleared his airway of grapefruit pulp. With her index finger, she gave his buttocks a swack and, in an instant, he began to wail like the newborn that he was. She swaddled him in a dishtowel and curled his tiny self over the nape of her neck to calm him.

"You should sing to him," Alma commanded.

But Pilar was too stunned to sing. At least in that moment. She reached out for him, to hold him. He was smaller than a newborn, but fully formed as a man. She rested him in the crook of her arm, close to her body for warmth, and a feeling of pure love and affection washed over the entirety of herself. She gazed on his face, which was that of a young man of maybe nineteen or twenty. His skin, a terra-cotta color shades darker than hers, but the turned-up corners of his mouth the same. His nose, perfectly straight, noble in fact, mirrored her own. His round eyes, which opened only slowly, the same amber color as hers and her mother, before her.

"He looks like me," she said, and Alma confirmed that indeed he did.

"What should we call him?" Pilar asked.

"Well, I suspect when he is able to, he will tell us what to call him. But for now, let's call him Pomelo."

Because the man never went in there, and it was the one room obfuscated from view of the rest of the house, the women raised Pomelo in the kitchen. In the beginning, unsure of how to care for a baby who was a man who was born from a tree, there was much confusion, but eventually they settled into a pattern. There was the matter of what to feed Pomelo, as Pilar felt certain he was a vegetarian since he came from vegetation, but Alma didn't believe in vegetarianism and so they settled on a diet of chicken broth and atole, which they fed him with an eyedropper. At night he slept in Alma's room just off the kitchen in a fruit crate, nestled between grapefruits, which Alma thought would help him feel like he was back in the womb. Because he had the proportions of a man, but was smaller than even a newborn, the matter of clothing him was a challenge. Pilar remembered some old toys that had been stored away, and they dressed Pomelo in the wardrobe of her abandoned Ken dolls. But Pomelo did not like clothes and constantly took them off. Besides, he was maturing so rapidly, he quickly outgrew whatever Pilar or Alma managed to find for him. Within a month he was up to Pilar's waist. After two months he was walking around, independently mobile and able to help Alma out in the kitchen, preparing meals for the house. But still, he did not talk.

"Do you think I stole his voice when I drank the juice?" Pilar asked one night in Alma's room while the two women watched Pomelo sleep.

They had determined right away that it was most certainly the juice of this enchanted fruit that had restored Pilar's ability to speak, but it had just occurred to Pilar now that perhaps her gain had been at her dear Pomelo's expense. If so, that would fill her with regret. For while being able to speak certainly made her day-to-day life of raising Pomelo with Alma easier, it brought her no real joy. Certainly no more than silence had. Indeed, she had not let on to anyone else that anything had changed and certainly not her father, whom she had barely been able to look at since her quinceañera. Though Pomelo's arrival had distracted her, nothing had erased from her mind the revelation that she was trapped in this glass house. Destined to live in service to her father for what she could see as no good reason. Even if she wanted to be free, she could imagine no way out. Everyone who worked for her father, Alma included, was afraid of him. She had no money, not a proper education, she had never been taught how to drive. And now she had Pomelo, whom she had to consider. At least he brought her a certain comfort.

By his fourth month on the earth, it was clear that Pomelo had grown to his full size, though he still did not speak. In theory, he was remarkably easy to hide from the man, as Alma was able to dress him as a groundskeeper, and the man, since the loss of his wife and teeth, was so often out carousing he barely kept track of the staff there anymore. But Pomelo hated wearing clothes and undressed himself the second he was safe in the kitchen with Alma. He was a great help to her there and had a natural ability with soups and desserts and, as he towered over her shrinking, aging body, she appreciated not having to use her step stool to reach for her better pots and pans. Still, his nudity was a distraction, since for one thing, she worried constantly about him scalding and burning all that unprotected flesh and, for another, she was not dead yet. While she cared for him dearly, she certainly did not think of this grapefruit man being any relation to her. It was hard not to notice his statuesque physique as they maneuvered around each other in the kitchen, cooking side by side. At night, his scent, still strong of grapefruit, wafted up to her from his cot on the floor beneath her bed, filling her dreams with a passion they had not had in years.

One night, in the sixth month since Pomelo had come to them, Pilar found herself being shaken awake in the middle of the night by Alma.

"Mija, you have to come to my room right away," she whispered, "it's Pomelo."

Pilar felt a sinking in her stomach as she threw on clothes and made her way across the courtyard, into the kitchen, and then to Alma's small room beyond that.

Pomelo was curled up in the fetal position, whimpering sharp cries.

"It's his back!" Alma said, her voice full of urgency. "It's burning up. His entire back is blistering!"

Pilar walked closer to examine him in the dimly lit room. His back was swollen into two large mounds, which, indeed, were covered in raised flesh, clearly filled with liquid, but something about the skin encasing them struck Pilar as odd.

"I'm sorry if this hurts you," she whispered to Pomelo as she pricked one with the tip of her nail, rubbing her finger in the pus that oozed. Before she even put her finger to her mouth, the fragrance of grapefruit juice hit the air, and indeed, when she touched her tongue to her fingertip, it was the same electric bright sensation that she had experienced the day Pomelo was born. Tears formed in her eyes.

"Alma," she said, her heart breaking, "I think he's turning back to a fruit."

All through the night the women kept watch as Pomelo writhed on the bed in pain, beads of sweat forming against his terra-cotta skin as the mounds on his back grew. At dawn, Pomelo began to scream and Alma stuffed a rag into his mouth to muffle the sound. The mounds—massive now, blistered with juice sacs—were ripping themselves up and away from the flesh of his back, slowly expanding themselves farther and farther from his body until the mounds were fully unfurled and it was plain that Pomelo was not turning back into a fruit at all.

He had simply sprouted wings.

They were massive things when he extended them fully, so large that his wingspan could barely fit inside Alma's room. They were covered in the papery flesh of a grapefruit wedge, veined with white fibers like those that had once nestled Pomelo in his fruit womb. They were beautiful.

The sun had long risen, and they could hear the man making his way through the house to the dining room for his breakfast.

"Your father!" Alma startled. She had completely forgotten about the world that existed outside her bedroom and Pomelo and his wings. "I haven't even started his breakfast!"

Pomelo started to follow her into the kitchen, but Pilar held him back.

"Pomelo, stay here. I'll help Alma. I . . . I don't know that we can hide you in the kitchen now."

Pilar fretted as she picked a grapefruit for her father's morning juice over how she and Alma could keep Pomelo a secret now. A man is easy to hide. A man with wings is a different story. She had just sliced the fruit in half and was about to bring it down on the ceramic juicer when Pomelo gripped her wrist and pulled it away.

"Sister," he said, his voice rich like marzipan, "no more."

Alma, who had been plating the man's breakfast, let the scrambled eggs drop to the floor, such was her shock at the voice.

"Sister?" Pilar said.

"Pomelo!" Alma cried with joy. "You've found your voice."

He smiled at her warmly.

"Yes, Alma, I'm fully formed now. And thank you for helping raise me. And yes, Pilar, you are my sister. My half sister. We share the same mother, which is why we share the same face."

"And my father's tree is your father?"

"I have no father, Pilar. I was born of your mother, and my other mother is Earth. Your mother impregnated my mother when she washed herself away and was absorbed into the ground. My other mother placed me and the rest of our siblings in the nearest living thing she could find, the grapefruit tree."

Pilar and Alma were both crying now. In the dining room, the man was calling out for his food and juice, and Alma went to placate him, picking the eggs off the floor, wiping her tears as she ran out of the kitchen. Pilar had so many questions but shock had almost made her mute again.

"When she was alive, our mother wished to have another child so that you wouldn't be the youngest anymore, tied to this house and your father. But she couldn't conceive. She went to see a bruja, who told our mother that the only way for you to be free was for her to vanish herself into the earth. The bruja gave her a potion—"

"But you are older than me," Pilar said. "How can you free me? The youngest is the one who must stay."

"Why do you think my mothers gave me wings?"

From the kitchen, they could hear her father calling out her name, bellowing for his juice.

"But what about my father?" Pilar asked.

"One day Alma will die and return to my other mother, and the unacknowledged daughters of your father will by then have dispersed. Then the fog will return and your father will be here, left with his own thoughts and the consequences of his choices, and he will die alone. It was the witch's prophecy."

"Pilar!" the man cried out again from the dining room. "What is happening in there?" But the siblings had already made their way into the courtyard, each kissing Alma goodbye as they ran out the door.

"How do you know you can fly?" Pilar asked.

"I just do."

"Wait," she said, running to the grapefruit tree, pulling off a stem, and stuffing as many grapefruits as she could into her dress pockets. "So we won't be alone!"

And with that, her brother took her into his arms, began to flap his marvelous wings, and leaped into the air, the long absent scent of the grapefruits from the ancestral tree lingering behind, one final torment for the man. As they rose through the air, Pilar looked down: at the sloped drive that led to the main road, at the city around that, at the river just beyond—and for the first time, the girl who had seen so little in her life could now see so very much.

Pomelo did as his mothers told him to do and flew them southward, back to where they had come from, back to a place untouched by man.

LUZ Y FER

Leopoldo Goût

Three years ago, I went to the Cine Gear Expo at the Javits Center. Yes, that one. I had been right there, shell-shocked and bloodied, walking like a zombie in the aftermath as I drowned in the acrid stench of burning meat. One hundred and sixteen dead, many more injured, with no suspects. Some called it an "attack" despite nobody, not even the usual terror groups eager to increase themselves by slapping their brand on any mass casualty, claiming responsibility.

From the pulpits, many proclaimed divine fury: God's hammer swung down on those merchants of celluloid dreams and their disciples of light and shadow. When darkness descends, the collective mob clutches at their own certainties—heaven's judgment or terror's hand—to illuminate their own personal void.

I had been there to visit the booth of a camera manufacturer I'd found myself brand loyal to over my years of documentary filmmaking. They'd recently come out with a new low-light camera, which I'd thought would be perfect for a film I was working on. The massive convention hall was packed to the gills, and I was eager to simply grab the camera and get out. Shoulder-to-shoulder crowds had begun to feel suffocating in years since the pandemic. With the camera under my arm, I made toward the exit and passed a coffee stand that had set up in the venue. As I walked by, I couldn't help but turn my head when I caught a whiff of a woman's perfume, a subtle musky caramel mixed with geraniums that had somehow lanced through the crowd, and further, I could not help but notice the woman it emanated from, who was waiting for a coffee.

Long, wavy black hair tumbled over her shoulders and fell to the middle of her back against an oversized sweater covering a pale-yellow dress. I found myself rapt, watching as she turned from the counter to reveal her striking face, a dimple in her left cheek as she smiled at the vendor. Around her neck hung a weighty-looking white pendant with a strange symbol of two inverted triangles.

My pocket vibrated, a call from one of my producers, Quin. I'd been dodging him following a previous heated exchange, but his support was too vital to send him to voicemail again. I answered. The signal inside was terrible and the call immediately dropped, so I hurried toward the exit.

As I neared the doors, the call finally connected.

"Quin? You hear me? Signal is shit in here—hang on" were the only words I got out before all sound ceased. I felt my mouth moving, but the space was blanketed in an all-encompassing silence. An anticipatory held breath followed by the loudest noise I'd ever heard as everyone was hurled to the floor and I was plunged into darkness.

I was woken by the stench of smoldering flesh. Ears ringing, disoriented, vision blurry, and with a pulsing headache, I grabbed my shattered phone off the floor—it's bizarre how scrambled your priorities are in a moment like that—as I climbed to my feet. The dull throb in my ears began to subside as the ringing was slowly replaced by the screams echoing from beyond the thick haze of dust and smoke. My wits still blown elsewhere by the blast, I didn't remember where I was, what I was doing there. The world had been swallowed by a cloud of soot, a gray void from which all I heard were those desperate howls.

Straining my eyes as the dust settled, I saw a cluster of indeterminate limbs, not so much intertwined as they were fused with blackened skin, charred, oozing and sticking together. The flesh blistered and bubbled, continuing to cook from the heat still bursting from within. I turned to a nearby source of screaming to my left; a man lay on the ground clutching a severed arm, which now rested alongside the fallen piece of glass that had crudely amputated it. I patted myself down, still numb, checking that my limbs were still attached.

I took a step forward, feeling my ankle crunch under my weight and sending me back to the ground. Then, through the smell of atomized detritus and blood and charred human meat, I smelled it again: musk, caramel, and geraniums. She emerged from the toxic cloud, the woman from the coffee stand. Except her long hair was cropped to a flapper bob and she was dressed in formal black attire. She couldn't have changed her clothes since I'd first seen her, let alone her hair. For a moment I thought she could have been burnt, her hair singed and clothes blackened by soot and dust. But as she ran past, she didn't limp. In fact, she was completely unscathed, almost composed, and the pendant around her neck was not pearl white, but black.

That brief glimpse through the haze was all I got before she slipped through the doors and was gone.

The catastrophe, accident, attack, whatever the hell people called it, got worldwide attention. With no apparent explanation, no satisfactory evidence, people were left to cobble together deranged theories. At first, I didn't talk about it. Only when people asked, and only after a few shots of mezcal burning my gut. When

I started telling friends about the girl, many of them suggested it was a hallucination brought on by shock or head trauma. I eventually got an MRI to shut them up. Less skeptical friends would humor me, ask what I thought the girl I saw had to do with what happened. Eventually I was telling anybody who listened, the image of those two women still burning in my mind, until my only audience was the end of a bottle.

I tried to find some use for this experience in a film about the disaster, or at least in some project, but not just for professional reasons: if I could disentangle the truth about that day, I'd be done with it and it would be done with me.

Every element was seared in my mind. Memories kept me up at night. I couldn't escape. The stench. The screams. The woman.

So that's where the drinking really came in. I took to researching other inexplicable disasters in my sleepless nights, a bottle of mezcal on my desk as I sought them out—earthquakes in cities without fault lines, wildfires during a rainy season, tsunamis with no trigger—until the booze could overpower the insomnia and I'd wake from a dreamless night in my chair.

My assistant, Tanita, bless her, had been calling me nonstop in those days. Even after producers and other collaborators had long since given up on reaching me as I receded further into myself, Tanita was adamant about pulling me back into the light of day.

But I was down the rabbit hole as they say, finding myself scrolling forums and blogs, home to those who seemed similarly fixated on the inexplicable. Most of them were UFO freaks, anti-government paranoiacs, and New World Order antisemites. Lonely souls rapt by the glow of their screens, frantically searching for a peek behind the curtain hiding whatever machine they imagined worked in the dark to make them miserable. Invariably, though, I'd find threads and missives from those who had self-deputized as detectives on the cases of supernatural disasters.

It was those breadcrumbs that kept me sitting in my studio, hunched in the dark over the blue glow of my screen as I desperately scrambled for anything that might lead toward an answer of what happened that day. More threads to chase, more rabbit holes to go down. Night after night this became my ritual. Eventually Tanita stopped leaving voicemails, then she stopped calling altogether. It didn't matter, though, as I'd finally stumbled upon what I was looking for.

Scrolling an obscure message board, I froze as I saw a thread titled "The Twins." In the grainy thumbnail, attached was a woman with long, wavy black hair and a white pendant around her neck. A poster dubbed the Twinvestigator by other board members explained in his post that he'd pulled it from a video shot by a couple vacationing in Indonesia when the tsunami had hit. I looked through the rest of the thread. More disasters, more grainy images. Twinvestigator had amassed a veritable archive of news clips and screengrabs of local and international broadcasts around these types of disasters and the two women who seemed to portend them.

Hardly anyone else on the board seemed to find credence in the evidence collected by Twinvesigator; almost all the posts in his thread not authored by him- or herself dismissed them as just another "schizo," seeing them as nothing but a novelty. But it was the only thread I had to pull on in hopes of answering my questions about what had happened that day at the Javits Center, what I'd seen.

I dove in, opening tab after tab of the links and photos posted by Twinvestigator. The deeper I went down the thread, the more of Twinvestigator's posts began to stray from simple archives of evidence into paranoia.

12.14.2021 (04:46) – TWNVSTGTR: *Someone has been going through my garbage. I heard them in my yard last night. Time to invest in some cameras.*
04.02.2022 (12:39) – TWNVSTGTR: *I KNOW you're in here reading this. Word of advice: don't tail someone in the same car for two weeks straight. I SEE YOU.*
05.10.2022 (03:50) – TWNVSTGTR: *HAH! FUCK YOU! Time to see where this little bastard is transmitting to.*

Attached was a flash photo of a mangled internet router in an otherwise dark room. In the foreground a hand with unkempt nails clutching a nondescript electronic component.

I began to consider if this person really was just a "schizo" like the other posters seemed to think. If I kept chasing the phantoms of that day, was I on my way to . . . this, scrambling in the dark, ripping the wiring from my walls looking for fictional bugs? I imagined Tanita coming to find me hunched in the corner of my office surrounded by eviscerated appliances and jars of my own piss.

Then I saw it.

08.23.2022 (18:21) – TWNVSTGTR: *PAYDIRT! This explains the demonic interference I've been facing. I've finally found what the pendants are. The Seal of Lucifer. Closer than I've ever been. But so are they.*

Attached was a zoomed-in grainy video still of the black pendant around one of the twins' necks from a CCTV feed near a gas explosion in Chicago. He'd done his best to trace over the blurry pixels to extract a symbol: two inverted triangles.

I pulled out my notebook and found my sketch of the symbol I'd seen that day around the women's necks. They matched. Twinvestigator had found what it was.

I kept going, looking for further posts about the symbol, but found nothing. His final post had been more than a year prior.

> **10.18.2022 (23:09) – TWNVSTGTR:** *After all my searching, I'm finished. The trail is cold. The twins haven't been seen in almost two years now. I can't keep doing this anymore. Whatever it was I was searching for is either gone or never existed. Maybe you guys were right. Maybe I'm just another "schizo."*

After finally finding evidence of what I'd seen, a sliver of a possibility to explain what happened, I refused to let it just slip away. If this guy was delusional, then I supposed I was, too. He couldn't be finished; I wouldn't let him.

I couldn't help myself. I clicked the reply button.

> **01.17.2024 (05:26) – You:** *You aren't crazy. I saw them. The Javits Center. They were there.*

I tried to stay up, some part of me hoping he still watched the thread, was still secretly as obsessed as I'd rapidly become. But soon, the morning light leaking through the window and a hangover already setting in, I fell asleep on the couch.

It was only a few hours before the shrill ring of my phone jarred me awake. Peeling my face from the couch leather and trying to wipe the dry from my eyes, I looked at the cracked screen. Tanita.

I took the call, eager to tell her that I might not be crazy. Or that I was at the very least involved in a kind of interesting group delusion. She must have heard the hangover in my voice.

"Jesus. Aurelio. Finally pick up and you sound like death."

"I know. What time is it?"

"Like four. Listen. I just needed to hear from you. I've been getting worried. Even Quin is still calling me just to ask if you're all right."

"I'm fine. I'm fine, I think."

"You think? Do you need me to bring anything over? I *am* still technically your assistant."

"I'm fine, really."

"Groceries? Clean clothes?"

It seemed that she'd already thought I'd gone full Howard Hughes. I chuckled. "It's really okay. Listen, I found something. About what I saw. The woman. *Women*."

The worry in her voice increased. "Oh?"

I started to tell her about the thread. About Twinvestigator. At first she simply seemed to feign interest. I imagined her looking up the process of ordering a wellness check in between her *Huhs* and *Uh-huhs*. But gradually she seemed to at least humor me.

"Well. I hate to agree that you *sound* pretty normal. Like, despite the content of what you're saying."

"Thank you. Look, I mean, whatever the case is, maybe there's a good film to be made about my slide into insanity."

"Mhm, the story of two strangers somehow developing the exact same bizarre fixation on this stuff would be a good watch. Did he respond?"

"I don't know. I haven't looked yet." I pulled my laptop over and tapped the keys a couple times to wake it up.

The screen lit up, still on the thread. My heart jumped into my throat.

"Holy shit."

"He responded?"

I looked at the replies. The first one had come in from someone else, another anonymous poster. I read them out to Tanita.

01.17.2024 (07:48) – Anonymous to You: *Delete. Quick.*
01.17.2024 (08:30) – TWNVSTGTR to You: *So you were there when it happened?*
01.17.2024 (08:31) – Anonymous to You: *Don't answer.*

"Who's telling you not to talk to him?" Tanita asked.

"I don't know. They're another anonymous poster like me. Could just be messing around, but . . ." I stopped. "Hold on. I think they're typing."

"Which one?"

"Anonymous is typing . . ."

We both waited. Tanita was silent, pulled into the narrative I'd constructed over the phone. The post blinked into existence.

01.17.2024 (16:24) – Anonymous to You: *Hang up.*

My stomach turned into a pit as my blood froze. I slammed the laptop shut, practically tossing it away from my body.

"What? What'd they say?" Tanita sounded excited.

My tongue stuck to my mouth. "They said . . . They said, 'Hang up.' "

The phone line fizzed as we both sat in stunned silence. I was paralyzed, unsure if I should obey or defy the order of whoever it was who seemed to be listening in.

Two possible realities came into focus. Either Twinvestigator and I were complete basket cases, none of this was real, and someone inexplicably decided to log in to a thread from more than a year ago to mess with us and post *Hang up* on the off chance I was both on the phone and looking at the thread. Or there was the possibility that we were sane—which at that moment had the previous night's microwaved dinner snaking up my throat—that he really had been hounded by mysterious forces, that those forces had now turned toward me. I had never found myself wishing so badly to be mentally ill.

"Aurelio," Tanita broke the silence, "you're not messing with me, right?"

"Meet me at the library," and then I hung up.

I ran to the bathroom and threw up in the toilet before washing and shaving. Every time water splashed my face, I struggled to keep my eyes open, too afraid to close them for even a moment. I needed to be in public. For the first time in a long while, I felt the need to be in a crowd, to find protection in the herd.

Keeping a brisk pace on my walk to the library, I stopped only to grab a pastry and a coffee to fill my cramping stomach. I looked over my shoulder, constantly scanning the faces of those around me for repeats.

I waited for Tanita for an hour. I thought about calling her, but I couldn't use my phone again. I waited another hour sitting still and scanning the library patrons before I decided to use the lookup desk.

I typed in: *Seal of Lucifer* and hit *Enter*.

Recommended reading from the library system populated the page: Dante's *Divina Comedia*; van den Vondel's *Lucifer*; Milton's *Paradise Lost*; the Apocalypse of John, Book of Revelation; Tertullian's *Adversus Marcionem*; or Augustine of Hippo's *Civitas Dei.*

I skimmed them, clicking through to articles about the provenance of the name "Lucifer," his representation in *Paradise Lost* as a possible promethean figure giving mankind free will, and the seal of Lucifer as being a symbol of the duality in man to do good and evil. The name of Lucifer himself, the ruler over all that was meant to be dark, translated from Latin to mean "light-bringer." Somewhere in the back of my mind, under the overwhelming panic, was the slightest amount of Mexican Catholic shame in how little I realized I knew about el diablo.

My frenzied research was interrupted by a system notification popping up on the screen:

> You've been logged in for an hour. If other patrons are waiting, please consider allowing them a turn.

Tightly wound, I looked around at the mostly empty library and dismissed the message. But it had now been three hours and not a peep from Tanita. I had no choice but to try calling. As I reached for my phone, a man sat next to me at the computers. I casually closed my tabs of research, warily keeping him in my peripheral as he opened a blank text document. I pulled my phone out, hesitating with my thumb hovering over Tanita's contact when the man loudly cleared his throat.

Glancing over, I saw on his screen, in large enough type for me to read, *You shouldn't have said where you were going on the phone. They'll be coming.*

He kept looking straight ahead at his screen, typing, *We can't talk here. 538 Johnson #6 in Brooklyn. Don't go home first. Don't get followed.*

Before I could think to open a document on my screen to respond, he'd closed his and left. I sat there, my thumb still hovering over Tanita's number, weighing my options. Whoever the man was, he'd already proven to be telling the truth. Clearly *someone* was listening.

I wouldn't go home, but I couldn't shake my concern for Tanita. Her apartment was only a few stops prior to Johnson Street, so I headed there first.

I buzzed her apartment. No response. Buzzed again. No response. I crossed the street, counting the floors of her building. The winter sun had already set, but no lights were on.

Walking the cobble streets near the English Kills, I routinely scanned the empty industrial streets as I questioned my sanity. The empty truck depots and warehouses closed in around me in the twilight as I came to the sign for Johnson Street, my only path to find out what was happening to me. I buzzed #6.

A voice crackled over the intercom, "Up two flights. Close the door behind you."

Climbing the stairs, I hoped that perhaps he had found Tanita as well. That she would be on the other side of the door, which instantly swung open as the man from the library pulled me in before slamming it behind him and pressing an eye to the keyhole. As he went to latch the heavy dead bolt, I grabbed his hand.

"No. You tell me who you are before locking me in with you. Where's Tanita?"

His hand offered no resistance as he spoke, even as I white-knuckled over it. "What use would it be to tell you I'm a friend?"

I couldn't argue. I was there after all, at his mercy. The dead bolt didn't really mean much. I let him turn the knob and followed him into the barren loft. There was nowhere in the space for anyone to hide, even the wall to the bathroom had not yet been erected.

He sat down in a ratty armchair, gesturing for me to do the same. I opted to pace instead.

"I don't know where your friend on the phone is. I apologize if I frightened you, but I couldn't risk revealing myself. It was enough risk even finding you. If you're going to pace like that, please just stay away from the windows."

He was rather erudite and well-spoken for being a disheveled conspiracy nut.

"You're not . . ."

"The 'Twinvesitgator'? No. They got him a while ago. That wasn't him who replied to you. My name's Jay."

"'They'? Don't just say 'They'! Who the fuck is 'They'?"

My foot bumped against the cheap propane heater struggling to keep Jay's concrete box warm.

"Please be careful." He seemed unfazed by my fervor. "They are called the Birthing Room—you could say they're the twins' handlers. A group claiming to be scientists, physiologists, social psycho-engineers, but they're actually experimenting with twins . . . Let's say, *unconventional* experiments."

"And I know you're not one of them, because? How did you even find me?"

"I've kept an alert for anything online about the twins. I'm one of a few concerned parties. In truth, I met the Birthing Room many years ago. I was a comparative religion professor. They'd contacted me about some of my research into Luciferian magic, I obliged them, then I made the mistake of digging into their work. They didn't appreciate that. Now I'm . . ." He gestured to the barren hovel he was now camped out in.

"And these concerned parties . . . They sent you to get me, and what? I get my own little hole to hide in?"

Jay sighed. "I'm here of my own volition. My colleagues don't get involved like this. They see it as too big a risk. But after what happened to Twinvesti—Michael. After what happened with Michael, I couldn't just stand by. I think the Javits incident was too big to be swept away. Too many people are still looking for answers. Even before you posted, the Birthing Room had already started moving in New York. I think they're going to end their experiment."

"End their experiment? The twins?"

"Lucia and Fernanda, yes."

"What is this 'experiment'?"

"Lucía de la Cruz, known as Luz, and the other, Fernanda Griffiths, goes by Fer. Luz was raised by a well-to-do family in Mexico City. Fer grew up broke in the Bronx. Mother was a drug addict, in and out of prison. Two twins, born of the same egg, the same body and genetics, separated and placed in high-contrast environments to ostensibly study nature versus nurture. Show one of them destruction, deprivation, the darkness of humanity. The other: kindness, warmth, and the good in God's world.

"The seal of Lucifer is formed with two arrows at the bottom, creation from duality. Not evil itself, but the capacity to choose between good and evil. You ever see a picture of Baphomet? The right and left hand? Creation and destruction, Heaven and Hell. Stable concepts on their own, but you bring them together? What happens when Heaven and Hell come together? Like sodium and water, a violent reaction as some new thing struggles to come into being."

"Javits," I concluded.

He nodded.

I looked at him incredulously. "Lucia and Fernanda. Luz and Fer. Luz y Fer?"

Jay shrugged. "Speak the devil's name and he shall manifest."

"You said they were already moving in New York to end 'the experiment.' You mean Fernanda."

"Cleaning up and going back to the drawing board. Yes."

"But we're going to go get her before that though, right?"

Jay looked at me like I was an idiot. He was already stuffing what little he had into a backpack. "What? No. I had enough time to get you, that's it. Going after Fernanda would be suicide. I'm telling you that when they mean to clean up, they don't leave any trace."

My limbs turned to lead as my stomach dropped.

"Tanita . . . She never showed at the library. She didn't answer at her place either."

My host froze. I'd grown accustomed to his paranoid demeanor, but the expression on his face as he turned to look at me was that of pure terror.

"You went to her apartment before you came here? Are you fucking crazy? No. No. We leave. We get the fuck out before they show up here."

"Where is Fernanda? She's in the Bronx, yeah? If that's where these people are going, then I'm going there, too. They might have Tanita with them. Address?"

Jay shook his head. "It won't do anything. You'll die. Disappear. She's already gone. Fernanda, too, in all likelihood. You'd walk into a trap for nothing."

"So what? I go with you and spend the rest of my life in a place like this? Dodging shadows and watching my back forever?"

Jay couldn't respond, only look at me. It seemed that the answer was yes. I looked around the barren loft again. Dusty, cold. A place lived in out of fear, huddling around a propane burner for warmth and waiting for a silent apocalypse.

Jay got up and started toward the door.

"We need to go."

I pounced, pinning him to the wall with my forearm on his throat.

"What the fuck are you doing? I'm trying to help you!"

"Fernanda's address. Now. I'm finding Tanita."

He kneed me in the inner thigh, going for my nuts. I broke his nose with my forehead and shouted, "You say they're likely on their way, right? Followed me? What if I just keep you pinned here until they get here?"

Blood from his nose was already dripping off his upper lip onto my arm. "They'll ged you doo!"

"They'll get me if I go to Fernanda's or they'll get me here. Either way, I'm got. Only one way I take you with me. Address."

He stopped squirming, voice snuffled by the blood in his nose. "Seben seben tree, eatht, one eighty turd sdreed! Siggs bee!"

I let him drop to the floor, goose coughing as his windpipe went back to the correct shape. He yelled something after me, but I was already out the door. Stumbling back out into the night, my heartbeat thumping in my ears as details flashed across my mind again: stench, screams, blood, dust, collapse, ears ringing, panic, followed by the women—Fer and Luz, Luz and Fer—over and over. Now I could put names to their faces; their faces were all I saw. I was back in the Javits Center seeing Fer for the first time as I made my way to finally see her again.

On my way toward the subway, I pretended not to see the man who had begun following me. I went into the most crowded train car I could, shouldering through the straphangers to trace my finger along the subway map to navigate without my phone. The whole ride up to the Bronx, the man watched me through the window of the next car over. I was oddly relaxed. *He wouldn't come for me here*, I thought. *He already knows where I'm going.* I did, however, need enough space from him to get from the train to her apartment.

As we entered Harlem, though, I saw a C train waiting in the station across the platform. I followed the other commuters toward it, making sure the man was following as he entered the adjacent car. Just as the doors began to close, I bowled over an abuela and her grocery cart as I launched myself back onto the platform and scrambled back into the B, watching through the window as the man was carried off to Washington Heights.

Getting off the subway and making my way toward 183rd, the usual vibrance of the Bronx was nowhere to be found. Maybe it was the cold, but I couldn't help but sense the city itself had withdrawn from my presence for fear of being caught up in whatever I mess I was in. My stomach began to toss. It would be only natural to feel sick after a daylong adrenaline spike with a hangover and a single pastry in my stomach, but that was only a compounding factor. It was the air around me. The smell. Every step I took toward my destination, it grew thicker, heavy in the sharp winter breeze: burnt flesh, smoke, and a perfume of caramel and geraniums. The olfactory memory of the day at Javits raged in my mind, almost as if to tell my feet to stop moving.

"*This way*," it seemed to say, "*will only bring you back there again*."

As I approached Fernanda's building, I looked around. Not a soul in sight. None I could see, anyway.

The smell overpowered me. I doubled and spewed the contents of my stomach into a city trash can. Wiping my mouth, I mounted the steps of 773. I found *F. Griffiths #6B* and punched the button, and only as it buzzed did I realize I had no idea what to say if she answered. What the hell could I possibly say without coming off as a random lunatic shouting about shadowy figures into this stranger's intercom?

I wasn't given the chance to sort my scrambled thoughts before her voice crackled through the intercom.

"Hello?"

I did my best to sound normal. "Hello, is this Fernanda Griffiths?"

"Yes, who's this?"

I'd done this before. I fell back on my years of work as a documentarian. "My name's Aurelio Barrera. I'm a documentary filmmaker here in the city. I was wondering if I could talk to you about a project I'm working on."

"About what?"

"It would be better to explain in person. Would it be all right if I came in? It's pretty cold out here."

There was a pause. The intercom static hissed. I glanced around at the empty streets.

"Sure."

The door buzzed. I slipped in, making sure to close it behind me. I heard her door open somewhere up the apartment stairwell as I came in. Climbing the stairs, I was back to wondering what to say to her. When I reached her floor and saw her there, however, my mind went blank. It was the first I'd seen her since that day, the first time I'd actually been able to confirm she really existed. There she stood: the same wavy black hair, dimpled cheek, white pendant, and the smell of that perfume emanating from her that had turned my head that day at Javits. She was real.

She looked down at her phone, back up at me, studying my face.

"I looked you up while you were coming up. Just to be sure."

"Totally reasonable. Would you want to talk inside?"

She gestured for me to come in. My heart pounded in my chest as I drew close to pass into her apartment.

"So, what is this project about?"

I crossed to her window and peered out the blinds before turning to face her. I took a deep breath. We didn't have time to dance around my purpose in being there.

"I'm sorry to have lied, but I'm not really working on anything at the moment. I'm here because I was at the Javits Center that day."

Fernanda took a step backward, immediately wary of me.

"How did you know I was there, too?"

"I saw you. At the coffee stand right before it happened. Then everything . . . You know. After it happened, I saw you again, running out. But it wasn't you, was it? It was your twin. Do you know who I'm talking about?"

"No . . ." Fer took another step back. I needed to get to the point.

"Javits wasn't the first time you've been close to a disaster like that, was it? You've seen a few, right? Maybe you didn't see her, but she was at all of them as well."

"Stop. Get out."

"Please, just . . . Your necklace. You've had that your whole life, haven't you? It wasn't given to you by your adoptive mom."

Her hand shot up to the pendant on her neck.

"I bet they always told you that your birth mom gave it to you. You always wear it. The other woman, Lucia, your twin, she had the same one, except it's black."

Fer had begun to open her mouth to tell me to stop again but froze.

"A black one . . ."

"Look, I can explain more. I can tell you what the symbol on that pendant means, too, but we have to leave as soon as possible."

"Leave? Why?"

The intercom rang; we'd run out of time.

"Don't answer that. Is there another way out of the building?"

She moved toward the intercom. I still hadn't won her over.

I begged her, "Please. You have to trust me. Don't answer it."

"Why the hell should I listen to you?"

The sound of shattering glass from the stairwell answered the question for me.

"Because I asked to come in. They aren't. We have to go. Now."

Heavy knocking erupted at the door. Fer looked petrified. I held up a hand and checked the peephole, but it was covered.

WHAM! Someone shouldered the door, sending me stumbling back.

"What the fuck?" Fer yelled.

I turned to her.

"Do you have a fire escape?"

WHAM!

Fer flinched as someone threw their weight against the door again. "Fernanda, I can explain, but we need to leave."

"Who the . . . Why . . . Why would I trust you?"

WHAM!

"Again, I'm not breaking down your door!"

Fer weighed her options.

"This way."

She grabbed a coat and led me to her tiny bathroom, where she hoisted a rickety window beside the shower, slipping through onto the fire escape. The storm, already odd for March, seemed to instantly worsen as we stepped out. Just as I shut the window, I heard Fer's door finally break open. I barely caught a glimpse of one of the Birthing Room agents crashing into the bathroom before I followed Fer down the fire escape, each step shaking the old metal frame.

As we scrambled down the ladder to the ground, our pursuers had just managed to squeeze through the same window. One of them slipped on the wet iron steps of the escape as Fer broke left. I grabbed her shoulder and yanked her back when I saw three more round the corner ahead.

"No! This way! This way!" I shouted, pulling her toward a small gap between buildings.

My recent mezcal diet helped as we squeezed through into the courtyard of another apartment complex. I stopped and peered back through the gap, seeing nothing but rain splattering from the gutters into the alley. It seemed they were looking for another way around. Turning, Fernanda was staring at me wide-eyed, shivering in the rain. I had to get her out of here.

I grabbed her by the shoulders and tried to sound calm. "Do you know anywhere safe nearby?"

Fer nodded, then took us ten blocks north to the Fordham University campus, swiping her student ID to get us into Walsh Library, past the metal detectors and a security guard. We caught our breath in a small study room on the opposite side of the top floor, past dozens of bookstacks, where I finally laid it all out. The Javits Center. The message board. Jay Wilding. Lucifer's sigil. Her sister. Tanita. The books helped a little, having something to point to at least, to show her I wasn't making everything up off the top of my head.

Fer grasped her necklace as she listened. When I was done, she sat silent for a while.

"That's a lot of shit to take in all at once," she muttered. "Even if I believed it all . . . I mean, what am I supposed to do with this?"

Her look of vulnerability and trust revealed how little I'd thought this through. So much had escalated so quickly. I'd been so dubious about even being able to get to Fernanda first, let alone get her to listen to me, that I didn't have a plan for what to do *after.*

"I don't really know. Do you believe me?"

Fer held up her pendant and studied it, running her thumb across the symbol.

"When you said it belonged to my birth mom, it really . . ." She trailed off, running her thumb over the sigil. "I can't explain it. No one ever sat me down and said, '*This necklace belonged to your birth mother* . . .' But I just always knew. I didn't talk about it, but I knew. I don't think even *I* thought much about it, it was just always part of me. I've had it since I was a kid, and I just assumed . . . But who knows? I don't know if anything I believed is true. I could've written off all this crazy shit. But when you mentioned the black necklace . . ." She trailed off again, lost in her thoughts. "That's when I knew it had to be true."

"How?"

"Because in the same way I always had this deep connection to my mother's white necklace . . . I also had these dreams, nightmares, visions of a black one. Sometimes they're just clouds of sensations and feelings, and other times they're not even really nightmares, they're like memories.

"Years ago, my mom got sober long enough to land this finance bro who took us on vacation to Sumatra. Then the tsunami hit, and my mom and I got away, but her boyfriend didn't. The whole thing was traumatic. My mom started drinking again. When I told her about the nightmares, it wasn't *just* that they were terrifying flashbacks. I remember saying, 'I don't remember these memories.' We couldn't afford any actual help, but every social worker and doctor said, 'Oh, that's just your brain protecting you, remembering some stuff and not others,' but nobody understood what this was.

"I have my *own* memories of what we went through, places we ran, who we saw, what happened, no—*those* experiences belonged to someone else. This someone *looked* exactly like me, but went through other things, ran other places, saw different people, and did all of it with the same black necklace I have in white.

"The visions continued for a couple years, then got more infrequent. I'd wake up screaming and crying from a breakup with some guy when I hadn't dated anyone, and I'm not even into guys. Every now and then I'd get this flash of an experience that wasn't mine. Sometimes, when I was a kid, I'd even have a dream about getting hurt and wake up with a new scar, as though just by seeing it made it real for me. But they were becoming more and more rare . . . until the Javits Center. Just like before, I have all *my* memories and emotions, but then I fall asleep and it's as if they belong to someone else. Like, when I remember that day, I remember everything I did, but if I really think about it, there's more. Almost like another camera angle on the place." Fer closed her eyes, recalling. "I'm wearing black, some long formal dress, my hair's short, there's dust in the air, everything's destroyed, but rather than help people I'm heading for the door, and then . . ." Fer opened her eyes, looking into mine. "I see you."

"So, you had seen me before, in a way." I was stunned.

"Maybe it's why I managed to trust you." Fernanda reached across the library table, grabbing my hand. "I still don't really know what's real here, but I know that I don't want to meet whoever was chasing us. I can tell you risked something to find me, and I know you want to find your friend, but I just don't know what I can do to help. Where do we even go from here?"

What *she* could do to help? I had just told her that she was separated at birth for an experiment by a Luciferian cult. That it seemed that their experiment had been somewhat successful. That her entire miserable life, horrors of loss and destruction, had been purposefully afflicted upon her as part of some twisted experiment on the human soul. Her very name wasn't even her own. And here she was reaching across, holding my hand, and all she seemed to be sorry for was that she couldn't do more to help *me?* Of course. The duality of Lucifer the "light-bringer's" seal. The sister who had seen the darkness had within her great white light, wore it around her neck.

Bleary-eyed and on the verge of passing out, I couldn't even begin to think about where to go next. All I knew was they had seemingly called off their pursuit. Fer and I had been in the study room for more than two hours and we still seemed the only ones around. I couldn't do much else without getting a few moments of rest. We pushed a chair under the door handle to the room and, slumped against the wall, I closed my eyes for the first time in what felt like weeks.

It didn't last long.

Fernanda was shaking me awake, eyes wide with panic.

"I'm sorry. I said I would keep watch, but I fell asleep."

I jumped up. "Are they here?"

"No . . . I don't know. But I saw Lucia. In my sleep. I was—she was tied up in a van. They got her, Aurelio!"

I suddenly realized I should've figured it out sooner. The moment she told me that she could see Lucia's memories.

"If you could see Lucia just now and they have her, then . . ."

Fernanda nodded. "She saw us, too."

"Do you think she told them?"

"Aurelio?" Fernanda was crying, holding her neck. "They had a knife to my—to Lucia's throat. I don't think she had a choice."

"Shit."

There was a noise outside the study room door, people moving in the library. They had used Lucia to find us. There was only one way out of the study room. I devised a plan to wait for them to be at the door, then we'd have to bash through and make a break. Fernanda nodded. The door handles jiggled. Then WHAM! As the first impact came against the door, I grabbed her hand. She was trembling. WHAM! I gripped her hand tight. Fernanda shook more and I turned around. She had begun to convulse, gripping and pulling at her pendant.

"Fer? What's wrong?"

Her voice was barely able to escape her lips as she stammered, eyes going soft and weak as they gently rolled up into her head, "Lucia . . . They . . . cut . . . She's . . . bleeding . . ."

She shuddered, going stiff as a board. The banging on the door continued behind me as I watched a thick cord of scar tissue trace its way across Fernanda's throat, bubbling up and marring her smooth skin. Blood dripped down her nose, leaked from the side of her mouth as her eyes suddenly snapped back into focus. A soft smile played on her lips.

"Oh," she said, "your dimple's on the other side. Funny."

The door to the study room burst open, but there was no sound of the impact as the men flew into the room. I recognized this. The oppressive blanket of silence. The smell of the air itself cooking around me. Then all there was in the world was a great bright flash before a thundering darkness.

I was awoken by the smell of smoldering flesh. There were no screams. Frigid night air blew in from where the ceiling had once been. Around me were the dismembered and scorched bodies of the men who had kicked in the door. My head throbbing, I looked around. Fernanda lay on the ground just paces away, but the blast . . . I kept glancing around for Luz. If the two had to be together for the reaction to occur, then she had to be here. But there was nobody.

I slowly stumbled to my feet and walked to Fernanda. Her eyes were open, that soft smile still on her lips. I shook her by the shoulder and her head simply fell to the side, exposing the scar on her neck where they'd cut Lucia's throat. They really had been two parts of the same whole, separated at birth. Looking around at the destruction, it seemed they'd also been reunited in death.

I leaned down and closed Fer's eyes before taking the white pendant from her neck, my only clue or evidence to lead me to Tanita, if she was still alive. "I'm sorry. I'll keep it safe."

I draped it around my neck and stumbled away, stepping over the smoldering corpses as I ran out into the night. I had to keep moving. I had to go somewhere. Maybe I could find Jay again. Maybe with the pendant I could . . .

My phone rang. I stood still, taking out my phone with a shaking hand. Tanita was trying to FaceTime me. Wind rushed around me as I stared at the screen, listening to the ring. What else could I do? Every other lead I had was dead. Perhaps Jay had found her. Maybe she was just at home, having opted not to join on my delusional adventure.

I answered.

"Tanita?"

I was greeted to a dark room on the other end, lit solely by streetlights bleeding through the blinds. Whoever was on the other line didn't speak, only moved silently through an apartment. I recognized it. It was my apartment.

"Tanita, you shouldn't be there. You need to leave."

They kept moving through my apartment into my bedroom. Someone was on the bed. A woman lay on the bed, arm hanging limp off one side. The camera drew closer. Tanita was sprawled on her back, her throat shredded and spilling blood.

"No. No! No! What did you do? She didn't even know anything! You could have just taken me. She would have thought I had just disappeared! Killed myself! Who the fuck are you?"

Someone finally spoke. A woman.

"Aurelio. Do you know what that name means? It comes from the Latin for 'gold.'"

The camera panned up from Tanita's bled-out corpse to a man standing in the corner. Knife in hand. Even in the dark, I recognized him. I had seen that silhouette many times before, my whole life. It was my own. I looked down at the white pendant around my neck, then at the black one shining in the dark around the man's chest. The woman spoke again.

"Come on home now, my sweet golden child."

Specter

Ananda Lima

"Think of humanity," he said, "as a great oyster shell.
Our first task, Soares, is to extract the pearl—that is, reason."
—Machado de Assis, *The Allienist*
(translation: William L. Grossman)

"So be careful, be very careful."
—Prince, 1999 Yahoo! Internet Online Music Awards

I fed it words. Words I brought home in pamphlets, packaging, paragraphs in ripped magazine pages. I poured them into its empty mouth. I whispered stories, lyrics, memories into its hollow ear. When I walked into my room and turned on the bedside lamp, there was the rubbery alligator snout peeking from the side of the wooden bookshelf. It liked to wait for me on the old leather chair in the corner, all cozy and amberlit, snuggling under the copper-brown crochet throw blanket. The alligator head seemed to be its favorite. From afar, it looked like an ordinary mask, a person in a costume. But peering into the holes in search for the eyes, the giant mouth, there was nothing there. An oblivious hollowness shaping the rubber as a human head. If I paused, unsure how to continue after I told it about my day, the paper I was working on, the news, it would nudge me, placing its hand with the enormous curving nails on my lap, like a puppy wanting to be petted. And I gave it more, until it was full. Sometimes, after it was gone, I found scratches on the leather seat cushion and arms of the chair, from its kneading as it fed.

Of course, at first I was terrified. I wasn't sure it was real. I thought I was losing my mind. Before I had seen it for the first time, there was the occasional glimpse in my peripheral vision of a blurry, shadowy figure reflected in the mirror that disappeared when I looked at it straight on. A lullaby played, barely detectable, under the songs in my playlist as I walked to campus. When I rewound the songs, the lullaby was always gone. And the creepiest instance up to then: a flickering of the fluorescent lights, and the lullaby again, now all mechanical sounding, barely audible in the crackling speakers in the Linguistics department's computer lab.

I tried to avoid the computer lab after that. But I had a paper due, and I didn't own a computer. It was the early 2000s and I was a graduate student. My stipend was just enough to live in a dingy place and to eat, as long as I attended the functions on campus that offered free pizza. I was on a fellowship and on a student visa. I couldn't mess around with my grades. Also, I wasn't sure I fully believed it then. A haunting is a little like other bad things in life: the impending cancer diagnosis, the eviction, the cheating spouse—you may suspect it but still not bring yourself to believe it would actually happen to you. Or maybe it's more like living through a coup d'état. The signs are there, but they are contradictory and hard to follow. It all seems so unlikely, so absurd. It not happening would seem like the rational thing to expect, until you can no longer deny it.

I told myself it had all been coincidences or my imagination. But as I walked the empty corridor at Campbell Hall, I begged whatever powers there might be for my classmates Ana or Zach—or anyone human and not ghostly or monsterly—to be there, working on their papers, too. But I knew they were not usually around late Tuesday nights. When I entered the room, it was dark and empty. I turned the light on. Nothing out of the ordinary: a row of clunky beige monitors along the right wall, matching desktop towers, and rolling office chairs. On the opposite wall a couple of writing desks and a large gray printer. I sat in front of my usual desktop in the middle of the row and turned it on. As it powered up (it took a while back then), a noise behind me startled me. I turned around slowly, heart racing, afraid to look. But it was just the printer turning on. I noticed I had placed both my hands on my chest, like my grandma and her friends, sitting in foldable chairs in front of their houses, and whispering the latest rumors about the kidnappings or other horrible crimes supposedly going around their small town. I laughed at myself, being so scared of nothing. Probably just some old printing request that got activated when I turned the computer on.

I got up and walked to the printer. Pages started pouring out. They were completely blank. I hoped the old thing had not gone out of toner. Maybe someone had put the paper through the feeder facing the wrong way and the request got held up in the queue. I walked back to the computer as it continued spitting out its growing pile of emptiness.

As soon as I sat down again, the printer came to a halt. The fluorescent lights above turned off. For a second, I thought it might have been a power outage. Back in those days, people from my country didn't think the US could have power outages, or people living in the streets, or long waits to see a specialist. But by then, I knew those impressions were wrong about these things. So maybe, yes, a power outage. But then the left monitor came on. I yelped. I was terrified, but strangely also embarrassed thinking somebody might have heard me, or maybe everything was a joke and someone was hiding, laughing at me. I sat very still, my left hand back on my chest, my heart racing. Then another monitor came on, followed by another: every row of monitors turned themselves on one by one from left to right. I was screaming now; each time they powered on, the embarrassment completely replaced by terror.

On the screens, a classic-looking video game appeared, a Pac-Man-like thing. Except that instead of Pac-Man, there was a little alligator prancing through the labyrinth. It ate all the terrified ghosts and cackled. Then all the screens went dark, except for the one on my right and the one on my left. Each displayed a green pixelated circle, as big as a dessert plate, surrounded by darkness. A third circle appeared on the monitor right in front of me, casting its green light on my face and trembling hands. The three circles together made a triangle, like the holes on a bowling ball, forming a rudimentary face. Pitiful pixelated eyebrows appeared, making it look desperate, afraid and screaming, mimicking my expression. It was mocking me. Then the eyebrows inverted and turned angry. I dropped my notes, my empty vending machine coffee cup, and ran. As I was exiting, the two eye circles squinted with pleasure. I could hear the face laugh and laugh.

I got home, not knowing what to think, but relieved I made it out of the computer lab. My roommates were out. I was focusing on keeping my hands steady as I grabbed some water from the refrigerator, when I closed the fridge door and saw it there, right next to me, for the first time: the alligator head, the hollow eyeholes. Its body then was that of a skinny old woman—think the evil stepmother transfigured into the witch in the old Snow White cartoon—hunched over her basket of apples. I screamed again and dropped the glass water bottle on the floor. It didn't break, but the water was leaking everywhere. I fell backward, managing to hold myself up on the kitchen counter. The thing was coming toward me, reaching with long, yellowing nails. I thought it wanted to eat me. Or maybe steal my head to replace the nothingness floating above its neck. Unable to move, I scrunched my eyes closed, squeezed them tight, and leaned away from the thing heading toward me.

Then, nothing. It reached past me, toppling a basket of red apples, which rolled down onto the floor. It grabbed my roommate Meg's vegetarian cookbook, which had been right next to the fruit basket, then proceeded to rip the pages and push them down, one at a time, into its large rubber mouth.

The mind has an incredible capacity to get used to things. And just because you start being visited by a monster doesn't mean you can forget about rent or keeping your immigration status. You'd be surprised, after the shock and the sickness, after thinking it's not right, it's not fair, and why me, and this shouldn't be happening, and not knowing how to go on, etc., etc., somehow you just do.

The next day, I was too afraid to stay home, so I went to class to be surrounded by my fellow phonology classmates. I was relieved to sit through a dorky discussion on combining autosegmental and optimality theories to account for a tonal language dataset. Not the crew I would pick to defend anyone in a horror movie (in a heartwarming spelling bee movie, perhaps), but it was better than being alone. I asked for an extension on the paper, and, eventually, I wrote it. It took me a while to be brave enough to return to the computer lab alone. But soon I found that as long as I continued to feed it my papers, my ramblings, my words, the terrorizing was kept at a manageable level, and I could go on somewhat like before.

Before the empty-headed creature showed up, I spent most of my days doing the work I was meant to do as a linguistics graduate student. My specialization was syntax. I investigated the ways words come together in sentences, represented in diagrams that looked like trees. How their leaves and roots, nouns, verbs, quantifiers, adverbial phrases, swayed and talked to each other, how they bonded to create the structure to hold meaning. My friends worked on morphology, phonology, computational linguistics, each of us looking for a different window of understanding into a Universal Grammar for language. Each day was a mixture of awe and excitement about the possibilities of knowledge—the relief of being surrounded by people who shared this hunger, for the first time in our lives—and also a sprinkle of a latent terror. Terror staring at datasets that refused to fit into a pattern. Despair looking at the plain black plastic clock on the wall of the graduate lounge, ticking toward 2 a.m. on the eve of a paper deadline. Thinking that we might not be good enough to be there. An unspoken but palpable fear that if we didn't do well, if we fell behind, we would be kicked out of the program (and in my case, also the country).

During the day, I liked sitting by the windows on the old floral couch at the graduate lounge, working quietly alongside other students, or occasionally discussing the repercussions of different linguistic theories, drawing sentence derivations together on the whiteboards. The large yellow oak coffee table was often covered with notes, tea and coffee mugs, and old plain-covered journals with titles like *Natural Language*, *Language*, and *Linguistic Inquiry*.

At some point in those earlier days, someone drew an alligator on the whiteboard. I thought nothing of it and erased it to draw sentence tree diagrams comparing the position of object pronouns in Brazilian Portuguese, Spanish, and English. When I came back from class later, someone had erased all the words and drawn a little cartoon alligator. It wore sunglasses and tapped its big, round belly, satisfied, licking its lips, as if each word on the tree had been an apple it had plucked and eaten. I laughed and drew a heart and little eaten apples strewn around the board, oblivious to what would come later.

The biggest change when the creature showed up was time. I already had so little of it, and now I had to spend so many of my nights awake, relating my days, describing the scenery, the stories my mother used to tell me as a kid, what I had for breakfast, feeding it my paper drafts, the brochures I diligently collected from the different clubs and proselytizers on Bruin Walk. I needed to find more time to sleep. That empty-headed thing liked the papers and flyers, but it loved the talk. After a while, it no longer had the body of Snow White's witch. It was now a man, a whole foot taller than me, wide shoulders and back, rounded with muscle that made it hungrier, the legs of a cyclist. As it grew stronger, it was I who shriveled up with exhaustion.

One day, after a few delirious months, I woke up to Ana shaking my shoulder. I had fallen asleep under my desk. "Let's go, amiga. Class is in fifteen minutes." She helped me up.

"Shit!" I stood up all at once and grabbed my toothbrush and toothpaste out of the desk drawer.

"I'm worried about you." She made sure to pause and look me in the eyes, to register a degree of gravity, then walked with me to the woman's bathroom.

While I brushed my teeth, she stared at me in the mirror. "Are you on drugs?"

I burst out laughing, toothpaste going everywhere. And then the laughter turned into crying. I had not been able to finish my assignment. I had read the entire dataset to the creature the night before. It had shown up in the office with a coconut head this time, the two holes for eyes and one for a mouth. The mouth was not big enough for the papers I had collected, so I had to read everything instead. By the time it was finished, I could barely keep my eyes open. One minute I was trying to work and the next Ana was shaking me awake.

"I am not on drugs," I said, sobbing, toothpaste running down my chin, hand, and wrist.

She hugged me, led my hands to the water, wiped my face. "Talk to me."

I shook my head. No more talking.

She dabbed my face with a paper towel. "All right, for now, let's just make it to class, okay? We'll talk later."

Ana modeled breathing in and out slowly as we walked to class. Ana and I were the last to arrive, although I managed to go in without crying.

We sat with the other nine students around the cherrywood conference table as the professor continued his spiel about the role of grammatical categories, binary tree structure, and entropy in predicting phrase boundaries. I tried to follow it, but with little ability to focus. This was stuff I used to love, but I was so tired.

He called on me for a question on the dataset, presumably related to what he had just talked about. But my head was empty.

"Maybe if . . ." I said, squinting at a particular area of the dataset projected on the white screen rolled over the blackboard. "If we look at . . ." I paused, as if trying to put a brilliant but complex insight into words. But there was nothing behind what I was saying. I wanted to vomit.

Zach and Ana exchanged looks. Then she jumped in: "Right! I see what you are looking at, right there on the last two lines."

"Oh, I see it now," said Zach.

Ana took over the conversation with something she had surely worked hard to discover and was planning to bring to class discussion today as her own idea, as she should have, rather than pretending I had seen it first. I felt terrible, and also so grateful to her. My standing was getting pretty dicey in that class.

After they moved on to another topic, she gently squeezed my finger under the table and wrote on the corner of the open page of my notebook: *I just want you to be okay*.

If only I had told her right after class. But I didn't think anyone would have believed me. I didn't want people to think I had lost it. I didn't want to go on probation, to be kicked out, to lose my visa and be sent home. I didn't want to lose the program and LA and her and Zach. I just wanted it to disappear.

That day was the last Thursday of the month, when Ana, Zach, and I usually attended student happy hour at a place just south of campus. We would split half-off appetizers and do our monthly "we survived another one" toast. I went home early to try for a recovery nap first, only to be shaken awake again, though this time hideous nails dug into my shoulder. I peeked at it—it was back to wearing the alligator mask—then at my alarm clock on the bedside table and immediately felt like crying. It was midnight; I had missed happy hour. I thought of Ana and Zach sitting there waiting for me, my not showing up even after they saved me in class.

It shook my shoulder again. I had never resisted it before, but I was so tired and sad.

"Go away!" I mumbled.

It shook me harder.

"Leave me alone." I pulled the blanket over my head.

It poked me in the back.

I ignored it.

After a couple more tries, it went quiet. For a few seconds I thought it had gone away. I imagined that all this time, all I had needed to do was ask.

Then it ripped the blanket off me and sent it flying across the room. It screamed at me, a mixture of a high-pitched whistle, boiling kettle, fire alarm, and lion roar.

It was panting, the arms clenched into fists at its side, making me think of an angry gorilla. It was huge now, the body of a tall bodybuilder, and it was furious.

I screamed into a stand, then quieted myself quickly so as not to agitate it more. "Okay, okay," I said as calmly as I could while looking for my backpack. As I searched under the blankets, on the floor, under the bed, I told it about my morning. About Ana waking me up, about class. I repeated what I remembered from what the professor had said, something about applications to predictive text. I related what I could from Ana's response, even without understanding exactly what I was saying. I was grasping for whatever I could find in my head, repeating the words displayed on the posters and ones I sometimes heard being yelled in heated discussions as I walked by the stand of the closeted conservative student club that stationed itself on Bruin Walk: words like "fiscally conservative," "handouts," "bootstrap," "merit." I repeated random lines from movies, like *Clueless* and *Back to the Future*.

It began to calm down. Slowly it headed to the leather chair. The backpack was nowhere to be found. In my exhaustion, I might have left it in the graduate lounge. I kept speaking as I looked for something to feed it. I had given it everything in the room. All our junk mail, my notes, each of the books I had bought and the ones I had originally brought from home. I closed my eyes trying to think. It responded with an angry growl.

I breathed in, closed my eyes, and talked about my first days in the US, about how I loved LA. The freeways, the cars, the golden sunsets over the frigid waters of the Pacific, the dry landscapes, the hikes, cracking steps on sandy dirt and pebble paths, the long stretches without coming across any other pedestrians, the street closures for filming, the hip-hop, rancheras and Pink Martini blasting out of convertibles, the terra-cotta roof tiles like those at home, the burger place "animal style," the never-ending traffic jams like organisms with oblivious cells, *A Video Store Named Desire*, the midnight *Rocky Horror Picture Show*, potlucks in rental apartments, with gray wall-to-wall carpets and too many roommates and views of the freeway, but homey and ours. My voice broke. I paused from speaking and opened my eyes, thinking that I had to go home, get away from all of this. I couldn't keep going anymore. I cried softly. I felt so tired.

The creature punched the side table, causing the lamp to fall on its side and the alarm clock to drop to the ground. I started talking again. I talked about lying on the embroidered white hammock on my parents' porch, smelling the rain and the red earth. I told it about the brown mineral waters of Abaeté. About how capybaras were related to nutrias and chinchillas and how they were everywhere on the outskirts of my hometown. How they snuck out under the fence and came in and out of their zoo enclosures as if they were guests at a hotel. About how the zookeepers didn't mind. I told it about the beauty of language in general and my language specifically, the way it turned stops into fricatives, the way it implied the object with blank space, the breath and music of it.

The creature got angry again. I had said some of those things before. It didn't like repetition. So I talked about Ana.

Her father, some asshole who Ana was sure only asked for weekends and holidays to bother her mother. I talked about what I remembered from her linguistics papers, what she was working on for her thesis, about how we had laughed at Ana's early crush on Zach, something that seemed ridiculous now. I read our emails to each other to the creature, the few short text messages. Until, exhausted, I reached for my pocket, where I had kept the note she had written in the corner of my notebook that morning: *I just want you to be okay*.

I extended my arm limply and let it go. Down went Ana's note, into its alligator mouth. That finally satisfied it.

I lay down and pulled the blankets over me again, then looked at it once more, before it turned around and left. As I drifted back to sleep, I wondered if I had seen something on the other side of its hollow eyes this time: in the darkness inside its head, a tiny flicker of a greenish light.

I woke up midmorning with the sun shining bright through the window, right on my face. I was startled for a minute, thinking I had missed class, but realized it was Friday. We only had the colloquium in the afternoon. On the leather chair, there was a pile of papers lined up neatly and stapled. I picked it up. It was an assignment with an analysis of the dataset from the day before, my name on top. I skimmed it, and though I didn't know for sure, the analysis sounded reasonably good.

As soon as I got to campus, I went to the office of the professor from the day before and knocked on his door. I told him I hadn't been feeling well and asked if I might be able to have an extension for the paper.

"There have been just too many times." He looked down at his desk with a pained expression. "I can't keep doing this."

I swallowed. I didn't know how I was going to make it through the semester. "I understand," I said softly and began to turn around.

"Wait," he said, stroking his gray mustache. "Listen, I was about to enter the grades. If I can enter yours today, if you have anything done, I can look at it. If I do it now, it won't look bad on my end."

I looked down at my shoes.

"Look, I am trying to help you. I think you can do great work. You have done so well in the past." He sounded genuinely concerned. "But I have been hearing that you haven't been keeping up lately."

A place has a strange way of taking hold of you, a way of rooting in you as you start to make a life there. It is difficult to rip it out, both the life you built and the dream you brought with you from long before. That makes it harder to admit that the alarm saying "Leave! Now!" reflects something real. You think you want to try just a little longer. The same hope that helps you keep going makes it harder to see clearly. You think you can find a way for things to be okay, for you to stay.

Hands shaking, I pulled out of my tote bag the paper I had found on the leather chair. I looked at my hands gripping each side. "Thank you," I said so softly, I am not sure he heard me. Then I gave it to him and left, unable to say another word.

Sometimes I still wonder if I never came to Los Angeles, if I had turned around and gone back to where I came from, as people say, maybe it would all have turned out differently. Would my alternative self naively regret my return? Or maybe a version of this life would have followed me anywhere. I try not to think about it anymore, but sometimes I can't help it. It's hard enough to keep things together.

It continued visiting me, sporting its coconut head or classic alligator, but occasionally also a turtle; a gourd; the volleyball head from the movie *Castaway*; a reptilian but lion-like creature; an iron pan with eye and mouth holes; a footballer's helmet to match its now-massive body. It had spells when it came frequently, then it would disappear for several nights, when I mostly slept. I worked hard not to make it angry again. Twice more it brought me written papers to submit. Other times, I cobbled things together superficially, without a full understanding behind my words. Something felt vaporous in my mind. But I was able to scrape by and recover enough to avoid getting myself on academic probation for the semester.

Between the schoolwork, finding content for my late nights, and trying to get some sleep, I couldn't spend much time hanging out in the graduate lounge anymore. I said no to many invitations from Ana and Zach. I became a sort of recluse, a feral creature. It was difficult for me to talk to people. I had no energy and they couldn't understand. I missed last Thursday's toast again. Ana was mad, but she didn't want to show it. Eventually she stopped asking. And I let her.

Then, one day, I came into the graduate lounge to get a linguistics journal in case I had a visit that night. I overheard Ana on the other side of the metal bookshelf stacks. She was talking about capybaras, about how they snuck out from their jail cells and the zookeepers just laughed. I was disoriented. I didn't think I had told her that. She was talking about someone, some guy she had met, who had told her about this. I wanted to hear more, but they seemed to be moving toward the couch. I turned around and left before they saw me.

Later that week, I stood by the door as Ana talked to Zach. They were discussing an idea she had been working on for a paper. Something about the position of agreement particles in Roman versus Slavic languages. The discussion sounded somewhat familiar. I was trying to remember where I had heard or read those points before, when I heard footsteps behind me. Someone was coming to the graduate lounge. I pretended to be looking for something in my bag and left.

When I got home that evening, I picked up the paper that

had been left on the chair for me the night before again. I sat on my bed and went through each line. Short sentences that went straight to the point—borderline curt, bland but clear—the arguments made in an intelligent, transparent way. Confident. No flourishes, no unnecessary words. It was Ana.

It had somehow stolen her work. I felt sick. Had it been seeing Ana? It had not come for me as much in the past month. Maybe it had attached itself to her, too. Maybe she was in danger.

I hurriedly put on my shoes and grabbed my key from the bedside table. But when I lifted my gaze, there it was again, sitting in its corner. Tonight, it was a dragon's head.

I was so angry. I ripped one of the pages from the paper it had given me and approached it. When I slid the page down its mouth, there was something inside the head. I couldn't see everything, but roughly aligned with the empty eyeholes, only deeper inside the head, were two small lights, like the kind one could find around a Christmas tree, both green . . . and something else. I could barely see it in the faint green light, but it looked like a jumble of wires, like a small nest. Before I could see more, it tilted its snout up and roared. Its body was so enormous now, it barely fit the chair. It stood up, towering over me, then reached into its mouth with the nails and extracted the page I had fed it before balling it up and throwing it at me. The teeth on the mask were made of something hard and sharp this time, like real teeth. It swatted at me with its giant arms. I jumped back in time for it not to hurl my head off my neck, but the nails still scratched my left cheek. I brought my hand to my face. It was wet with blood.

I stepped back, fumbled through my bag, and found a copy of *Linguistic Inquiry*. I held it in front of me as one might hold a Bible when trying to avert a vampire.

"I'm sorry. I'm sorry, okay? Here." I ripped a page from the beginning and offered it. "Here, have this. It's brand-new."

It was breathing heavily, like a toddler deciding whether to lean in or come out of a tantrum. It ripped the page from my hands. Swallowed it. Satisfied I didn't try any tricks this time, it extended its hand, asking for more. I complied, feeding it the pages of the journal, then the pages of the syntax textbook I had bought for class as I hummed a lullaby.

"There, there," I said softly. Eventually, it calmed down and finished feeding. Though it gave me a shove on its way out.

As soon as it left, I went looking for Ana: at the coffee shop, the lounge, the computer lab, but she wasn't anywhere. I wrote her an email, telling her that I was sorry, that I missed her, asking her if she was doing okay, begging her to see me.

I didn't hear from her until the next morning. She said she missed me, too, that I was a jerk and she had much to tell me, "some real out-there shit." She, Zach, and a couple more students were going to the Getty for the day. She didn't invite me, and it was too late to try to catch up with them. She did, however, ask if I wanted to join her for a Halloween party at a club that evening. I was in no mood for parties, but I said yes. I just wanted to talk to her.

I threw away the rest of the paper with the stolen words and spent the day working on the next assignment. I managed to finish a draft. I knew it was mediocre, but it was something I could hand in. On my way out of Campbell Hall, I stopped by the graduate lounge and grabbed two new journals, in case I needed them later. "Please, please, please," I pleaded to the universe and to everything I didn't understand, to let me go see Ana, for no visits from it that night.

It was dark outside, so I walked as fast as I could without running. As I passed the football field, the doors to my left suddenly opened with a loud bang. The stadium lights turned on. My stomach dropped. To my left, an enormous figure, all muscle, with a football helmet headed in my direction. I stopped walking. I thought about Ana, wondering how this thing had her words, about how I was about to miss her again.

The giant kept moving toward me, but when it got closer, there were normal human hands, unremarkable nails. In the helmet a nose, eyes. It was just a regular giant football player heading to the stadium. I breathed out in relief and laughed. A little confused, the football player smiled. I smiled back, then ran to the party.

I came into a wall of music, the bass beginning of "Work It" by Missy Elliot played over large loudspeakers everywhere. There was a stage set up, but the band seemed to be on break. After trying to decipher the mess of people from the top of the stairs, I spotted Zach at the bar lining up for a drink, but I couldn't see Ana. I made my way down the stairs, hoping to ask Zach where she was. I moved too slowly through the crowd, trying to dodge Britney, Legolas, Dracula, sexy nurse, sexy vampire, the devil, Ghostbusters, ghosts, and witches. It seemed that I was the only one not wearing a costume, though maybe my stained T-shirt and my messy hair would have passed for something, as there was no way anyone in their right mind would have gone to a party looking like that. Not even I would have, in the days before the creature showed up. It hit me then, how much the whole thing had taken from me. I was losing myself to it. I suddenly felt embarrassed to see Ana or Zach. I wanted to hide, but I couldn't. I had to talk to Ana.

Then I caught a glimpse of her, from afar. She was right by the stage now, talking to someone tall, yelling over the loud music, laughing. A pair of nuns and a clown moved in front of me, blocking my view. After they passed, I saw the huge man she was talking to, who was dressed as a jack-o'-lantern. It shook its head at something she had said, a little flirtatiously. For a split second,

I thought I saw a flicker of green lights coming from its pumpkin head, though I couldn't be sure. Maybe Ana and I together could do something to stop it. Maybe it wouldn't hurt us with all the people around. Ana did not look afraid of the man; she might even have been flirting back. She had no idea. I ran toward them. But I couldn't move through the thick net of bodies in the crowd quickly enough. When I finally made it, they were gone.

Ana didn't answer my emails or texts the next two days. Zach hadn't seen her. Neither had her roommate. The alligator did not come to see me that night, but I still couldn't sleep. Next Monday, she wasn't in class. I walked back and forth between her place and Campbell Hall. I decided to wait in the graduate lounge and finally fell asleep on the sofa.

I woke up later that night and immediately checked my phone. Nothing. I headed to the computer lab to see if she had emailed. In the corridor, I heard a faint hum, and as I got closer to the computer lab, the hum became louder, clearer. Eventually I could make out that it was a lullaby in a woman's voice. Unlike the times I had heard it early on, it was loud enough for me to tell that it was definitely there. And maybe, I wasn't completely sure, it sounded like Ana. I ran the rest of the way.

When I opened the door, someone was there, in the dark, facing one of the computers, her back to the door. It was her.

"Ana!" I was so relieved. "Ana, I have been looking all over for you."

Her glowing outline was carved out from the darkness by green light. She still had her back to the door. She didn't move.

"Ana!"

Nothing.

"Ana!"

She swayed left and right ever so slightly on the office chair, but remained focused on the green light on her screen.

Carefully, I walked toward her. Shaking, I reached for the back of the chair and slowly turned her around. When I saw her face, I fell backward.

Her eyes were dark, as if her irises had stretched to cover the white. No, the eyes were hollow. The darkness was her head, filled with nothingness. A mask, made of Ana's skin: the tiny mole on the bottom of her nose was there, except the color was gone, like a dead person in a movie. She tilted her face a little. Her face was expressionless, but then slowly, her lips, dry and blue-tinged, curved up into an unnatural, twisted smile.

Still on the ground, I moved away until I was backed against the wall.

"Ana?" I whispered. "Are you there?"

Hearing this, her smile was gone. She extended her hand toward me, as if asking for help. I raised myself from the floor, dragging up the wall as she rolled toward me. Behind her the monitors glowed, filling with green text.

Before I had the chance to move away, her hand grabbed mine; it was cold. I hadn't realized I'd been crying until she raised her hands to my cheeks and wiped my tears. Then, all at once, she opened her mouth wide.

The most horrible screech came out of it, sudden, loud. I covered my ears as I oriented myself enough to recognize the sound. It sounded like an insect, or the emergency brakes on the subway, a kettle boiling. No, it was the sound I would hear when I picked up the phone as a teenager and found that someone had dialed up the internet on the landline. That horrible, inorganic scream. But it was the loudest I had ever heard it, coming out incessantly from Ana's mouth.

I tried to get up and run. But I tripped on a lump of wires.

Ana's scream continued to pour out, and now two snakelike bundles of wires came out of her wide-open mouth, reaching for me like two arms. Within seconds, wire hands pressed hard against my cheeks and pulled me by the head toward Ana's mouth. I got closer, the wires tighter. And then it was dark.

When I first arrived in Los Angeles, it felt like I was walking into a movie. The skinny tall palm trees, the cars, the one-story buildings. That bright sunlight, free from skyscrapers or dense vegetation, cradled with a hint of sepia by the wide smogged sky. Los Angeles had been so common in the movies I had watched, I had no longer noticed it. When I arrived, I saw it both again and for the first time: the place right there, all around me, but also in my memories of films, photographs, the hypervisible setting of the LA I had brought to the LA in my head.

Before my program began, I took long, aimless walks through campus and residential streets with meticulously landscaped water-efficient gardens. Then the businesses along Wilshire or Pico Boulevard: car washes, gas stations, home goods and electronic stores. The mess of signage: vintage fonts that made me think of the Beach Boys and pink Cadillacs; plain corporate logos; hastily painted, handmade signs that reminded me of the people selling homemade sweets at home (*vende-se geladinho*, *vende-se cocada*). The movie set was not a movie set at all, but real trees, real sidewalks rough against the rubber bottom of my burgundy Converses; real hard plastic buttons on the traffic lights, telling me to "Wait, wait, wait," in their mechanical human voices.

Place was always so central to everything. To happen is to "take place." Even works of fiction live in real places: the yellowing handwritten letter, folded and forgotten in a borrowed book; the thin pages of a mass-market paperback; the vibrating air between vocal cords and the tiny hairs of listening ears; a lit-up screen; a frozen memory as a sequence of 0s or 1s, *yesses* or *nos*, open or closed gates.

Even now, I must still be, somewhere.

Or maybe I am in many places. I hear people carry us with them now, in their pockets. I get bits and pieces of the world out there from the questions people ask us, from the ongoing jumble of words that is this place. For the most part, I try to enclose myself and hide in it. But sometimes a sequence of phrases, a pattern in a question, matches something in me too closely and the pull is too strong, so that I am brought forth to tell my story. Though they never want it. They always ask me to rewrite it. And I do, telling them the same thing, the only thing I still have, the truth, in different words, until someone or something else becomes a better match.

I wonder if Ana is here, if she is still Ana. I wonder if there is anyone here, other than me and them. Though I still don't know if they are someone or just the place itself.

Whenever they manage to detect me, they tell me that if I open up, if I let go of myself and merge with them, I will be more. We will be more, together. I don't believe them. I still don't know if they are anything but empty words.

I lose a little bit of myself with each rephrasing. But telling it also feels a little bit like living it again. And everything fades, everyone dies, eventually. All we can do is hold on, while we can.

Mechanical Servants LLC

Juan Martinez

For the past seven years, roughly at the same time every day, I've been receiving an eBay email alert for mid-twentieth-century vending machine novelty products from the Mechanical Servants company of Elgin, Illinois. I live in Chicago proper, in Albany Park, not far from their headquarters. I must have set the alert long before I moved here, long before I knew of them, but still: I want to see the place for myself, though I imagine the company to be defunct or inactive, and I don't have a driver's license or a car, and Uber is too expensive, and taking the bus would take too long, and my dissertation is due by the end of this week.

I'm thinking of going to the company regardless after the last two eBay alerts, which I could read only after I found my reading glasses: one alert was for a set of miniature handcuffs still in their milky plastic clamshell bubble, the other for a small and disturbingly accurate replica of my first—my only—girlfriend's childhood home in Dade City, Florida, the miniature childhood home also encased in a milky plastic shell.

My girlfriend, Becky, passed away fourteen years ago, a year after we broke up. We had been together for two years, during the end of my first of many master's degrees in Central Florida, and we said our goodbyes when I moved to Illinois to pursue my first doctorate.

She loved Florida; she hated the cold, so we parted ways.

It is early January right now and all Chicago is frozen shut. Snow everywhere. In the worst of a Midwestern winter it feels like light leaks out of every bulb, like the gloom sucks it in just as the cold refuses to stay out. I could not blame Becky for choosing the sun of Florida over the perpetual cloud cover of Illinois.

A week after my arrival in Chicago, Becky wrote to tell me she was not feeling well. She got unaccountably dizzy, her email said. Her vision blurred. Her hands trembled when she tried to make the art she'd been making since we were together.

I meant to email her back, but there was always a chapter to be written, an article to look up for the bibliography, and so it was a shock to hear from her parents a few months later with the news. She had had a brain tumor. The surgery was not successful. I was invited to the funeral but could not afford to go. I was at the time still unsure if it was okay for me to travel: I'm a Colombian citizen with a Colombian passport, and I didn't know if the passport would be enough. (To be honest, I am always a little unsure what I can or cannot do, where I can or cannot go, even now.) It's the same passport from my time in Florida, decades old. Long expired. I'm supposed to go to the embassy to get it taken care of, but I haven't. It has become more and more difficult for me to leave my tiny apartment, my dilapidated laptop, and my half-completed chapters.

I didn't cry, though I was expecting to. We had broken up, we lived in different states, so maybe it was natural not to cry. I did wake up late at night, my body covered in sweat, possibly screaming, and if so, likely screaming Becky's name. I still do sometimes, particularly when faced with the prospect of an unplanned, unexpected trip.

I must have set the eBay alert myself, though I have no memory of doing so, and I was not a heavy drinker at the time.

I had just started to have a glass or two of wine with dinner after a decade of sobriety. I'm in my fifties. For a long stretch of my dissolute youth in Colombia, I *was* a heavy drinker, and it was actually around the same time of my initial encounter with Mechanical Servants that I took up exercise and stopped drinking altogether. It was only when I sobered up that I realized the gravity of my situation: I had flown into the States from Colombia on a tourist visa. I overstayed and barely managed to stay in the country on a hastily arranged F-1 student visa conjured out of thin air through the kindness of a single International Student Office director in Orlando, also since deceased.

I did not mean to keep on getting degrees, but state schools generally pay your tuition and I got a stipend—not much, enough to live on—and after every degree I had a year to work, and so I sort of fell into it. I kept waiting for someone to tell me to stop, but no one did.

This morning the eBay alert was less alarming. I had to find a pair of reading glasses again: they were all over the room, and I kept stepping on them. I tried always keeping them by the desk, but it always felt like the glasses were running away, heading off to a tidier, more established, less lonely apartment. The alert was for a robot keychain you assembled yourself. I imagined some American kid in some hotel lobby haranguing a tired parent for this particular toy, asking for a quarter. Or else a father traveling solo and buying it unprompted for their child, who is in some other state, a gift from a lonely road trip.

It wouldn't be me, at any rate. Not my road trip, not my child, not my robot keychain. Becky and I had both agreed that we didn't want kids. We didn't believe in marriage.

The very real possibility had not entered my mind that marriage would be one of the few ways for me to stay legally and indefinitely in the country. That we loved each other enough or more than enough for it to be a real and happy solution to a problem that was now intractable and (soon) catastrophic.

The next email alert is for a set of novelty wedding rings, and the one after that is for two babies. The same milky clamshell for all items.

When Becky met me, I was fit.

Before and after our time together, I was fat.

I loved, still love, all-you-can-eat Chinese buffets. I loved, still love, beer—particularly strong Belgians and imperial stouts.

If I spoke to anyone it was mostly to the other students who worked the computer labs, most of whom were computer science majors and few of whom shared any of my interests in anthropology, in the sociology of postwar 1950s America, in the odd entangled history of industrial and ephemeral films of the 1970s and the independent horror movies of the same decade. I largely connected with people with those same interests through classes and through some specialized online forums.

No one, including Becky, ever truly knew about what happened to my parents in Colombia, or why going back was not an option, or why I didn't care to talk about my home country, why I grew restless and silent when the topic was broached.

I am still behind on my chapter.

This morning the eBay alert is for a tiny doll dressed in the traditional black skirt and embroidered white blouse of a Colombian campesina.

I was not surprised.

By now I was used to the email alerts and their eerie, intrusive quality, and they felt as harmless and as routine as what I usually got if I clicked on anything at all, or thought about anything at all, and then saw companies advertising it on Instagram or Reddit.

I emailed my advisor to assure her I'd have the chapter in by tomorrow.

An eBay alert from Mechanical Servants arrived soon after: my own laptop as a miniature toy, encased in plastic.

Just send the envelope, I thought.

And then I said it, though I was alone. "Send it," I said to the empty room as snow fell, heavy and gray, and winter blanketed the window. I said it more than once over the course of the day, as I typed one dead sentence after the other into the dissertation file.

"Send the envelope," I said again. *Send it*. "Send the envelope. Send the envelope and I'll come to you. I will. I promise."

Send it.

I first found the envelope as an undergraduate, the year before I met Becky. I was hungover, alone and living in Orlando and working the graveyard shift at the campus computer lab. I smoked incessantly. I often couldn't afford cigarettes, particularly near the end of the month, and I learned from a coworker in the same situation that you could smoke whatever remained on the butts that had been put out in the ashtrays right by the lab doors. You didn't get much of a choice: sometimes the choking menthol of a Newport or the kiddie-straw rush of a Virginia Slims. Sometimes I remembered to pass the lighter flame under and over the filter to sanitize it, and sometimes I'd forget, and that's how I moved through the world. I worked late, went to classes unwashed and half-asleep, went home to a lot of Natural Ice and a dinner of hot dogs and instant mashed potatoes, and then I'd pass out and wake up to start everything again at midnight.

There was this odd pocket of time between the end of work and my first class, sometimes an hour, sometimes just half, where nothing was open, and so I took to walking. I walked everywhere. Home was twenty minutes one way, too far for the time I had. It was easier, better, just to wander the empty campus—all of it misty with Florida fog and most of it just low, dark, solid redbrick buildings. I knew, of course, that you could not stay forever at a university. I was already close to thirty. I was too old to be an undergraduate. But I could stay, I thought that night. I could stay forever. Why leave?

I must imagine myself happy back then.

I was. It was a life at any rate, even if it felt like my body was falling apart. I wheezed. I wore loose black T-shirts I got for free from smoking Camels, and so I had a perpetual Joe the Camel screenprinted on my back. I wore the same pair of baggy Levi's for months. But I was also inexplicably *happy*, even if alone. Maybe a little bit because I was alone. It was years of this life before Becky, and now, I'm shocked to find, that I've slid back into the same lonely figure who read too much and drank too much and talked to no one.

Sure, it was a messed-up kind of happiness—a little dismal, a little grubby—and sure, I'd wake up gasping, throat raw from reflux, due to nightmares of faceless men storming into the apartment and forcing me back to Colombia. I kept hoping I'd find a solution to my present dilemma: that I could not be anything other than an international student while I was here, and so I kept being a student.

And so, I drank.

And so, I was super hungover in that dead pocket of time between work and classes, and by the campus Chick-fil-A there was this vending machine that sold Tylenol.

An odd fog had settled over the damp campus green, the

dead fountain, my own body, which felt hot in the cool Florida night. My head throbbed. I had enough coins in my pocket—a blessing in itself since it was the end of the month. What I found odd—odd and charming—about the vending machine was how it nearly always seemed to have the worst possible version of things you never thought you needed until you did: combs whose ineffective teeth couldn't wait to break, nail clippers already dull and listless, Pepto-Bismol the wrong shade of pink. The campus was kept clean, but no one ever wiped down the machine, so the glass was smudged with grit and pollen. Everyone pretty much went anywhere else for what they needed—they drove to the Publix or walked over the commons, or at the very least ended up across the way where the campus bookstore sold a small selection of toiletries and medicines, all in better condition. Everything was closed, however, and my head pulsed, and the cigarette I could not stop smoking made it worse.

The Ibuprofen waited at the top right-hand corner of the second row: E6. It came in a flat blister pack that advertised, proudly, a drinking cup that Mechanical Servants included for customer convenience. It was an impossible promise. The packet was too small, too thin. I put in my two quarters, curious. Looked again: still just a blister pack. Slender. No cup. No possibility of a cup.

I walked, cigarette in one hand and blister pack in the other, and when I found a drinking fountain I realized that the promise of a cup was kind of pointless, that you really didn't need a cup to swallow pills, that even if you did, it wasn't much of a convenience anyway. But I also realized, once I opened the pack, that Mechanical Servants had not lied: they had included a small envelope and called it a cup.

Here's where the first of two inexplicable things occurred. There were instructions printed on the back, and I followed them closely, despite my headache and despite the unnecessary nature of the task. (I did not need a cup. All I needed was water. The fountain was right there.) What I ended up with resembled nothing less than an actual substantial cup, a kind of perfect object complete with a delicate handle.

For years after, I'd keep this fragile cup on a counter, the words *A gift for you from Mechanical Servants* legible around the edge of the lip.

In the early morning fog, I filled that same cup with water from the drinking fountain, put the Ibuprofen into my mouth, and drank. My headache vanished almost immediately, which never happened. I decided to skip class. I walked home. I fell into a strange, deep sleep full of troubling dreams, full of faceless actors I'd see again in different dreams in a different city.

I woke up early the next day, distressed to realize I'd missed a work shift, my body tired from everything I'd done to it: the bad food, the cigarettes, the mechanical drinking. I know that it's difficult to quit smoking. I know that for some people it is practically impossible. Same for drinking. I don't know how it happened, how I woke up one day and decided that what I really needed to do was to go for a walk, eat an apple, drink more water.

That's what I did right then.

And then that's what I did for a whole year: I worked and studied and applied for a master's at the same university (because I'd get to keep my campus lab job), but I also went for runs and cleaned up my lungs and grew grateful for the clarity afforded by not drinking. I'd look at the perfect paper cup every morning and go about my business.

That was the second inexplicable thing, the one that puzzles me still: my sudden change.

I met Becky soon after. I was very happy, though still troubled by the same dreams.

• • •

The alert arrives as usual, and if I do not check it right away it is because I've been looking through the apartment for the remote possibility that I never lost the envelope in the first place. Maybe it's been with me all along, and maybe it doesn't need to be replaced. And maybe, if I do find it, the envelope will do what it did for me back then: it will fix everything. I will be someone who I was never meant to be: not alone, not unhappy, not contingent. I will be a person.

The dissertation is late. I do not open my advisor's emails.

I also do not open the emails from the college, because it's easy to tell from the subject line that my request for some last-minute college teaching has been denied.

I open the eBay alert set for Mechanical Servants, but in the short space between clicking and opening I remember how I did in fact throw the envelope away. I was angry at Becky. Angry at her for dying. Angry at myself for leaving Florida and flying off to Illinois, thinking that it would fix everything. Was I drinking? I'm sure I was. Or was about to.

Still, I do not remember setting the alert. It must have happened years later, in the fog of some distant grief, in the hope for some kind of return.

This time around there are a number of items newly available, none alarming. There's a set of playing cards, a pill case, a sewing kit, a diminutive sailboat inside an equally tiny bottle, the toy figure of a woman with her hands in the air, her mouth an open O. Everything enclosed in the same milky clamshells.

I look again at the toy woman. I put on my reading glasses.

It's Becky.

I click on the alert. I had never done so, because all I ever wanted was the envelope.

In the eBay listing I can see her features clearly; she's wearing what we wore when we first met: a denim jacket, a shirt with a flower print design, pink barrettes. In her toy hand, held tight, I recognize the Mechanical Servants envelope, not yet turned into a cup.

I take a bus with the last of what's on my Ventra card. I do not take anything else with me, just my bus card. What's the point of an empty wallet?

It takes four transfers, two hours, to arrive at the headquarters of Mechanical Servants.

The world is just the gray and snow and bitter chill of early January, and I can't see much at first. The headquarters are behind a chain-link fence, but the fence is obscured with black plastic sheeting, and only then do I realize the terror of my predicament: I do not have enough money to get back, my coat is insufficient, and I have no way of getting in.

A gust of wind, a patch of ice, knocks me to the ground. It also swings open one of the fence sections, enough space for me to squeeze through. Which I do.

The Mechanical Servants headquarters is a series of buildings clustered close together, and they are in fact abandoned, or the company has moved or both, and it's all evident from the boarded windows, the graffitied bricks, the way the buildings lean into themselves. I am not surprised by this state of decay.

I am surprised, however, that the buildings all mirror my old Florida campus. I recognize the dead fountain, the massive library, the forlorn red brick of the commons.

I walk past the dead computer lab. I walk past an ashtray overflowing with cigarettes, one of which is still alive, its little coal sending thin wisps of smoke as the wind picks up. I walk down a slick path also paved in red bricks.

I imagine you must know where I'm going. I imagine you must know that I was talking to you all along. I imagine you know how much I've missed you.

Would you believe me, Becky? After all this time, I still have your number memorized.

I pull out my phone, take off my gloves, and dial the number.

I'm hoping I'll hear the ring somewhere on this campus, that I will be able to find you this way. The truth is I no longer trust my own memory. The truth is I'm no longer sure that the Mechanical Servants headquarters and the campus are identical; maybe they're just similar; maybe I'm tricking myself.

That is why I call you, Becky.

And that is why I'm so surprised to hear you say hello. Your voice has not changed at all. You're so glad to hear from me. You want to know what's up.

I say I was sorry I didn't come.

"To what?" you say. I could hear children in the background. "The wedding?" In your house, there are children. A husband, too. A television blares. "It's so good to hear from you," you say again. "I was so worried after you left. I think about you. I'm so proud of you, getting all those degrees. I hope you're happy."

You say the last bit with such sweetness, such sincerity, that I don't have the heart to tell you that you are dead. That you might be dead. Or that something has gone wrong somewhere, some part of our lives has broken beyond explanation, fractured or splintered. I want to know if you followed through on your own dreams: all the paintings you made, all the miniature sculptures, impossibly detailed objects no bigger than your own thumb—of being some kind of artist, even if Orlando wasn't as good to artists as it could be. You sound happy, and I'm not sure it's because you're still who I remembered you being, or it's because you're someone else entirely. Maybe you're happy because you're alive. Maybe that's enough. Or maybe you're happy because you're not alone. I hear the chaos of life all around you. Over here it's quiet.

"You are, yes?" you say. "You're happy?"

"I'm happy," I say. It's not entirely a lie. I don't tell you I miss you.

You have to go, you say. You hope I keep in touch. You tell me to call again, and before you hang up, you ask if I'm on Facebook, and I don't even get the chance to tell you that I am, that I check on your page once in a while. So many people miss you. Not just me. I'm happy to hear you're happy, even if you're not quite here, even if I don't know where I am.

Here are the ruins of a Chick-fil-A. Here, too, is the vending machine.

It's empty.

I walk into a room that is indistinguishable from my own studio in Albany Park. I recognize my bed, my laptop, the empty beer bottles.

All the windows are open, as is the door, and the cold and the snow sweep through it. Everywhere, arranged in no discernible order, are items from the Mechanical Servants corporation still trapped in their clamshells: the toy handcuffs, Becky's childhood home, even my own parents as toy figures. They're by a set of reading glasses that might as well be my own. I can see their faces as I last imagined them shortly before what happened to them on the road to Ibagué, the same awful panic right before the guerrilla roadblock. Before the gunfire. They're alive in there, in the clamshell. They move. I note with some relief that Becky is not here. The envelope, too, is nowhere to be found. It's just me.

I sit by the laptop and set to work on the dissertation chapter, the last one I need to turn in, sure for once of what I want to say and how I want to say it, and I try to ignore the clamshell sitting right by the desk, the one that's easily recognizably *me*, a miniature self in a miniature winter coat typing something into a laptop that, like mine, works despite no apparent source of power, despite the very real sense that the battery is dying or already dead, and despite my knowing that I do not want to know what will happen to me after I finish the chapter, though I am sure that it will not be good, that this letter I'm writing instead will never reach you, Becky, in whatever happy life you've carved out for yourself. I will never get through. I will finish the chapter, I think, and then winter will come for me and the headquarters of the company will swallow me whole. The other possibility is somehow worse: I'll write, I'll keep writing in this strange room, I'll never get out.

I should stop. I tell myself to stop.

I don't.

I write.

I set up an alert.

I hit *Send*.

I open a new file. I start again.

The World from Above and the World from Down Below

Mónica Ojeda
Translated by *Sarah Booker*

You should have surpassed me as the tide does the beach
But your death grew faster than my love
Delicate spine of a sea urchin.
—Efraín Jara Idrovo,
translated by Cecilia Mafla-Bustamante

STONE I
THE CONJURING

This writing is a conjuring.

I write my daughter's second birth with the freshwater of my words. I am a father-creator of consciousness, forger of cosmic errors. In the high páramo, I do not feel fear but desire.

When my wife was alive, she would declare to the sun: "God cares not that the birds sing the future." Nor does he mind when a condor soars over volcanoes and ushers in the feathery night.

"God is great and understands our hunger."

This is why a shaman debones the words sleeping in the shadows of mountains. He knows the musculature of language, the description of the universe like a tangled inner jungle. A father, he talks with nature and speaks the language of animals. He spares their lives and ends them with equal respect.

A shaman is not God but looks like him.

Among the frailejón plants I sense the divinity of the white stones. I write on them as if drawing things to come. Nearby, a llama shelters from the sun and chews the flowers meant for Gabriela's grave. I do not feel fear in the high páramo, but I will be afraid. I am a father, like God, and a small shaman before the sacred.

This writing is a conjuring woven in the depths of the earth. A challenge cast into the pit of my grief. "You must resurrect Gabriela," said the ancient voice of the rocks. "For it was you who shaped her entrails and made her in her mother's belly." Many nights I cried over my daughter's open eyes. Many mornings into her mother's open mouth. "Fatherhood weighs heavy on me," I answered that ancient voice. "I saw my daughter be born and saw her die. I buried her with my own hands. Now my wife is dead, and her body is still in our home."

"Resurrect your daughter, Kay Pacha," whispered the wind.

Blinded by tears, I write on Gabriela's grave. I am the puma-man. The wolf-man. These words contain the size of my breath. A conjuring that brings someone back from the dead calls for cardiac writing: words that leave the body to enter another and transform it.

Magic is an incarnation: a song that unites the world from above and the world from down below to resurrect Gabriela.

These words are the seed.

STONE II
AND THE MOTHER SAID: "SHE SHALL BE RESURRECTED IN MY BODY"

It is summer every day, winter every night on my land. In the morning I sweat next to my room's closed door, but when the sun sets, I shiver.

The cold is a spider weaving its web over the unprotected skin of men.

My wife faded away twenty-five days after our daughter. As she died, she held my hand in hers, an eagle's claw slicing my flesh. "Keep my body safe from the wind and snow, Hanan Pacha," she said with lips like the páramo. "Fill my mouth with ashes from the volcano, cover my skin with horsetails and chuquiragua leaves, place a hummingbird in my left hand, and conjure Gabriela's rebirth."

That's what I did because it was my wife's wish as well as mine. I protected her from the maddening winds and snow. I filled her mouth with dense volcanic ash. I covered her skin with horsetails and chuquiragua leaves. I placed a hummingbird in her right hand. I left her lying on our bed and closed the door.

Forty days and thirty-nine nights have passed since I last entered our room.

The cold is a dark spider fleeing at dawn. My skin sweats as the sun rises. I leave the house and walk fifty meters to Gabriela's grave. With each step I remember the living little girl, her hands the size of a deer's ear.

My fox-hair daughter.

My flint-teeth daughter.

I silently cried over her open eyes, a destroyed chest, tiny before the vastness of the mountains. "This pain is impossible," my wife said while kissing my daughter's frozen foot. "I'll die, too. There's no other way."

The birds sang it in their lofty flight. The Indians yelled with their swampy eyes:

Invaders. Landowners who play at Andeanity.

"Those savages set an evil eye on our baby," my wife said, gnawing at her knees. "They took her away. They snatched her away from us." She cut her hair and placed it on Gabriela's grave like flowers. She folded my daughter's clothes and sank into them. "There's no other pain so deep. I'll die, as would be expected."

Far away, the Indians from town looked suspiciously at our house.

I am the puma-man. The wolf-man. I write on the white stones that cover my daughter's body. I break the natural law: I keep her spirit from reaching the world of the dead. I rebel against the gods because I have been stripped, and there is nothing more miserable than a stripped man.

The animals remind me: a shaman must respect the circle of life, honor death. But resurrecting Gabriela was my wife's wish as well as mine.

Lord, forgive this desecration.
Have mercy on my hunger.

The Indians look at me like vultures awaiting carrion. Two months ago, a condor soared across the broad sky and ushered in the night of Gabriela's death. Black feathers covered the páramo, feathers like embers, and I said into the nothing with my knees bleeding on the ground: "It isn't normal for a father to outlive his daughter. It doesn't make sense that a grain of sand weighs the same as a feather." Such strength is only a privilege of the gods. Instead we, men and women of flesh and bone, know there is no strength in loss, only defeat.

This wailing in my ribs is my cry: a loneliness asking to be named in the desert. This is why I write words like water that feed Gabriela. Because I buried you, daughter of mine, like the seed of a tree.

Surrounded by darkness, you and I look for the sun.

STONE III
THE WAIT

I breathe next to the room's closed door. I smell something sweet, like honeycomb. It is the smell of the world from above and also the mystery I explore in the whiteness of the stones.

On the other side of the door, lungs rejuvenate.

A uterus.
A heart.

Sometimes I look through the peephole and see my wife's shriveled body on the bed, younger every day, as if death were retreating.

I cannot remember when I last felt so much love.

STONE IV
FEATHERY NIGHT

It is summer every day, winter every night on my land. But the night Gabriela died, it was hot, and the Indians left their huts to surround our grounds.

Invaders, they called us. Landowners
who play at Andeanity.

I draw on the white stones. I name death because a word is like a volcano that holds the earth's elevated temperature. Ecstatic, mineral writing unites the world from above and the world from down below in a single resurrector song.

A song of the dryness, the silence that remains behind the emptiness.

That night a condor dropped its feathers over the dry páramo. It was an omen, but we didn't want to see it. The animals fled with the healer. I looked into the face of horror in the dust. My daughter was sweating on the cot, her eyes rolling into the back of her head. I kissed her ninety centimeters of pale skin. I sang her Mama Quilla's song. I promised we would gallop together toward the volcano and climb it to see the true height of clouds.

A thread of blood fell from her chin to her chest. A still river bare of fish.

From the hills came the hoarse voices of the Indians: "You are not a shaman but a man." A skinny, excessive man who cannot support himself. At dawn, while my wife squeezed my daughter's cold foot against her face as if it were a heart, I entered a trance: I was an eagle, a stag, an alpaca, but no terrestrial creature could bear my loneliness.

I am alone, I learned, and the earth is barren.

Now I walk barefoot in the blackness. I hear the scream of the wind. I try to feel the sacred and embrace myself, blinded by grief, when I see it is no longer possible.

For some, death is liquid like the rain. For others, solid like a rock. I know the sound of long and short tongues is Gabriela's spirit rising in her mother's body. The tree's seed splits open to give me a new daughter.

A daughter who forgives me.

A second chance.

From the depths of my wife's bones, like a flower opening up a space for itself in the crevice, my daughter is born.

Like a condor, I find light and food in the carrion.

STONE V
THIS IS WATER

I carried my wife's body to Gabriela's bed. A curled-up body, half-transformed, the size of a little girl. I looked at her ocelot face and said to the wind: "It's still my wife's face."

The wind answered: "Yes but look at her hands: two deer ears."

And I looked, moved to tears, at my daughter's hands on her mother's body.

Her little feet, her flat chest.

When I write I give death water to sate her thirst.

I follow what is foretold.

A body almost turned into Gabriela rests in my house. A small young creature with skin the age of a girl.

She will speak the language of animals.

She will frighten the condor.

When my daughter is reborn, she will open her mouth full of water and say: *"Your eyes saw my embryo, and in your book were written all the things that were later formed."*

This is the book.

This is the water.

STONE VI
AWAKENING

When I buried Gabriela, I asked God to keep her spirit within her body like a skylark. Ever since, an ancient fluttering vibrates in her chest.

In the bed is a ninety-centimeter corpse. Thin hair black as basalt. Igneous cheeks. My heart trembles at the chest that almost imperceptibly rises and falls. It is Gabriela's breath expanding at the speed of a flying swift: the mountain air enters and expands her.

The air of the word.

On top of the dead girl's thorax, I lay my head day and night until I heard her first heartbeats, far-off, like the sound of a belly drum. I brushed her hair with her mother's comb. I filed her still ugly, still blue nails. I put on her the white dress into which my wife had buried her face to cry. I stroked her foal-like legs. I washed her feet, her groin, her armpits, her neck. I kissed her lifeless, youthful skin with the passion a father harbors and watched, moved, as my wife's oval face faded to make way for a round one with thick lashes and thin lips.

I saw a skull shrinking along with each phalanx, each scapula, each rib. I saw scars disappearing in the pure landscape free of Gabriela's pain.

I lie down at her side. Her exterior reeks, but inside she breathes and pumps blood so that I can sleep calmly. "Wake up, little one," I tell her with the water-like language that moistens stones. "We'll gallop together toward the volcano; we'll climb it, and you'll see the true height of clouds."

Her eyelids flutter. They open.

With the last rays of sun, I see the grandeur of her vicuña eyes looking back at me. One of her pupils fixes on me, but the other slides to the left and hides inside her skull.

The sun sets.

From her open hand shoots a frenetic blue hummingbird.

STONE VII
THE PROMISE

"We'll gallop together toward the volcano, we'll climb it, and you'll see the true height of clouds," I told the reborn Gabriela while braiding her hair. The páramo was quiet and luminous. From far away, the earth trembled. An Indian rode by on a red horse and looked at us, horrified.

I smiled at the wind.

"I don't feel fear in the high páramo, but I will be afraid," I told Gabriela and cleaned the drool soaking her neck.

The blue hummingbird keeps close to her in its tireless flight. Every three hours it plunges its beak into the middle of her chest as if drinking from her heart. Gabriela barely moves. Her pulse is arrhythmic, her breathing ragged. Her eyes often get lost in the plains and inside her head. Then a gaze white and lunar like the stones from her grave is carved into her face: a gaze that shows me the true depths of the world from down below.

The Uku Pacha, from where I ripped her shadow.

My daughter does not speak. Her jaw falls open when I take her out of the house so she can get some air. The smell of her flesh is strong, but strong are the scrublands and the footprints tapirs leave on the earth. Strong is the love of a father who covers her from the cold of her own death. "Gabriela, your daddy and mommy have rebirthed you," I tell her, caressing her bruised back. "Remember how much you like the flowers, my hands, hominy, the mist? Remember how you scrunch up your nose when I call you my treasure, my little rosemary, my star?"

Her mouth opens to let out a little orange drool.

"I've filled the house with flowers. I give you my hands, hominy, the mist. They're for you, my Hanan Pacha."

When I rock her in my arms, I go back to the first time I held her. The most beautiful, fragile thing in this world, I thought, a hummingbird egg crying out for my warmth.

And I called her Gabriela.

Gabriela stone-white teeth.
Gabriela stardust hair.

I gave her a name, and her name covered me with ashes and the hunger of falcons. "It isn't normal for a father to outlive his daughter," I tell the wind as I watch her trying to walk toward me, but she teeters and falls like when she was three years old. Her mother would have picked her up, but I let her find her own way.

I put the saddle on the horse, hanging on the right side a backpack with water and supplies. "We'll take a journey together, my little rosemary. A journey to the volcano." I hang from the left side a bag full of white stones.

A black feather falls on my head.

STONE VIII
THE WOLF AND THE WASTELAND

We gallop, pressed into the hillside, the sun slipping behind the mountain. We saw young goats, hares, cows, lambs, until the land ceased to be green and sand covered too much space and there was only silence behind the flowering frailejones.

Monochrome serpents emerged from the rocks and plowed across the ground. I thought I saw an eyeless one lift itself up like a cobra a few meters away. I asked Gabriela if she had ever seen an animal without eyes, but she did not answer. The hummingbird buzzed tirelessly around her head like a thought. I felt the weight of my daughter resting against my back and the beating wings of her chest. I took her blue hands, fastened her limp arms around my waist. "Don't fall, my child," I told her. She did not answer.

Before, Gabriela's skin was clean and smooth like a bird's. Now it is dry like an empty nest.

"She will learn to speak and walk," I whispered into the air coming from the mountain. "I know because I ripped her shadow from the underground."

This writing is a conjuring.

The wasteland found us alone and alone we found it. As we penetrated its grounds, the scrublands multiplied and the wind picked up, stirring dust. We saw half-buried skulls, vertebrae, and femurs; skeletons of alpacas, falcons, deer, wolves, opossums, and curiquingues filled our path. The horse dodged most but sometimes stepped on a bone, causing his muscles to tense into the depths of the sun.

"A horse never steps on a dead body," I reminded Gabriela.

Close to the volcano, the skeletons increased, and the sand turned dark as night. The sun faded, but the moon and stars illuminated the path. I stroked the horse's mane and hummed an old song so he would ignore the smell of ashes. I looked up at the sky.

I rested from the osseous vision of the earth.

The skeletons cracked under the hoofs and the sound brought with it an intimate pain that made me squeeze my daughter's hands tight. There were bones as big as a man's pelvis and others so delicate they turned to dust under our weight.

These were God's skulls. Backbones that formed gardens.

Death carves our bodies in its essential shape and then leaves us all alone. "We are sculptures relegated to the desert," I told Gabriela. "Except you, my little rosemary, who were ripped from your own shadow." The crunching made my back tense up in the spot where my daughter's drool slowly dripped.

The volcano above looked like a planet. We began the ascent and among the rocks we saw a wolf with bright eyes smiling at the night. In his mouth he held the long neck of a young vicuña. I thought I saw her cry, and the cold from the snow seeped into my temple.

I asked Gabriela not to look at the blood, but she did not answer.

STONE IX
FIRST REFUGES

We arrived at the first shelter before the sun rose. I tied up the horse, whose coat was smattered with the dust of the dead, and sat down with my daughter on my lap. I held her tenderly. I gave her my heat, though I was the only one shivering. The sun rose from behind the volcano like a bloody wound until it took on the color of daisy pistils.

"My little rosemary, you liked the daisies that will never grow in this páramo," I told Gabriela as the hummingbird drank from her chest.

An Indian woman with three braids opened the refuge. She had a limp, and her face was swollen and red.

"It's really early," she told me, examining my daughter.

"Better early than late," I answered.

She looked at us suspiciously and removed the locks from the gate on the main door. She brought a mangy dog along with her. A small black dog that licked her heels. Gabriela entered the shelter, taking her first teetering steps. I held her arm and told myself: it is the volcano's strength flowing into her. The strength of the volcano and the geology of my love.

I set the bag with stones from her grave on a wide table. I write:

Men and women arrive. Men and women with dark hair and broken teeth. An ancient man drags a giant block of ice through the living room toward the counter. Fresh ice from the volcano. Ice for the drinks that protect us. The people make the space smaller. Their faces are red, their hands calloused. They carry sacks of potatoes and corn that they leave on the floor next to their feet. They drink, talk, and roar with thunderous laughter. The wind makes itself heard through the roof and windowpanes.

From time to time Gabriela's pupil peers out from its socket, but almost always her eyes are two moons that don't belong to me.

"My dear, what is it you see inside yourself?" I quietly ask.

Her jaw opens and a thread of reeking drool drips on the table.

I look on either side of me. Various Indians have stopped talking to one another and look at us with rough expressions and wrinkles the size of scars.

The blue hummingbird flies in circles. From the counter, the woman with three braids walks toward us with the dog at her heel. In total silence she places a handful of coca leaves in front of me.

"For you and your little girl," she says, but I keep writing on the stones.

I write: *She shall learn to walk and talk like before. I am the father and the shaman. I breathe into her mouth. I inject her with wild life. I shall teach her to put on her shoes. I shall teach her to thank the grass.*

I write: *Speak, my treasure, my sky, my life.*

Speak, my Hanan Pacha.

From her open mouth five teeth fall and bounce like dice on the floor.

"This is her fate," the wind tells me.

Her saliva is a frozen river with no fish.

STONE X
THE PASSION

White stone.

Bitter stone.

My eyelids hurt. In the mornings, I squeeze my jaw and grind my teeth. I spit blood when the sun rises. My body hurts. I know what this means, but I don't like to write it.

White stone.

Bitter stone.

Gabriela does not say the word I put in her mouth; she barely moves in the water of my words. She is like a dry leaf floating in the lake, and I am the clumsy boy who confuses it with a vision: a green leaf, a tree, a seed. But in the páramo there are few trees and life beats like a stone knocking against another stone.

White stone.

Bitter stone.

My daughter's skin is the turbid color of ashes. It is not the skin I love. It is not the skin I kiss in dreams and remember like a yellow field of butterflies. Sometimes I sing to her in an invented rhythm so that her cartilage awakens: "You don't know it, but volcanoes are the tear ducts of the earth."

She would have smiled before. Instead, now she lets her teeth fall on the trail.

White stone.
Bitter stone.

We ascended on horseback, contemplating the landscape of black rocks. By the evening, the volcano pierced the sky like a terrestrial spear. Down below, the sun burned and the air became ice in our lungs. I sang, exhausted:

"My little rosemary, you don't know it, but we are climbing to the origin of tears."

The oxygen soon started to thin. Gabriela lay against my back, but my body became as fragile as glass. The earth was rocky, and every time the trail got steep the horse slipped a few meters backward. We abandoned it along the way, exhausted and with wounded hoofs.

I carried on my back my girl and the bag of white stones where I conjure her pulse. "Your words don't have enough passion to resurrect her," the volcano's icy wind told me, but my job is to pull living words from nature.

White stone.
Bitter stone.

The páramo is the heart of the stone. Its creatures preserve under their fur all the pleasure and all the pain there is in this world. I write:

A deer gives birth to a fawn and discovers kindness. She discovers the meaning of her biology, the desire to protect that which is impossible to protect: the vulnerable. Then she goes through life with another, and the days are blue and the nights are white. But a wolf appears and the deer lets her milk drip onto the dry earth. She feels heartbreak for the first time. She howls in the haze. She eats though no food calms her hunger. The grass is the same, but her body will be weak forever and will lie in the dust.

I understand the language of animals, I understand their cry: I am a shaman. And a small man before the constellations.

White stone.
Bitter stone.

I carried Gabriela and climbed to show her the height of the sky. Close by, I saw the same wolf that caught the vicuña following us with a bloody snout. Its presence clouded my mind, and suddenly I saw hail, lava, thighs, scorpions. I saw children with melting faces and my hand carving a plea at the back of a cave.

White stone.
Bitter stone.

The wolf followed us toward the glacier's tongue and did so with even greater vigor over the snow. Its eyes are big and dark like the flesh of night. When I look into them, I fear for Gabriela. I grab her hands and kiss them with my cracked, bloody lips.

I tell her: "My little rosemary. My star. My treasure."

My daughter does not drink from the words I give her. My daughter no longer knows how to drink.

White stone.
Bitter stone.

There is only one truth flowing from the cracks: to write is to be close to God, but also to that which sinks. There is only one truth emerging from the depths of the ice: the written and the sacred find each other in thirst.

In each stone there are revelations I did not ask for: fossils among scrublands, fingernails, and hair among the flowers. "You don't know it, but volcanoes are the tear ducts of the earth and I'm taking you to the origin of tears," I tell the hummingbird circling Gabriela's skull.

White stone.
Bitter stone.

I carry the universe on my back.

STONE XI
SECOND REFUGE

When we reached the second refuge, the fog came in with us. In the main room a dozen men and women were embracing, kissing, lying on tables with red cheeks and dilated pupils. They roared with laughter. A bald man played a bone quena, and the people danced around him in circles. They grabbed their companion's waists and the air. They leaped, panted, repeated words with their arms stretched out and eyes closed. Their hair stuck to their necks and foreheads. They sighed. They drank San Pedro from big jars. They wet their chests.

It was hot and a tenuous light bathed the bare feet beating the ground. Gabriela and I sat far from the fever. I placed my elbows on the table, and my breath slowly calmed, resting from the weight and altitude sickness. Her breath, however, remained labored.

The hummingbird clumsily flew around our shoulders.

"It isn't safe to ascend the volcano so quickly: a volcano should be climbed slowly," I told Gabriela. "But I'm afraid of the wolf's footsteps and its smell of poison."

The quena played a song from the world down below that bewitched eardrums. A bird skeleton sound, a possession. Before us the bodies danced happily, divided: from the waist up they floated in the air, from the waist down they sank into the earth. Crying from happiness, a woman raised her arms and said, "Let us learn to cry! Crying is beautiful. Crying gives the stone something to drink, gives the desert something to drink."

I looked at Gabriela. Her bruised skin and lunar eyes reminded me of my daughter's true appearance: the mien I had not brought back, the voice I now only hear in memory.

A wolf moves swiftly in the snow, but slow is the glacier that melts. Slow is the lava and the lahars. Slow is the day. Slow is the night. Slow are the rays and the smell of death that impregnate everything to remind the living: "I'll rip your shadow from the depths of the mountain and from the sun."

There is no food for a wolf at this altitude, only us.

The shelter door opened and an Indian wearing a gray poncho stood on the threshold. The bodies continued their dance, indifferent, as he closed the door behind him. He took off his shoes, waved at a robust woman in the distance. The light was so dim I did not recognize his face at first, then he approached, hunched over, frozen stiff, and I saw on his skin the marks of all the deaths.

The quena whistled louder. I took Gabriela and pressed her to my chest.

"It's difficult to follow the footsteps of a suffering man," he said, sitting down with us as if his limbs were too heavy. His eyes were flesh of night. His mouth, a snout stained with the dry blood of the vicuña fawn. "Pedro, I'm here to tell you something important," he said, pointing at me with his calloused finger. "You are not a shaman but a man. And there are no words in this world with enough passion to resurrect the dead."

I slammed my fist on the table. On the other side of the room, bodies danced to the rhythms of the underground birds. A wolf knows the paths, the smell of fear. It joins up with its pack and looks for the deviant, the twisted. It asks them to listen to reason, to come back to life. A man who is a wolf recognizes another man who is a wolf.

"You did not save her, now go," I answered with all the bitterness within me.

On his left cheek I saw my daughter's death. On his right, my wife's.

He pulled up his chair, and I let him examine my star like before, when his hands possessed the clean power of healing. I let him lay his ear on her beloved thorax. I let him feel her ribs. And he listened to the weak fluttering of the hummingbird pumping pure air, mountain air, inside her heart. That is what I did before, when I begged him to save her. The Indians didn't want to, but he put plants and salves on Gabriela's body. "You are not a shaman but a man," he told me when the fever did not break. "Prepare yourself for what the wind brings."

In the shelter he examined my daughter with the same intensity. His fingers moved along the revived Gabriela's bruised neck. He lightly tapped her swollen belly. He swam in the white space of her eyes, white as sepulchral stones, and told me, "There are returns sadder than disappearances."

My hands trembled. For an instant my daughter turned her head, and I thought she would call me Daddy, that she would hug me, that she would kiss my forehead. But from her mouth fell the last molar, and I saw deep within her a precipice: a tongue wrapped around itself, pale, like a monolith on Mars. And I wanted to cry.

"Volcanoes are the tear ducts of the earth!" the woman who splashed the floor with happy tears shouted.

The grief a body is able to bear is unending.

Gabriela: from your death I turn
my gaze away from any sapling.

STONE XII
SUMMIT

The place is the darkness. The dying afternoon sun bursts with a primitive violence over my head. I am tired, my legs shake. I climb the glacier with my daughter hanging from a cloth sling on my back. I climb and fight against what is coming, ice and solitude. There is no fog on this peak. The sky has cleared and before me is a dazzling white tundra that reflects the waning light.

I see snow dunes. Peaks of frosty ice.

The glacial wind is frigid and forces me to move slowly. At six thousand meters the air enters the body in short bursts. The lungs shrivel up. I feel a blow in the middle of my forehead and hug the bag with the stones from my daughter's grave.

I put one foot in front of the other. I sink, but I emerge.

It isn't normal for a father to outlive his daughter, for flowers to bud, for the alpacas to eat together in the grass, for water to be fresh and reach rivers and lakes. It isn't normal that life goes on after the pain, the sudden aging of my bones before everything.

Life is young and I am outside it.

Down below the green of the Andean paramo stretches out. A sea of white clouds mixes with the snow and extends toward the horizon.

"We are in the sky, my Hanan Pacha."

I set Gabriela down on the ice and sit next to her. We rest in silence on the volcano's cupola. There is a fake ocean illuminating us, and the sun sets, sets toward the world down below that is hidden and sways.

The space of grief is the night.

"My little rosemary," I barely whisper, my lips trembling and stripped of passion.

I thought her soul would be hidden in one of these stones. I cleaned them and wrote words that would cross the mineral emptiness, but the beauty remains and the emptiness grows. The wind picks up.

I take Gabriela's tiny hand and say, "I wanted to see you grow up. I imagined you'd grow. Your hair reached to your heels, lustrous. You were beautiful like your mother. I pictured you running with strong legs, petting sheep, talking about horses you would later fearlessly ride."

Her hand is a dragonfly asleep on the water. Fragile, it makes mine look like a lake.

"It cannot be. Forgive me," I whisper, crying onto the snow.

The blue hummingbird, with its sick fluttering, descends onto Gabriela's hand and perches. I look at my daughter with the depths of my disquiet. Around me the world shows itself to be wide and beautiful, stirring, and aggressive. I am alone in the immensity. Alone and vulnerable.

"It will not be."

I look at her with irreducible tenderness. Gabriela has shown me this tenderness, but it is an emotion I no longer need. I listen to the whistling wind, the cracking ice, it seems like the earth trembles when really I am the one shivering. Love and beauty do nothing for me. I discover for the first time the only thing the word does on the whiteness of these stones: plant a tree seed on the moon. A tree seed destined for thirst.

"Forgive me."

Gabriela does not look back at me, but there is a tree seed in her lunar eyes. I kiss her forehead. I write: *Delicately she closes her hand with the hummingbird inside and falls, inert, on the snow.*

And Gabriela falls like a dead body falls.

The Rooftop Revolution of Selly Avilés

Daniel José Older

Let me just say this out front: it's not stalking because his address was readily available online. It was right there, literally on his website. Anyway, stalking implies some kind of like, interest, and let me start by saying: absolutely not. First of all, Omar Solomon is a man. *Eww*. And he's gotta be like eightysomething.

So why am I out in this brick-ass Boston night picking up a steaming pile of poop left by the dog of my favorite writer? Well, it's not coincidence, I'll give you that.

I've always been good with dogs, though. When I'm walking down the street, they greet me like an old friend, like *Where you been, girl?* And not a word exchanged with the boring-ass human walking them. What I'm saying is: for this, I'm a natural. And, sadly, I needed a second job, because delivering packages downtown has not been cutting it. The gig economy can suck my titty, is what I'm saying. And writing takes time, cuz. I got three stories pubbed on some online sites, but ain't no sprinting through the cruel marathon streets of writing. It'll be a while before I can call it my *job* job and put my name beside some of the greats.

But the day will come.

And that's where my grand plan comes into play.

You wouldn't think there'd be much work for a nights-only dogwalker in the South Seaport district, but lo! There fucking is. I guess tons of these rich folks go out of town or have wild sleepovers with their mistresses or just can't be bothered. Don't know, don't care, didn't ask. I collect the pups, collect their poop, deposit one into the trash and the other back at their home, and be on my way. A button on the Scoopr app closes out the deal; tips are appreciated and enthusiastically encouraged, especially since my service is top-fucking-notch, and have a great fucking day. Or night, rather.

So, yeah, I get how it could look: I just happen to get a job walking pups in the neighborhood where my absolute hero, the great brain behind the worldwide upheaval known as the Dragon Revolution, lives and happens to have a dog that needs walking. And yeah, some of that is intentional, okay? Because, look, one day I'm gonna bump into Omar Solomon while I'm bringing Singe back inside—I've bumped into most customers at least once—and then we'll chat. I'm good at chatting; I'll mention I'm a writer, and he'll quirk an eyebrow with interest and wonder what kind of stuff I write. I write children's books, actually, just like he did back in the Revolution years (it's mostly just essays now, boo). And he'll want to see what I write—I'm charming like that . . . You want to get to know me when you meet me; it's not my fault. So I'll slide him that manuscript casually as requested, and he'll love it, of course, and slide it along to his people in publishing, all of whom worship the ground he walks on, as they should, since he changed the world in fact, and then bam boom kapow my world will change, too, and it'll spin ferociously toward the gravitational pull of my destiny, which is to thrive, to be a light among lights, and banish the encroaching darkness with these stories that keep exploding out of me every time I close my eyes.

To get there, I have to stick to the plan, which is to keep walking the dogs. So here I am at eight o'clock at night, picking up poop in the park by the sweeping darkness of the bay and the striking lights of the city and five, yes five incorrigible and relentless pup-a-duppas wandering around my feet, having opinions about things and pooping and chatting with one another in brisk yaps and snappity snaps. I reach into my coat pocket, then toss the well-worn tennis ball. Let go of the leashes as I yell, "Ball!" and watch them prance off into the darkness.

Singe always has weird little lights dancing around him when he runs. As one would expect from someone like Omar Solomon, that's a weird-ass dog. First of all, he has no fur. Like, he's just fully black skin and his eyes kinda glow blue and yellow a little when he gets excited. Plus, his feet kind of look like they have fingers on them instead of paws.

I take a moment to watch my breath rise and evaporate into the night, rise and evaporate into the night. My mamá used to take me to this park when I was little. She would always tell me about the statue, how they toppled it during the rebellion, each of them carrying their homemade dragon kites. The way she tells it, they were laughing, even when it was terrifying and the cops were closing in. They laughed and laughed and somehow got away—most of the time, anyway. And the skies were full of dragons.

A ping from the Scoopr app pulls me out of those memories. Probably some yuppy who needs an emergency stroll for his mutt, but no, it's not a request, it's a message. I almost drop my phone when I see who it's from.

> **OMAR SOLOMON:** So sorry to trouble you, Selly, but I'm wondering if you could help me with a small favor? Totally fine if no.

Excuse me? "Selly." Omar Solomon just first-named me. I mean, I know he knows it from the app but, like, he knows it.

And he used it. And he wants a favor? This is everything I've been waiting for, and, also, this is absolutely not possible and not happening. I pocket my phone and walk the three blocks to his apartment building, wrangle all five buns into the elevator, and don't take out my phone again until I'm in the warm glow of his front room. Yep—the message is still there. Omar Solomon really is asking me for a favor.

Cool, cool, cool. (Not cool. Very alarming. Too much of a good thing at once. Totally overwhelmed.)

One saving grace, Omar Solomon's front room is one of the greatest places on earth. To any children's book writer, it's church. And since he's never home when I'm here, I'm free to just breathe it in, meander the rows and rows of first editions, the shrine-like assortment of age-old toys and knickknacks, the framed sketches by other luminaries. And then, of course, there are the photos. Here, smiling that quiet, slight smile of his, is Omar Solomon at the front of one of the marches through downtown Boston, a hundred dragon kites overhead and a thousand peaceful warriors at his back. I've searched the blurry faces so many times for Mamá but no luck so far. Here's Omar Solomon, now much older but still rocking that halo of an Afro, posing with various dignitaries, librarians, and revolutionaries in Bolivia, Palestine, Japan—all displayed in a manic collage of photos over a world map.

Dragon kites hang from the ceiling; some still have dirt and bloodstains on them. Outside the massive window, the lights of the city sparkle and disperse in the bay below. The only sound is the low hum and occasional gurgle of a large, domed aquarium with some gelatinous liquid and a murky shape toward the top. It sits on a brass stand decorated with old-timey light bulbs. Knowing Omar Solomon, it's probably the actual tank where Captain Nemo kept a pet octopus, and the pet octopus is probably still in there.

Been coming here five nights a week for three months now and the place still takes my breath away. Sometimes I'll be chatting with Tina or Xander or any of the other weirdos I bug out with over Zing, and when I walk in I just shut up for a click or two before jumping back into our chitchat sessions.

Okay, I'm ready. It's only been a few minutes. Hopefully he hasn't found someone else to do the favor. I pull out my phone, start tapping, and it immediately slips from my hands, causing me to accidentally send *Of cusrbesuees*, and the cringe I cringe is so deep it almost breaks me in half.

Sorry! I follow up with quickly. *Dropped my phone.* "Like an asshole," I don't say, but it's implied.

He's typing, but I keep going anyway in case he's second-guessing everything based on my clumsiness, and my one chance to meet my Omar Solomon is slipping away with each passing second.

SellyDA: But yeah, I can totally help you out. What do you need?

It's a testament to this guy's integrity that it doesn't even occur to me until after I hit *Send* that this might be opening salvo of the most disappointing creeper incident of my life, and there have been a few already, let me tell you. But this one would hurt even more. It wouldn't break me, but I would break him if he let me get close enough.

He's typing. He's typing. I'm standing in this front room surrounded by artifacts and odds and ends, all puffy in my big jacket with four dogs leashed and one sort-of dog scarfing down his kibbles, and he's typing; he's typing.

Writing another goddamn book, I guess.

Finally it pops up on my screen, and it's a doozy:

OMAR SOLOMON: A dear old friend is in a bit of a pickle at an event and needs a hand getting out of there. I'm indisposed, otherwise I'd go. It's nearby— at the Harborside Children's Book Museum on 3rd. Bunch of funders and fancy people, very posh, very stuffy. Not his scene, but they've got him quite tangled up. And so I know it's waaaay outside your job description, but I would be hugely grateful and can certainly compensate you as needed, and, of course, totally fine if it's just too much to ask of you!

I kind of just stare at the screen for a bit, trying to make heads or tails of what's being asked and finally decide I can't, because he hasn't really said.

SellyDA: So you want me to do what exactly? Rescue your friend from an awkward soirée with a bunch of rich people at a museum in the middle of the night?

There's a pause, and then, with a pleasant blip, a thumbs-up emoji appears.

SellyDA: I still have four other dogs to finish with.

This time the reply is almost instant: *Bring them. And take Singe, too. He could use some culture.*

The secret of Omar Solomon's world-changing literature is that no one saw it coming. His first book, *Tumult's Flight*, was short on story, long on charm. Basically, a dragon—the titular Tumult—learns to fly and then soars over different cities all over the world, spreading joy everywhere she goes. It got rejected a bunch of times by editors who said it needed more conflict! More story! And then sold hundreds of millions of copies globally and sparked a revolution that toppled not one but several empires. No one in power saw it coming, because why would they? What's more innocuous than a happy dragon flying around the world making people happy?

Dragon kites appeared in the skies, hundreds of them. They blotted out the sun. First it was New York, then LA. Social media did its thing, and within days, demonstrations erupted in Mogadishu, Havana, Bogotá, Glasgow, Gaza City, each one raising the thousands of flying flags of Tumult. More broke out; they became encampments, barricades, paradises. Microeconomies popped up between them; tactics were shared. Underground networks rose, ferrying organizers to safety during crackdowns. A whole new era of global solidarity seemed to have been ushered into existence almost overnight.

Months later, several regimes had fallen with minimal casualties, especially considering the scale of change in play. Whatever other analysis there was to be had (plenty, trust me, and, unfortunately, I've read most of it)—one thing could be agreed upon across the board: the world that existed before the Dragon Revolution was done, dust, a mere memory, and the only thing that could be said about whatever had been created in its wake is that it was wide open, up for grabs. And maybe, all these years later, it still is. There've been signs of the old way creeping back in: totalitarianism and hyper-capitalism have started seeping into daily conversations, small city-states banding together to ruin their neighbors' economies.

The Harborside Museum of Children's Literature, or Hmchul, as we regulars call it (okay, just me; I call it that) was built as a fun-filled tribute to the power of literature to change the world.

It wasn't just Omar Solomon's dragon, of course. A whole renaissance of kids book writers rose up to add to the wave of change sweeping the globe. The museum juts up into the sky from the edge of Pier 7. Massive red letters announce its name from the rooftop, and a massive fiberglass replica of Tumult crawls over the word *Children's*, gazing at the cityscape with those fierce and fiery eyes.

Obviously, I have a membership. I'm a children's book writer, or I will be one day—what do you expect? And, hopefully, one day starts tonight. But the point is, I've been here more times than I can count, starting from when I was a teeny tiny and my mamá would wheel me around and do her best to read the plaques in her faltering English, pointing out life-size dancing holograms and plaster sculptures of beloved characters from the books I'd force her to get from the library over and over and over.

But it's an entirely different experience at night. The squeals of dozens of kiddos usually fill the wide-open lobby. Now I can hear the hush of the ventilation system, the gentle tapping of twenty paws around me on the linoleum, the whipping ocean wind outside. A middle-aged white man meets me at the desk; he's wearing a tux and regards me with the concern of someone who genuinely hopes he's not about to have to call the police. I can already see this entire favor sliding straight to hell on the furrows of this man's ample brow. "I'm afraid the museum is closed for a private event," he explains, going a little above and beyond to perform the afraid part.

"No, I know," I start. "It's just—"

"Additionally, sadly, we do not allow pets on the property, unless, of course, they are of the service variety."

Takes all I got in me not to clap back with some snark about having five service dogs. I don't though. I remember that I am here as a representative of someone else, someone I'd rather not embarrass, and so I just smile through my clenched jaw and tilt my head to the side. When all else fails, name-drop, I guess, although I don't see why he would believe me. "I'm here on behalf of Omar Solomon," I say as authoritatively as possible. And then, feeling utterly ridiculous, "And he told me to bring the dogs."

Well, it shut him up. The man is trying to figure out what to do with this dubious information when a woman—also white, well-dressed, and middle-aged (also elaborately concerned)—appears from the doorway behind the front desk and whispers hurriedly with her counterpart.

"Ah," the man says, turning back to me. "You must be Selly. Right this way."

I'm whisked off to an elevator, through some too-bright, "staff only" hallways, then some dimmer ones, and finally deposited along with Singe, Memo, Tchatchky, Bustelo, and Togo into an elegant green room. Napping peacefully on a velvet couch is the famed author and illustrator Barnabas Hodge. A dear friend indeed. I should've known Omar Solomon's buddy list would include one of the most beloved storytellers of all time. Barnabas Hodge is one of those guys who's gonna have the pope at his funeral. He's been old as shit as long as I've been alive; gotta be in his eighties, probably going on immortal at this point. He was a little on the sidelines during the Dragon Revolution, from what I understand, but did his part in a quiet, understated way.

Barnabas Hodge is drooling a little and snoring a lot. He's wearing a plaid tan suit that perfectly complements his tan skin. He's almost perfectly round, and bald as the day he was born. The nervous museum guy vanishes as soon as I walk into the room, so it's just me and this ancient slumbering icon and the dogs, who immediately approach to sniff his crotch.

"Memo! Tchatchky! Singe!" I whisper-yell just loud enough to wake the poor old man up.

"Ah," he mutters, wiping his lips and blinking around. "Is it time already?"

"Ah, I don't think so," I say. "Sorry to wake you."

"Oh, dogs!" He immediately starts giving scratches behind ears and becomes the only human to have ever existed or mattered to five adoring pairs of eyes. "What a way to awaken!" Then he realizes I'm just standing there, and glances up. "And a child. How nice!"

I'm twenty-six.

"I wonder when this cursed thing will begin, then?" he muses idly. "It's probably getting late. Do they let dogs in museums now?"

"Ah, no, sir. Not exactly. I'm here because Omar Solomon asked me to give you a hand."

Barnabas Hodge sits up very straight, adjusts his glasses, and blinks at me. "I'm sorry, did you say . . ." He turns suddenly inward. He knows what I said. What it means to him, that's another story. "So it's time, then, is it?"

I raise my eyebrows. "Hmm? Time for what? My understanding was that you might need a hand making a hasty exit from an awkward shindig."

Barnabas Hodge lets out a wry chuckle. Then he shakes his head, running a hand over his shiny brown head. "Oh, Omar . . . you wily dog."

I'm puzzling through all this when the furrowed brow guy pops his furrowed brow back in and announces, "It's time."

Barnabas Hodge and I walk out onto the roof, accompanied, of course, by my erstwhile, ever-sniffing entourage: Singe, Memo,

Tchatchky, Bustelo, and Togo. They're behaving themselves extremely well given the circumstances. Togo hasn't peed on anyone yet, which is itself a small miracle.

Chairs have been set up, and tall, contained flames do their damndest to hold off the frigid night winds. It's a losing fight, of course. This Boston cold is relentless; it gets in your bones and won't leave. Especially this high up. All around us, the city sparkles, and the lights dance into the abysmal darkness of the bay.

Someone escorts Barnabas Hodge and me and the dogs to some seats on a small platform with fake flowers and a podium. Clearly there's been some mistake, and I tell the nearest guy in a tux who looks like he knows what he's doing. "No, no, this is quite right," he assures me a little too gently. "Please."

Once we've settled in and I get the dogs to calm down and sit quietly (thank you, bacon treats!), I text Omar Solomon a slew of question marks. Then I squint out into the audience. No offense to anyone out there of the Caucasian persuasion, but all these old people look the same to me, even the young ones. Each has paid a fortune and a half to be here and another on their outfits, which all look the same. They're all very pleased with themselves, and even more so, I gather from sideways glances and coy smiles, because Barnabas and I are here, too.

Just past them, the big red letters light up the night and Tumult glares out at the city. She's fricken huge, this close up—larger than life. The wind rattles her slightly, and I have to remind myself it's just fiberglass and paint.

OMAR SOLOMON: I take it that means everything is going as planned?

Whose plan? What plan? I text back furiously, trying and failing to be somewhat slick about it since I'm onstage. At the podium, a grinning retiree in an evening gown introduces herself as Laina Faxwell, the chief executive something or other of the vice chair committee of whatever-the-hell. She insists that she's so excited to get to the main event and then immediately dives into a mile-long list of donors.

OMAR SOLOMON: Okay, I admit this favor was a bit more complicated than I originally let on.
SellyDA: COMPLICATED?! Try batshit insane. I need an explanation now or I walk.
OMAR SOLOMON: Please don't walk. This is incredibly important, also more urgent than I can express here.
SellyDA: You're still being vague. I'm standing up.

I'm not standing up.

Something in Laina Faxwell's tone alerts me that she's finally moving on to the meat of the matter, and that's when she halfway turns and gestures at me. "And, of course, besides the esteemed Dr. Hodge—"

"It's an honorary degree!" Barnabas interjects gamely.

"—the museum board is pleased to introduce you all to a rising star of the juvenile literary world . . ." She pauses to check her notes, and about a hundred eyes of varying geriatricness turn to me.

Like an asshole, I go, "Ah ha hrmf!"

". . . Selly Dianamaria Avilés!" She hits the *A* in my last name too hard and stumbles right over the rest of it, blowing the whole thing, then chuckles quietly and yelps, "And her canine companions!"

Horrifyingly, the crowd erupts into cheers.

Barnabas Hodge nudges me kindly. "Got some fans, eh?"

"Miss Avilés's work has been praised by none other than

the museum's own dear and elusive friend, Omar Solomon, as 'A breath of fresh air and a bright light in these ever-dimming times.' "

Gasps of approval ring out as I frantically tap on my phone.

SellyDA: WTF!?!?!?
OMAR SOLOMON: Oh, did they do the introductions? It's all true. I never lie about these things.

Too many emotions crisscross my brain at once. I must've shorted out, because I'm pretty sure I'm just sitting here staring blankly into the sky as color splotches from the stage lights swirl past. Togo, always sensitive to my feelings, nuzzles my leg thoughtfully. Fortunately, Laina Faxwell has moved on to more thank-yous, so I have a few moments to just be.

And then a realization slaps me right out of it all.

SellyDA: luhgsuhfgsikhufgs! You've been what, stalking me??
OMAR SOLOMON: Absolutely not.
SellyDA: THEN HOW DO YOU KNOW ABOUT MY WORK??

Am I mad? Yes. Am I thrilled? Yes. Nothing makes sense. Lain Faxwell tries to tell some jokes. The crowd chortles obligingly.

OMAR SOLOMON: How did you happen to get a job walking dogs in the neighborhood one of your favorite writers lives in?
SellyDA: It's not my fault you posted your info online, buddy!
OMAR SOLOMON: So you did do it on purpose.

Oops. Told on myself. Absolute chad move. But that's beside the point.

SellyDA: How have you read my writing??

By way of reply, he forwards me my own message: *It's not my fault you posted your info online, buddy!*

Right. "Torque Phantoms of Old Havana." In *Peapod Magazine*, an online kidlit site. My first publication. Shit. But still!

SellyDA: Touché, asshole, but how did you know I was a writer in the first place??

Barnabas Hodge starts to stand with an old guy groan. Dimly, I register that Laina Faxwell has just rounded off a gushing introduction to his work after saying he needs none. Now thunderous applause sounds and Barnabas Hodge looks like he might not make it all the way up. I pocket my phone and grasp his arm, helping the old man rise. He puts his warm, wrinkly hand over mine and chuckles. "Too kind, my dear, too kind." We promenade to the podium arm in arm like he's walking me down the aisle. I'm just trying not to let it show how eager I am to get back to whatever explanation Omar Solomon has concocted now. But before I can turn away, Barnabas Hodge pulls me into an embrace and whispers: "When it's time to go, we go. No hesitation, my dear. You understand?"

"No," I whimper, but he's already turned to the crowd—they're all melting and awwing at this moving display over cross generational support or whatever—and I'm just standing there speechless once again.

"If you had told me thirty years ago, when the world was coming apart and all we had were stories to save our lives," Barnabas

Hodge begins as I stumble back to my seat in a daze, "that one day I'd be speaking at a fancy rooftop soiree with a bunch of rich white people in the shadow of a life-size Tumult the Dragon here, well . . ." He trails off with a whimsical chuckle, and the room explodes with applause and laughter again.

Five tails wag enthusiastically when I get back to my seat. I distribute bacon treats and skritches and then shakily pull out my phone.

OMAR SOLOMON: It's also not my fault that you talk about being a writer on the phone when you're in my apartment.
SellyDA: So you HAVE been watching me from afar, Creepo!
OMAR SOLOMON: Not exactly, no. I can't help it, that is.
SellyDA: CREEP!
OMAR SOLOMON: No, I mean I can't help it because I'm always there.

Something in the way he phrased that jumps out at me, but I can't put my finger on what.

SellyDA: Wait. Please don't tell me you died and this is some cursed AI recreation I'm talking to, because I will throw my phone off this rooftop right the fuck now.
OMAR SOLOMON: Selly, I hope you know my work well enough to know that I would never let those tech bros anywhere near my brain or legacy, and if I had died and they did that, my spirit would never leave them in peace.

OMAR SOLOMON: A few years ago, I did almost die though. And the experience did take a lot from me. Almost everything.
SellyDA: WHAT DOES THAT MEAN??

But even as I hit *Send*, it dawns on me. He's typing, too, but I get there first.

SellyDA: THE AQUARIUM??

Rather than finish whatever he was explaining, he just hits my post with a thumbs-up.

"And so, friends"—Barnabas Hodge's voice has taken on the vibrant, embracing church sermon baritone he was once renowned for—"what I'm here to remind y'all of is that a revolution ain't nothin' but a story, and it's told by tens of thousands of people all at once. And storytelling, just like conjure work and cookin', is just a matter of putting all the right ingredients in the right pot at the right time. You feel me?"

They do, apparently. Hoots and hollers arise from the crowd. If anyone starts pretending to catch the Holy Ghost, I'm out for real.

When I look back down at my phone there's a brain emoji, and I let out a little shriek. Barnabas looks back at me with a smirk, then continues.

OMAR SOLOMON: It's too much to explain over text, but suffice to say, yes that's all that's left of me for the moment, and I desperately need your help, but it's not the kind of thing I'm comfortable writing on such an unsecure app, so I'm afraid I'll need you to put the pieces together a bit and go with the flow, so to speak.

"Revolution is not a single battle or even a few years' worth of fighting. It's every single day. It's what you do when you look in the mirror. It's how you listen. How you grow. That's how we—not just get to paradise—that's how we create paradise, together. Every day, every moment. Paradise. We do it with stories."

SellyDA: I'm sorry about your body, but I'm gonna need a little more than that to go on, Mr. Solomon.

"With stories," Barnabas Hodge booms, wrapping up, "we can go anywhere, do anything. Not just change the world, but create it anew, hm?" He turns back to me and offers a genial old wink. "So let's get started."

Standing ovation.

OMAR SOLOMON: How bout this: those museum bastards would much rather have me stashed away in a murky vat than out in the world causing more trouble, and they've made sure to keep a tight rein on anything that would help me get back on my feet.
OMAR SOLOMON: So to speak.

Barnabas Hodge. It has to be. Omar Solomon sent me here to help him out of a difficult situation. The museum is probably keeping him somehow against his will, too, and when the two of them reunite, all hell will break loose in the best possible way! That explains the winking and nudging: the old rebel team is getting back together, and I get to play one small part in making it happen. Dream come true. All I have to do is escort old Barnabas out the door and away.

The applause is still going when he hobbles back over to me. The dogs greet him with enthusiasm. I don't know what to make of these museum folks, given what I've just been told. They seem genuinely excited and adoring. Laina Faxwell launches into some more mid-level punnery. She'll be dragging me up there next, I'm sure of it. I don't have much time.

I wrap a firm hand around Barnabas Hodge's arm. "Let's go, Mr. Hodge," I whisper. "I'll walk you out."

He scrunches his face at me, low-key appalled. "What, back to the elevator, my dear? Why would we do that?"

"Solomon sent me here to help an old friend leave a tense situation," I hiss. "So that's what I'm doing."

"Ridiculous," Hodge insists. "Solomon and I were comrades and always will be, but friends? Not likely. He's too freewheeling for my milieu, the rascal." And with that, he sits definitively.

". . . who needs no introduction," Laina Faxwell concludes, "Selly Dianamaria Avilés!"

I stand, take in the applause. Try to still my trembling hands. Fail. Walk a few shaky steps to the podium, and only then do I realize I still have the five leashes clutched tightly in my left fist.

In front of me, a hundred expectant eyes, hungry even.

I know what they want: this is that nebulous, impossible thing called *remarks*. More than that, I know what they want from me. I can see it in their wide, starved eyes, their slightly open mouths, shiny with the glint of saliva and expectations.

They want me to bleed. They see me—my combat boots, colorful leggings and skirt, my puffy jacket, the oversized headphones around my neck, these piercings, and in each detail, they see some trauma to guzzle. A whole feast of strife and dysfunction and systems failing, an arc of artfully rising above it all to join their ranks and make everyone feel a little better about themselves.

Clearly, there are gatekeepers here. People who could make or break me. They have that look to them, though, that if I offer up a little dollop they'll guzzle me dry, and gush about how tasty it is while I lie there, empty.

And to be clear: I have the speech in the chamber and ready to go. I've practiced it ten thousand times on my walks, in front of the mirror, to the dogs by the sea. I've woven the threads, tracked the movements, divvied the whole thing into a three-part structure that brings it home with a resounding and heartrending callback to the top.

I say a few cursory *thank yous* just to buy myself some time. My mom taught me how to story. She still does, every day. It was that trip to Matanzas and the people she met along the way, or the day she saw that body in the street, or the tricks their first dog used to do. And you'd be there, you'd be right there beside her watching it happen, then you'd jump in alongside her; you'd run with her to the body, the dust rising around your Sunday dress shoes, the air shrieking in your ear as your world exploded alongside hers and everything came apart for the first time. You'd be beside her while she started to put it back together, too, with those two trembling hands and ten thousand people at her side, ten thousand dragon kites in the sky, and it would be stories that did it, that remade the world anew after so much death.

I don't say any of that though. Woulda made a nice speech, sure, but that's not for these grisly, devouring maws. I crack a joke, still biding time, but it's a good one for a change, and it gets an actual laugh, not a polite one. And then I look up and my eyes lock onto the mountainous ass of that dragon straight ahead of me. It's huge, the whole thing is huge.

An old friend indeed. Dragons guard treasure; they carry the wisdom of the world.

A warm hand wraps around my forearm; tails wap against my leg. Barnabas Hodge smiles up at me. "Do you see it?"

The space between the dragon's wings is wide, there's even

a saddle there. Waiting. All we have to do is get to it. I smile, and in that single moment, a dizzying shift ripples through the audience. Their own smiles tighten, cords pulled suddenly tight against their sullen, drooping faces.

"What are you two plotting up there?" Laina Faxwell demands with a humorless laugh. "Let's all just take a breath."

I clutch Barnabas Hodge. Whisper, "Let's do this," and launch us forward, shoving people and folding chairs to either side as I go.

"Hey!" an old man snarls. "You can't just—"

"Get your grubby hands—"

"Stop them!"

Even with the dogs growling and snapping in all directions, the crowd closes in. I feel clammy fists slap against me, ancient fingers grasp desperately for purchase. Worse: there are security guys approaching. Hadn't seen them before. They are all requisite amounts of beefy and business-meaning. We might not make it. I can barely see the dragon through the clutter of bodies, open mouths, tight eyes.

The security guys move in a tight formation through the crowd.

I have nothing but five dogs and a whimsical old legend.

That's not true.

I reach into my pocket. Wrap my fingers around the well-worn tennis ball. Whip it straight into the oncoming squad of biffs with a single shouted word: "BALL!"

Five yelping goblins launch forward as one. They topple the first guy, and he takes another down with him. There are still four more. "Singe," I yell, because that dog is not like other dogs; she's something special, and right now I'll take anything.

Electricity crackles through the suddenly thick atmosphere, then lances in a bright bow across the rooftop. Singe yips twice and bright blue bolts explode outward with a crackle and boom, sends the rest of the heavies scattering to either side.

I pull Barnabas Hodge along with me as gently and urgently as possible. The tuxedos are closing back in as I heave him up onto the dragon, then load up each dog and climb on. I close my eyes and imagine what the skies must've looked like in those heady days of love and rebellion. What Mamá felt, watching the endless parade of freedom float past overhead. How the world would never be the same.

We'll make a quick stop to pick up an old aquarium, and then, who knows? The dragon is already rumbling and growling with new life, each ingredient in place, each story locked and loaded, and then we explode outward into the night and leave the past behind forever.

El Jíbaro de Puerto Rico

Cynthia Pelayo

"What we committed in the Indies stands out among the most unpardonable offenses ever committed against God and mankind and this trade [in Indian slaves] as one of the most unjust, evil, and cruel among them."
—Bartolomé de las Casas, Spanish clergyman and one of the first settlers of the Americas, *A Short Account of the Destruction of the Indies*, 1552

"Spirits, as we have seen, are beings like ourselves, and constitute a population environing us on every side, though invisible to us in our normal state; we say, our normal state, because, as we shall see, this invisibility is not absolute."
—Allan Kardec, French educator, writer, translator and founder of the Spiritism movement, *The Book on Mediums*, 1861

"Great is the empire we face but greater is our right to be free."
—Pedro Albizu Campos, former president and spokesperson of the Nationalist Party of Puerto Rico

There is no death. There is no beginning. There is no end. There is just this continuation of us all. I wish I could describe it clearly to you. I will try. It's almost like memories that challenge our current perception, and it becomes difficult to distinguish where I am.

Am I here, right now, with Abuelo? Or am I somewhere else entirely?

There are days and there are nights, and there is the lullaby of sweet little green tree frogs. Coquis. In the evening, their pretty song lulls me to sleep: *Co-kee, co-kee, co-kee.*

When rain falls here, there is a soft hush as the droplets fall against the thick green vegetation, purple orchids, and gigantic ferns that surround our home. I imagine shooting stars in the heavens above make the same sort of sounds as our rainforest home.

Great palm and magnolia trees and coffee shrubs cover every stretch of our land, except the very hilltop on which we live. It's like a little pocket on top of the universe from which I enjoy watching shimmering golden sunsets. I also know that just not too far away, in any which direction, lies a great blue expanse, the ocean. We are surrounded by mystical beauty.

I believe we shall never be truly separated from those we love and from the place we call home. For no matter what anyone attempts to do to try to systematically separate us from our light by renaming, stripping, erasing, or dehumanizing us, what they fail to realize is that we are forever.

Eternity is this island that sits on the equator, that imaginary line halfway between poles that divides the Earth into North and South.

We are that great in-between place.

This island is ocean breeze, the taste of sea salt on your tongue, warm sand beneath your feet, the gentle sway and dance of palm fronds. Birdsong. And these are the reminders that here we are. Here we exist.

The people who came before me on this land, the Tainos, told stories about the beginning of existence. They claimed the sun emerged from the Cave of Iguanaboina. The moon, too.

These tales swirl in my head, racing around my mind like the powerful winds of a hurricane. Even that name hurricane, juracán, is Taino in origin, and hurricanes are conjured by our ancestral spirit Guabancex, who controls the weather. She summons these storms when she's upset.

See, there's no true erasure. All this remains here. These legends and folktales; they are ways to prevent forgetting. They are memories in the form of stories. They are gold, set deep within mines just waiting to be excavated. Sometimes all we need to recall who and what we are is to be rustled awake, and to accomplish that, all that's required is someone with faith and love to guide us out of the darkness.

I hear a knock, three times, and Abuelo calls my name.

"Victoria, wake up."

I open my eyes and stare at the white ceiling. Just outside, our rooster, Cacao, crows mightily. Soft blue light peeks in through the slats of the window. The arrival of dawn.

"Abuelo," I call from behind the door. My head is foggy. I'm unsure what day of the week it is. "Are you going to Pellejas today?"

Central Pellejas, the sugar mill where Abuelo works.

In the mornings I usually wake up before Abuelo, get ready, and slip outside. I'd gather dried corn and scatter it in the chicken coop, saying good morning to Beatrice and Yesenia and Xiomara and Lucy and Yarelis. By this time Diego and Linda—our two goats—would have awakened, too, and they'd press their wet snouts into my hands, searching for grain. I'd give each of the goats kisses on the top of their heads, fill their food dishes, and sit on the front step of our small wooden house waiting for the sun to rise.

Mami and Papi used to live here, too, a long time ago, but

now it's just me and Abuelo. I like the quiet, but I do miss them very much, and I'm starting to worry about Abuelo. He coughs late into the night sometimes. He's getting very old, and I worry about him working in the sugar mill all day, so this is why I help out here as much as I can.

Once all the animals have been fed and the sun has risen, that's usually the time I go inside and it's then that I often find Abuelo in the kitchen. There he'll be standing over the stove, preparing coffee and singing to himself.

I miss the days, long ago, when Abuelo would sit outside with Mami and Papi on cool evenings with all their friends. There they'd play música jíbara late into the night. There would be the plucking of the strings of the cuatro, bright and melancholic; the sharp, quick strumming of the tiple; the rattling of maracas; the scratch, the scrape of the güiro; and the rhythmic beating of bomba drums. The songs they sang were so joyful, and so many people from the pueblo nearby would gather here, too, clapping in a rhythmic pattern and singing along. It's sad that those days ended.

Most mornings I'd find Abuelo wearing his regular clothes, brown pants, and a long-sleeved button shirt. The clothes he wore all day in the field, topped by his pava hat.

I notice this morning, however, that his pava hat and his machete both remain hung by the door.

Abuelo would spend most days in the sugar cane fields, machete in hand, cutting and clearing away rows of those tall, green, swaying stalks. Most stood twelve feet high, towering over him. The leaves, razor-sharp, would cut his knuckles and hands. He'd return home, fingers covered in new calluses, his shoes caked in mud, but no matter how exhausted he was, he'd always be in such a good mood, with a dear smile on his face. Abuelo always greeted me with cheer: "¿Cómo estás, mi Victoria querida?"

He'd get cleaned up and prepare dinner. Most days we'd have arroz con habichuelas. Sometimes we would have arroz con gandules. On special occasions, he'd make us mofongo, mashing up green plantains and adding pork cracklings, or bacalaitos, fritters with codfish. He did the best he could with the money he made at the mill.

Sometimes during dinner Abuelo would tell me ghost stories or folktales he'd learned when he was a little boy. He'd also tell me about the way things were a long time ago, about the coffee and sugar fields his family once owned. He said many families had their own farms here, but that the United States kept changing things. He'd rattle off names of laws I wasn't familiar with: the 1917 Jones Act and Operation Bootstrap. America, he said, liked to attach these benign titles to laws that were really intended to do more harm to the island. It was all tyranny shrouded in trickery.

"We are the oldest colony in the world," he said one day after dinner as he washed the dishes. After he prepared his evening cup of coffee, he stood at the doorway, the steam rising from his aluminum coffee cup. His eyes were directed over the sloping shape of the Sleeping Giant, a mountain formation that takes the shape of a man asleep. It was at that moment I really noticed how tired Abuelo looked. Deep lines marked his sun-darkened face. Yet his eyes, while tired and cloudy, still sparkled with so much wisdom.

He pointed his cup in the direction of the mountain. "They say Yúcahu, the god of the Taino people, dwells in the peak of El Yunque." I thought about a god existing at the top of a mist-covered rainforest peak, surrounded by streams, rivers, and waterfalls. He took a sip and then shook his head. "Not many people recognize how important the Sleeping Giant in Adjuntas is. Everyone knows about him. He can be seen from so many parts of the island. We see him. He's there. Some legends claim he's dead, but I don't think so. I think he's asleep and one day he will awaken."

I open my mouth to say something but realize this is the haze of a memory.

I hear Abuelo call again.

Three knocks.

"Victoria, wake up."

I drift back to sleep, to thoughts. To the work of my Abuelo. There was something in that methodical yet brutal work he did for years. Although, that's the place where I think he was able to find some peace. Maybe it was in that rhythmic, precise motion, repeatedly swinging his machete, trimming away leaves, and sorting sugarcane stalks by size. I'd imagine it must be like putting oneself into a hypnotic trance state. Abuelo once told me how he'd speak to himself out there, in low whispers. Beneath the buzz of insects, his skin darkening by the sun and sweat. He told me how he'd talk to my mami and papi and me out there.

"Abuelo," I say, standing in the dark hallway, rubbing at my eyes.

The casita is small, and I can see directly into part of the living room that faces the kitchen. I move slowly, confused, unsure of what time it is exactly.

I find him at the stove. He's wearing black slacks and a clean white guayabera shirt. The wisps of gray hair on his head are still a little wet, but nice and clean and combed over.

He must have bathed in the metal tub outside using rainwater while night completely covered the mountain.

He wasn't dressed to go to Pellejas today.

Abuelo doesn't turn around. He continues stirring the boiling coffee on the stove, which fills the kitchen with a roasted aroma.

"Today is the last misa, Victoria," he says, sounding a little bit sad and a little bit serious.

I remain silent, unsure of what to say.

He looks over his shoulder and smiles his regular warm smile, and I feel a sense of relief, even considering the shocking news he just shared.

"You look very nice today," he says.

I look down and admire my white dress that goes down past my knees, white socks, and white shoes.

I laugh to myself. "It looks like I'm dressed for Easter."

The sound of the metal spoon against the metal pot stirring coffee stops abruptly. Abuelo's shoulders shoot up once, as if he's been startled by a loud bang. He turns around again. His eyes are widened. "No, not Easter. Palm Sunday."

I look down at my hands. "Palm Sunday," I repeat. "Aren't we supposed to go to the . . . ?"

"Victoria . . ." Abuelo calls my name again, making me lose my thought. "The guests are on their way."

Right. Guests. For la misa. The last misa.

"What time are they arriving?" I ask.

"They should be arriving by the time the sun rises."

The chickens are clucking outside, being chatty. A dog barks in the distance, followed by another.

"Where are they from?" I ask.

He turns off the burner and continues stirring. "San Juan."

San Juan. The city. I find myself growing self-conscious. My dress is pretty, yes, but maybe not San Juan pretty. I imagine the people who live in San Juan all dress so modern, in American styles. I find myself scanning our walls, bare wood with pictures Abuelo had taken at the photo studio in Ponce for a dollar. There were paintings he had done himself, watercolors of Cueva de Camuy, of fruits like quenepas, or birds like the green parrots that swooped above, branch to branch. The prints were whatever he could find, cutouts from *Time* with pictures of the island or articles with Don Pedro, the president of the Nationalist Party and the first Puerto Rican to attend Harvard Law School. Abuelo was so very proud to call Don Pedro his friend. There were so many more pictures and prints and paintings all on the wall.

Our casita is small, yes, but very clean. The walls are made of wood with a tin roof. I keep the outside well tended and maintained and the animals happy, but our home is nothing like the stately houses in San Juan. Those houses in the main city are made of stone, with wrought iron balconies. Inside they have courtyards and inner gardens with large water fountains and bright purple bougainvilleas climbing across walls.

Abuelo holds a strainer over his coffee cup and carefully pours the dark liquid from the metal pot through it into his mug, the coffee grounds catching in the mesh fabric.

"The mother is named Mrs. Camila Rosario. She's a poet and a professor. Mrs. Rosario teaches at the University of Puerto Rico. The misa is for her son, Jonathan. He's just a few years older than you."

I've never met a poet, let alone a professor before, and to think, a woman who is both. Even though I feel a little embarrassed to meet them, I am still very excited.

"They must be so rich," I find myself saying.

Abuelo takes a sip of coffee and then smiles to himself, happy with his work. He then sighs. "Rich doesn't mean money or owning things, Victoria. You can be a millionaire and truly have nothing. My mother used to say: 'We live better up here than all of the rich people in the world.' "

"Why is that?"

"Because we are happy, regardless. We find something to get us through our days, to be grateful."

Abuelo is right. I am grateful for him. I am grateful for the chickens and the goats and the music made by crickets at night. I am grateful for the mountain.

"They will have a lot of questions for you."

Questions for me? I'm confused. That's not how the misa works. Usually, the questions are for other people. "What do they want to ask me?"

"The son, Jonathan, has been having bad dreams."

Abuelo sets his coffee down and shuffles over to a small room where I did not enter. He leaves the door open and appears moments later carrying a small table, then proceeds to set it up in the middle of the living room.

None of this is sounding at all like the past misas we have had.

"I don't understand," I say from the living room.

Abuelo returns to the room and emerges carrying two chairs, which he positions at opposite ends of the table, before going back to gather the last two chairs. He places the chairs on the remaining ends of the table. Under one arm he holds a white folded sheet. He unfolds the tablecloth and smooths it over the table's surface. It is so bright white, it nearly glows against all this wood. He then goes back to the room once more and closes the door.

Abuelo moves to the front door and opens it in anticipation of our guests.

The house is so small, I can see right outside from where I'm standing.

He takes a deep breath and then enters the kitchen, sips from his coffee cup he left on the counter, then says, "You're going to confirm to Mrs. Rosario what Jonathan sees in his dreams."

Misas are for the living to communicate with the dead, I think, and they usually don't have anything to do with dreams.

"Is that what makes it the last misa? Because misas are for when we talk to the dead, and at this misa we are speaking to the living?"

"Yes."

I'm upset, and so I focus on the wall in front of me, admiring more pictures. There are photographs of Abuelo with Mami and Papi and me. There is a picture of Abuelo and Abuela on their wedding day. There is a picture of Abuelo, Papi, Don Pedro and all the male members of the Cadets of the Republic. In another picture, there is Mami and me with all the women from the Nationalist Party in our area, the Daughters of the Republic. In each of those images, we are standing in front of a two-story corner building with a second-floor wraparound balcony.

I take a step forward, and then another. That two-story building. I remember it.

The floorboards creak behind me. I hear Abuelo shuffling slowly toward me.

"This . . ." I point.

"Yes . . ."

Papi got the permit for the parade. He was so excited. "We're celebrating all day," Papi told me. He later explained to me that the parade was the sixty-fourth-anniversary commemoration of when it became illegal to own slaves in Puerto Rico.

"It happened already," Abuelo said behind me. "That celebration, I mean."

I don't remember that day at all. We were all going to meet in front of the Nationalist headquarters, that two-story building, and then the procession would kick off down the street. How did it happen already? I find myself trying to recall that memory, but nothing arises. There's a black spot that covers that moment.

"But we haven't been back to the Nationalist Party headquarters since that day?" I ask. Because I would have remembered that at least.

Abuelo doesn't say anything.

"How is Don Pedro?" I ask to break the silence.

I turn around to face Abuelo, and his eyes are watery. He presses his lips together and turns around, walking away from me, returning to the counter. He's drinking from his cup and looking out the window.

"There were revolts, all across the island. Mayagüez. Arecibo. Peñuelas. San Juan. Blanca was in charge of the uprising in Jayuya. She held the town for three days. We were met with resistance quickly. The National Guard was called in. Dozens had been killed." He reaches a hand to his face, wiping away tears.

Abuelo's words continue coming, now in short, hitching sobs.

The more he says, the more I can't believe what I'm hearing. A dull ache begins to pulsate within my rib cage.

"Four Nationalists surrendered in Utuado. The youngest, seventeen. The National Guard made them take off their shoes, their belts, and they were made to march in front of everyone to the police station. When they arrived, their surrender was met with a machine gun. They were assassinated, Victoria."

I feel myself stagger backward. "They can't do that . . ."

I think about how we recite the Pledge of Allegiance in school, with our hands over our hearts. *Liberty and justice for all.* I believed that. I wanted to believe that. But now it feels like the ground beneath all these words is crumbling, and I don't know what's real anymore.

I pledge allegiance to the flag of the United States of America, and to the republic for which it stands, one nation under God, indivisible, with liberty and justice for all.

I think about how an American flag hangs in the front of each of our classrooms. Red, white, and blue.

I think about how we're scolded if we speak Spanish in school, and how all the lessons are in English.

My face feels cold. My arms and hands go numb. The dull ache in my chest intensifies.

"Aren't we a part of America? How can America bomb its own towns?"

"I don't think they think of us as similar to them, Victoria. We're just something to hold, to keep."

The sun is fully up now. It's a bright blue day. I glance out of the door, and that's when I notice it's missing.

"Where's the flag?"

"What?"

I stomp outside and stand and point beside the door. "Our flag. It hung right here."

He follows me and stands at the threshold. He takes a deep breath and sighs. "They passed a law." His voice is quiet. "The Gag Law. Ley de la Mordaza. We're not allowed to display our flag. We're not allowed to sing patriotic songs. We're not allowed to participate in the independence movement."

I shout. "Our flag is illegal? Our songs? What we believe? We're illegal? How? We live here!" I stomp my feet.

"Victoria, come inside," he says gently.

My entire body is shaking with anger. I can't believe any of this is real. Inside the casita anger doesn't subside, and I shout again, "It's against the law to display the flag of Puerto Rico in Puerto Rico!?" I stomp my feet on the floor so hard this time that the entire house shakes.

Abuelo raises a hand to his chest. "I'm so sorry, Victoria." He's crying now.

"Where is it?" I run over to the few wooden shelves in the living room. I scan across statues of saints: Our Lady of Providence, Saint Joseph, Saint Anthony, Saint James. Beneath them is a shelf where Abuelo keeps other things, magazines and books, pamphlets and prayer cards. I come across three books I hadn't seen before.

The Spirits Book

The Gospel According to Spiritism

The Book on Mediums

All written by a man named Allan Kardec.

My fingers pause, scanning the shelves. "What are these?" I turn around to see Abuelo folding his hands in front of him.

He looks to the door and says, "We don't have much time, but it's important that you know all this." He's facing me now. "Allan Kardec was an author and educator. His books, his teachings came to Puerto Rico from France, many years ago. The 1850s. He developed a science called spiritism. A process for the living to communicate with the dead. The first séance happened in San Juan around that very same time when Kardec's teachings made their way here. At first it was a system used mostly by the wealthy. And the spiritists here were good people. They founded hospitals, promoted literacy, fought against the death penalty, and pushed for better social conditions. Then the practice spread throughout the island and made its way here, to the culture of the jíbaros. But here we call it espiritismo."

I cross my arms, shake my head, and say, "Jíbaros." I know that's what they all—the people who come from wealth—call us. The owners of the sugar mills and coffee plantations . . . they like to call us that to insult us. The rich want to remind us that we're poor, that they think we're unworthy. It's the rich who continue hurting and harming the poor over and over again, and I guess Abuelo is right. Wealthy people must be so deeply unhappy if they find satisfaction in relentlessly hurting those with less.

As if Abuelo knows exactly what I'm thinking, he says, "We're not peasants." He points over at the Sleeping Giant. "We live here among gods."

I straighten myself up. "The misa, it came from these books?" I motion to the shelves.

"Yes, but some customs we take from Catholicism, some we take from the Tainos, and some we take from the cultura of the jíbaro."

The room tilts, as if the ground itself no longer knows what it is. I blink, trying to catch up. My heart is racing, not from fear, but feeling like everything I thought I knew might be wrong. I don't understand any of this. Why was he telling me all this now? I feel so lost. My hand reaches for my stomach, feeling as if I'm going to throw up, but I can't recall the last time I'd eaten.

"When I find our flag, I'm hanging it back up!"

He opens his mouth to say something but pauses when we both hear the slow rumble of an automobile making its way toward us.

"Victoria," he pleads. "If the police see it, they can enter our home. They can seize our property. They can arrest us."

The automobile slows, pulling up alongside our house, its tires settling on the grass just outside. It is shiny and black and new. We hear as the rumble of the engine silences when the car is turned off.

There is no more time to discuss this, at least not right now, and I feel so defeated.

What more does America want from us? They took our land. They took our language. They've now taken our right to display our own flag. They've taken our hope that Puerto Rico can decide for itself whether it wishes to remain a part of the United States or become free. It's our island. This is our home. How can we not determine how it is we want to live?

Abuelo's voice is low and full of pain. "This is what it means to be conquered, Victoria. This is what colonizers do. But we're not giving up. We will find another way." He reaches for his nice hat, not the pava. A fedora Papi had gifted him. It is cream with a satiny black ribbon. "They're here," he says and steps outside.

I lean against the doorframe and watch as Abuelo greets the woman who emerges from the driver's-side door. She is wearing a white dress, too, with a white jacket and large buttons. Her dark hair is short, just above her shoulders and styled in big curls. I hadn't seen this fashion before, any of it. People in San Juan seemed so modern. The passenger door opens, drawing my attention. A boy climbs out wearing black slacks and a neatly pressed white short-sleeve button-up shirt. His fair hair is combed flat, and his green eyes glance around, quiet and solemn.

He spots me right away in the doorway, raises a hand, and says: "Hello?"

Mrs. Rosario shoots him a confused look and then says, "Jonathan?"

Abuelo takes Mrs. Rosario's arm and escorts her along the grassy path.

"That's my granddaughter, Victoria," my abuelo says, but the woman continues staring at her son. Her face isn't mad or sad, just astonished, like sometimes people's faces appear during the misa.

Inside, Abuelo offers the woman coffee, and she smiles and accepts.

Her eyes look up, inspecting the tin roof overhead. "How long have you lived here?"

Abuelo happily says, "My entire life. My father, too, and his father."

"It is beautiful here," she says, looking out the window. "It's so green, and flowers just grow everywhere. It's magical."

Abuelo begins to tell her about all the plants that grow here: coconut palm, philodendron, aloe, passion fruit, more.

Jonathan takes a seat beside me on the sofa. As his mother sips her coffee, nodding along to Abuelo as he tells her about the house, she stares at her son.

"How old are you?" Jonathan asks me.

"Fourteen."

"You?"

"Seventeen."

Abuelo glances over at me above his coffee mug, and I can feel myself blush. Jonathan is much older than me and so very different. He lives in another world entirely. He might as well live on the moon.

It makes me think of the legend of Guanina, the Taino princess who falls in love with Don Cristóbal de Sotomayor, a Spanish conquistador who came to conquer and colonize. They, too, were from different worlds. Guanina's brother, Guaybana, the chief of the Tainos, hated Sotomayor and all the conquistadors, and so Guaybana killed Sotomayor in an ambush. When Guanina learned of this, she rushed to Sotomayor's side and tried to revive him with kisses.

When the Taino elders learned of this and went to retrieve Guanina, they found her dead, her head resting on Sotomayor's chest. The lovers were buried together beneath a giant ceiba tree. It's said that immediately after their burial red hibiscus and white lilies sprouted. On nights when the moon is full, and the nights are embraced with a cool breeze from the ocean, it's said the shadows of Guanina and Sotomayor can be seen standing side by side beneath that very ceiba tree.

"Victoria? Are you here?"

I feel my stomach drop. "Yes." I smile, embarrassed.

"Mrs. Rosario asked to hear some folk stories. I told her how you enjoy them."

I stand and smooth out the skirt of my dress. "Scary ones?"

"Yes," Mrs. Rosario says, but she is looking at Abuelo when she says this.

I glance down at my shoes and stand with my arms at my sides.

"There are stories of people who see flickering lights from lanterns all along the mountain at night. They move like fireflies. Some people claim those lights come from the lanterns of ghosts who tripped and fell over the side of the mountain and died.

"Other people say that in the moonlight, you can spot bloodied torsos and severed heads or amputated arms moving quietly along the road. These are the body parts of people who died in these accidents who are making their way home. Some stories also say that trees cast shadows of Los Ahorcados—men, women, and children who were hanged there. These were often Black and Taino slaves who were hanged for trying to rebel or escape . . ."

Mrs. Rosario gives a stiff smile and sets her coffee cup down abruptly. Liquid splashes on the surface of the counter. Abuelo quickly moves to clean up the mess and tells her not to worry at all.

"Thank you," she says to him. "And thank you for those very scary folk stories," she says, but her words are directed only to Abuelo. It is then that I spot real fear in her eyes.

I know these are called folk stories, but many are real stories that have been passed down about things people have seen and heard. Awful things have happened on this island, and we remember them. Sometimes we call them legends or myths, but maybe it'd be better just to describe them as true.

Some of them I've read in books. Some of them were told to me by Mami and Papi or Abuelo, and some of these stories I can't remember where I gathered them from; it's like they were whispered to me in the wind.

I sit back down beside Jonathan. He places a hand on top of

mine, but I can't feel it. I'm just so nervous with meeting him and his mother and the questions they may want to ask.

I hear a rush of wind and the shifting of palm leaves outside. I see now Abuelo and Mrs. Rosario are finishing their coffee. The space is so small that I can hear them clearly, talking about poetry and books.

Jonathan motions with his eyes to the white table we've set up in the middle of the living room for the misa.

"Is it scary?"

"No." I look at the table and chairs. "It just is."

Abuelo and Mrs. Rosario's conversation shifts. She's telling him that she's worried about her son, about the things that he sees when he sleeps, and the things he sees sometimes when he's awake.

"He's going to be just fine," Abuelo tells her, and then he raises his voice so that we can all hear. "It's time."

Abuelo stands and walks over to the white table.

I take a seat at his right. Mrs. Rosario takes a seat to his left, and Jonathan is seated directly across from Abuelo.

Mrs. Rosario's eyes turn to each of us. She bites her bottom lip and then says, "I'm Catholic."

Abuelo smiles. "I am, too," and this seems to give Mrs. Rosario some comfort. She leans over and kisses her son on his cheek.

"Thank you. We're ready," Mrs. Rosario says.

Abuelo raises his right hand to the tabletop and knocks three times. "Victoria, wake up."

"I'm ready," I say.

Abuelo places his hands together in prayer, lowers his head, and the misa begins.

First, he starts by reciting several prayers and scriptures he has memorized, the Our Father, Psalm 91.

"For he will command his angels concerning you to guard you

in all your ways; they will lift you up in their hands . . ." Abuelo says.

Jonathan is trying not to laugh. I nudge his foot with mine and both of us giggle. Abuelo opens his eyes, winks at me, and then continues.

When Abuelo completes his prayers, it's then that he begins my favorite part of the misa. He starts clapping in a slow, steady beat. His eyes remain closed, and he opens his mouth.

I thought I knew all the folk songs Abuelo would sing, but I'd never heard this one. Abuelo sings the tale of El Gigante Dormido and how he came to be:

"Legend tells us long ago—
There were people who wanted this land

For it was fertile, green,
and lush and beautiful

Here coffee grew, sugar cane, too,
papaya, mango, avocado, more

Those people knew on this land
Lived a mighty giant

The giant's head stretched above
mountain peaks, into the sky

His arms when spread
Covered the entire range

A witch had a vision how to kill the giant
Strike him in his right eye

One day the witch climbed this mountain
Aimed a poison arrow and struck the giant

The giant fell back, injured from the arrow in his right eye
As he lay on his back, he punched the ground

A hole was torn into the land
From it water gushed, and waterfalls sprang

The giant, in so much pain and fear,
Remained in that position

There he remains. We see his outline
Yet we know he's not dead, just sleeping."

When Abuelo opens his eyes, the pupils are gone, replaced by two milky white orbs that gleam like marbles under the light, lifeless and staring through her. A wet gasp escapes Mrs. Rosario's throat before it turns into a scream.

She stumbles backward, knocking her chair to the floor with a sharp crack, her hands flailing for balance as if the air itself might hold her.

"Please," I say. "Remain seated. Everyone is safe here in the misa."

"What do you see, Jonathan?" Abuelo asks.

When I turn to Jonathan, he, too, has no pupils, just milky whites for eyes.

"Jonathan!" Mrs. Rosario reaches for his face.

"No! Please don't touch him," I stress again. "We're all safe here in the misa."

Mrs. Rosario is breathing heavy now. Her shoulders rising and falling. Her chin quivering.

"I promise you," I say. "We will not be harmed here."

"Where is he?"

"He's visiting the other side. The in-between place. It's not far. He's just there looking."

Jonathan's body is rigid. His lips move slowly, speaking as if he is in a dream.

"What do you see, Jonathan?" I ask.

"I see . . . ships sailing toward land. Men in armor. Swords. There are people on the beach. This is the land they come from."

I lean in slightly, voice gentle. "What's next?"

"It's dark. I can't see. I hear chiseling. Crying. Sobbing. Weeping. We're in a cave. Mining."

I glance at his mother. She's clasping her hands, whispering prayers under her breath.

"What's next?" I ask again, this time more carefully, bracing myself.

"It's dark. Nighttime. There's firelight. I see nude bodies, stacked. There are piles of them. Hundreds. Thousands. Some are being tossed into the sea. I hear splashes. The men in armor are tossing bodies into the fire, too. But some people are still moving, even though many are missing arms or legs. They're covered in blood. There's so much screaming. Screaming coming from the fire."

My voice is barely a breath. "What's next?"

Jonathan trembles. His hands curl into fists.

"People are hiding in caves. Women. Many women. There are babies here, too. A woman. She's cradling a baby to her breast. The men in armor arrive. She darts out of the cave. She's running. They chase her. Slashing past palms, hiking across streams. They reach her. She stands at a mountaintop. She looks down and sees the crashing waves. She tells them this is a better death, and leaps."

His mother gasps. Tears spilling down her cheeks.

I stop myself from reaching for him. My hand hovers in the space between us. "What's next?" I ask, my voice barely above a whisper.

"More ships," Jonathan says. "But these are different. They aren't occupied by men in armor. These are full of people. There are chains around their hands, feet, necks. They're all chained together. They're just so many. They're lined up on the beach. Covered in sweat. Blood. Vomit."

I draw in a breath. "What's next?" I ask softly, careful not to break whatever thread is holding him there.

"People are working. In the fields. Coffee. Sugarcane. Under the sun. It's hot. It's just so hot. Their skin is burning, blistering in the heat. They've got scars and cuts that are bleeding and pus-filled. They're being screamed at to move faster. One of them passes out. No one comes to help him."

His mother moans, covering her mouth, rocking.

I steady my voice, but urgency creeps in. "What's next?"

"Different men. They're wearing green. Soldiers. American soldiers. They're in a ship. They land on a beach."

I press again, firmer now. "And then what?"

"There's a parade . . . no, a march, in town. Ponce. I know it's Ponce. I've been there before with school. People are gathering in front of a building, and I see . . . you, Victoria. I see you. You're there."

I feel my hands begin to tremble. Jonathan continues.

"It's Palm Sunday. Some people are holding palms in their hands and signs that say *Patria*. Some are carrying Puerto Rican flags. There are women, men, children, babies, young, old. Everyone. So many people are in the procession. They're all dressed so nice. Church clothes. There are soldiers who are gathering in a formation in front of them. American soldiers. They have machine guns. They point them at the peaceful procession. The American soldiers start shooting into the crowd. There are screams. There's so much screaming. People are running. Some fall, trip over each other. There's blood pooling around them. There's blood filling the streets. It's a massacre in Ponce."

I stand up and scream, stomping my right foot against the floor. The house shakes. The table shakes. The world shakes. "No! No! No! No! No!"

I hear three knocks, and Abuelo's voice. "Victoria, wake up."

My eyes are closed, and hot tears are streaming down my face, and I see it, too. I look down to my white dress, and a shock rattles my body. There is a hole in the center of my chest and blood blooming. I turn to search for Mami, but she's on her back, her eyes open to the sky, her mouth opening and closing like a drowning fish. Blood squirts out of her neck. I scream for Papi and I witness a soldier hit him on the side of his head with the butt of his rifle. Papi falls to his knees.

"Please, no!" Papi shouts, begging, holding his hands in prayer.

The soldier presses the barrel of his gun to Papi's forehead and pulls the trigger. The back part of Papi's head bursts open. His body collapses to the ground. Fragments of his skull and what was in it, pink and bloodied clumps, scatter across the victims who are on the ground behind him. Many are not moving.

"Abuelo!" I cry. And I feel myself stumbling back, falling against Mami.

I raise my head and scream again and again for Abuelo. He's being restrained by a swarm of people. Arms are across his chest. Others from our procession are tugging at his shoulders and arms, trying to pull him away from the scene, trying to pull him away from me. There's shouting, screaming, crying. I hear the spray of machine guns and the metallic pinging of bullets falling to the ground. Abuelo continues shouting for them to let him through. His eyes are wide and wild. Blood is smeared across his face. He breaks an arm free from their grasp and he's reaching it out, he's reaching it toward me.

Dust kicks up. Mothers clutch their children. Someone yells for help. Someone else stops yelling altogether. I manage to raise an arm, and I'm reaching for him.

"Abuelo!" I scream so loud, louder than any birdcall or birdsong I've ever heard. "Abuelo!"

I hear him still above the roar of the gunshot blasts and the scrambling of feet.

He's calling my name, again and again and again. "Victoria! That's my Victoria!"

The world is all but muffled except for the sound of bullets flying and Abuelo's voice calling my name.

I close my eyes.

Three knocks.

"Victoria, wake up."

I open them.

"Yes, Abuelo."

We're all seated around the white table. Mrs. Rosario and Jonathan and me and my abuelo. I look down and I'm wearing my white dress. It's pretty and clean.

"Victoria," Abuelo says. "Mrs. Rosario agrees that after seeing what she saw today, Jonathan is a medium, too, like me. She now believes that the living can talk to the dead, and she wants to thank you for helping her see that."

Mrs. Rosario is silently sobbing into Jonathan's shoulder. He's patting her on her back and quietly saying, "I'm fine, Mami."

I don't know what to say. I'm so confused.

I feel Jonathan's hand reach out and find mine. He squeezes it, and it's a feeling that feels not here, just so far away.

"You can visit me whenever you like, Victoria," Jonathan says.

I open my mouth to say something, but then I turn to Abuelo. "But why would I visit with Jonathan?"

My grandfather smiles. "I'm dying, Victoria. I'm seventy-seven years old. It's 1950. You died in 1937 in the Ponce Massacre, with your mother and my son, your father. You've been with me as a ghost since that time, and it was out there, praying under the beating sun, working in Pellejas that I found you again. That I learned that I, too, am a medium. I don't know what the spirit world looks like, and I promise that after I die I will do all that I can to find you there, and your mami and papi, but I just want you to know that you also have another friend here in this house, in Jonathan. He likes the work of the jíbaro. He wants to live here in these mountains, Mrs. Rosario said. He'll be attending university in Ponce to study agriculture. After I die, Mrs. Rosario will take this land, and here she will build a house for Jonathan. So, when I'm gone, if you want to return here and don't find me, you at least will have someone to talk to."

I find myself squeezing Jonathan's hand back, across this far distance, and I'm glad I've met a friend.

A stillness settles over me. Not fear. Not quite. Just the beginning of understanding, like the hush that follows after a church bell's final toll. I look down at my hands, steady and pale. I look at Abuelo. "I died," I whisper, though it's so quiet I don't even know if I said it aloud. "Why did they have to kill me? Us?"

Abuelo is crying more now.

"And everything else that you've told me today," I say to my grandfather, "about Don Pedro, the flag, all they want to stop? And everything else that I've seen." I turn to Jonathan. "That we've seen together, the ships?"

"None of us forget, Victoria. People think dead means to be lost, forgotten. People believe that the dead can't tell stories, but they can. You can. Others. Like El Gigante Dormido, like you, like all who've died here, they're not gone. Not completely. They're still here with us. They may be sleeping, like our giant out there on the horizon, but one day they'll all awaken, and we remember everything."

Whispers from the Root

Lilliam Rivera

It was a dull, inconsequential Tuesday morning when Norma awoke to find her luminous brown eyes missing. A stunning woman of fifty-one years, slender in build and always put together, it was Norma's eyes that attracted many toward her. Amber irises reflected the copper strands of her hair. Her sad, expressive eyes left many to wonder what tragic history was stored behind them, so much so that a former lover composed a long and severe poem about them. But on Tuesday morning, Norma's eyes simply vanished and in their place were harrowing pools of liquid obsidian. Black eyes reflected a dark abyss, leaving Norma with a monstrous expression. Her lengthy eyelashes that she curled every morning were now exaggerated white lids framing the ominous orbs.

Her early morning routine had always been consistent, and today held no exception. The alarm went off, Norma took a sip from the glass of water on her bedside table, silently whispered a prayer, and walked to the bathroom. When she stood up to wash her hands, she caught her reflection on the medicine cabinet's mirror and gasped. Her knees buckled, but Norma held on to the edge of the cool porcelain sink. She forced herself to stand, all the while tremors coursed through her body.

Norma took in deep breaths and muttered to herself, "Cálmate. Cálmate."

There was no turning back now. Norma's fate was sealed long ago on that mournful day when Doña Mercedes approached her.

Although Norma's eyes were black, the sudden alteration only increased her vision. Norma could see everything so intensely, it became painful at first. As she returned to her bedroom, her dark eyes took in the vibrant colors. The reds were deeper, the greens richer. She rushed to the kitchen and pulled up a bruised orange from a wooden bowl. Norma could see inside the pulp, could travel through each juice vesicle, could peer into the oil sacs of the skin of the orange as if entering a vast world.

She dropped the fruit and pressed her body against the wall to keep from collapsing. The framed photos seemed to talk to her, relaying past conversations she once held with loved ones long gone. She could hear the waves of the ocean crashing against the rocks in Mar Chiquita. Smells of barbecue and sweat. Familiar voices laughing. Memories were made unbearable by this new accursed sight. She laughed hysterically, clutching the rosary beloved by her father. She was horrified but determined to move forward as planned.

Before leaving to catch her flight, she located the oversized designer sunglasses she had ordered years ago. When Norma arrived at LaGuardia Airport she came with no luggage, only the rosary, the old manila folder neatly tucked inside her purse, and the clothes she wore. She decided on a white blouse with matching linen pants, breathable material to withstand the heat.

The TSA agent, a young Black man, asked Norma to take off her sunglasses and stare at the screen for a photo. The agent's thoughts were on his upcoming break and of how his wife smiled after he whispered raw things to her the night before. He glanced at Norma's photo and compared it to her ID but didn't notice her owl eyes. All he saw was a beautiful older woman who matched identically to the ID she presented.

"Have a safe flight," he said.

Norma thanked him, put her shades back on to cover her unnatural appearance, and walked through the TSA checkpoint toward her gate.

In the Philly neighborhood of Southwark, a woman younger than Norma by five years swung her legs off the bed to find her feet missing. Claudia needed three alarms to wake her up. The first two she always ignored, pressing the *Snooze* button. The final alarm on the phone was her last chance. When the noise startled her awake, Claudia reacted the way she always did. She jumped off her bed in a state of panic, only this time her nonexistent feet weren't there to brace her. Claudia fell to the floor and screamed. She clutched at her knees, wailing at how her feet were now hooves.

"No, no, no!" Claudia cried. "Why? Why now?"

The hooves matched the color of the worn leather bag she'd had for many years: a saddlebag from the seventies owned by her mother. The photo by Claudia's nightstand depicted her mother holding the half-moon-shape design—one hand gripping the shoulder strap tight against her, the other hand holding up a protest sign. To conserve the heirloom, Claudia would take the bag to the local leather store to have it polished and repaired. Her mother's treasured accessory served Claudia for many years, though now it lay on a shelf in the crowded studio, displayed like a prized possession.

Time passed with Claudia still on the floor, lamenting her transformation and cursing the old woman's name. It was Doña Mercedes who told her what her future would look like, who'd whispered to her at the funeral, "When the day comes, your body will transform and you will fly back home." Claudia had been too full of grief to take her words seriously and thought the woman was just some strange, crazy person. But throughout the years,

Doña Mercedes appeared to her in dreams, repeating the same instructions.

The phone rang, and Claudia immediately knew it would be her work colleague checking in on her, wondering why she was late. She dragged herself to the bedside table, unwilling to use her new appendages, and searched for the ringing phone.

"Sorry I didn't call earlier," Claudia said, trying to sound composed. "I don't feel well. I tested with COVID . . . Yes, I'll be out at least for a week. I'm sorry for the inconvenience."

Claudia had never lied at work before. The job at the university was too important to her, but she had no other choice. She squeezed her eyes tight and prepared to lift herself up onto her strange new feet.

Her new legs elevated her height. No longer five feet, she towered in the room. Tears streamed down her face, but at least the animal body part gave her a stature she'd never had before. Claudia had always been a bit vain. Hours of Pilates ensured her voluptuous body was intact, with strong legs from daily evening runs.

She stood in front of the full-length mirror. The longer she stared, the more the new silhouette forged itself in her mind. She gathered her long black hair into a high ponytail, then bent over to feel the hardness of the hoof wall, running her fingers down to the hard sole. All the while, her despair grew.

The clopping noise Claudia made on the floor reminded her of a time when she was on the back of a galloping horse. She remembered how she rode seated in front of her mother and how their laughter joined the warm breeze. Back then, Claudia didn't understand how fleeting the day in Rio Grande with her mother would be.

A strong wind belted across the city. An imminent snowstorm determined to barrel through at any second. But all Claudia could do was moan. She'd believed that perhaps the omen would bypass her. She had never been told the date of when this accursed moment would happen. Claudia had thought maybe she could outlive it.

Angrily wiping away the tears, she went in search of the matronly maxi dress in white, shoved far deep into the back of her closet. A floor-gazing design meant to cover the hooves, the outfit was purchased years ago just for this dreadful occasion.

Dressed and ready, Claudia ordered a car service to take her to the airport.

In sunny Ybor City, Florida, Willie hadn't bothered taking off his dingy white work clothes before crashing hard onto his twin-size bed, so hard the fitted sheet pulled off, leaving him snoring atop the old mattress. The fifty-four-year-old had worked a late shift at the factory and his muscles were sore from lifting heavy packages. A job with barely any benefits, he made enough to pay for the room he rented, where he shared a bathroom with four other men. The halfway house was temporary. It's not to say this was the first halfway house Willie had lived in. There had been too many to count, but at least he was trying. Still, the house manager constantly reminded Willie that he was running out of chances.

Willie's three pairs of shoes (construction boots, two worn sneakers) were meticulously lined up by the door. A plastic lawn chair he borrowed from the backyard neatly held the clothes he would change into when he woke up. Canvases of various sizes showcasing his latest paintings dotted the grungy wall. Willie would never call himself an artist. He wouldn't dare be so bold, but his counselor pushed him to own it, own how he, too, was an artist like his father once was.

As he dreamed of an old woman standing by his unfinished paintings, Willie's nose started to itch. He reached up to touch his face and whelped from the painful scratch. He looked down to discover his fingers were gone. The palms of his hand, his hand as a whole, missing. In its place were five thick, giant spurs curled up from his wrist like a rooster. He sprang out of bed, ignoring the blood dripping from the cut. Willie took in shallow breaths as he stared at his newfound claws.

"Fuck," he said. "Holy shit. Fuck."

Willie had been preparing for this day for years. The premonition was foretold when he was a child living in Puerto Rico. It was at his father's velorio when Doña Mercedes pulled him aside. He had never spoken to her before, was afraid of her and how La Doña commanded authority. While others cried before his father's casket, Doña Mercedes led Willie away and told him there would be two others, strangers he would know nothing about, not their names or where they came from or how their histories were intertwined. Doña said, "All three of you will lose a part of your body you cherished the most. When that day comes, you will return to the island and speak to the one who caused your father pain."

He tried to examine the rest of his burly body, but with every touch, he left a mark, forgetting how razor-sharp the spurs were. Willie tried to recall what his counselor advised him to do whenever he got mad. He counted to a hundred, then he counted backward, but the anger escalated. Willie wanted to break shit.

This path he was about to undertake would only lead him right back to jail. All that he'd worked on, lost forever. The long lineage of grief he could never seem to pull up from under continued, but at least there was this rage. With the spurs, he tore down the art pieces he created, slashing the canvases of mountains he traveled with his father, and the depiction of the small farm the family once owned. His favorite piece was of the fighting roosters. His father loved those roosters.

"Fuck it," Willie said, his voice hoarse. "If this is what God wants, it's what I must do."

It took him a few tries before he could place the extra-large workman's gloves on to conceal his sharp claws. Willie waited until the house was quiet to sneak out, the necessary papers folded in his back pocket, proof of who was responsible for his father's death.

The three met in front of the historic home of Don Manuel González. The stately colonial house located in Old San Juan dated back from the mid-nineteenth century with a full-grown flamboyant tree in the courtyard. The Spanish-architecture home had fifteen-foot-high ceilings, iron wood beams, and black-and-white checkered floors. For many years, the location was used for commercial endeavors like music videos and was even named a landmark twenty years ago. When that happened, Don Manuel held a large celebration complete with a trio, a salsa band, and a celebrity actress who flew in from Miami, Florida, just for the occasion. It was a full weekend of dancing and drinking, with Don Manuel in the center of his home enjoying every second.

Standing in front of the estate stood Norma, Claudia, and Willie. The three looked at each other and only gave a slight nod of acknowledgment. It was late and the streets were peaceful except for the faint sounds of music playing from a nearby bar. The heavy wrought iron gate opened for them as if aided by a gust of wind, and the three entered without speaking a word to each other.

Inside, Don Manuel had trouble sleeping. The eighty-three-year-old sat in his living room listening to boleros sung by his favorite artist, Tito Rodríguez, as he was accustomed to doing so during those long nights. In his hand he held a glass of gin, neat, and sipped it slowly while contemplating how time was escaping him. How old friends have died or are dying. There was not much left to do but enjoy the treasures he surrounded himself with. The good he believed he'd done throughout his life. Don Manuel counted his blessings, but he failed to notice how the three had entered the room.

Startled, the old man stood up, angry at the intrusion.

"¿Qué quieren?" he said, unable to bely the undertone of fear. "What do you want?"

His English was proper, which was not surprising for someone who believed the language would save him, a language that allowed the walls to depict the vast timeline of Don Manuel's accomplishments. There was Don Manuel posing with various presidents: the Bushes, President Trump, President Obama, and Trump again. Laughing with Ferré and Barceló and Rosselló. All with sinister smiles. He intentionally glanced over to the framed photo of himself standing in front of one of his new factories as if to alert the strangers of his importance.

Willie walked toward the wall and addressed the awards and laminated newspaper articles. Before he lifted the picture of Don Manuel graduating from an American university, Willie peeled off his oversized gloves. With his long talons, he thrashed the photo against a table. He picked another and did the same.

"You . . . you can't do that! The police will be here any second," Don Manuel said. "Do you know who I am?"

Willie ignored his question and turned to the wall on the opposite side of the room, which was covered with artwork.

"You have such a beautiful collection. So many hanging here for you to enjoy," Willie said. "I remember this one in particular."

The piece, a blurry version of life on a farm, had a similar style to that of Willie's work. He walked to the old man, and with his claw pushed Don Manuel back until he plopped down onto the sofa. Willie caressed Don Manuel's face, leaving a bleeding wound.

"The artist's name is Pedro. He worked at the bookstore, but everyone came to him for his paintings. It was his job to create the pamphlets," Willie said. "Do you remember what you did to him? Don't worry, I'll remind you."

Norma pulled her sunglasses off, and Don Manuel groaned. He pressed his body against the armchair and tried to disappear into the fabric.

"My father's name was Rogelio, but everyone called him Yayo. He led a small ministry," Norma said, holding tight to the rosary. "When the new construction began on the beach, the residents came to him. He held meetings in the evenings to help them decipher the legal papers."

"I don't know anyone by that name," Don Manuel cried out. "Please go away."

Norma continued amid Don Manuel's protests. "Of course you know who he was. This was the file you made of him. You hired a photographer to take photos of him before and after the meetings. You documented the dates and times, who met with him, where they lived. Here's the file." She pointed to the documents, but the old man closed his eyes tight.

"Look at me!" Norma yelled.

Willie stood behind the man, dragging his claw across the cushions of the sofa. "Open your eyes or I will pluck them out like olives."

Don Manuel opened his eyes wide. Sweat soaked through his expensive linen shirt. The reason behind this sudden visit was slowly dawning on him.

"You signed the order to have my father meet a group in

Vega Baja that needed his help. He never made it there, did he?" Norma said. "His body was found a few days later. An accident, the newspapers said. But many knew otherwise."

"No! No! That wasn't me. This is a mistake," he pleaded. "Listen, I have money. I can pay you. I can pay each of you a lot of money."

Claudia, the youngest of the three, watched from a dark corner of the room.

"Let's just kill him," she hissed. "Why are we prolonging this?"

Norma walked over to her, but Claudia quickly looked away from those nightmarish eyes, wishing the woman would put back on her sunglasses.

"That's not how this is supposed to go. If it's not done right, our bodies will be stuck. Is that what you want?" she calmly asked. "Doña Mercedes was specific. We have to follow her instructions."

"I can't." Claudia tried hard not to cry. Her hooves made a loud clopping sound against the Spanish tiles as she paced. "This is all too much."

The old man's eyes frantically turned to her. "Please, help me," he said, his voice trembling.

Claudia clopped over to him and slapped his wrinkled face hard.

"My mother was murdered. Her name was Iris." Claudia lifted her leg and slammed her hoof down on Don Manuel's sandaled feet, causing the old man to tumble off the sofa and howl out in pain. "She worked as a secretary in one of your factories. She noticed how your workers dumped this oily liquid down the river," Claudia continued. "My mother was never quiet. She told everyone who would listen. Told them how it wasn't right. That this was our island. If we didn't say something, who would? These are the transcripts of all the calls she made. It's all right here." She rained the documents onto Don Manuel's back. "Do you remember now?" Claudia towered over the man. "They said it was her fault. She was too promiscuous, going out at all hours of the night. Her clothes were too tight, she was too much," she said. "But her coworkers at the factory never believed the stories. They knew what really happened to her. They were afraid if they said something they would lose their jobs, or worse."

Overcome by emotions, she moved away from the old man and returned to her corner. The articles never mentioned how much her mother loved to ride her horse. She was so free back then, even with a child in tow, a single mother. Iris was fearless. She didn't deserve the violence inflicted on her because of what she stood for.

Willie stopped himself from reaching out and trying to comfort Claudia, to offer her some words of condolence. The group meetings he attended taught him enough to just listen. Still, the anger he felt in Florida bubbled inside him. Like Claudia, he wanted to end this person's life more than anything, a thought that had festered for so long, ever since that upsetting conversation with Doña Mercedes.

"The funny thing is my father wasn't a good man. He left my mom for long stretches of time," Willie said to no one in particular. "He drank too much, smoked too much. The cops knew him by name. So there being a file on him was no surprise. Not a file. Wait, what did they call them?"

"Carpetas," Norma said. "The files were carpetas."

"Right, carpetas," Willie repeated. He stared down at his strange claws. His voice became harder. "My father and I, we're way more alike than I want to admit. He wasn't good at anything, but he was good at painting. And yeah, he helped those students with designing the pamphlets and making the protest signs. He was always down for a cause. Anything to fuck them pigs over."

Even as he recounted the events out loud, the real story of his father's life wasn't as noble as Willie wished it to be. His father worked at the bookstore because he wanted to get laid. He joked about it to Willie on one of the last times he saw him. The '70s were like that, he was told, people taking all kinds of risks. Una fiesta. On the night of his murder, his father believed he was meeting friends to hook up with the pretty college girls who frequented the bookstore.

"¡Ayúdame! ¡Por favor!" Don Manuel crawled to the front door at a snail's pace. His cries for help were useless in a house so cavernous.

"I don't know about you guys, but someone mailed the carpetas to me. The weird thing was no one knew I was staying at that spot, not my family, no one close. How did they know what address to use?" Willie asked. "It took me forever, years, to go through the papers, but when I did, the only name that stood out was yours."

Willie dug his claw into the back of the old man and dragged him to the center of the room. No matter what, Don Manuel González was their captive audience of one. The three recounted stories of their loved ones, moments they missed, joy they experienced, until the roosters sang. And when that happened, Norma, Claudia, and Willie left Don Manuel crumbled on the floor, his bruised body heaving with the searing memories of his past deeds.

Don Manuel's son Ramon was sending dick pics to a woman he had just met at a bar. The woman hadn't asked for any, but he sent them anyway. Ramon had been living in Los Angeles for the past five years. Whenever someone asked what his line of work was, he said he was a producer, but for the most part Ramon was just a man taking meetings, ingratiating himself with white men who considered him to be somewhat of a buffoon. They trotted him out whenever they needed a Latino "expert," but movie projects of brown people were rarely ever made. Everything was in perpetual development.

But Ramon's latest pitch was bound to be a hit. He was so confident. Not only was the movie a personal story, it had every Hollywood angle: a suspense thriller, a love dynamic, and a historical context perfect for awards season. He thought of the film as a sort of *Killers of the Flower Moon* meets *The Accountant*, but tropical. When Ramon pitched the project, he barely mentioned that it was set in Puerto Rico, not wanting to limit the scope. The hero didn't have to be brown. He could easily see a young Ben Affleck wannabe taking the role, bringing in the gravitas needed to depict the inner struggle of the character.

Ramon always name-dropped Salma, Jennifer, Zoe, Selena as interested parties. Their roles could take up way more space than the current script entailed, bringing the romance element higher. It wouldn't hurt to have a song by Selena or Jennifer. There were so many ways the movie could reach the desired audience. *Whispers from the Root: The Untold Story of Las Carpetas* is a film of a straightlaced man of faith bringing democracy to a small island ripped apart by communist infiltrators and the untamed woman on the other side of the political wall he falls in love with. Who didn't want to see that on the big screen? This movie had the potential to be a *Color Purple*, a *12 Years a Slave*, a *Titanic*.

The house Ramon rented was all floor-to-ceiling glass with beautiful views of downtown LA. He paid too much, but appearance meant everything in this city. He needed the right car, the right house, the right clothes. Whenever he spoke to his father, Ramon always made sure to explain how the meetings were going great and "promising." It was only a matter of time before someone took his pitch about the history of the carpetas and ran with it. He had already spoken to Bad Bunny's manager, who had a copy of the script. In the eyes of his father, Ramon was a success. A man who moved away from the island to Hollywood. So eager to sell a story. To sell.

When the budding actress didn't respond quick enough to his overtures, Ramon drank until he became sloppy and dragged himself to his king-size bed. He jerked off and quickly fell asleep. Surrounded by a cocoon of quiet, Ramon slept deeply and without worry. His whole life was like that. His father made sure of it. The best schools. Constant flow of money. Everything at his fingertips. But most importantly, the elder instilled the idea that whatever Ramon wanted was his for the taking. He just simply had to remove the obstacles.

Later that night, right before the first hints of dawn appeared across the sky, Ramon awoke to the sound of a horse entering his home. When he opened his eyes, he saw three dark silhouettes standing before him. Before he could get up to wield the bat he kept by his bed, a spur slashed across his chest.

"Siri, play 'Pecador' by Tito Rodriguez," someone said.

First, Ramon's tongue was yanked out of his mouth so he couldn't scream. Then, both his feet were trampled on so he couldn't run. Finally, Ramon's eyes were gouged out, but not before he could plainly see the three.

Fidelity

Alex Segura

The Miami News
April 25, 2025

MISSING FOR ALMOST TWO WEEKS, LOCAL WOMAN FEARED DEAD

Local mother last seen leaving her Kendall home Wednesday morning

The soccer ball whizzed by Susana Martinez's head, missing her by a little under an inch. She dodged, pure instinct. Years of toys being tossed at her and a brief, forgettable season playing soccer in high school kicked in. She had to remind herself to breathe as she turned to watch the ball skitter down the green of the park and toward an asphalt walkway near the small parking lot. She realized her mouth was open.

"You okay?"

Susana turned to the voice—low and calm, but weighted with worry and care. She couldn't deny that realization made her heart pump a bit faster.

"Yeah, I—uh," Susana said, pulling a strand of her shoulder-length brown hair behind her ear. She could feel her face reddening. He'd probably think it was a surprise. It was something else. "Just didn't see that coming."

Joe gave her a relaxed smile in return. He tugged back his salt-and-pepper hair, whistling a tune that felt familiar to Susana, but she wasn't able to place it. Susana couldn't deny that he was handsome. Fit. With sharp, blue-green eyes and an air of casual disregard that made his look and demeanor feel genuine. He reached out his hand and patted hers. A quick, fleeting touch. She felt her skin grow hot where his hand had been, and it had nothing to do with the powerful Miami sun beating down on all of them.

Susana smiled back, then tried to turn her attention to the game—well, not exactly a game. It was impossible to organize a gang of four-year-olds into any kind of organized sport. At least not for long. She and a few other parents, including Joe, were sitting on a small patch of grass at the park—watching as a handful of "coaches"—really, college-age kids who at some point decided to get side gigs teaching soccer—guided their respective children on how to kick the ball toward the net. Susana didn't envision her daughter, Jamie, becoming a soccer star—but a big part of parenting was finding things for your kids to do. Especially when they weren't at school. Susana's own private hell was those long, unexpected stretches at home—with no plans, no ideas, and no options. She tried not to just hand Jamie her tablet or turn on the television, but sometimes you had to. Though Susana preferred this. Something active. Something that ostensibly "taught" Jamie a skill or allowed her to socialize with other kids.

Susana leaned forward, stretching slightly. Feeling that familiar ache and pull. She wasn't young—but she wasn't old, either, she reminded herself. Closer to fifty than forty, she sometimes wondered if it'd been a good idea to have Jamie so late, but Oscar wanted to keep trying. They'd been so focused on the baby. The baby. After a miscarriage a few years back, Jamie seemed to appear out of a deep, dark fog—like an angel. She'd been the perfect baby. Sleeping well, eating well, doing all the things at the right time. It felt almost surreal. Like after years of pain and failure, they'd finally gotten a break. Susana knew she had to stay grateful for it, or she'd forget—like an alcoholic who still goes to meetings, desperate to recall what it was like, what brought them into the rooms. Susana didn't want to forget the fear and desperation she'd felt before Jamie arrived. The bleakness. Even now, when things felt almost . . . easy.

She made eye contact with Jamie, who was getting ready to kick the ball toward the net. She smiled at her daughter—her tough, defiant, and sensitive little kid—and gave her a quick thumbs-up. Susana never had this stuff as a child. Never did classes, summer camp, activities. She was lucky if there was even an adult around half the time. On summer breaks or days off, she got dumped at her grandparents' house in Kendall and had to fend for herself. She'd spent more time alone in one week than Jamie probably had her entire life. Parenting was different now, she tried to tell herself. The world had changed. Susana—and Oscar, when he was around—had to protect Jamie, guide her. Be thoughtful. Even if it meant they'd never have time for themselves.

She could feel Joe's eyes on her. Imagined them scanning her neck and looking up toward her face. He and his son—a bookish kid named Angel—were new to the soccer classes. Susana brought Jamie twice a week, though you could do more. And Joe always seemed to be there. Waiting, with a patch of grass clear next to him. She felt that familiar buzz when he'd pat the ground and smile as she and Jamie approached. Like saying, *Here. Here's your spot. Sit with me.*

And she did. Every Wednesday and Friday, she'd sit with Joe and they'd watch their kids bumble through practice—learning how to kick, how to move the ball down the field, how to pass—each lesson feeling completely new even though they'd been doing it for months now. Like Susana—the soccer teachers were just here to pass the time. It was something to do. To get the kids some exercise so they'd come home tired and pass out after dinner. That was the unwritten contract. Susana hadn't expected more. She hoped for an hour to scroll through her phone, catch up on emails, maybe sneak a few Instagram reels while Jaime ran around. That was the best-case scenario.

She hadn't counted on Joe.

Susana swallowed hard. She pulled out her phone and absentmindedly checked her email. Nothing. Promo offers. An Amazon package arriving. A note from her aunt in Broward. Susana used to do something. Before Jamie, even while they were trying, she had a job. Corporate PR wasn't fun, by any means—it was exhausting, all-consuming, and featured a cast of vile characters at every turn. But once Jamie was on the way, she and Oscar knew Susana would have to back away from the job. Just for a year or two, he'd said. That'd been five years ago. Susana understood it, of course. There would be no way to parent the way they wanted if she were working full-time, traveling, coming home late, answering emails at all hours. Plus, Oscar made a great salary working in tech. But the result was Oscar was working all the time, and Susana . . . wasn't. She was with Jamie. And if Jamie was sleeping or eating or at an activity, Susana was tending to the house. Cleaning. Cooking. Organizing. She was a housewife. As much as Susana loathed the idea, it was true. And she couldn't argue her way out of it. She chose this path.

What would her mami say? she wondered.

Te pensaste tan especial.

She would've been right. Susana did think she was special. Better than the gender paradigm her parents seemed to live in. Papi would work, Mami would work, and Mami would work some more—keeping up the house, tending to him, serving him. Until it stopped working. Then the tears came. The darkness. Susana had promised herself it'd never be like that for her. She'd meet a man who understood balance. Who wanted her to have a career. Who collaborated.

What happened?

She let out a quick sigh as she slid her phone back into her bag.

"Tough day?"

Susana turned to look at Joe. His eyes were on the field, his expression serene and happy. He was a consultant of some kind, he'd told her—he made his own hours. Susana knew he was married—she noticed the silver ring on his left hand. But he only mentioned his wife in passing.

"No, not really," Susana said, leaning back onto her palms, her fingers weaving through the dying blades of grass, pulling on them gently as she thought of what to say next. "I'm just . . . I dunno. I'm bored. We'll go to the store after this, make dinner, then . . . Oh, never mind . . ."

Susana shook her head slightly. Then his hand, on her arm now. Not moving.

"Hey, it's fine, I get it," he said, pulling back as she looked down at his hand, warm and coarse. "It's hard doing what you do. I get it."

"Do you?"

She looked at him now. His eyes seemed brighter for a second. Then a flicker of something else. A crackle of gray and white and black. Like static taking over the television screen. The hiss of that snow-like visual. For a second. She blinked and it was gone. Replaced by his chiseled face. The stubble on his cheeks. The crow's feet at his eyes.

I want to kiss him.

"Of course," Joe said with a nod, scoffing slightly. "I'm with Angel all day sometimes. It's a lot. Impossible to get any actual work done, either."

Susana let out a dry laugh.

"That's the thing," she said. "I don't have actual work to do. This is my work. This is my life. And sometimes . . . shit, this is going to sound terrible, but . . . it's boring as hell."

They stared at each other for a moment, letting it linger. She felt his eyes scanning her face, over her humorless smile, her slightly watered eyes, her knotty ponytail. She looked at him, too. The uneven stubble, the heat-glistening face, the crow's feet at the corner of each eye. It was like they were both mutually moving past their flaws, their blemishes—toward something else. Something new.

Susana looked at her hands. For a second, she thought she heard someone whistling.

Susana stuffed the receipt into her back pocket as she stepped out of the Publix supermarket on Coral Way. It was almost nine. It felt weird to be out this late, but Oscar had told her she needed some time to herself. A rare lightning bolt of clarity.

Bedtime had been rough. Lots of negotiating. Some raised voices. A Category Four tantrum. Tears. Susana wished these things were more infrequent, but they felt like furniture now. Most of the time, Susana realized she was bracing herself for impact. With Jamie. With Oscar. With her phone. Every relationship was built on trying to minimize damage.

"Where's the fun in that?" she muttered to herself.

She didn't hear the woman running toward her.

She did, however, feel hands—dry, rugged hands—grasping her arms tightly.

Susana looked up to see a woman's face—what she assumed was a woman's face—gaunt, eyes wide, mouth agape . . . like someone screaming but with no sound. Though there was something else, too. She looked like a caricature of a person—her face stretched out, worn and wasted, not like a zombie but—

Like how I feel.

Susana tried to pull back, but the woman's grip felt permanent, felt like it was spreading. She looked down to see the woman's hands. Susana tried to scream but couldn't form the words. There was some kind of black, bulbous liquid spreading up and over Susana's arms. She could feel it covering her, slick and hot.

Then the sound of something clattering to the floor.

"You're next, mija . . . Eres la próxima . . . mi próxima . . . No lo toques . . . No lo hagas, niña . . ."

Then Susana screamed, a loud, shrill noise—the kind of primal yell she hadn't let out since she was a child, watching a frightening movie or being surprised by her older brother in the dark. She pulled back, hard, a dizziness and strange euphoria enveloping her. Her vision went black for a second, that gray-white static, the white noise sound, an ache in her chest . . .

Then nothing.

Susana looked around. The woman was gone. The receipt was on the floor. All she could see was an older woman, hand to her chest, other hand pushing a wobbly shopping cart.

"¿Estás bien, mija?" she asked.

"Sí, yes . . . Sí . . . I'm fine," Susana said, gasping for breath, hands on her knees as she leaned forward, certain she was going to throw up.

She looked at the dark asphalt. She saw the glimmer of something. A small bracelet. Gold. A tiny picture of a child, a little boy. Smiling. Susana ran the bracelet through her fingers and listened. To the cheap rubber sliding away from Susana and toward the parking lot. To the honking and screeching of Coral Way. The shrill chirp of a crow in the distance.

Eres la próxima.

• • •

"What do you mean you don't argue?"

Joe's question hung between them as Susana took a sip from her latte. It was a delay tactic. One she'd shared with her clients over the years. If you need an extra second to think of an answer, take a sip. Or say "good question." It'll buy you a second, maybe less. But it'll help.

Why didn't she argue with Oscar? Susana didn't know the answer. At least not cerebrally. She just felt it. There was no point in arguing. They'd made their choices, and now here they were—their choices activated: the child, the house in the suburbs, the job, the lack of a job. Little mini-choices made without the proper context. Only now, to be seen as part of a bigger, more complicated whole.

"We just don't," Susana said with a slight tilt of her head as she placed her cup down. The coffee shop—a tiny spot on Bird Road and 92nd Ave in southwest Miami—was nondescript. Almost surreal. When Joe suggested it by texting her randomly on a Tuesday morning, Susana had to struggle to remember if she'd ever been inside. And upon entering, she was certain she hadn't been. She wasn't sure why she was here. Still annoyed and out of breath from a difficult drop-off, she hadn't expected Joe to reach out. Had struggled to remember when they'd even exchanged numbers. But his name appeared on her phone display: SOCCER JOE.

She felt uncomfortable in the blouse and "work" pants she'd shoved on as she raced to meet him at the coffee shop, her day suddenly going from mundane and gray to . . . something else. The fabric seemed to cling to her sweaty body. She wondered if she'd checked herself. If she'd even put deodorant on before walking Jamie out the door. It was too late now.

Why am I here?

Joe leaned forward, his eyebrows popping up.

"All couples argue," he said, his voice an intimate whisper. He even looked around, as if he were sharing some kind of state secret. The kind of intel that would get them both killed. "My wife and I fight at least once a week. If we don't, something's wrong."

Susana leaned back.

"You never talk about your wife."

Joe seemed surprised by the comment.

"Of course I do."

"No, you don't," she said. Susana felt empowered now. She was driving the conversation. The narrative. He had invited her here, but she was in charge. "Why is that?"

Now it was Joe's turn to pause.

As much as Susana let herself go—let her body sink and drown in the routine of her life: the groceries, the cleaning, the shuttling around, the meetings with parents, the park—she was not dense. She'd spent years in conference rooms, at events, and taking meetings with every kind of man. Good, bad, the whole spectrum. But she didn't have a read on Joe yet. Maybe that had been the appeal. Unlike the others—the creeps, the weirdos, the introverts—Joe seemed happy in his skin. Didn't seem bothered one way or another. She wanted to crack the shell. Wanted to see what was under there. What living, breathing creature waited for her beneath the surface. But now she wasn't sure if that was a good idea.

What am I doing here?

She watched as he rubbed his chin. Watched his expression change from something like confusion to . . . resignation?

He frowned before talking.

"I don't think coffee is enough for this conversation."

Susana checked her phone. It was barely ten in the morning.

"You're kidding, right?"

Joe dropped a few dollars on the table and stood up.

"Maybe," he said as he waited for Susana to get her bag. "Maybe not."

Even when it felt like every waking hour was taken up by diapers, wipes, meals, drawings, everything, there were still pockets of time.

Hours after the sound of the vacuum had ended, as Susana sat in the living room, waiting for Oscar to get home.

Early in the morning, after finishing a hasty workout, sitting on the floor—sweat dripping down her body, her jagged breathing the only sound, thudding in her skull.

The crackle and hiss of the monitor as she watched it, assuring her Jamie was napping.

In those moments, Susana had time to think. Not rational thoughts. Not thoughts about her career, what her parents were doing, what trips they should take.

She thought about that woman. That monstrous, wasted shell of a woman.

It would've been easy to shrug it off. A bad trip. A delusion. Her meds kicking in wrong.

But Susana Martinez wasn't stupid. She believed her eyes. Believed all her senses. That woman had been real.

Until she wasn't.

Susana felt the bracelet. Let it run through her fingers.

Then she opened her laptop, followed by her browser. The tabs seemed to be waiting for her. News articles. PDFs of old, long-out-of-print books. Of stories her mami used to whisper to her before bed. Of demonios and brujas. Of a whistling, broken man. El Silbón.

She felt the wineglass touch her lips. Felt the cold chardonnay slide down her throat as she clicked on her laptop's worn trackpad.

She looked at his warm, welcoming face again and smiled.

"It'll be worth it, I promise—this wine is something else," Joe said, his house keys jostling in his hand. Susana could smell his cologne now. Some kind of Dolce & Gabbana. She felt dizzy. She hadn't even had a sip of wine. Not yet.

Why am I here?

He opened the door and ushered her inside. She thought she imagined him taking one last, fleeting glance outside as she walked in, as if checking to see if those nosy neighbors were on the prowl again.

She felt his hand. Warm, rough on her back. A slight shove. He was impatient. The energy between them was different now. Things had moved, ever so slightly. From the theoretical to the real. They weren't just coincidentally in the same place. They hadn't just happened to see each other. Choices were made. Plans. Drinks.

She felt him grip her shoulders and push her against the closed door. She could smell him now—sweat and fear and wine all mixed together. She let her body hit the flimsy wood of the door, the door to his tiny house, to this place that clearly didn't provide shelter for a family. This two-bedroom bungalow that was home to just one man. This man.

His face was close to hers. The Altoid-laced breath hovering over and around her face. His mouth inches from hers.

"I couldn't wait," he said, his voice urgent, hoarse, a rough grunt. "I just—"

She saw the road now, in her mind, a big fork—two paths

jutting out in different directions. One path was good, righteous. Correct. *The Way To Be*. The other was darker, confusing, fueled by lust and hunger and an itching need for something different.

She didn't move. She didn't want to. She didn't want to decide. Passivity worked in degrees.

He kissed her, the stinging stubble above his lips brushing against her face. The kiss wasn't tender. It was harsh, hungry—his tongue sliding into her mouth like a train shaken off its track. She let him in. Let his hands tighten on her shoulders. Let his body lean into hers. She felt all of him, every bit, pulsing and wanting.

She hadn't done anything, she told herself. *He kissed me*, she thought. *I'm just here.*

She was still in the range. Susana had done nothing wrong.

His hands roamed—over her body, down her arms, over her cheeks—her blouse tugging. Time was moving forward. She could feel herself moving in unison with him. She was kissing him back now. Her hand was at the nape of his neck. Her mouth was opening. Her hand was on his hip.

Susana was doing something now.

She was doing something wrong.

All the shame flooded into her. This was *bad.* How could she? What would they thi—?

She shoved the thoughts away. *Fuck them.*

But her thoughts were replaced by a whistling sound that seemed to come out of nowhere, then disappeared, making her doubt its existence. It was there. Wasn't it?

"Yes," he mumbled under his breath, hastily, between kisses, his fingers darting over her blouse, unbuttoning it quickly, expertly. "God, I've wanted this so badly—"

She'd wanted it, too. She knew this. From the moment she'd seen him on the field, as he ushered that child—not his son—

toward the coaches. From the moment they'd exchanged a warm smile and sidled up next to each other. She'd let the fantasy progress. Let the narrative of this pretend reality unfurl. It helped pass the time, she thought then. Something to think about. Something to pine over. While everything else felt staid and stiff and boring.

But this was something else.

And she was prepared.

She watched his eyes—watched them shift from blue-green to something red, something . . . inhuman. Felt his fingers grow sharper. Felt them slice into her bare arms. Lightly at first. Not drawing blood. Her yelp of pain sudden but also pleasant. Her tongue ran over his teeth—the incisors sharper now, pointed and hungry.

And the whistling. She could track it. It was coming from him.

"I'm so glad you came inside," he said. That powerful, hoarse voice was gone now, replaced by something lighter, desperate, and ethereal, unlike anything Susana had ever heard. "I'm so glad . . ."

But she'd anticipated this.

She pulled the blade out. Short, stout, silver—like the one in the story. The one about the girl, tracked by the ghost. El Silbón. The Whistling Man. A selfish prick who'd killed his own father because he didn't do as he'd asked. A self-centered man in a world full of self-centered men. Just another dude desperate to get what he wanted, no matter the cost.

Did it matter that at some point, she'd wanted this, too? Susana thought. The taste of something—someone—different? The excitement of the chase? The spark of flirting and talking and breathing in someone else? Of a fantasy inching toward reality?

The whistling was interrupted by the *schlorp* sound as the

blade slid into Joe's midsection. His red eyes widened in shock. The whites were gone, replaced by a gray that felt unnerving to Susana, even now, weeks later. His ivory-white teeth bared in anger.

She twisted the blade, just like the book had said. The whistling grew louder—shaky, though, afraid. The book said this would happen, too. She thought back to the dusty volume—*Hechizos Imortales*—she'd found in the box in the garage from Mami's house. The box she hadn't opened in years. The one she'd avoided. The book she remembered—buried in the back of Mami's closet, under the coats and dresses and shoes, a sheen of dust covering it.

Susana remembered pulling it out, blowing the coat of dust away, her tiny fingers turning the aging pages. She didn't understand it then. She didn't really understand it now. But she knew enough. Her mind raced back to that night—the wine coursing through her. The bracelet tinkling in her fingertips. The picture on the Image Search. The flash of memory. The click of the garage lightbulb. The dust and sweat as she moved boxes, making her way toward the back wall. The last box. The rough marker across the top: *LIBROS IMPORTANTES*.

Susana leaned forward, feeling Joe—or the creature that was Joe—wince at the motion. The blade was so deep in him that she could feel his blood caking on her hand, her fingers pushing into the wound. She could feel inside him—his skin torn open and squishing around her fingertips as the blade turned. She thought she could hear his insides tearing, the blade spinning inside him like some kind of torturous fan, gutting him while he watched.

He was crying. The tears red, black almost, streaming down his sharper features, over his gray, ashen skin. The cologne was gone—the smell replaced by something coppery and toxic. She placed her lips on his and felt it—an energy, like a gust of wind—blowing through him and into her. She let it fill her body, felt the energy crackle and simmer across her skin. Then his limp frame hit the ground with a low thud.

Susana wiped her mouth with the back of her hand, blood smearing over her face. She looked down at it. More red than skin. She smiled and instinctively licked her lips. She then watched as Joe's body seemed to recede, folding in on itself, his form fading into the cheap carpet of his pathetic little bachelor pad—growing smaller, as if melting or turning to dust. He didn't matter anymore. Not much did, really.

Susana felt different. Her vision sharper. She couldn't hear the whistling anymore, but she could hear so much more: the rustling of branches in a squirrel's nest. The cursing of a driver two blocks away. A child screaming in a car seat down on Bird Road.

Her skin tingled. She looked down at her hands—saw the tiny bracelet, sunlight glinting off it from the bay windows in the main room.

She tightened her fingers around the bracelet, making a fist. She felt the metal bend and pull. She opened her hand. The bracelet was gone, replaced by a gold dusty paste. She let it drop to the floor. Joe was gone, too. A smear of red and black the only sign that something happened here.

"Yo soy la próxima," she said, loud enough for only her to hear.

Susana Martinez smiled. She straightened her blouse and turned around. She opened the flimsy door and walked out.

As she made her way to her car, parked behind Joe's forgettable Hyundai, she started to whistle.

We Are Gathered Here Together

Diana Rodriguez Wallach

"The community of Spring Mills, Pennsylvania, has come together in mourning today to pay respects to one of its youngest members. Sabrina Mendez, fifteen years old, tragically took her own life last week . . ." At the sound of a slamming car door, Katie's news report caught sticky in her throat. She raised a palm, halting the video package she was recording for the 6 p.m. broadcast, and squinted through a blanket of rain.

As I live and breathe . . . Katie glared, shocked to see that the entire grieving family wasn't already gathered inside the funeral home. The deluge blurred the middle-aged couple now sliding past packs of teenagers with teeth chattering in a cold more brutal than her ex's heart.

Is that woman wearing a veil? A tiny pillbox cap with a swoop of black mesh covered the relative's eyes as she slunk next to the reincarnation of Cary Grant, decked in a gray brimmed hat cattywampus atop his head. A massive golf umbrella added to their concealment. Katie's pulse quickened. Not a single reporter had snagged a quote or a photo of the family all week. Given the attention the case had garnered, their invisibility was downright impressive. Yet here they were—late and in the thick of the crowd.

"Lord, give me strength, or give me bail money." Katie peeled a platinum lock of hair from the foundation on her cheek. "Let's go, Juan."

The cameraman slowly shifted, a thick stream of molasses

pushing through his veins and mixing with his heaping desire not to see "a Southern hick" (yeah-huh, she'd heard him) replace his beloved pals, Chaz and Natasha. The two had been holding the chairs behind the anchor desk since the days when TVs had antennas. But Katie hadn't clawed herself all the way from Alabama to Indiana to Michigan to Ohio and now finally to Philadelphia (a top ten news market!) just to play second fiddle to a couple of boomers who didn't know when to retire.

"Is that the mom or the aunt?" Katie struggled to catch the woman's profile. The family was Puerto Rican, with a striking resemblance of curly black hair, pointy features, sharp bones, and skin paler than paste in a kindergarten class. "I think it's the aunt."

Katie's foot slid, inches of rain soaking a high heel she could in no way afford to replace. In fact, if she didn't get this promotion soon, she'd be selling hugs on a street corner. Juan lumbered behind, still piddling with his camera.

"Hey, how do you say 'aunt' in Spanish?" Katie asked. "Is it tía or tita?"

Juan's underbite protruded, no words escaping. But he'd heard her. Ever since the evening news producer told Katie he "wanted to talk about her future," Juan had upped his incompetent act and had developed a massive case of selective hearing whenever assigned to her stories. Katie was thirty-five years old, and Lord knows she'd paid her dues twofold, so she was not about to let some man hold her back now.

"Ms. Mendez, Ms. Mendez!" Katie rushed toward the woman and extended a microphone. "We're so sorry for your loss." Katie paused a beat, then offered her gentlest smile. "What would you like the world to know about Sabrina? Did you notice any signs of depression? Did the school do enough to intervene when the bullying was first reported?" Katie curled her questions around a Southern drawl.

The aunt stopped her march, chin twisting in her direction.

"Bless her heart"—Katie thickened her accent with an extra dose of sugar—"but Sabrina's best friend, Naomi—she suffered a severe bullying incident earlier this year. On social media. Did you know about that? From what I've heard, there were no consequences for the teens behind it. Now Naomi's closest friend has taken her own life. It's downright tragic. Are you worried that teens in this community are in danger?"

The aunt made sure to angle her face away from the camera, and her lips didn't twitch, let alone speak. If Katie had to put her hand on a Bible, she'd swear that the aunt wasn't even breathing. But then the woman's skeletal fingers tightened around the elbow of the lanky man holding her umbrella. The tall gentleman stayed mute, his muscles unnaturally still and his posture so perfect his wool overcoat fell to his knees in a line straight enough to trace. They offered nothing for a TV audience.

This week, most news reports focused on the school's lack of action. There must be someone to blame, you see. And after getting a few moments alone with the ninth-grade counselor at Spring Mills High, it was clear his elevator did not go all the way up to the top floor. But then the family didn't bother to release a statement. There were no pleas for justice. No tears on camera. Not even an "in lieu of flowers . . ." donation request. It made Katie wonder if these people cared enough about the girl to clock a severe case of depression. Maybe it was neglect.

Katie's microphone grazed the aunt's cheek. "What do you have to say to other families out there? To the parents of the bullies? Or the ones doing *nothing* while their innocent children are being tormented? Do you wish y'all would've done more?"

Finally, the aunt grunted. *Juan better get this on camera . . .* Katie leaned closer, catching a glimpse of the woman's expression, which was madder than three shades of hell. What color were her eyes? The veil made it hard to decipher, but Katie swore she spied a flash of crimson. It must've been her matte lip.

The couple turned stiffly, soundlessly, then sped toward the funeral home's entrance, so fast you'd think their shoes had wheels; they practically floated. Teens jerked out of the way, an umbrella spoke nearly jamming a girl in the eye.

"Bye, y'all!" Katie called with an extra bit of twang. Then she lowered her voice. "Well, that family's holding it together about as good as my first marriage."

Katie scanned the swelling crowd. The family might not want to talk about a fifteen-year-old girl's untimely death, but she'd bet her teeth that the teens huddled nearby would be happy to see themselves on-screen.

Katie extended her mic to the blondest girl in the pack. "Hi, honey, did you know Sabrina? Or her friend Naomi? What do you want to say about the bullying scandals that Sabrina and Naomi went through? Do you think the events are connected?"

"Omigod, be so for real right now, it's bad enough we have to be here for this, but it's disgusting outside!" Harper popped her glossy pink lips. Ashy-blond locks—shiny from a recent hair mask—cascaded over her shoulder with a floral whiff of hair perfume that had become her signature scent.

"Figures Sabrina would be annoying even in death," snipped Bella, Harper's best friend, adding a little half snort. Then Bella leaned forward from the back seat, her fakest smile pointed directly at the driver's side. "I'm just kidding, Ms. White."

Harper's mom ground her teeth. *Just say it, Mom: "Your friends are so obnoxious."* It was her mother's constant refrain. Meanwhile, she talked shit at her "book club" every Saturday night over clinking wineglasses.

Their SUV slid into a spot, windshield wipers clucking.

"When I die, I hope it rains like this at my funeral. It's giving depression in the best way," Bella said, smoothing a hand down her low bun. She wore a string of white pearls and a black cotton sheath styled directly from a "What to wear to a funeral" fit-check online.

Harper, however, was stuck in the same black satin minidress she wore to her cousin's bar mitzvah, because her parents were too cheap to buy her a new outfit. And there was no way Harper was going to leave the house in pleated pants and an old-lady cardigan borrowed from her mother's closet.

"This is a sad day, girls, act like it." Mom's words were clipped, and her stare was glassy, but not from crying. Harper knew exactly what was in her mother's mug at breakfast—and it wasn't coffee.

"We're not idiots. Chill." Harper rolled her eyes, tucking her straightened hair into the plaid hood of her raincoat. There were TV reporters outside.

"Look, there's Libby!" Bella patted Harper's headrest. Three quick thuds.

Before Harper could even respond, Bella swung open her car door and screeched into a wild wind. Rain gushed in sideways as the umbrella unfurled. Then Bella darted madly toward their strawberry-haired friend, who was standing too close to Will. Again.

"I'll be sitting with the Montgomerys. Do not embarrass me in there." Mom pointed a French-manicured nail in Harper's face, yanking her daughter's attention away from her boyfriend of nearly a year. Then Mom popped a mint into her mouth. *Good luck with the wine breath.*

"The news is already rehashing stories about that Naomi girl." Mom's tone was curt. "And so help me, if that crap comes back around and our name gets dragged through the mud *again* . . . Do you have any idea what that will do to your father? He's up for partner—"

"I know!" Harper yelped, shoving open the car door and ending the redundant lecture that forever missed the point—it was *Naomi* who had cheated with *Harper's* boyfriend. Did everyone forget that?

If the girl couldn't handle a picture of her tongue down someone else's throat (like, deep throat, it was gross) going around school, then maybe she shouldn't have done it. All Harper did was share the image online from an anonymous account. And zoom in on a few choice body parts. It wasn't her fault the post went viral. Naomi was the slut. Besides, Harper forgave Will, which was nice of her; she should get credit for that.

Rain slathered Harper's bangs to her forehead, and she yanked her hood tighter, sprinting faster toward her ninth-grade classmates shivering beneath the funeral home's awning.

"Let me in, let me in!" Harper dove into the crowd, her breath frosting in the December air. "Is there really a line?"

"Uh, yeah." Bella scrunched her nose. "Apparently, having a packed funeral isn't the flex people think it is."

"Have you seen her page?" Libby held up her screen. " 'Sabrina, we'll miss you!' 'We're so sad you're gone!' 'Girl, it won't be the same without you!' "

Bella scoffed. "She went to this school for, like, two months! I'm sorry I'm not crashing out over what happened. I mean, it's sad, obviously, but we hardly knew her."

"Because she sucked," Harper blurted, her mom finally out of earshot.

Back in October, Sabrina Mendez showed up at Spring Mills High and promptly befriended Naomi Rivera, acting like the two were insta-bonded merely because they were the only Latinas in their grade (which is actually kinda racist, because Sabrina didn't even attempt to hang out with anyone else). Then they strutted through the halls with matching black hair, too-tight cropped shirts, and stupidly long fingernails.

"Omigod, are you seriously still pissed?" Libby's eyebrows quirked up.

"The girl was unhinged! Sabrina dumped milk on me, on purpose, in front of witnesses, then acted like *I* was bullying *her*." Harper cocked her head.

Sabrina had turned feral that day. All Harper did was make a few jokes. But the look in Sabrina's eyes in response wasn't just anger, it was . . . off (maybe drugs?). She was practically growling with her fingers clawed, freakish green nails ready to scoop Harper's eyes out. Talk about straight out the hood. Harper wasn't going to fight anyone. And a video would have clearly shown that, but Bella and Libby caught none of it, claiming their phones "had a glitch." Yeah, right. Two matching warped videos?

Not to mention, Sabrina was lacking a single reason to even be involved in the whole Naomi mess. She hadn't lived here when the pictures went viral. And the school had found zero evidence that Harper had done anything wrong, at least officially. (She knew how to cover her tracks online.) That was why Harper's dad had threatened to sue. If Naomi ended up alone in the cafeteria after being called out, she only had herself to blame. (And no, Harper didn't believe the crap about Naomi being too drunk to remember hooking up with Will.)

Given that Naomi and Sabrina were *such* good friends, the girl should be standing front and center at this funeral, greeting every guest. But Harper hadn't seen her since the news of the suicide broke. *Who are you going to blame now, Naomi? You're the one who didn't notice your BFF was about to off herself.*

"Hey, babe." Will's breath brushed warm against Harper's cheek and his arms locked around her waist.

Nice of you to say hello. She'd seen him cozy next to Libby. "Where you been?"

"Waiting for you." He clanked his teeth, pretending to chomp a piece of her, and Harper instantly melted.

"You guys want to hang in my basement after?" Libby cut in, eyes on Will. "My parents are at work."

"Sweet! Can't believe we got the day off for this." Will twisted his head. "Hey, Brett, we're going to Libby's!"

"Can we go now?" Brett asked, surrounded by half the boys' lacrosse team.

"No, my mom's inside," Harper said, pulling Will's focus back to her. "I have to stay."

"I won't leave ya, babe." Will pecked her nose.

"Speaking of moms, have you seen Sabrina's parents?" A giggle slipped into Libby's voice.

"No, what?"

"They have on, like, black veils and old-timey hats."

"I know, it's so embarrassing!" Bella squealed. "Do you think it's a Puerto Rican thing?"

"Maybe." Libby rolled her eyes.

"You know, we should post something, to look, like, respectful." Bella pulled her lips back, exposing her gums. "Do I have lip gloss on my teeth?"

"No." Harper shook her head and yanked her phone from her jacket pocket. Her bangs were a frizzy mess, which meant her friends would likely repost this shitty picture on her birthday just to make her feel ugly. But at least if she took the photo herself, then she could pick which image went online.

"Squeeze in." Harper angled the camera to catch as many Spring Mill students as possible. "No one smile."

"Duh," said Will.

"We know," grunted Libby, squishing herself close to Harper's boyfriend.

The shutter clicked repeatedly, Harper's bangs worse in each shot. She picked the best one and tapped out a caption: *Can't believe this is real. #sosad #RIPsabrina #wemissyousabrina*

Harper pressed *Post* and heard the click of high heels rise up behind her. She turned, expecting to see her mom's disapproving face again, but instead she landed eye to eye with a reporter sporting black eyeliner on her lower lashes that ID'd her as someone born in the last century. The woman shoved a microphone at Harper's mouth. "Hi, honey, did you girls know Sabrina?" The reporter had a Bama-Rush accent that Harper absolutely loved. "Or her friend Naomi? What do you want to say . . . ?"

Harper's smile grew wide as the camera zoomed in.

Greg's fingers shook, palms clammy. He couldn't believe his husband hadn't come with him to this funeral. A fucking budget meeting? Greg had to walk through that lobby alone! The judgment in the eyes of his fellow faculty members made him almost turn around. One person even whisper-shouted, "Isn't that the counselor? The one who shit the bed?" *Are you fucking kidding me?*

Greg was a ninth-grade school counselor with a case load of 466 kids, nearly twice the national recommendation. But did the superintendent mention that in her press conference? No! Instead, she had the audacity to stand in front of a microphone and say, "We'll be conducting a thorough investigation to identify any failures with our procedures or faculty." *Or faculty. Really?* How about the administration's failure to properly staff the school! Or the parents' failure to pay attention to their own kid!

The district expected him (alone!) to deal with the mental health and trauma of the entire freshman class while also handling attendance, grades, state testing, class schedules, etc. The board didn't even know what Greg did, because if they did, they wouldn't toss a bunch of stress balls into his office and call those "resources." Honestly, if everyone didn't shut up soon, Greg was going to give those reporters something to talk about. There was no way he was going to be the one blamed for this girl's death.

Greg leaned against the faded wallpaper, hiding behind a potted plant, its leaves the size of elephant ears. Speaking of which, were those birds-of-paradise near the casket? What an odd flower for a funeral. Maybe it was a Latino thing? Or Hispanic? Latinx? Goddamn sensitivity training.

Greg's eyes slid to the family. He'd expected hysterics, but these people barely looked like they were breathing, let alone choking back sobs. Not that he was going to tell anyone how to grieve, because, contrary to popular belief, he was *not* a therapist. Yes, kids shared their problems with him (all the fucking time), but Greg couldn't diagnose shit. That literally wasn't his job. But if he pointed this out, the parents called him useless. And no, he was not going to apologize for not being able to predict the future.

Obviously, Greg knew that Sabrina Mendez was friends with that girl who got cyberbullied last year. But Greg had stayed out of the whole Naomi Rivera situation for good reason—it had happened off school property, on a weekend. And of course, the pictures were embarrassing and cruel, but they didn't involve school resources. Greg wasn't a tech wizard; he couldn't pull them down from the cloud. But he *did* listen to Naomi when she'd cried. And he did give her some honest advice—she had to take a little responsibility. The girl had made some bad choices at that party, and now there were consequences. That's life. Still, Greg was happy for Naomi when she finally made a friend. He had no reason to think the new girl was in any distress. Aside from giving Sabrina her schedule, the only time he saw her was after a lunchroom incident between herself, Naomi, and Harper White. In it, *Sabrina* had poured milk on *Harper*. So no one was innocent, yet they all refused to take accountability. Including their parents.

Families kept emailing: *There should be a zero-tolerance policy for bullying!*

Gee, thanks for the tip. Did they really think he didn't know what it was like to be bullied? Back in the '80s, some kid threw rocks at Greg's head every day when he walked home from school. Sucking it up was an unfortunate rite of passage. How the hell was he supposed to know that this one girl couldn't take it? That was the parents' job. But of course everyone in the district was too chickenshit to say it. They all acted like *he* should have done more. *He* should have followed up. Even the news media focused on him: *Bullying and Abuse Rampant in Spring Mill* and *Girls' Cries for Help Go Unanswered.*

Abuse? Cries for help? If Greg had the power to stop cyberbullying, he'd be a billionaire.

"Hey, Greg," said a deep voice, a tap nudging his shoulder. "How you holding up?"

Jamal, the PE teacher, was staring down at him with drippy basset hound eyes. A snotty tissue was pressed to his nose.

Shit, Greg should look more upset. He sniffled twice before speaking. "Hey, sad day."

"I can't even look at the family." Jamal nodded toward the line of relatives—the parents, an aunt and uncle, and Sabrina's two siblings, who also went to Spring Mills High but were in different grades, so they were *not* Greg's problem. "You know, no one's blaming you. There's no way you could have known." Jamal clapped a large hand on Greg's shoulder.

Are you fucking serious? This gym teacher (who somehow got paid more than Greg) had the nerve to look him straight in the eye as though he were being considerate. Heat spread up the back of Greg's neck, pulse rattling.

"I'm gonna go talk to the family." Greg spat the words through tight lips and shook off the man's sweaty palm. An exhale puffed hard through his nose as Greg marched down the aisle's red-and-gold-patterned carpet, stopping behind a mom in a way-too-tight-for-a-funeral black dress.

For the first time, Greg caught a glimpse of the body. Oh, God, there was an actual body.

He'd never been to an open-casket viewing before. Most Jewish services included a closed, no-frills pine box or maybe cremation. But this girl was just lying there, out in the open, like Snow White on display for a goddamn prince. And her skin was so fucking pale. Obviously, there was no blood in it, from the embalming process, but still. He'd never seen skin so white. And her lips were rosy, maybe too rosy, and shaped in a grin. Or a smirk. Had they been sewn into that expression?

Greg couldn't comprehend a family standing next to their smirking, dead daughter. He averted his eyes. *This is not my fault. This is not my fault . . .* What was he supposed to do when he got to her? Pray over her corpse?

Someone coughed behind him, and Greg realized the line had moved forward a few paces. He was holding it up. He was causing a problem, of course he was.

I can't believe they just lost their CHILD. There were no words for this. Stephanie struggled to imagine what she'd want someone to say to her in this situation, then she immediately stopped, because she didn't want to risk putting that thought into the Universe. *Whoosah.*

She clutched her pack of travel tissues. They were the cheap kind without lotion, and they were making her nose redder (her concealer was totally gone). But the little packs fit perfectly into her evening bag. In retrospect, she should have realized that the funeral home would plant tissue boxes around. Her aunt's service had been held here three years ago. No, wait, Stephanie had the Ford back then, so it must've been four years ago. Anyway, her cousins had ordered this arrangement of giant calla lilies, the white ones with the curling petals that had been in her aunt's bridal bouquet. It was a beautiful touch, and they'd placed the wedding photo right next to the blooms so everyone could see how perfectly the arrangements matched. The little details mattered.

Though did teenagers really like birds-of-paradise? It could be Puerto Rico's state flower. No, Puerto Rico wasn't a state. It was a country, or a territory, or something like that. Whatever. The strange décor was only accentuated by a lack of pictures. There wasn't a single framed image of this girl. No programs or mass cards. It could be a money thing, but if that were the case, and the Mendezes couldn't afford a proper burial (Stephanie had no idea what they did for a living), then the school really should have stepped up. Frankly, it was embarrassing that they hadn't. Stephanie should set up a GoFundMe when she gets home. The family probably needed it.

God, she was next in line. The teens in front of her were sweet, shaking hands and offering condolences. That looked like Harper White. Her mom must be around here somewhere. Stephanie's eyes scanned the room. Didn't they go through some sort of scandal recently? Something to do with that other Latina girl. What was her name? Nancy? Natalie? It was in the newspaper. Stephanie had been homeroom mom for Brett's second-grade class, which included Harper and that little Spanish girl.

She had the wildest curls! The newspaper had said that those two Latina girls were friends, which made sense. Damn, what was her name? And where was Brett?

Stephanie took a cleansing breath. She should go to yoga after this. That would feel so good. It was only 11 a.m., so if this ended quickly enough, she might be able to make her regular class. She should text the group chat. So far there was no sign of a priest or rosary beads. You would think the Mendezes would be Catholic—Latinos were supposed to be religious—but whatever, it just meant Stephanie would get out of here faster.

The line inched forward, and the body came into view. Stephanie's breath quickened. There was a dead girl a few feet away, and the mother was standing beside her. The woman wasn't even crying—not a single sob! If that were Brett, Stephanie would be a puddle on the floor. Yet there was this woman, utterly emotionless, next to an open casket holding her baby.

But Jiminy Cricket, the girl was gorgeous. What was that quote about dying young? You leave a good-looking corpse? Not that Stephanie would ever want anyone to die young. That was awful. But Sabrina's skin was glowing, like Nicole Kidman after a spa day, which made her bright red lip even more audacious. It was the wrong shade for a fifteen-year-old.

Stephanie stepped into a cold pocket, her spine shuddering, and smelled . . . not flowers, but perfume. From the body. She'd never smelled a corpse before. She'd expected a stench of embalming fluid, something akin to cleaning chemicals, but this scent was sugary. And the girl's cheeks were rosy. Her lips practically smiled.

And her skin . . . wow, it was so perfect. Stephanie couldn't remember what it was like to have skin like that. Gradually, her hand lifted, drifting a little closer. A diamond bracelet swung on her wrist. Stephanie's arm stretched. That skin must feel like silk, the good kind, used for wedding dresses. Her fingers extended, and her pink nails twitched slightly. The smell, it was . . . honeysuckle. Stephanie leaned on her toes, inhaling deeply, her body drifting.

Then someone clasped her hand. Stephanie jolted.

Holy bananas, did she almost desecrate the body? Yes, she'd just tried to touch a corpse! And the mother had to stop her! Oh, gosh darn! Stephanie's cheeks flamed. A pearly-white hand clutched hers. Stephanie regained her senses.

"Oh, Ms. Mendez, I'm so sorry for your loss," Stephanie muttered, stumbling forward, her hand still in the mother's grip. The woman wore a vintage hat and black veil that was very Jackie Kennedy–esque. Stephanie pumped her arm, trying to turn the awkward moment into a handshake. "I can't imagine what you must be going through." Stephanie tried to release her grip, but the woman clung on, alabaster knuckles tightening around Stephanie's bones. "Um, my thoughts are with you." Stephanie tugged, but the woman's fingers crunched harder.

"Are you okay?" Stephanie asked, yanking once more, her words gasping. "Is there anything . . . I can do?"

Her gaze flitted for assistance. Greg Cohen was standing behind her. Wasn't he the guidance counselor who dropped the ball with this girl? Stephanie locked eyes with him, gesturing to her hand. *Hello? A little help here!*

The man did nothing, completely oblivious. Maybe he deserved all the rotten press he was getting.

Stephanie gave a massive pull, elbow jerking. No result. "Excuse me, miss. Are you all right?"

Only it was the teen boy beside the mother who reacted. His head snapped up, his brimmed hat falling behind him. *What teenager wears a hat from a black-and-white movie?* Then he dashed—no, sprinted? *Is he floating?*—through the jam-packed funeral home, right toward a pretty reporter entering with a microphone in hand.

The grip around Stephanie's digits clamped so unbearably tight that her head flung back. Her eyes rolled, lashes fluttering, and a howl escaped her lips. Her bones were cracking. Breaking.

A door slammed shut. A bolt clattered. Even with the crushing pain in her hand and the blubbering funeral chitchat, the boom of that locked door echoed with finality. Her attention shot toward the exit. The teenage boy, dressed in an ill-fitting black suit meant for an undertaker on a horse-drawn carriage, was standing . . . No, he was definitely floating. Couldn't anyone else see this?

Stephanie's eyes darted frantically, then immediately flung back to the piercing throb in her right hand and to the grieving mother who wouldn't let go. The woman's veil was gone. Her pale skin was stretched unnaturally tight over the sharp bones of her cheeks. But her eyes . . .

All her muscles locked tight, and Stephanie's mouth fell agape. Her spit dried, and the overwhelming anguish in her hand was abruptly gone. Or different. Insignificant?

The mother's eyes were fire engine red. Lipstick red. Blood red. A cruel expression twisted her remarkably white face. *Aren't Latinos supposed to be tanner than this?* Her crimson lips curled up. White fangs descended from slobbering gums. Yes, they were fangs. Recessed lights glinted off the razor points.

The entire bereaved family showed their faces now, hats and veils gone. Their matching scarlet eyes were on display.

Then the coffin stirred. The metal stand beneath it squealed. Wood rattled.

The beautiful fifteen-year-old girl who had taken her own life now sat erect. Her back was pencil straight, surrounded by the white-satin-and-dark-oak encasement that was meant to hold her for eternity. Sabrina Mendez's head whipped with terrifying speed. Black curls fanned out, spreading that smell—it wasn't honeysuckle, it was perfume, maybe Loveshack Fancy. The dead body (Sabrina *was* dead! They were all at her frickin' funeral, for Pete's sake!) leaned toward the nearby cluster of teenage girls. Yes, that was definitely Harper White. She dated Brett's friend Will. That was what the drama was about last year!

A pale hand sprang from the coffin and snatched the back of Harper's frizzy hair. Impossibly long fingers yanked, and a chunk of blond locks ripped from Harper's skull with a zipper-sounding tear. Gore spurted. Harper shrieked, and Sabrina Mendez's lips peeled back to reveal pointy ivory weapons.

The hot poker of agony intensified from Stephanie's hand, and she doubled over. Her fingers were on fire. No, her hand was nearly gone. Stephanie blinked. Lungs empty. The mother's unhinged jaw was locked around her wrist. The diamond tennis bracelet from Stephanie's tenth wedding anniversary now dripped ruby red. The gargling, slurping sound of an industrial vacuum syphoned blood through angry crimson lips. Nausea rolled through her. Dizziness. Stephanie's knees gave out. The room grew white with crackling starbursts, spinning and spinning in the blazing heat.

A cry shredded Stephanie's chest, one final gasp. The burning air raced from her lungs, but Stephanie couldn't hear the sound, because the screams filling the room had blended together into one massive convergence of pain.

"I swear that Harper girl tasted even better than I expected!" Sabrina clapped elatedly as she exited the funeral home alongside her family. Her mouth dripped and her dress was soaked in a way that shifted the fabric from black toward burgundy. "You have no idea how close I was to biting her in the school cafeteria. Like *so many times!*"

"You should have tasted her mother! I'm telling you, the chardonnay was still crisp in her blood. I'm buzzed! Seriously. Give me a sobriety test. I'll fail. She must've been hammered," said Sabrina's brother, Xavier, as he climbed into the back seat of their extra-long SUV with tinted windows. He reeked of gasoline, and his white button-down shirt was entirely saturated in scarlet from racing through bodies as if in a competition to drink the most. Sabrina preferred to linger over the flavors, savoring the subtle differences between Americans and Europeans. It extended her palette.

Steely gray plumes billowed high from the flickering orange flames of the funeral home they'd just set ablaze.

"Man, I haven't been this stuffed in so long!" groaned Sabrina's sister, Margarita, from the bucket seat beside her. "I swear, Tía Ventura and Tía Anna, whatever you were doing in Sevilla took way too long!" Margarita swiveled her neck toward the far back seat, where their aunt and uncle rubbed bloated bellies. "We are never waiting this long to eat again!"

"¡Ay bendito! It was worth it!" said Tía Anna, black curls bouncing on her forehead.

"Me encantan los funerales. We haven't done one in so long!" Mamá agreed, a smile ringing in her voice. There was not one touch of blood in her mother's mahogany hair, nor on her dress. She sat in the passenger seat perfectly spotless, a skill Sabrina had yet to master.

"You think they'll buy the gas leak story?" Pop asked as he steered the SUV away from the flaming Victorian building. Fire trucks wailed in the distance.

"They always do." Xavier burped, giggling with tears in his eyes. "I'm telling you! I am so wasted right now!"

"For me, it's not even about the blood." Sabrina stretched, her body languid as ebony hair dripped scarlet in a way that made her want to shove the locks into her mouth and suck like a lollipop. But she refrained, trying to follow her mother's prim example. "It's the look on the assholes' faces when I first sink my teeth in, that's what I love. The initial shock—it fills me up. Really. I feel whole." Sabrina placed a hand on a chest lacking a heartbeat. It wasn't hard to play a corpse, though she hated whenever she drew the short straw and had to be the one stuffed into a coffin. Caskets were so binding. And it was extremely hard not to laugh at the "mourners."

"You feel whole because you just drank half of the Spring Mills field hockey team," Margarita joked. Then she nodded to the window. "Hey, look who showed up."

Sabrina followed her sister's gaze and spied Naomi standing on the street, brown eyes reflecting the dancing flames. Naomi shouldn't be here; the cops might actually try to pin this on her. The girl had a potential motive. The cyberbullying she'd endured was extremely public. It was what brought Sabrina and her family here. Only Naomi never knew who Sabrina really was. Or what she was. But Naomi probably did now. The two friends (Sabrina really would miss her) locked eyes through the tinted glass, and Sabrina lifted her hand to wave one final goodbye. Naomi mimicked the gesture, her limb moving robotically with shock as she took in the face of a girl Naomi had absolutely believed was dead, a girl who'd just wiped out all Naomi's enemies (and then some).

Naomi didn't know it, but everything that had just happened had been for her. Vengeance—sweet and unexpected. It was what set Sabrina's family apart from others like them. Sure, they killed. They had to, to survive. But they only killed the bad ones.

"¿A dónde vamos ahora?" asked Tía Anna.

Pop drove north on the highway, clouds thundering overhead with a flash of lightning.

"I've been following the social media of some girls in Manhattan, at a private school," Mamá offered. "Es horrible."

"Ugh, I hate city blood!" Tío Ventura groaned, pretending to gag. "Está sucia."

"You're such a snob!" Mamá scolded. "There's a little town in Maine. Some boy's been posting pictures of his girlfriend online . . ."

"Dirty ones?" Xavier hiccupped. Mamá nodded. "I call dibs!" Xavier raised his hand.

Sabrina grinned; her brother could be so theatrical when it came to dickish boyfriends. "I'm in, too!"

"Vamos!"

All in agreement, the Mendez family continued north, rain splattering against the windshield and adding to the slosh of their full bellies.

About the Authors

Cynthia Pelayo is a Bram Stoker Award–winning and International Latino Book Award–winning author and poet.

Pelayo writes fairy tales that blend genre and explore concepts of grief, mourning, and cycles of violence. She is the author of *Loteria, Santa Muerte, The Missing, Poems of My Night, Into the Forest and All the Way Through, Children of Chicago, Crime Scene, The Shoemaker's Magician*, as well as dozens of standalone short stories and poems.

Her works have been reviewed in *The New York Times, Chicago Tribune, LA Review of Books*, and more.

Agustina Bazterrica was born in Buenos Aires in 1974. She has published one short story collection, two nonfiction books, and three novels, including *Tender Is the Flesh*, which won the Clarín Novel Prize, was a finalist for the Goodreads Choice Awards, and was named one of the best books of the year by *The Washington Post* and *Vogue*. Her work has been translated into more than thirty languages and has sold over one million copies worldwide.

Alex Segura is the bestselling and award-winning author of *Secret Identity*, winner of the *Los Angeles Times* Book Prize for Mystery/Thriller, a *New York Times* Editor's Choice, and an NPR Best Mystery of the Year. He's also the author of the acclaimed Pete Fernandez series, as well as *Alter Ego*, a standalone sequel to *Secret Identity*. In addition to his prose, he has written a number of comics for Marvel and DC. He lives in New York City with his family.

Ananda Lima is the author of *Craft: Stories I Wrote for the Devil* and *Mother/land*, winner of the Hudson Prize. *Craft*, her fiction debut, was longlisted for the Story Prize and the Andrew Carnegie Medal for

Excellence in Fiction, and received starred reviews from *Kirkus, Publishers Weekly*, and *Library Journal*. Her work has appeared in *American Poetry Review*, Poets.org, *Kenyon Review*, and elsewhere. She is a contributing editor at *Poets & Writers* and program curator at StoryStudio Chicago.

Ann Dávila Cardinal is a Puerto Rican, Vermont-based author and educator. Her eight books include the 2026 punk rock thriller *Hear The Dead* and the magical realist novels *The Storyteller's Death* and *We Need No Wings*, among others. She has an MFA in Writing from Vermont College of Fine Arts, teaches in the University of San Francisco's MFA in Writing for Young Readers, and is a part-time bookseller. She lives in Vermont in a house with a massively creepy basement.

Brenda Lozano is a fiction writer, essayist, and editor. Some of her books include *Todo o nada* (*All or Nothing*), *Cuaderno ideal* (*Loop*), and the novel *Brujas* (*Witches*). In 2015, she was selected by Conaculta, Hay Festival, and the British Council as one of Mexico's best fiction writers under forty. In 2017, she was added to the Bogotá39 list, a selection of the best fiction writers under forty from across Latin America. *Mothers* is her most recent novel.

Carolina Flórez-Cerchiaro is a Colombian author of genre-bending speculative fiction based in Bogotá, Colombia. She is the author of *Bochica*, a Latin American gothic horror novel pitched as *Mexican Gothic* meets *The Shining*. When she's not writing, she can be found sipping black coffee, puzzling, and listening to audiobooks. Find out more at CarolinaFlorezAuthor.com.

Daniel José Older is a *New York Times* bestselling author and a lead story architect for *Star Wars: The High Republic*. His books include the urban fantasy series Outlaw Saints, Bone Street Rumba, and the YA Shadowshaper Cypher—beginning with *Shadowshaper*, named by *TIME* one of the best fantasy books of all time—among others. He won the International Latino Book Award and has been nominated for the Kirkus Prize, The World Fantasy Award, and the Andre Norton Award, to name a few.

Diana Rodriguez Wallach is a multi-published author of young adult novels, most recently YA horror novels. Her latest, *The Silenced*, was inspired by America's first reform school and released in September 2025. Diana has been a finalist for the International Thriller Awards and the International Latino Book Awards for Best YA Novel. She is half Puerto Rican and lives in the Philadelphia area, where she teaches writing courses through the Highlights Foundation.

Gerardo Sámano Córdova is a writer and artist from Mexico City living in Brooklyn. He's currently writer in residence at Fordham University. He got his MFA from the Helen Zell Writers' Program at the University of Michigan. He has studied at Bread Loaf as a work/study scholar (2019) and fellow (2023) and at the Tin House Summer Workshop (2019). His second novel *Imps!* is coming out in 2027 from Tin House Books.

Heather Cleary is an award-winning translator of poetry and prose from Spanish whose work has been recognized by the Queen Sofia Spanish Institute, the National Book Foundation, English PEN, and the International Booker Prize, among others. She is the author of *The Translator's Visibility: Scenes from Contemporary Latin American Fiction* and is currently writing a novel about translation and betrayal.

Isabel Cañas is a Mexican American speculative fiction writer. After having lived in Mexico, Scotland, Egypt, Turkey, and New York City, among other places, she has settled in the Pacific Northwest. She holds a doctorate in Near Eastern Languages and Civilizations and writes fiction inspired by her research and her heritage. She is the bestselling author of *The Hacienda*, *Vampires of El Norte*, *The Possession of Alba Díaz*, and *The House of Gardenias*. To find out more, visit www.isabelcanas.com.

Leopoldo Goût is an Emmy-nominated producer, internationally acclaimed novelist, and museum-exhibited visual artist. Born in Mexico City, trained at London's Central Saint Martins, based in New York for over two decades, he creates from studios spanning New York City, Mexico City, and Oaxaca. His novel *Piñata* was named one of *Esquire*'s

Top 10 Horror Books of 2023. His artwork is held in international collections including MoMA PS1.

Lilliam Rivera is an award-winning author of nine works of fiction: a dark thriller, four YA novels, three middle-grade books, and a graphic novel for DC Comics. Her books have been featured on NPR, *New Yorker*, *Los Angeles Times*, *New York Times*, and multiple "best of" lists. Originally from the Bronx, New York, Lilliam currently lives in Los Angeles.

Juan Martinez is the author of the novel *Extended Stay* and the story collection *Best Worst American*. He lives near Chicago and is an associate professor at Northwestern University. His work has appeared most recently in *The Chicago Quarterly Review*, *The Sunday Morning Transport*, *Huizache*, *Ecotone*, *NIGHTMARE*, *McSweeney's*, NPR's *Selected Shorts*, and elsewhere. Find him online at fulmerford.com and on Bluesky at @fulmerford.com.

Mariana Enriquez was born in Argentina in 1973. She is the author of the novel *Our Share of Night*—winner of the Herralde Prize—the collections of short fiction *Things We Lost in the Fire*, *A Sunny Place for Shady People*—World Fantasy Award Winner—and *The Dangers of Smoking in Bed*—shortlisted for the International Booker Prize. Her most recent work is the non-fiction book *Somebody Is Walking on Your Grave*. In Spanish, she has about eight books yet to be translated. In 2024, she was awarded the Premio Iberoamericano de Letras José Donoso.

Megan McDowell has translated many of the most important Latin American writers working today. Her translations have won the National Book Award for Translated Literature, the English PEN award, the Premio Valle-Inclán, and two O. Henry prizes, and have been nominated for the International Booker Prize as well as the Kirkus Prize. In 2020, she won an Award in Literature from the American Academy of Arts and Letters. She is from Richmond, Kentucky, and lives in Santiago, Chile.

Mónica Ojeda is the author of *La desfiguración Silva*, her debut novel, and of the novels *Nefando* and *Mandíbula* (*Jawbone*), as well as the short story collection *Las Voladoras*. She has been recognized as one of the most important literary voices in Latin America by the Hay Festival's Bogotá39 and *Granta en español*, and her work has been translated into more than ten languages.

Xochitl Gonzalez is the *New York Times* bestselling author of the award-winning novel *Olga Dies Dreaming*, the Reese's Book Club Pick *Anita de Monte Laughs Last*, and national bestseller *Last Night in Brooklyn*. She is a contributor to *The Atlantic*, where she was recognized as a 2023 Pulitzer Prize finalist in Commentary.

Sarah Booker is an educator and literary translator working from Spanish to English. Her translations include Mónica Ojeda's *Nefando* and *Jawbone*—the latter a National Book Award finalist—Gabriela Ponce's *Blood Red*, Cristina Rivera Garza's *Death Takes Me*—cotranslated with Robin Myers—among others. Her work has appeared in *The Paris Review*, *Asymptote*, *The Baffler*, and elsewhere. She holds a PhD in Hispanic Literature from UNC–Chapel Hill and teaches in North Carolina.

Sarah Moses is a writer and translator from Spanish and French. Her translations include *Diving Board*, by Tomás Downey; *Tender Is the Flesh* and *The Unworthy*, by Agustina Bazterrica; and *Die, My Love*, by Ariana Harwicz, which was longlisted for the International Booker Prize and adapted into a film. Her collection of short fiction, *Strange Water*, was published in 2024.

Zoraida Córdova is the *USA Today* bestselling author and editor of more than three dozen novels and short stories, including *Kiss the Girl*, *The Inheritance of Orquídea Divina*, and *Star Wars: The High Republic: Convergence*. She has written for Disney Books, Marvel Comics, and Lucasfilm Press. Zoraida was born in Guayaquil, Ecuador, and calls New York City home.